The Herodian Stones

by

GAYNOR LYNN TAYLOR

GODSEND

Published by Godsend Publications Co. Ltd.
Registered Office: 33 Highfield Lane, Chesterfield, Derbyshire S41 8AZ
www.godsendbooks.com
e-mail: gtaylor@godsendbooks.com

Printed in England by RPM, Print & Design, 2-3 Spur Road,
Quarry Lane, Chichester, West Sussex PO19 8PR

Cover design: Two By Two Worship Ltd.
134 Norwood Avenue, Chesterfield, Derbyshire S41 0NH
www.twobytwoworship.com
e-mail: info@twobytwoworship.com

This is a work of fiction

For my Law class of 2006:

Daniel
Deborah
Emily
Jonathan
Kiren
Lee
Rachel
Rebecca
Sabrina
Sarah
Sigourney

With thanks to Glynn Botham and Gwyneth Armstrong

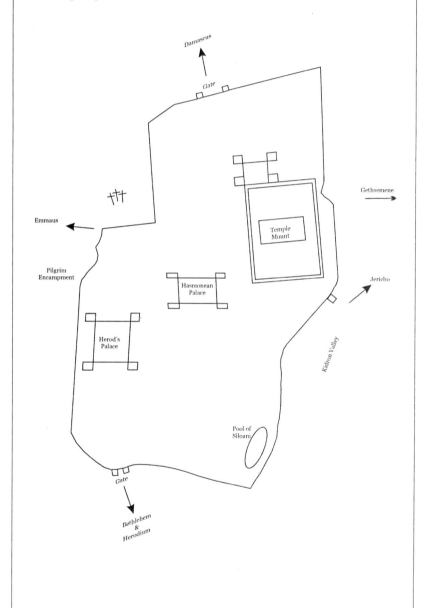

Rough guide to Jerusalem

Damascus

Gate

Gethsemene

Emmaus

Temple
Mount

Pilgrim
Encampment

Hasmonean
Palace

Jericho

Herod's
Palace

Kidron Valley

Pool of
Siloam

Gate

Bethlehem
&
Herodium

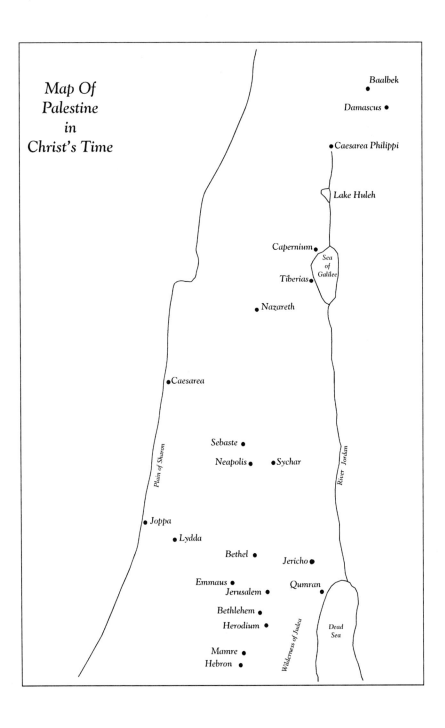

Map Of
Palestine
in
Christ's Time

Baalbek

Damascus

Caesarea Philippi

Lake Huleh

Capernium

Sea
of
Galilee

Tiberias

Nazareth

Caesarea

Plain of Sharon

Sebaste

Neapolis

Sychar

River Jordan

Joppa

Lydda

Bethel

Jericho

Emmaus

Qumran

Jerusalem

Bethlehem

Herodium

Wilderness of Judea

Dead
Sea

Mamre

Hebron

Characters

Abel	Father of Gaius
Aemilia	Wife of Marcellus
Anna	Wife of Joel
Anthony Avitus	Brother of Rebecca and son of Sabina
Aziz	Father of Daleel
Baraka	Slave of Herod Philip
Barnabas	Young pickpocket
Claudia Procula	Wife of Pontius Pilate
Cornelius Sulla	Great, great grandson of Roman statesman
Crassus	Theatrical director
Daleel	Marc's guide
Daniel	Slave of Rebecca Victor
Deborah Avitus	Wife of Anthony Avitus
Dimitri	A Guard
Drusilla	Wife of Herod the Great
Flavius	Chief administrator of Pilate
Gaius	Assistant to Marc Tiro
Herodias	Wife of Herod Antipas
James	Friend of Lydia
Jerome	Scribe at Qumran
Joel	Husband of Anna (deceased)
Jonathan	Younger brother of Daleel
Judas	Convert living in Damascus
Julius	Slave of Cornelius Sulla
Justin	Young actor
Keren	Sister of Daleel
Leah	Abel's housekeeper
Lydia	Lady trading in cloth
Marc Tiro	Ex Commander of the Praetorian Guard
Marcellus	Wealthy member of Jerusalem's society
Mary	Follower of Jesus
Miriam	Wife of Dimitri
Nadeem	Brother of Daleel
Philip	Historian in Herod's palace at Caesarea
Pontius Pilate	Governor of Judea AD 26 to AD36

Portius	Slave of Cornelius Sulla
Prissi	Prostitute
Rachel Victor	Daughter of Rebecca, skilled water diviner
Rashidi	Recluse in Baalbek
Rebecca Victor	Architect, half sister of Anthony Avitus
Rufus Tiro	Marc's father (deceased)
Sabina Victor	Mother of Anthony Avitus, owns a tannery
Salampsio	Daughter of Herod the Great and Mariamne
Sarah	Slave of Deborah
Saul	Tentmaker in Jericho
Silas	Caretaker of Herodium
Sydonie	Granddaughter of Marcellus
Theo	Jeweller in Jerusalem
Tribune Polybius	Court magistrate in Jerusalem

Historical Characters

Archelaus	Son of Herod, ruled Judea, exiled AD6
Augustus	Emperor before Tiberius, 63 BC – AD 14
Barabbas	Leader of the Zealots in the time of Christ
Herod Antipas	Son of Herod, ruler of Galilee and Perea
Herod Philip	Son of Herod, ruler of Iturea and Traconitis
John Hyrcanus	Hasmonean high priest, died 30 BC
Mariamne	A wife of Herod the Great
Pompey	Roman commander, 106 – 48BC
Sejanus	Praetorian commander, died AD 31
Sulla, Lucius C.	Roman consul, 138 –78 BC
Tiberius	Emperor after Augustus, 42 BC – AD 37
Tiro, Marcus	Slave of Cicero, invented shorthand 63BC
Varro, Marcus	Roman writer, 116 – 27 BC
Vitruvius	Architect in time of Augustus

1

It was one of those days towards the end of winter when the occasional sun has some warmth but the wind can still bite. A man was sitting quietly, almost invisibly, on a square stone pillar lying on its side providing a perfect bench. He had been there on and off for several days but everyone was too busy to notice him. He seemed to be reading, sometimes drawing, but his main purpose was watching. A narrow concrete aqueduct surfaced in front of him from a tunnel cut into rock, and a small wooden bridge allowed access to the town's market.

The man had become familiar with the variegated colours and smells that emanated from the other side of the waterway but continued to be entranced and entertained by them. Fruits and vegetables of deep red, orange and purple provided a background for clothing and cloth of different textures and hues that billowed in the breeze, as the sellers displayed them for prospective buyers. Several bystanders were admiring the latest fashionable footwear, bejewelled sandals with leather straps. There was everything available for the citizens, both rich and poor.

The town was now under Roman occupation. He knew how much this ownership had cost the Empire, having seen the deaths, smelt the blood, heard the anguish, understood the hatred and experienced the valour. How he had loved it! What is life if it is not conquest? Winning was the only thing that mattered, the how or the why were irrelevant.

A glint caught his eye. He stood up and crossed the bridge, needing to be closer. Casually he walked towards the woman who had become the focus of his attention, and pretended to examine some artefacts on the neighbouring stall. The days of waiting and watching were at an end.

Keeping a low profile, he followed her round the market until her basket was full of the necessary provisions. She left the square at the top left hand corner, so did the man. Her journey took less than five minutes. She turned through an archway into a small courtyard, from where she climbed some stone steps and entered the back of a house. The man took note. Now he would wait a little longer. An elderly woman emerged from the house next door. He approached her.

'I wonder if you can help me. I am sure I recognize the lady who has just entered this house. I met her and her husband two years ago. Could you tell me her name?'

The woman looked up at him. She was rarely asked a question by a stranger but was only too willing to oblige him.

'You may have met her, but I doubt you met her husband. She doesn't have one. There's just her and her youngster. Shameful! Her name's Simone – that's all I know. Some say she was once from a noble family, but noblewomen don't behave like her.'

She was looking for some sort of support for her argument but none came. The man had the information he needed and she was dispensable. He ignored her. Realizing her audience had lost interest she shuffled away.

The man was wearing a long grey tunic tied with a belt and covered by a reddish brown woollen cloak. His hand reached inside to check he had what he needed. He stood a while longer on the opposite side of the narrow street, but became impatient and not a little cold since the sun was now disappearing and the buildings afforded no protection in the late afternoon chill. He shivered and pulled his outer garment more tightly round him. The walls of the passageway were roughly hewn and caught bits of wool off the cloak. The soft leather shoes made no noise on the steps; the back of the house was quiet; the door was not locked.

'How foolish!' he murmured.

He entered into a large room with multi coloured raffia mats on the floor and an open fire in one wall. Warm dancing light filled the room, reflecting on the walls. There was very little furniture, just a rough wooden table and two chairs, but several earthenware pots.

A girl was playing with some pebbles, throwing one in the air and picking up others catching the airborne pebble before it hit the ground. There was a gentle click as it knocked against those she already held in her hand. She looked up at the face of the giant in the doorway. She noted the crookedness of his nose, the fullness of his lips and the blueness of his eyes; the two scars on his chin reminded her of lightening streaking across the sky. She stood up, terrified, yet she spoke bravely.

'Who are you? What do you want? My mother is asleep.'

She did not feel any easier when he gave her a smile; it was somehow cruel and had something of a sneer in its execution. The eyes were cold and without feeling.

'Where is she?' he said.

It was an unnecessary question because there was only one place she could be. In the corner, near the fireplace, were some more stone steps leading to a higher level in the house that were the sleeping quarters. Four or five strides were all that was required.

The woman lay on a low bed that was clean and comfortable. She was waking up from the disturbance of the voices and lifting herself from her elbow into an upright position. She had no chance to get to her feet. The man did not hesitate but drew a dagger from beneath his cloak, grabbed her long black hair and pulled back her head. The silken blade was smooth and lethal as the woman slipped easily from sleep to oblivion. The girl who had been standing in the entrance screamed and turned to run. The giant picked her up as if she were an empty garment and lifted her level to his face; she was barely six inches from him. For a second or two he paused, but knew he could not let her go.

'I'm sorry,' he said, and threw her forcefully across the room. She struck the opposite wall and slipped to the floor like a doll made of rags. He walked across to the lifeless form and was satisfied. He pushed the woman's body off the bed onto the floor and stripped the mattress. He knew what he was looking for but his search was only a partial success; his face was a mixture of anger and frustration.

The blood on his cloak was congealing into the same background colour. He was so skilled with the knife that he knew how to keep away from spurting blood, but of course some was unavoidable. The back of his hand brushed it into the fabric until it was barely visible. Satisfied that he still looked fairly respectable, he left the way he came, closing the door behind him. He had a small pang of regret about the child, but it was just one of those inevitable consequences.

He had just one more task before his long journey home to Rome. The city of dreams with its magnificence, its splendour, its sophistication; it was at the forefront of ideas, open to all and above all it welcomed him as its son. He walked through some winding back streets until he came to a small shop front tucked away from sight in a narrow alley. His visit to the proprietor did not take long. But when he emerged, he was filled with hostility and bitterness. The disappointment of plans foiled at their instigation was revealed in the snarl of his mouth. When he went aboard a ship headed for Rome, he had a third murder on his hands.

2

-Sixteen Years Later-

The ship rose and fell gently as the port of Caesarea came into view. Light from a sun low in the sky deflected on the water, broke into millions of tiny specks and danced on the waves. Marc Tiro was on deck enjoying the early morning air on his face, relieved to escape the unwholesome atmosphere below. A storm near Crete had caused a number of passengers to be violently sick and the smell of vomit still hung in the air, unable to be cleansed by repeated douches of salt water.

The wind unexpectedly changed direction and caught his thick unruly hair. He ran his hand through it to no avail and felt the stubble round his face. Standing with his feet apart he clasped his fingers behind his head, stretched his elbows and tightened his muscles. The material of his tunic rose up and folded into the small of his back as he leaned all his weight over one thigh and then the other.

He breathed in deeply, expanding his chest, and slapped his stomach a couple of times with a short sharp gesture. He may once have been fit and fast, but now he just felt fat. A decade in the seat of a military saddle had been replaced by longer in the seat of justice. He was aware of the subcutaneous layer that had crept uninvited over his body like a slow growth, imperceptibly enlarging his frame as it did so. Fortunately, the length of his upper body was still able to conceal the worst of it, but he knew it was there.

'Good morning, not long now!'

Marc sighed, puffing out his cheeks irritably. It was impossible to have a few quiet moments without interruption. However, when the ship's captain stepped alongside him, he looked down offering a smile that had just the right calculated measure of boyish charm.

'The journey hasn't been too uncomfortable for you, I hope?'

Why did this man, so highly skilled in seafaring, feel the need to ask such a fatuous question? What was he supposed to say? That he didn't object one bit to being thrown about like an unleashed log and covered in the stench of other passengers' semi-digested food? Fortunately, years of practice dealing with the delicate egos of Roman politicians had taught him the art of pouring out dollops of honey to sweeten his own acerbic remarks.

'Well I must say I prefer travelling by land. Give me a horse any day. But as far as sailing is concerned, this has been as good as it can be and I would like to thank you for making it so.'

The captain was noticeably pleased. He looked up at the dark energetic eyes and slightly irregular face; the smile was friendly, the teeth enviable – always a matter of concern for the captain as he ran his tongue over his own gaps and jagged projections – they had been the bane of his life.

He had come to recognize the onset of a determination about his passenger's mouth and jaw, a slight downward turn of the head combined with a penetrating upward glance. That was the time to expect an incisive or challenging comment that many times broke desultory after dinner conversations and led to some stimulating discussion, even laughter. The erudition of the man exposed self-confidence. Yet the captain detected no hubris that invited ill will from lesser mortals, just respect, although he could well imagine how the more insecure members of the Roman elite might perceive him as a threat.

'We're just waiting for a space. This harbour was dredged and deepened so we can take the ship very close to shore. There's a lot of docking area but the port has become so popular that we usually have to queue. I actually miss seeing all the small boats that used to line up to take passengers ashore when we anchored further out.

The competition was so fierce ferrymen would knock one another into the water. I'm afraid there's no such entertainment for us these days, but the whole process is much easier, particularly for the ladies.'

Marc looked at him with some surprise. He had not noticed any women aboard on this trip.

'Do you get many ladies sailing with you?'

'Oh yes! Often they are with their husbands but sometimes they're alone. They are the ones who need a bit of special looking after. It's trade that does it, you see. There are many ladies nowadays who sell goods and buy from abroad. Had a lady not long ago, name of Lydia, trading in cloth. She brought a lot of stuff with her, samples I believe they were, had a lot of courage, if you ask me. Obviously wealthy! Good luck to 'em, I say. Are you intending to stay long?'

'I'm not sure.'

Marc really did not know the answer to this question. He had been invited to complete an assignment in this strange new place for a man called Cornelius Sulla. An investigation of some importance was required – that was all he knew. A crewman arrived and started to prepare the hawsers. The captain excused himself and walked over to give instructions.

Close by, Marc noticed the sun glimmer on a writhing mass of silvery movement as a young man tried to haul a net frantically from the water. His triumph was marred by his lack of vigilance. He had failed to notice the large ship that was bearing down on him. He had to make a decision, lose the fish or lose his boat, possibly his life. Balancing in his small craft as it moved violently in the swell, he looked up at his observer, shook a fist and uttered expletives. Soon, thought Marc, fury will turn to a sense of failure, followed by a renewal of faith. He questioned how many times a man has to experience the first two emotions before the third is extinguished, and all hope is lost.

The approaching harbour was a magnificent tribute to Herod's great works. Rising from the shore was the city, an arc of stone walling standing protectively behind it. Marc watched the new sun reflecting on stepped white buildings broken by the occasional red tiles of a Roman villa. The scene was interspersed by orange and lime groves, olive, fig and palm trees. The interplay of colours triggered memories of rambles through the Roman back street bazaars with his maternal grandmother, artisans displaying their wares on trestles.

He took in another deep breath and expelled it slowly. A feeling of deep peace enveloped him. At last he was out of Rome, away from the political intrigues, the power mongering and the duplicity. He had been reprieved.

As he relaxed, a sharp stab of pain made him lift his left hand to massage his right shoulder, circling his elbow as he did so to relieve the stiffness. Marc was reminded of the intense animosity on the face of Lucius Sejanus, as he had raised a serrated edged dagger and aimed it at his chest. If it had not been for a small movement to the left, he would not be alive. The intellectual and psychological battle he had fought for many years with the chief commanding officer of the Praetorian Guard had come to an end in a vicious physical confrontation, as was so often the case.

The quay bustled with disembarking passengers, vying for wooden wheeled carts and barrows provided by baggage handlers for a price, amidst much shouting and arguing. On either side of the walkway were high protective stone walls, preventing daredevils from inadvertently falling into the sea, or being crushed by a ship's side. A boy, who had escaped his father's grasp, was already testing his physical climbing skills, unaware of the dangers. Retribution was swift. No doubt Felix would do the same. The challenge was too enticing for any ten-year-old.

He wondered what his son would now be doing. Perhaps taking his lessons or working on the estate just outside Rome where Marc had been raised by his humble, hardworking grandparents. They had nurtured the fertile land until its lush olive groves sustained a highly successful business in olive oil production, a substance that was part of the staple diet of the Roman Empire.

His father, Rufus Tiro, had been a cavalry officer. Amongst his many campaigns were the ill fated exploits fought in Germany. Injury brought the offer of retirement and a pension, but he chose instead to join the Roman city police force and fire-fighters, the Vigiles Urbani, newly created by Augustus. The early city guards had a hard task, preventing robberies and groups of rapists from plaguing the lives of women who dared to venture out after dusk. Nobody was safe on the streets of Rome before the police force was established. But by the time Augustus died, eight years later, and Tiberius took power, the uniformed guards, with their specially decorated breastplates, were respected, their training intense.

Marc had seen little of Rufus. He could not remember if he was happier when his father was away on campaigns or at home. He looked forward to the visits, but always looked back in disappointment. Rufus was a big man, with an even bigger irascible disposition and pugnacity that caused disruption and disharmony wherever he went.

His mother died in childbirth so he never knew her; there were a series of 'step-mothers' who Marc soon realized were the result of his father's womanising. There was one in particular; he struggled to recall her name. She was very pretty. His father beat him when he caught him watching her brushing her hair, naked from the waist up; if the aim had been to make him forget, it had not worked.

Marc hated his father's ill temper whilst secretly acknowledging to himself a similar tendency in his own personality. As he grew older, he watched with interest the way his paternal grandmother carefully manipulated her son's temperament by listening with empathy she did not feel, and waiting until the time was ready to impose her own will. Adopting and practising the same techniques undoubtedly helped his career.

Marc had loved riding and asked his grandfather for larger or more challenging horses. He feared his father would call him a coward. Joining the cavalry, however, was not to please Rufus, but through personal selection. His excellent horsemanship had been noted. He had tenacity, acquitted himself well, and won the regard and loyalty of his men. He was invited to join the Praetorian Guard, special bodyguards of the Emperor, Tiberius. For the first time, Rufus said to him, 'I'm proud of you son.' Although the approval came too late, Marc recognized his father's contribution to his own drive and personal ambition.

The cohorts of Praetorian guards, police and fire fighters were stationed at a garrison in Rome. There were plenty of opportunities for promotion. At thirty he was given his first magistracy. When ten years later he became a Praetor, his judgements were an important source of Roman law, as well as of life and death. Little did he suspect then that, a few years later, his father's death and the incident with Sejanus would encourage him to ask to be relieved of his duties.

The crewman was shouting. 'Sorry sir, 'fraid you'll have to move – got to get the gangplank ready.'

Marc moved to one side. Whilst deep in his thoughts, the ship had sailed effortlessly through the gap from the open sea into the large square port enclosure. Oars were withdrawn; hawsers were thrown to the dockworkers; the ropes were secured; the anchor was dropped. The whole process was done with such skill and precision that hardly a jolt was felt.

He was experiencing an emotion that he had not felt for a long time, anticipation tinged with excitement. Whatever changes the next few weeks or months might bring he was determined to make the most of them.

3

-Cornelius Sulla-

Roman administration was cautious about movement of people round the Empire, always looking out for would-be troublemakers. A soldier, wearing a strong leather cuirass with a short cloak pinned to each shoulder looked up and observed the tall, well built man approaching him. He prided himself on being able to identify the nationality of most of the people who stepped through his barriers. They came from all parts of the world but this one definitely looked Roman.

The soldier lifted himself from the hips, stretched his waist and chest, to appear taller. He did not like others looking down on him, especially not in his official position. He stopped Marc by raising his palm.

'May I have your papers please, sir?'
This was not a request. The guard made an art of adapting his voice so that there was no doubt that it was a command. He looked down at the information presented to him and making a fist with his right hand, brought his arm across his chest, a salute in acknowledgement of the visitor's equestrian rank.

'Welcome, Commander! It's good to meet you, sir. Will you be staying long?'
That confounded question again, thought Marc. He gave the same answer he had given the ship's captain. As he proceeded through the barrier to the waiting area, a young man in a white tunic bounded towards him.

'Commander Tiro?'
'Yes.'

'Please follow me, sir. Cornelius Sulla has sent his chariot. I have arranged for your bags to be sent up shortly.'

Cornelius Sulla was at least twenty years older than him and had achieved his high rank through military exploits. He knew him by reputation and had met him on a few occasions, mostly at honour-bestowing ceremonies, but hesitated to call him a friend.

The chariot ride was a delight. Marc stood back and enjoyed the view. The city streets were narrow and bustling with business. He noticed that the people were expensively and fashionably dressed. Doorways were freshly painted with decorated architraves. The streets, clean and well maintained, had foundations of large stones topped by smaller ones and bonded by cement. A surface of cobbles completed the infrastructure. There were no unpleasant smells in these streets. Herod had used Roman expertise to install underground sewers, waterways and drainage systems. The pervading feeling was one of health and prosperity.

Progress was a little slow through the city because of the number of people, but the young man was not averse to cracking his whip to warn pedestrians of his imminent arrival. People scurried to one side to avoid the chariot with its extravagant red and gold motifs.

By the time they reached the city gate the horse had picked up pace and they galloped through the large stone archway in Herod's wall. Immediately to the right was the hippodrome for horse and chariot racing, built with a base colonnade and extravagantly designed entablature resting on its pillars. It occurred to Marc that his driver was likely to be familiar with the inside of the building. Further round to the right, requiring him to turn his body to see it, was a semi-circular theatre facing seawards. To his left, but further away, was a double storey amphitheatre for gladiatorial games; and beyond that was a palace. The buildings were as grand as those he had seen in Rome, an observation that surprised him.

Meanwhile, Cornelius Lucius Sulla was pacing back and forth in his wide atrium. His dogs sat to one side, watching, disconcerted by their master's lack of ease. Cornelius was unused to visitors. However, this was necessary. A solution needed to be found to the problem but he must stay in control; must know what progress was being made. That fool Pilate could not be trusted. He was too preoccupied with his own position and lacked the essential clarity of thought.

Cornelius was the great, great grandson of the infamous Lucius Cornelius Sulla, a statesman who assembled an army and marched successfully on Rome, but at a cost of civil war. His cruelty against his enemies was well documented, but he nevertheless restored constitutional government, run by a Senate and the aristocracy, before he retired.

That was what Rome needed, thought Cornelius, properly elected leaders managed by the elite aristocrats who have the education to know how to run the Empire, not these new Emperors who independently declare themselves, not only head of state, but divi filius – the son of a god. The people of the Empire were made to worship the Emperor as one more of their interminable idols. Everything his ancestor fought for was destroyed by the advent of Augustus, and now his fawning inadequate stepson, Tiberius Claudius Nero Caesar. At least Sejanus had guts.

Who was this Marcus Tiro who thought he had the right to stop him overthrowing these self appointed demi-gods? The question was rhetorical. Cornelius knew the answer. Marc had a reputation for being a good judge with mature political acumen. He kept his own counsel, which was why Cornelius had asked him to come. Furthermore, he was well liked by the Emperor. But we shall see what his limitations are, he mused.

One of the dogs approached cautiously and licked his hand.

'Yes, yes, Piso, I know, I am getting myself worked up over

nothing. It's always the same when strangers come through the doors. Help me to stay calm. I must be gracious and so must you. We will do our best will we not?' He patted the dog and the dog responded with pleasure at his master's attention.

Most of the residents of Caesarea lived outside the city walls. The chariot continued along a dirt road, compacted and even, until the ground started to rise and then more steeply. Fields abounding in vegetables and orchards, offering an abundance of different fruits, sped by on either side. Women were fetching water from wells; others were buying fresh commodities from the roadside. Most were pre-occupied and took little notice of the chariot, other than to brush their clothes as disturbed clouds of dust descended on them.

On a steep part of the hillside, the chariot came to a halt outside a small single storey house, specially built for a man who preferred quality to ostentation. A slave opened a pair of high wrought iron gates, the only access to the walled enclosure, through which could be seen the gardens. These were a haven of green foliage, trees and fountains arising from statues of Greek gods. A wide entrance porch hinted at the luxury within. Cornelius Sulla having reached an enviable status was reaping the rewards. He emerged from his home with two barking fearsome looking dogs on either side. One word from Cornelius and they were silent.

'My dear Marc, how well you look, welcome to my home. How was your journey?'

Marc was used to assessing the character and stamina of men. He looked down now at his host, observing the high cheekbones, hollow cheeks and deep set eyes. Where the thick eyebrows met two vertical furrows ploughed upwards into the forehead. The end of the nose was so broad that it divided into two bulbous tips, and the chin was similarly split by a deep cleft. His bearing was one that Marc had observed many times before, battle weary; the body challenged to a point that the soul no longer wished to abide there. The smile and the inanity of the words uttered by the mouth belied the darkness of the heart within.

'The journey was as they ever are, tedious, but I'm extremely pleased to be here.'

Marc jumped down from the chariot and extended a hand of friendship. Each man grasped the other by his forearm with a shake of something close to genuine feeling.

'Come in, come in and refresh yourself. Feel free to use my home as your own.'

'That's very kind,' said Marc, walking into the atrium.

The tessellated floor was adorned with beautiful mosaic artistry in the form of a racing chariot. The coolness struck his face and arms since outside the heat of the day was increasing. He breathed in the refreshing air and relaxed. To the left were some wide steps downwards, and to the right was a corridor leading to more rooms. From the hallway they walked through a square open courtyard, full of vines stretching their branches to the exposed sky. A sunken square impluvium for collecting rainwater stood in the centre of the floor. An ornate fountain was its centrepiece.

Wooden doors led into the main living area, a quietly beautiful room with exposed timber beams supporting the tiled roof. On the left were latticed shutters from floor to ceiling opening onto a balcony, revealing a view across the garden to green hills. The cerulean backdrop made it impossible to distinguish sea from sky. A low square wooden table with a glossy patina stood in the middle of the room. Sitting on it was a bronze tray with two lavishly crafted glass goblets. Either side of the table were long couches, sumptuously covered in rich red velvets, and on the far side was a wooden chair with arms and a leather seat. An intricate tapestry covered the wall behind. On the right, a fireplace with a wide gaping mouthpiece displayed tall, exquisitely painted pottery jars. Above, there hung a portrait of a beautiful young woman.

Imaginary, real or lost, Marc wondered.

'Come! Let's have some cool grape juice to refresh you.'

He indicated to his guest to take the couch on the right of the table so he had the advantage of the view towards the sea. Cornelius clapped his hands and a young male slave appeared instantly with a glass jug artistically designed to match the goblets.

'Tell me, how is Rome? Sounds like there have been a tricky few years with Sejanus being found guilty of treason!'

'It hasn't been easy, but the Emperor has been generous.'

'I heard he allowed you to retire now that Quintus Macro is fully installed as the new Prefect. I hoped, with your insatiable curiosity, that you might want to continue with your investigative work.'

'That is perceptive of you, Cornelius. You are right, of course.'

'I'm grateful to you for coming all this way. We need the help of a distinguished man like you. Your experience in the imperial police makes you an ideal candidate for the job we have for you. There will be an ample reward.'

'I trust then that I may be of some service.'

'I hear you were largely responsible for the downfall of Sejanus?' Cornelius obviously did not wish to let the subject go just yet, despite his promise to himself.

'No, Sejanus sowed the seeds of his own downfall. It's a shame that power often corrupts. Due to his machinations, the Praetorian Guard became a threat to the Emperor, rather than a source of his personal protection. As you know, Sejanus was suspected of murdering Tiberius' son, Drusus, many years ago, but there was insufficient evidence. His final plot to kill Tiberius himself was properly uncovered, and Sejanus had to suffer the consequences of being a traitor, denounced and executed with his co-conspirators.'

'Is it not also true that sometimes it is better if power moves forward?'

Marc wondered what Cornelius meant. Whatever it was, he was too tired to argue. There were a few moments silence while he looked down at the juice left in his glass. His mouth twitched thoughtfully then he looked up at Cornelius without moving his head, his right eyebrow lifted slightly. His tone of voice left no doubt that this was his final comment on the matter of Sejanus.

'There's been enough change and bloodshed. I have never made a secret of my loyalty to the Empire that superseded the Republic. Augustus and now Tiberius have brought a period of relative stability. Gone are the days when wealthy elitists can raise an army against the state. But our power lies in winning the approval of all those countries we've annexed by force. We can't indefinitely bear the cost of imposing our rule. The Emperor and Rome are one and the same. They are universally powerful and can't be at the mercy of every man who takes up his sword against them. A failure for the Emperor is a failure for the Empire. A crisis of imperialism would return us to the days of individual power struggles using mercenaries. It's important that we retain the central power and if obeisance to the Emperor is what it needs, then so be it.'

Cornelius smiled and nodded, although Marc knew full well that his host's own ancestor had toppled Rome in the way he had just described.

'You're right, of course. It's a pleasure to meet a man of principle. I trust you'll enjoy a restful few days here before plunging into your investigations.'

'I look forward to that. You have a beautiful home.'

'Thank you! I'm glad you find it so. I've been here now for several years. Tell me, how is your father and son?'

'My father died. My son lives on the estate with the stewards of the business and his tutors.'

'I am sorry to hear of your father's death. He was one of Rome's progeny at the forefront of new developments. However, that means you are a wealthy man now. Like you, I inherited the lands here. I'll show you round tomorrow.'

Cornelius looked directly at his guest. Any tenseness had

disappeared, although Marc thought he was probably unused to having his privacy invaded by visitors and entertaining was not his forte.

'I am sure you are anxious to know the details of why I felt obliged to write to you. But first we must attend to your comfort. If you will excuse me, I have some business to see to this afternoon. We can talk later.'

Cornelius clapped his hands again.

'Portius, make the necessary preparations, our guest will be bathing soon.'

Despite his curiosity, after the long and wearisome journey, ablution was engaging his thoughts above all else, so after further pleasantries and shared memories of Rome's military exploits, he was escorted by Portius back through the open courtyard into the hallway, down the steps to the bathing area.

Marc stood at the marble edge and felt the welcome hot water glide over his body as he moved further beneath the surface. Frustrations and irritations floated away in the scented steamy atmosphere; his muscles relaxed and he was filled with unexpected peace and optimism. An hour or so later, clean and freshly clothed, he felt refreshed and ready for anything.

4

-Who Moved the Stones?-

The two men sat side by side on the balcony drinking wine and enjoying the peacefulness of the evening. The dogs, now satisfied that Marc had their master's approval, were also relaxing at their feet. The grand buildings below looked small from up here, and the whole scene was enchanting.

Cornelius began.

'How familiar are you with the history of this country?'

'I know that it was ruled by Herod as its King until his death, that Herod was a supporter of Rome and a friend of our first Emperor Augustus.'

'Well, that's a good start. Herod was clever. He came from a Jewish background and knew how stubborn these Jews could be. He allowed them to keep their spiritual leaders – the Pharisees and Sadducees among others – because otherwise they would have been impossible to govern, but, of course, the seat of political and economic power lay with him and Rome. He made absolutely sure of that.'

Marc thought about what Cornelius had just said. Many times he had heard this story. Allow people some cultural and religious freedom and they are happy for political control to be elsewhere.

'Wasn't his land split up after his death?'

'Yes, it was divided between three of his sons: Archelaus, Herod Antipas and Herod Philip. Antipas and Philip are still ruling their lands but Archelaus, who was here in Judea, was eventually exiled in time.'

'What did he do wrong?'

'He seriously upset the Jews. There was an uprising in Jerusalem soon after his father died and Archelaus foolishly killed three thousand pilgrims. He also divorced his wife and married the widow of his half brother, which is against Jewish law. On top of that, he deposed any high priests who disagreed with him. The Jews were so upset they even got together with the Samaritans who live north of here - people they despise. Rome had no choice, he had to go, couldn't risk another uprising.'

'Where did they send him?'

'I think it was somewhere in Gaul.'

'So the people had power.'

'There's no doubt they have power. As you said earlier, we can't be everywhere. We depend on the previous leaders to still do their job, providing they don't overstep the line.'

'As I recall, a procurator was then appointed to govern Judea on Rome's behalf.'

'That's quite right. The first one was called Colonius. We are on our fifth now.'

'Pontius Pilate!'

'Yes, we'll meet him tomorrow. He has invited us to the palace where he lives when in Caesarea, which is most of the year. Herod built all the more spectacular buildings below us. He provided massive aqueducts - you can just see one of them from here – underground sewers, public baths, fountains and roads - not what the people were used to. And not only in Caesarea! Herod also transformed Jerusalem. He rebuilt the Jewish Temple with a magnificence that Rome would be proud of. He is undoubtedly the greatest king the Jews have ever had, even if the ungrateful wretches don't recognize it.'

Milo and Piso needed to stretch. They stood up and walked around then Milo rested his head on Marc's knee.

'Well, that's most surprising. I've never seen him do that to a stranger. He must like you and trust you.'

Cornelius seemed satisfied, as though the opinion of his dog was important to him.

Marc continued. 'How did Herod afford so much grandeur?'

'Very good question and it brings us to the point of your invitation here.'

There was a natural pause in the conversation while Cornelius poured some more wine. Marc made an appreciative noise as he took another draught.

'Fine wine, this! Does it grow locally?'

'Oh yes, Judea has its own vineyards, although we do import from many other countries. That's one big advantage of the Empire that people don't appreciate. Travelling has been made so easy. We have opened up the world. Let's toast the Empire!'

The two men lifted their glasses.

'We were coming to the point of my being here.'

'Yes, but I want to tell you a bit more of the background first. You asked how Herod financed his projects. Basically, they were built by Augustus, but the Emperor was no fool, he was generous because he knew of Herod's renowned personal wealth, and insisted that Herod should bequeath everything to him.'

'Where was the personal wealth kept?'

'Herod had a palace built some ten miles south of Jerusalem called Herodium. The treasures were kept in the vaults.'

'And did Augustus receive his bequest?'

'After Herod's death Augustus sent a contingent of his own personal guards to take an inventory of the valuables that were still in the vaults, and claimed them as his inheritance. He shipped some of the gold back to Rome and ordered a guard to be maintained at Herodium. It was rumoured that the gold was sunk in a storm so the Emperor was particularly sensitive about protecting what was left. When Augustus died some years after Herod, the order was never rescinded and so the guard remained.'

'What else did the treasures consist of?'

'Among his fortune were stones of lapis lazuli that had belonged to Mariamne, one of Herod's wives. They were of a unique quality and irreplaceable, over a thousand years' old, deep blue in colour with golden flecks, quite priceless. I heard that they had once belonged to Queen Cleopatra.'

'Are they still there?'

Cornelius paused before he answered this question. He seemed embarrassed.

'Well, this is the problem. When Pilate was in Jerusalem eighteen months ago for the Feast of the Tabernacles, he noticed how unhygienic the city was becoming with all the pilgrims who flood into the city at such times and decided that more public improvements were needed to deliver fresh water. He asked Emperor Tiberius to fund the projects. But Tiberius was reminded that Augustus had never claimed the rest of his inheritance and told Pilate to use Herod's wealth. When eventually the vaults were unsealed - the valuable lapis lazuli had gone.'

Cornelius leant back in his chair with a sigh. In a dramatic gesture, he opened his arms and turned his palms upwards, as though indicating that he had held the jewels in his hands and someone had snatched them from him. Marc looked out at the horizon. The sky had lost its blueness.

'So my job is to find the stones?'

'Yes, I see you understand perfectly.'

'Any suggestions as to where they might be?'

'None at all, I'm afraid. The vaults were securely shut. There was no sign of anyone breaking and entering. The embarrassing problem for Pilate is that nobody has any idea when they were taken. Emperor Tiberius is furious. Pilate may lose his posting for incompetence, which of course would end his career. He is a very worried man.'

'Was anything else taken?'

'No! That is also puzzling.'

'When were the vaults opened up?'

'About six months ago.'

'Who was present?'

'A man called Silas, who is in charge of Herodium when no-one is in residence, which has been the case for a long time now; he is Keeper of the Keys. Then there was Flavius, Pilate's chief administrator, who visits Herodium regularly, and two guards.'

'Was no inventory taken on a regular basis?'

Cornelius groaned as if in despair.

'No, I suppose it seems ridiculous to an outsider looking back on it now. But there honestly did not seem to be any point. The vault was regularly guarded. Nobody was making any demands. It was not until now, when money seems to have become an issue that anybody thought to look.'

'Not even when Augustus died?'

'No, I'm afraid not.'

'Are the rest of the treasures still at Herodium?'

'No, they were moved to Jerusalem last week on my orders.'

It occurred to Marc that knowing he was on his way to investigate it would have been more sensible to leave them where they were for one more week, but he said nothing. Instead he took another deep draught of wine and allowed the scratching of the cicada below to waft over his senses. This certainly did seem to be an excessive case of foolishness and negligence.

'I would like to see the vaults.'

'Yes, yes, of course, and so you shall. Pilate has to go to Jerusalem very soon for the Passover. We can ride with him and his guard. Any information is available to you that you ask for … if we have it, that is.'

Was that suggestion of support intended to comfort him? Normally it might have done so, but in most cases he dealt with there was at least some clue. When artefacts go missing someone usually has some idea of when they were taken. It perhaps was not so surprising that there had been no need of the wealth in the vaults. The Empire had been undergoing a period of consolidation. Maybe it was left in Jerusalem to be used in case of uprisings. He speculated no further. Tonight he had heard enough. His journey, the wine and the calmness of the evening were overcoming him in waves of tiredness.

'Well, I have had too much of this excellent wine to apply my mind to it tonight. I would like to know more about the lapis lazuli though, so I know what I'm looking for.'

'Pilate should be able to help there. Herod's palace is full of old records. But may I suggest that for now we finish off this jug.'

He poured out the remaining contents and the two men sat in a companionable silence until the chilled air encouraged them inside.

5

-Pontius Pilate-

Marc rose early, bathed and breakfasted on fruit, cheese and white bread. Portius and Julius, the young charioteer, obliged his every need. Even the dogs followed respectfully at a distance as he strolled round the spacious gardens, occasionally sitting under a group of palm trees to listen to fountain waters. He had been given many assignments about missing or dead persons but a burglary of this nature was a first, particularly one where the time frame was anything up to thirty years, with no clues as to how or by whom it was committed. Presumably the motive was greed so why take only the jewels? He mentally made a list of things to do.

Speaking to Pilate was probably the place to start, although he doubted he would hear anything other than what Cornelius had already told him. But at least he would know for whom he was working. Find out more information about the jewels, where they originated, what they look like, how many. Inspect the inventory if it still exists and any other archive material. Visit Herodium Palace and obtain the plans, search the vaults, check the guard duty list and look for anything unusual.

His thoughts were interrupted by the approach of Cornelius.

'Good morning, glad to see our Judean wine has not upset your constitution. How have you managed to so easily tame the dogs? I seldom have visitors and when I do the dogs are less than agreeable. I trust you had a comfortable night?'

'Very good thank you, particularly after so long at sea, and the wine was excellent.'

'Good. I must check my farm and the stables this morning.

You are welcome to join me. Later this afternoon I have arranged for us to meet Pilate at the palace. We are invited to join him for dinner and then at the theatre. Some actors from Corinth are performing "Oedipus Rex." I read it a while ago, forgotten it though, something about killing his father, solving a riddle and marrying his mother.'

Marc's maternal grandmother taught him the love of books, much to his father's disgust. Strange then, that when Rufus Tiro became very ill, he demanded that his son should read to him. Tears rolled down his cheeks, half eaten way by disease, as he grew to love recitation of the Greek tragedies. Any misspoken lines were greeted by a tirade of abuse, and when the rottenness of his tongue made speech impossible, he would lash out with his walking stick if the narrator skipped so much as a word.

Thus Sophocles' story of the King and Queen of Thebes was deeply imprinted in Marc's mind. Determined to avoid a warning by the Oracle that their new born son will kill his father and marry his mother, they leave the child in a wood where he is found and brought up by the King and Queen of Corinth. As a man, Oedipus unknowingly kills his real father and after solving the riddle of the Sphinx, he is made King of Thebes and marries the widowed Queen, his own mother. Retribution of the gods is fierce, leads to exile, self-mutilation and suicide. A typical Greek scenario!

Marc wistfully posed a question.

'What goes on four feet in the morning, two feet at noon, and three feet in the evening?'

Cornelius looked at him in surprise.

'Sorry, I don't understand.'

'It's the riddle that the Sphinx asks Oedipus.'

Cornelius frowned and speculated for a while.

'I don't know.'

'The answer is man. A man is a baby in the morning of his life and he crawls on four feet. He is an adult in the noon of his life and he walks on two feet. But when he is old, in the evening of his life, he walks with a cane, on three feet.'

Cornelius laughed and prophesied.

'Not me! I shall die on my two feet or not at all.'

Together they strolled through the main gates and down the hill. Cornelius' farm was on the left. He waved an arm expressively across the landscape.

'This is my land as far as you can see. My ancestors were Persian and settled here three hundred years ago. Although I was born and brought up in Rome, I inherited all this during the reign of Herod when I was just twenty. I decided to retire here.'

Marc followed the vista Cornelius outlined. The flat land in front of him would soon be a riot of burgeoning colour where blocks of different flowers and herbs were growing.

'We're cultivating anemone, narcissus, cyclamen, poppy, lavender, lilies and jasmine. Over there is a field of papyrus, caper, sage, mint, myrtle and wormwood.'

Cornelius made a pointed gesture with a spatulate index finger.

Marc was familiar with some of these plants from his own estate but had never seen so many. There were also plants that he did not recognize, presumably from the east. As the gradient of the land increased it was covered with pine trees, date palms, tamarisk, pomegranate, figs, olive, cedar and almond.

'Come on, I'll show you the distilleries where the perfumes are made.'

So this was the basis of his wealth. They turned left through a bower beyond which stood two long wooden buildings exuding the most exotic of smells. Cornelius led Marc along the line of equipment and explained the process.

'Perfumes are produced more quickly using distillation, other Egyptian methods take too long and make the perfume oil too expensive. Here is where the plants are crushed and placed in boiling water. The essential oils vaporise with the steam. Once it condenses the oil separates from the water and is collected and then blended with almond or olive oil.'

Both men and women were working in these wooden sheds. The perfumes were being poured into small, pottery and glass cosmetic jars or phials for distribution and sales at the local perfume shops.

'We sell to local shops but much is shipped abroad.'

Marc was impressed with the business ingenuity of his host. Herbs were either being dried or tied into fresh bundles for cooking and medicinal purposes.

Cornelius said with pride, 'Now, you shall meet my Arabian beauties.'

From the distilleries they walked uphill along a path through a grove of desert acacia trees until they were nearly back at the villa. The grove gave way to a spotless courtyard with low buildings on three sides, two of which were divided by stable doors. The third had a single door in the centre. Cornelius' love of Greek culture was apparent in the names of his horses.

'Let me introduce you. This is Artemis, goddess of the wild beasts; Dionysus, the wild one; Poseidon, god of the sea; and my favourite, Zeus, chief of all gods.'
He approached Zeus lovingly, and it was clear the horse loved him.

'These are the best and fastest in the land. They cannot be beaten in the ring. Zeus is their leader.'

All four animals were a light dapple grey and, harnessed together, would be a magnificent sight. These four made Cornelius a major competitor in the hippodrome. There were two other stabled horses; one had been used by Julius to bring Marc from the port. For some reason they had been given the names of Roman rather than Greek gods, Mercury and Vulcan.

Marc loved nothing more than the combined smell of horse and leather saddles. He reached out and stroked the mane of Artemis, then moved towards her muzzle. The horse jerked her head in the air with a snort but stood curiously still as Marc breathed into the animal's nostrils. Within minutes Artemis was nuzzling this stranger. Cornelius watched with interest and chortled.

'Well, you certainly do have a way with animals. First you beguile my dogs and now my horses. Are you as good with women?'

'No, unfortunately not, if only it was that easy.'

The accompanying long shed was filled with fresh straw, hay, oats and barley. Shiny four horned saddles, bits, bridles, leather girth straps and reins hung from the middle of one of the walls, together with rugs and cleaning materials for horses from hooves to manes. Several young slaves were bustling around, anxious to look busy and hoping for a word of praise from their master. None was forthcoming, however. Cornelius merely expected the best. Julius, the young charioteer, was in charge.

He said, 'I'll show you the chariots.'

They entered another wooden building round the back of the stables where the chariots stood. They were not like the large military chariots with which Marc was familiar, encased in metal like the one they had used the day before. These were racing chariots made of wood with little or no protection for the charioteer. Correct balance made the difference between life and death.

'We harness the four horses together. They're an unstoppable team. I have won many times and hope to pay for my freedom. The master has assured me that it will be so.'

Julius spoke with pride. Oddly enough, despite his interest in matters equine, this was a sport that had never appealed to Marc. He preferred to ride bareback and feel at one with the horse. Nevertheless, he had respect for those who risked their lives in the ring.

Julius continued, 'Our colour is red trimmed with gold.'

He pointed to some tunics and other pieces of leather clothing carefully hanging by the chariots, together with some lightweight gold helmets.

'I hope you will have a chance to see me in the ring before you go.'

'How do you cope with four sets of reins?'

'I wrap them round my waist; it helps me to control the horses.'

'And if you slip?'

'Then I will be dragged beneath the hooves. It has happened to many charioteers, but not to me. My gods protect me.'

With this, Julius opened the door and indicated that it was time to leave.

The rest of the day was spent pleasantly enough relaxing, resting and reflecting. The sleeping rooms were to the right of the open courtyard. The slaves' quarters were to the left down the steps that led to the bathing and food preparation areas. Marc's room was lavishly furnished with voile drapes round the bed to protect the sleeper from unwelcome winged visitors. The frame was made of wood; the mattress full of down with fine woven covers. Rugs covered the wooden floor; shelves and drawers were available for the convenience of the occupier. It was of a strangely feminine décor.

In late afternoon, Marc and Cornelius, driving the more substantial chariot that Julius had used the day before, set off down the hill to the city. They had changed into more traditional togas, rather than the tunics they had been wearing, in recognition of the formal affair they were about to attend. They turned to the right before reaching the city wall and headed towards Herod's palace, now the Roman administrative centre, and occupied by Pontius Pilate when in Caesarea. The palace was a square fortress around a large courtyard. Crenellated towers stood at all four corners. Marc had rarely seen a better administrative building in all his peregrinations round the Empire.

The two visitors drove passed the buttresses, through the fortress gates, under an archway and into the open square beyond. They were expected, and immediately relieved of their chariot by attentive slaves. Escorts showed them into the royal portico with marble colonnades on either side. Pilate sat on his seat of office at the far end. He rose and walked to greet them.

'Welcome to you both!'

Pilate was stocky and muscular. His face was square with a heavy jaw, full lips and thinning black hair. His eyes had a vitreous quality, yet there was an air of astuteness about him. He was an administrator not a soldier, a politician who had survived only by shrewdly compromising where his superiors were concerned. However, there was no such consideration for those he considered inferior. The conversation followed the usual platitudes. Pilate addressed Marc.

'I'm glad you've agreed to help us solve this mystery. I trust Cornelius has already outlined our problem.'

'Yes indeed, it's quite mystifying.'

In fact, Marc was not sure he could help at all.

'I thought it best for us to have a quiet meal together so we can talk in confidence. Let's eat.'

He led the way through one of the colonnades into a room used for dining purposes. A large, square highly polished table stood in the centre of the room with couches on three sides. The fourth side was left open to allow for serving. Double doors placed at intervals stood open, facing the quadrangle. They were draped with thin transparent vitrage blowing in the gentle breeze. The delicate smell of spring flowers wafted through the open spaces. The table was already covered with appetizers of eggs, raw vegetables, pieces of fish and shellfish. Pilate indicated to Marc to sit in the place of honour opposite the open end of the table. Cornelius and Pilate took the remaining two places.

'Tomorrow, Marc, I would like you to meet a young

administrator who shows great promise as an investigator, I believe. His name is Gaius. He has already detected anomalies in the imperial accounting system and has followed them up with a great deal of acuity. I think you'll like him and he can show you our historical records and files. You may find it helpful to have a trusted colleague to exchange ideas with.'

'Thank you! I shall look forward to meeting him. I will need someone to show me around.'

Marc preferred to work alone but was now in an unfamiliar place so he deferred. Pilate continued.

'Jewels do not vanish into thin air and must be somewhere. I hope you'll come with us to Jerusalem in a few days. I have to make one of my compulsory visits there during the Jewish Passover. It is part of my role as governor to make at least three visits a year. I usually go during the Jewish festivals. Not that I enjoy them. Never have I met a more difficult people to govern than the Jews. Do you know they have only one God? Can you imagine – the poor fellow must be run ragged trying to meet all the needs of their incessant prayers! And they consider us unclean, unclean! We are people who have turned bathing into a form of art.'

Pilate pulled down both sides of his mouth in disgust and raised both hands into the air in a gesture of disbelief. Marc smiled. Cornelius managed a small chuckle.

He said, 'They know nothing. Else they would be the victors and we the conquered.'

Pilate emitted a loud laugh at the preposterousness of the idea and slapped the side of his couch in mirth. Unexpectedly he sat up, his face enraged, and he shouted loudly.

'You idiot, I will have you flogged, do you hear, flogged.'

A slave had spilled a drop of wine on the table. He visibly trembled as he bowed, edging his way backwards from the room. Pilate smiled at his guests.

'I can't abide sloppiness. A good dose of fear never does anyone any harm, eh?'

How often Marc had observed these contradictory complex traits among the powerful who use their authority for entertainment, like a young bully prodding a caged animal, until, that is, one day the beast breaks free and devours its tormenter.

The main course of cooked vegetables and pork was accompanied by copious glasses of wine, and by the time the sweet pastries arrived, Pilate had mellowed considerably. His chief topic of conversation was a rehearsal of the story that Cornelius had already narrated the day before. But this time it was from Pilate's personal viewpoint and stressed his embarrassment, the impossibility of theft under the noses of his excellent staff, the Emperor's unreasonableness in blaming him, and his ineluctable shame if a solution were not found.

Cornelius looked sympathetic, yet somehow Marc doubted his sincerity. He seemed unmoved by Pilate's grievance and disdainful of his insobriety. There was an element within the man that was essentially inscrutable. He addressed Pilate as though comforting a fretful child.

'Well, I'm sure a solution will be found. Enough of this dispiriting talk! What time are we expected at the theatre?'

Pilate was jolted out of his depressed reverie.

'Of course, we have an evening to look forward to. My wife will be joining us shortly.'

The three men rose from the table when, as if on cue, Pilate's wife, Claudia Procula, entered the room. She was in her late thirties, slim and not unattractive. Her most engaging characteristic was her eyes; filled with a sense of fun. She was introduced to Marc and Cornelius. She had actually met them both before, but it was many years since she had spoken to Marc and she did not appear to recognize him. He decided not to remind her for the moment.

Her long hair was coifed onto the top of her head and decorated with sparkling diamantine jewels. Her elegant blue dress clung to a slim yet fulsome figure. In advance of the journey, she wore a dark cloak draped from the front over her left shoulder, brought round her back and under her right arm, then across her body, with the remaining material carried over her left arm. Pilate was clearly well pleased with his wife, and so he should have been.

'I'm delighted to meet you.'

Claudia addressed her remarks to Marc with a smile. He noticed her genuine warmth and wondered why Pilate could not rest his spirit in the arms of this woman. He also could not help noticing the way the material rested over her right breast, not covered by the cloak. Pilate, like his guests, was wearing a toga as a mark of his Roman citizenship.

The four illustrious visitors to the theatre were carried in litters on the shoulders of slaves. Marc was less than comfortable with this display of grandeur and suspected that Cornelius felt the same. Nevertheless, to decline would be churlish and rude. They were heartily welcomed by the theatrical producer and proffered prime comfortable seats for honoured guests. The seating was built in a rising semi-circle. An acoustic wall formed the backdrop of the stage which faced them, covered by painted wooden scenery. There were three entrances and exits.

The play began with several actors emerging on stage dressed in black. They were members of the chorus whose role was to fill in necessary details of the story for the audience. Messengers and prophets warned the listeners of the ominous outcome as a result of the evil that had been perpetrated. Costumes and masks were worn to indicate not only the type of person who was on stage, but also their emotional state. Women were not allowed to act. Young men, or boys, wearing white masks performed the female roles. Some of the actors played more than one character.

As the tragedy unfolded there were comments, gasps and cries from the audience. The natural light was beginning to fade as the play progressed. Clay oil lamps were lit along the front and side of the stage, creating mysterious livid shadows that simply added to the potency of the message. Marc was much moved by the performance and noticed Claudia was fighting back tears. Pilate was silent. Only Cornelius took in a deep breath that he expelled through his teeth and pursed lips, as though he were glad it was over. He was the first on his feet as the bows and applause came to an end. Pilate, however, was determined to meet the cast and asked Marc and Cornelius to join him and Claudia.

The actors formed a semi-circle and their theatrical producer, Crassus, introduced them in turn to Pilate, his wife and illustrious guests. Each one waited to be spoken to first, doubtless out of deference to the status of the visitors. However, in the line up was a boy, not quite a young man Marc thought, with soft feminine features and a voice barely broken, who played the part of Jocasta. He addressed Cornelius.

'What did you learn from the play, sir?'

'How stupid and ignorant even those who rule can be.'

The young actor pursued the questioning.

'The gods punish the proud – but punishment brings wisdom, don't you think?'

'I'm sorry,' said Cornelius, 'I'm not sure I can agree.'

Marc had folded his left arm across his body, supported his right elbow and rested his chin in his hand. He rocked back slightly onto his heels. He looked like a man patiently waiting. But that slight tilt of the head and eyebrows enabled him to miss none of the nuances of this snippet of conversation. He had a strong sense that these two men – the younger and older – had met before.

6

-The History Lesson-

The next few days were spent visiting the record office to discover anything remotely connected to this mystery. Pilate had personally picked the young man called Gaius to help Marc with his investigations. He prided himself on his ability to judge the qualities required for each role under his command, and identify them in his staff. He was, after all, a leader of men. Pilate took a few minutes out of his busy schedule to speak to them.

'Good morning, Marc, allow me to introduce to you my trusted young colleague, Gaius. He will help you with your research and make sure you have no difficulty gaining entrance to wherever you choose to go.'

Marc assessed that Gaius was in his late twenties. He was handsome and well proportioned but quite short, and this gave him the appearance of being younger.

'Just tell me what you want and I shall do it if at all possible. I'm very willing to help in any way I can.'

Marc could find no fault so far with the welcome and hospitality he had received. Gaius showed him through a labyrinth of corridors with more colonnades and pillars in the Corinthian and Ionic styles. Everywhere there was marble, mosaic and lavish furnishings. The two men walked side-by-side to the east end of the palace, and talked together comfortably. Marc asked Gaius about his work with Pontius Pilate.

'I'm not a military man. I have worked for the government since returning from university in Athens. I learned languages so I was employed as a translator.'

'Where are you from?'

'My father is a Phoenician nobleman from Syria. He made his wealth trading in jewels.'

They were heading for the enormous library filled with books, records and reference material of every kind. Marc took a few moments to peruse the great works and was pleased to find copies of the writings of his great, great grandfather, Marcus Varro. Gaius peered over.

'I read some of Varro at university. I can't remember much about it now though.'

Marc did not comment. It was part of his being.

There was no problem gaining access to the most private of papers. Among Herod's possessions they found a portrait of Cleopatra VII painted on wood, apparently received from his one time friend Mark Anthony. She was wearing a necklace of deep blue stones with golden specks.

Marc said, 'Cornelius told me he thought they had once belonged to Cleopatra. She was the good friend of Julius Caesar.'

'And Mark Anthony! She had children by them both.'

Gaius chuckled and his eyes twinkled mischievously.

'So how did Mariamne come to own Cleopatra's jewels?'

'It appears that Mariamne was the granddaughter of a man called John Hyrcanus. She inherited them from him.'

'Who was John Hyrcanus and how did he come to have them?'

'I don't know. We need to speak to an historian. I know just the person.'

The curator of the palace library was an elderly Greek scribe called Philip. They found him in a small room sitting at a desk updating a register of accounts. He looked up and welcomed them with a smile of recognition as Gaius opened the door with gusto.

'Good morning Philip! This is Commander Marcus Tiro. We need a history lesson.'

'You know me, Master Gaius. There's nothing I like more.

Please, come in both of you and take a seat. I'll move these out of the way.'

A table in the centre of the room was covered with parchment scrolls, untidily askew where they had been left undone. Philip removed other scripts from two chairs.

Gaius began. 'We want to know about John Hyrcanus, the grandfather of Herod's wife, Mariamne. Can you help us Philip?'

'Well now, John Hyrcanus was a Hasmonean high priest around the time the Romans took control of Jerusalem.'

Gaius repeated the name slowly enunciating each syllable.

'The Hasmoneans! Yes, I've heard of them, just remind us of who they were.'

'They were a particular group of orthodox Jews who felt very strongly about keeping the traditions of their religion. They ruled Judea for nearly a hundred years, until General Pompey and his Roman army came along and conquered them about seventy years ago.'

'Do you know if there was any connection between the Hasmoneans and Egypt, particularly Queen Cleopatra?'

'Yes, but we need to start a bit further back. Three hundred years ago, the Greeks were the main superpower, led by Alexander. Although he ruled the lands here in the east, he largely let the people govern themselves. When he died the land was divided between two of his generals, Ptolemy and Seleucis. Seleucis ruled Syria in the north. Ptolemy ruled Egypt in the south. Judea was in the middle of the two, and they were always fighting over it.'

He paused to see if there were any more questions. When none came, he continued.

'Egypt ruled Judea for a hundred years; but it was then conquered by Syria. The king tried to Hellenise Jerusalem, to make it return to the Greek culture and values. But the Jews didn't want to conform to that. They were very particular about whom they worshipped. So there was a Jewish uprising, led by a man called

Mattathias and his five sons from the Hasmonean family. That was the beginning of the Hasmonean dynasty which lasted about another hundred years.'

Gaius asked, 'There's a Hasmonean palace in Jerusalem. Was it built by them?'

'Yes it was. But by the later generations of Hasmonean kings. They weren't quite as ascetic as the early ones; they preferred palaces and the luxuries of the Greek civilization. Meanwhile, the Romans had conquered lands in the west and were beginning to turn their attention to the east.'

'How did Cleopatra get involved?'

'Openly the Hasmoneans were against Roman occupation even if some of them quietly approved of it. Queen Cleopatra saw this as a way of regaining influence in Judea, the land that Egypt had once lost, and she secretly fuelled their hostility. '

'Do you think she supported them financially?'

'Oh yes, master Gaius. That's more than likely.'

Marc removed his hand from his mouth and chin where it had been supporting his head.

'Interesting! So what happened to John Hyrcanus?'

'Well, he survived the change of control because he became a Roman sympathizer. There were always Judeans who were loyal to Rome, you know, despite what they may have said in public. King Herod was among them. Even though the Roman Senate gave Herod the title of King of the Jews, he was never popular with the Hasmoneans. He wasn't one of those true to the faith. But he was clever. He married Mariamne, who was not only a Hasmonean but also the granddaughter of John Hyrcanus. Although Herod eventually executed him – he was too popular.'

'So Mariamne might have inherited wealth that was accumulated as a result of Cleopatra's support,' commented Marc.

'Yes. That's highly probable.'

'Thank you, Philip, you've been most helpful.'

Philip beamed. He wanted to continue talking but the two men had heard enough for the time being, so they left him with a promise to return if necessary.

They took a break and wandered through the city and port of Caesarea. Gaius showed Marc where he lived, a small white Judean house, within Herod's wall, built of brick and mud and painted white. The house sat on top of an incline and reaching it required walking up a gentle cobbled hill. The front door opened directly onto the road. Gaius had painted it red. The white architraves were decorated with red and green leaves in the form of wreaths.

The downstairs room was plainly furnished with rugs on the stone floor. A wooden table stood in the centre of the room with benches either side. Pottery vases and other utensils were placed on shelves. On the wall to the left, inside a chimney, was a stove, filled with coals now cool. Across the room was a door that led outside into a courtyard. In the right hand corner an open stone staircase went to the floor above.

'This is where they used to keep animals,' explained Gaius. 'But I use it for cooking and washing. I live and sleep upstairs. There's a third floor but you have to go back outside and up the side steps to reach it.'

Gaius walked up the stone steps into a comfortably furnished room with a fireplace directly over the one below. He invited Marc to follow. He opened the shutters revealing a view of the harbour and sea beyond. Marc spent time at the window breathing in the air. As he turned he noticed some trophies proudly displayed in a corner of the room.

'What did you do to deserve those?' he inquired.

'While I was at university in Athens, I took part in Olympic foot races and javelin throwing. I enjoyed it and was lucky enough to win sometimes.'

'You are just full of surprises.' Marc said amiably.

He turned back and looked down into the communal courtyard with its well for drawing water. Two young girls were struggling with a wooden bucket, or at least one was struggling the other was watching. A voice came from the back of a house opposite and they both jumped into action.

'Why do you choose to live here when you could have the luxury of rooms in the palace?'

'It's simpler and more private. Besides, there's a very good place just down the road that sells excellent beer and good food. I'll just pick up some coins and then I suggest we go.'

They walked back down the cobbled street and turned left towards the harbour. Houses on either side were sometimes joined together forming an archway. The bar was on the quayside facing the sea. The barman was a large jolly man whose business was booming. He recognized Gaius immediately and slapped him heartily on the back.

'Beer?' he said. 'What about your friend?'

'Two beers please,' said Gaius, good-naturedly. 'And we'll have a plate of your excellent fish with garum sauce and white bread.'

They watched the fishing boats bringing in their catches, offloading and setting sail again. Marc felt more relaxed than he had done for many years. Adrenalin struck him uncomfortably in the gut as the tossing locks of a flower seller reminded him of Felix' mother. She had filled his senses and he missed her still. But then the moment passed.

When they finished and went outside, he looked beyond the city to where an enormous aqueduct walked like a centipede out of the hills, and buried its head into the sand as it disappeared underground. Life here seemed very good. It even occurred to him that it might be a good place to live permanently. It was time he wrote to his son.

Over the next day or two they found some old papyri legal and administrative documents from Egypt. Marc made notes.

'It seems the stones were mined over thirteen hundred years ago in Northern Afghanistan and sent to the king of Ugarit in Syria, where they were shipped abroad or sold to the wealthy merchant classes. Some were used seven hundred years later by a jeweller in Damascus to prepare settings for Cleopatra I, a Syrian princess, at the time of her marriage to Ptolemy, King of Egypt. The lapis lazuli was handed down to all the successive queens, until Cleopatra VII evidently gave them to the Hasmoneans.'

He looked up at Gaius.

'If the stones were unique then they wouldn't lose their value. That'll be why Augustus left his inheritance sitting in the vaults at Herodium.'

Gaius looked at Marc's jottings.

'What on earth is that language you're writing in?'

'It's called shorthand.'

'How did you come to learn that?'

'It was invented by my great, great grandfather. I was named after him. He was a slave of Cicero. Shorthand made him so valuable, writing speeches for the Senate, that he was given his freedom, and land to go with it. It has proved very useful.'

'Would that be the shorthand or the land?' Gaius joked.

 Marc always regretted that a few hours later this comradeship was fractured by distrust.

7

-The Fire-

One evening, having enjoyed some of Gaius' cooking, Marc returned to the villa. Portius greeted him and explained that Cornelius had left to carry out some business in the north, but expected to be back before the trip to Jerusalem. He was grateful for the time alone and sat in the splendid gardens listening to the fountains until he felt sufficiently relaxed that tiredness overcame him, sleep inevitable.

Because of the depth of his sleep, he did not notice the figure at the door of his bedchamber, nor did he see the arm raised ready to throw the dagger. The holder took aim and the dagger left the hand just as Marc stirred and moved from lying on his back to his side. With remarkable accuracy the instrument flew across the room and the blade sank deeply into the bed just behind him. At the noise of the soft thud, Marc turned back his body the way it had come, only to encounter cold metal. Instinct made him leap to his feet.

He caught a swift glimpse of the shape, shadowy behind the lighted torch that rose into the air and drifted onto the flammable coverings. Within a short time the room was ablaze since the floor, bed structure and other furniture was made of cedar wood. Marc ran naked towards the door. Julius appeared on the threshold dressed in a long tunic that had caught fire. He ran towards the open courtyard exacerbating his condition. The room where Marc and Cornelius had sat a few nights earlier enjoying the evening air was now alight, the furnishings, the tapestry and timber beams. Burning hay was strewn over the floor throughout the house.

As Julius reached the small courtyard, the flames were fuelled by the air from the open space in the roof above. He collapsed. Portius appeared with cloaks, throwing one over the burning body. Together they dragged him to the edge of the square basin and heaved him into the water, burning the palms of their hands as they did so. The superior element won and the flames were extinguished in a rush of steam. The body was badly blackened and Julius was convulsing. A stench of burning flesh filled their nostrils and throats, choking them with its acridity.

The wooden beams supporting the tiles were now in danger of collapsing and the two men, with the body of the third, struggled outside just before the roof caved into the main hallway. The tiles lay in violent array on the mosaic floor. There was little that could be done. People started to appear at the gates with containers of water, having seen or heard the fire and smoke that was by now filling the skyline with orange and black shadows. Portius opened the gates. Everywhere was chaos. Marc gently placed another cloak over Julius who was in a bad state of shock.

Whoever did this must have been young, speedy, agile and accurate. Marc thought of the figure he had seen in the doorway and remembered some trophies. His anguish soon turned to anger. He ran from the villa towards the stables, ignoring his nakedness. The door into the building where the hay and straw were stored was open. So this was how the intruder had started the fire, using hay as tinder, no doubt lighting it as he retraced his steps. The speed with which it had been done was astonishing. How had he got passed the dogs? There was no sign of them. They had not barked. Marc decided he would check when he got back from where he needed to go. Someone had tried to kill him; someone must know why.

He took a piece of cloth where the clothes hung, wrapped it twice round his hips, pushed the loose end between the two layers, passed it under his crotch and tucked the spare material into the waist on the other side of his body. This would provide him with some protection. He then threw over his head one of the tunics that Julius had so proudly shown him with its red and gold colours, tied some sandals round his ankles, lifted one of the bridles off its resting place and ran towards the stables. He bridled Mercury, jumped on his back and set off at a gallop down the hill to the city gates.

Marc banged on the red painted door. He needed an immediate response to help him assess whether Gaius was involved; he had to know whether he could trust him. Gaius opened the door, hardly conscious from his slumber.

'Tell me, Gaius, who ordered my death tonight?'

'Sorry, I don't know what you're talking about.'

'I think you do.'

Grabbing him by the throat with his right hand, he forced him back into the room and pushed him against a wall. The younger man's reactions were instinctive and fast. He drew his left arm across his body and with all his force hit the inside of Marc's elbow. The shock to the old injury in his shoulder produced sufficient release for Gaius to advance on his visitor with his left foot. He twisted his right leg round Marc and hit him sharply along the back of the knees, so that he crumpled and fell backwards onto the floor. Gaius reached for the gladius he kept by the door. But he didn't want to aggravate the situation. Having temporarily gained the upper hand, he took two paces back and allowed Marc, who was already on his feet, to stand without further attack. He dropped the weapon and held both hands in the air as if in surrender.

'Please, tell me what's happened. I swear I know nothing about any of this.'

'Someone threw a dagger at me, torched the house and a slave has been badly burned. There were only three people who knew why I was here. Cornelius wouldn't burn down his own villa. So that leaves you and your commanding officer. Does someone want to stop me working on this assignment?'

'If there is, it's not me, I have nothing to gain. Besides, who would want to kill you now? We have only just started the investigation. We are nowhere near the truth. Everything we've found so far is already public knowledge.'

Marc decided he believed him. If Gaius had been ordered to kill him, he would have continued fighting and claimed self-defence. He sat down on one of the benches. Gaius put the sword back in its place and took a seat opposite him.

'There's one thing, you're not dead, thank the gods. What has happened to Cornelius?'

'He's gone away for a day or two. Portius told me when I got back this evening.'

Gaius poured Marc a drink and had one himself. He wanted to know more.

'Did you see the person who threw the dagger?'

'Yes, very briefly, I moved slightly just as the blade hit the bed. It landed behind me. It was pure good fortune. Then someone threw a lighted torch and the whole room went up in flames. Whoever it was had planned what he was going to do. He'd been to the stable for dry hay to start the fire with. The slave Julius has been badly burned.'

'I'm sorry.' Gaius shook his head. 'Do you know how he got in?'

'He must have scaled the walls. I've not yet had a chance to check. The gates were still locked.'

'The dogs are trained to savage any strangers – they would have ripped him to pieces. Why didn't they stop him?'

'Good question! They must have been got at in some way.'

'Do you think there was more than one person?'

'The speed with which it all happened leads me to believe there was probably just one. It would be too risky getting away otherwise – it would take too long to scale the wall.'

'How big was the person you caught a glimpse of – could you

tell?'

'No, not really, they were in the shadow of the flames. But Julius appeared in the doorway not long afterwards, and he was certainly no bigger than him. In fact, I would say he was more your height. I'm going back now to see what I can do.'

'I would like to come with you, if you think I can be trusted.'

Half an hour later, Mercury had carried both men back up the hill. The sight was one of devastation. Cornelius' magnificent home was largely destroyed. The walls were still standing, built as they were with brick and concrete, and the mosaic, though deeply scarred, was still discernable.

There were several people present at the scene. Some were just observing; others, those who worked for Cornelius, were doing their best to clean up, trained and indoctrinated into believing that this was their role for their master. But the materials and ground were too scorched and hot and Marc advised them to go home before they too were injured. There were murmurings and everyone seemed shocked, but there was also an element of fear amongst the gathering, as though it was their fault, and retribution would come upon them.

Portius was weeping over the injuries of his friend. Julius had been moved to the house of a neighbouring doctor who said he would do what he could to help him, although everybody seemed to be certain that only the will of the gods would prevail. Marc inquired of Portius where the dogs were.

'I don't know, sir. I haven't seen them.'

Gaius and Marc walked round the side of the villa to the place where the dogs were usually fed, although at all times they were allowed to wander the grounds at will. Two charred bodies were visible among the still smouldering rubble. They were not tied down but had allowed themselves to be burned alive.

'Let's walk round the outer walls. There must be some clue as to how the intruder got in. He must have carried straw or hay over the walls. I'll find the dagger when the house has cooled down.'

Marc could not imagine who would want to kill him. Then a thought occurred to him. Was this some kind of posthumous revenge for the execution of Sejanus? If so, there might be another attempt.

A rope ladder with two grappling hooks on one end hung from the outer perimeter. It had been thrown onto the top of the wall enabling someone to climb up, turn the hooks round and clamber down on the other side. Pieces of hay confirmed his theory. The hooks were similar to those Marc had seen recently on the fishing boats at the port, used for hanging mammals such as dolphins or whales.

The muscles of his face were tense as he stood squinting at the mess. Am I getting too old? He thought to himself. Get me away from Rome and I behave like I'm on holiday. He was determined to stay focused and walked back to where Portius was still distressed over the horror of his friend's experience.

'Portius, tell me about the dogs. What did you do with them earlier?'

'I did what I always do, sir. I fed them early evening.'

'Did you check them before you went to bed?'

'Yes, and they were fine, lying on their sides with their legs stretched out.'

'And did you approach them?'

'No sir, I just observed them from the doorway. There didn't seem to be any problem.'

Marc ran his hand across his chin.

'Where do you buy the meat for the dogs?'

'I go to a stall down the hill. There's a farm on the right hand side. They sell the meat of wild animals and birds. I buy it fresh every morning. The master insists upon it.'

'Tomorrow, I want you to show me. Was there anything

different about the meat you bought in the last two days?'

Portius looked affronted by these questions. He was hesitant.

'Well, actually, yes, something was different. There was an old woman selling the meat. She said the farmer had wanted to get on with some work on the land, preparing his spring crops; she said she was standing in for him.'

Marc shifted his weight and rubbed the back of his neck. He needed some rest. He told Gaius to take Mercury and return home. Marc and Portius bedded down in the hay in the stable. But sleep was impossible.

The next day a representative of Pilate rode up the hill accompanied by Gaius returning Mercury. He insisted that Marc should come and spend the rest of his days at the palace before heading for Jerusalem. Cornelius would join them once he returned. All the resources of the imperial household were to be at their disposal. When they left, Marc asked Portius to come with him to the farm.

'Is this the only place where meat is bought for dogs?'

'Yes sir. The master was most particular about what was fed to Milo and Piso.'

'So, it wouldn't have been difficult to find out which farm enjoyed their patronage.'

The farmer was upset that in innocence he might have contributed to the cause of the fire. He was a sensible man who worked hard to provide a living for his family.

He said, 'The old woman came to buy some meat but then said she was very poor, and because of her age no one would employ her any more. She actually asked if she could mind the stall for me in exchange for the price of the meat. I was pleased to let her because this is a very busy time of the year for me.'

'What did she look like?'

'It's very hard to say. She wore a long black cloak, which was

pulled over her face. What I did see of her looked rather … well
….ugly, so I naturally assumed she was embarrassed. I made a
point of not looking directly at her. She asked me for work two
days ago and then came up yesterday. I was expecting her again
today but she never arrived.'

'What language did she speak?'

'Greek, but her voice was shaky and sometimes so faint that she
was difficult to hear.'

'Thank you for your help! Will you let me know if you see her
again?'

'Yes sir, of course, straightaway! I am so very sorry about this. If
only I had been more careful.'

'Please don't blame yourself. This whole situation has been very
carefully planned. No one could have foreseen the outcome of
such an innocent meeting.'

As he and Portius went back towards the house, Marc pondered
on which god must have been watching over him as he
opportunistically moved onto his side, and avoided a blade through
his heart – not for the first time. Perhaps there were gods after all.
He had earlier insisted that nobody should walk through the
burning remains in case there were more clues to be found, but he
doubted the validity of the argument. The night had been very
cold, as they often are during the spring before summer imposes its
heat, so the mosaic floors were now bearable.

He crossed what was left of a hall and living area whose
ambience he had previously enjoyed, and turned right into a short
corridor off which had been the room where he slept. It was not
recognizable. He looked for the spot where he thought the bed
had once stood in all its strangely feminine splendour, not what you
would expect of a hardened soldier. There amongst the rubble was
the dagger. Marc wiped its blackened blade and head, and looked
at it more closely. It was old and not Roman. Its blade was made
of bronze and on its hilt was an image of Medusa, the lady of

Greek mythology with the many heads. Despite its age, it had been well cared for and was very sharp.

Tucking the dagger in his belt, he headed for the stables. One of the slaves was mucking out.

Marc asked, 'Have you seen any strangers around here in the last few days? Anybody you would not expect to see?'

'Sir, there was a man here two days ago asking if we had any hay to sell but that's not unusual.'

'Did you get a look at him?'

'No, sir, he stood quite a distance away. I had the storeroom door open and he was at the other end of the yard. When he knew I'd seen him he shouted across and then turned and went.'

'Was there anything different about him?'

'Nothing, except that he didn't appear to have anything with him to carry hay in, even if we had any spare.'

'Have you seen him before or since?'

'No. Just that one time! But I'll ask the others.'

He raised his voice and another slave came running out immediately.

'I didn't see anyone round the stable, sir, but I saw a horse up here two nights ago, grazing, just down the hill in a copse. I thought it belonged to one of the farmers. I'm sorry if I should have done something about it, really I am.' He was nearly weeping.

'Have either of you seen a dagger like this before?'

They both shook their heads.

Later that afternoon Cornelius returned and reacted as Marc might have expected, angrily at first and then philosophically. He was concerned about his slave, but more it seemed because he might lose a good charioteer who knew how to handle his steeds. The villa worried him not at all. The loss of the dogs, however, caused him grief. They were buried with due dignity. He agreed that accepting Pilate's hospitality was the best plan for now. It would give him time to organise builders. He was, of course, concerned about who might have attempted to kill his guest.

'Death is never far from any of us, Marc. You must be more vigilant.' As if he needed to be told that.

'Cornelius, forgive me asking, but do you usually sleep in the room you gave me?'

'No, I have my own just across the corridor. That one is reserved for guests.'

'Do you know of anyone who might want to kill you or damage your property?'

Cornelius gave a hollow laugh.

'My dear Marcus, I have had many enemies but they are all dead. There is no-one left alive who would want to kill me.'

Marc showed him the dagger.

'That's an interesting weapon. Looks like it should be in a museum. It's in very good condition though.'

Cornelius could offer no more comment and went to the stables to issue orders for the further safety and protection of the horses. He wanted a slave on guard at all times through the night and threatened them with death if any mishap should befall his animals. Portius was to come with Cornelius since he was a personal slave who was familiar with his master's needs. So, after salvaging what they could, which was precious little, the two Romans took Mercury and Vulcan and headed for the palace. Portius was left to make his own way.

8

-The Viper-

Pilate and his household were making preparations for their trip to the capital city. Not that Pilate would admit that Jerusalem was the capital. At various times in the history of Judea it was unclear exactly which city was the most important. Jerusalem may be more important to the Jews, particularly now that, thanks to Herod, their precious temple had been rebuilt. But the port of Caesarea would be his preference, and since he lived here most of the year, this was the seat of power as far as he was concerned.

Pilate sent for Marc. When he arrived, Crassus, the theatrical producer, and Justin, the boy who had spoken to Cornelius, were both present. They bowed low before the governor.

Crassus began, 'Sir, we have a great favour to ask you. We understand that you are about to go to Jerusalem. We are due to perform "Antigone" in the theatre there, just west of the city. As you know, there will be hundreds of people and we have been asked to provide some entertainment. Would it be possible to travel with you? We will feel much safer. But we don't want to inconvenience you.'

Pilate consented.

'Of course you can. There will be no inconvenience. My wife is coming with us, which means we'll be slower than usual. She'll be travelling in her carriage. But the road south is fairly flat; it goes through the coastal plain. Even so, we'll not manage more than thirty-five miles a day so I have made arrangements for us to stop overnight at Lydda, a town inland from the port of Joppa. We have a garrison there so we can refresh ourselves and rest comfortably and safely.'

'Thank you, sir. That is most kind. We hope you will find time to come and watch us perform again.'

'No doubt about it! My wife wishes particularly to see you again; she was quite moved by your performance the other evening. I shall probably be leaving Lydda quite early in the morning and my wife will take the last part of the journey more slowly since it's over rougher ground. You're welcome to join me if you feel up to a hard ride.'

'Justin and I will join you, but the others may wish to come with your wife. We would like to get there ahead of them to find some accommodation in the pilgrim camp nearby. There will be a big demand with so many people.'

Crassus looked at Marc and lowered his voice respectfully.

'We were all very sorry to hear about your experiences the other evening, sir, and thank the gods that you were spared.'

'Thank you for your concern.'

'Would you also pass on our regrets to Cornelius?'

'I will. But you can speak to him yourself since he is coming to Jerusalem with us.'

'Are you any closer to finding the person who set fire to the house?'

Pilate interrupted, 'Not yet, but make no mistake, we will.'

He made it clear he now had more important matters, and told them to be at the palace the next morning. The two actors left.

Pilate turned to Marc.

'There's been more trouble in Jerusalem with these wretched Zealots.'

'Who are they?'

'An anti-Roman group, mostly from Galilee, who stir up the people against us. They feel grieved that they don't have as much influence as the Judean Jews. I cannot imagine why. They are governed sensibly. They have everything they need. We build them roads, aqueducts, public baths and rebuild their temple. We provide them with safety and security with our guards to police the area.'

Pilate had been gesticulating with his left arm followed by his right and back to his left in an effort to stress this list of obvious advantages.

'How should I govern people such as these, tell me that, Marc, how should they be governed?'

He did not expect an answer. In fact, he would have been deeply insulted had Marc attempted to make an answer.

'When we find the leaders I shall put them to death by one of the worst penalties I can impose, crucifixion. It's slow and very painful but gives them plenty of time to mull over their behaviour. It reinforces our power too. Puts fear into the rest. We have a whole road full of them sometimes, lined up on their pitiful crosses.'

Pilate sat down heavily as though the weight of those crucifixes was too much for him to bear.

'I know you'll be busy with your investigation but I would appreciate your help finding out a bit more about these rebels. You are new to the city and can make inquiries more easily.'

He switched to philosophical mode.

'People think power is easy. Once you have it, they say, you will never let go. I think it's the other way round. Once you have it, it will never let you go, not until someone takes it from you, of course. It becomes a drug that you can't do without. It's a trap. It dominates your life and you are no longer free just to be yourself. But I have seen what some men are like when they have been finally denied it. They are left with no resources to cope with life. They suffer painfully from its withdrawal and, with nothing to replace it, shrivel like an old fig and die.'

'In that case, perhaps it is better not to have it at all.'

Pilate retorted, coming out of his mood.

'Hah! That of course is nonsense. What is life without power and conquest?'

Marc reassured him.

'I will do my best to see what I can find out for you.'

The following day the large party was ready to move. Nearly everyone including the actors was on horseback. The exception was Pilate's wife, Claudia, and the soldiers driving wagons with provisions and requirements for safety and comfort.

Claudia was dressed very simply in a long linen tunic tied just above the waist, with a full-length cloak. Her hair was drawn up from her neck and pinned on top of her head but there were no sparkling ornaments today. Her carriage was enclosed and fully padded with cushions. Nevertheless, the journey would not be comfortable for her and would be a test of endurance. Marc admired her bearing and grace. She was uncomplaining and responded to the slightest indignity with humour. Affectionately and coyly she kissed her husband on the cheek and told him she would see him later. Pilate seemed too preoccupied to return the compliment.

There were six fully uniformed members of the cavalry accompanying the party, complete with decorated helmets, breastplates and swords. Their appearance alone should have been enough to deter any attackers. It was a pleasant spring morning, perfect for such a journey. As they took the firm flat road south out of Caesarea, the uninterrupted vision of the sea to the west became more distant as their path at first closely followed the coast, and then gradually veered inland. To the east were the mountains of Judea, bare and slightly monotonous but impressive nevertheless.

Once they left the city behind them, the richness and vividness of the land became apparent. There was a wealthy array of spring flowers. Some grew by the roadside, and others had ventured into the middle of fields adding gaiety and colour to ploughed land with its new green haze.

The hamlets through which they passed were small; some were little more than just a few mud huts, and the farmers eked out a meagre living supplemented by milk from a goat, or eggs from a few hens. Occasionally a solitary farmer could be seen breaking up the sods with a primitive plough, yoked across two oxen. The elderly sat outside peeling vegetables or simply sitting. Marc rode up beside Crassus. He looked delighted at the honour.

'These people are not impressed by us, are they sir?'
Marc had noticed that their passing produced very little reaction, except from the very young children who were fascinated by the horses and pointed and giggled at the cavalry helmets.

'I think they've been occupied for so long they know better than to overreact to anything anymore. They just want to be left alone to live in peace.'

'They must have their own culture to be proud of, their own songs, dances and stories. Much of it will be lost otherwise. Even when conquerors are tolerant of the people they conquer, the old ways gradually disappear.'

'Is that why you became an actor? So you can remind people of former cultures?'

'Yes, I suppose it is. While we go on performing Greek plays the great works will be remembered. It is sad that the young always want to be like the victors, to learn their ways and to be educated into their society.'

'I'm sure these folk, who live simply, won't forget their past. It's the wealthy elites of a country who are affected by domination most. They're the ones the victors want to change because they in turn influence the people.'

'Rome seems to have been very clever at getting people to think like them. Just look at Herod - a Jew, but more like a Roman. He even copied Roman architecture if Caesarea is any example. But the power of Empires is never as invincible as it seems. They have monuments of stone but feet of clay. The Persian Empire fell, the Greek Empire fell. Is seems impossible that the Roman Empire will go the same way, but who knows?'

Marc thought how the nature of this conversation would be unthinkable in Rome, barely short of treasonable. Yet he had sympathy with these people who did not want this foreign interference. An unaccustomed sense of humility came over him. Far from feeling proud as he rode by with this splendid troop, he felt embarrassed by everything it stood for. He doubted the rest of his compatriots experienced the same emotion. Pilate was busy talking loudly to a member of the cavalry about the insurrection they were facing, and how it would not last when the might of imperial justice was properly meted out to the insurgents. Cornelius looked unconcerned and was enjoying conversation of a lighter nature with two of the soldiers.

Pilate had ordered a break and Marc found a pile of logs to sit on beside the road quite near the carriage. Claudia slipped out while her husband was not looking. She smiled and walked over.

'May I join you?'

'I would be delighted.'

'I have met you before have I not, Commander Marcus Tiro?' So she had recognized him, as he had her.

'Yes. It was many years ago, when we were both at the palace of Tiberius.'

'I thought you very handsome. You looked so dashing in your uniform. I was too frightened to speak to you.'

Marc was taken aback by her ingenuousness.

'I'm flattered that you should have noticed, ma'am.'

Claudia looked directly at him and laughed.

'Well, I'm not frightened any more.'

Claudia Procula was the illegitimate daughter of Julia who was the daughter of Augustus. While Tiberius was still heir apparent, Augustus forced him to divorce his wife and marry Julia to secure the succession. When Julia and her father both died in the same year, Tiberius was kind to Claudia and adopted her. Marc felt they had something in common. In some ways, Tiberius had been like a father to him too.

'I'm very sorry to hear what happened to you. I have had no opportunity to speak to you since the night we went to the theatre - it must have been a horrifying experience. Have you heard anything about the slave Julius?'

'He's still alive.'

'I saw a lot of burn injuries while at the hospital in Rome.'

'You worked there?'

'Yes, for a while. I would like to have trained as a doctor, but the profession is not held in high esteem and my father was against it. Nevertheless, he couldn't stop me learning how to set broken limbs and heal wounds. I loved finding out about medicinal cures.'

'Did you learn about poisons?'

'Yes. Some! In small doses they can be curative.'

'Do you know of one that could induce paralysis in dogs?'

'Aconitum Napellus or Monk's Hood induces numbness, irregular heartbeat and then breathing stops. Henbane has the same effect – rapid heartbeat, then coma when taken in sufficient quantity. But one of the most deadly toxins actually comes from the Cone Shell, found in the Red Sea. It causes paralysis almost immediately. I'm not sure that's generally known though. Do you think Cornelius' dogs were poisoned?'

'Almost certainly – they would have barked and alerted us otherwise.'

'Who could have done such a terrible thing?' Claudia looked down and shook her head.

'I don't know – but I intend to find out.'

'Be careful – you have no idea who you can and cannot trust.'

Pilate was shouting to get under way.

'I would much rather ride, you know. But Pilate insists I travel in that awful carriage – it's supposed to be ladylike. He thinks we should be seen to be more patrician.'

She sighed. It was the sigh of a woman who, like other pre-nuptial young women, had thought her love would change her man.

Lydda stood on the slope of a hill and the land started to rise as the town came into view. Labourers were busy in the fields on the perimeter, working in the light of a declining sun. A Roman soldier rode out to greet Pilate. This was indeed an honour to have the Procurator of Judea and his wife and guests staying overnight. Everybody in the small fort had worked hard all day to prepare for this moment. Hot baths were in readiness, together with a banquet and comfortable sleeping arrangements within lavishly decorated tents. Marc was grateful for the hospitality. A day in the saddle had made him realize how little riding he had done in the past three years and how sore his muscles had become.

Later that evening, after the dismounting, the greetings, unpacking, the organising, the decision-making and the eating, Marc strolled round the encampment. A huge fire was lit near the centre throwing wavering light over the people seated round it. He leaned against a nearby tree and stood watching the scene feeling the warmth reaching out to him. Cornelius sat enjoying a joke with the cavalry officers. He shouted across.

'Marc, come and join us. We are just about to drink some well matured wine. Throw over that bag – the one beside the tree, just there where you're standing.'

Marc picked up a leather bag that Cornelius had slung over his saddle earlier and threw it towards him. Cornelius opened it and reached inside. With a yell, he was immediately on his feet. Fright and adrenalin mobilized those who were next to him. A snake had bitten his arm just above his wrist and its body was dangling towards the ground. Cornelius put his arm over the fire hoping to shake it off. The snake, sensing danger, lifted its tail and coiled itself round his elbow.

Portius, without a thought for himself, grasped the creature by the back of its head forcing open its mouth so that it let go of its prey. He uncurled the coils, grabbed the end of the tail and lifted it as high as his arms would allow. Then he threw the head away from him towards the fire and let go. He miscalculated and the snake fell further from the middle of the flames than intended. Now in a frenzy of fury, it slithered with great speed through the logs and embers and came out on the other side. One of the terrified soldiers did not move quickly enough and the snake struck again so fast that hardly anybody saw it happen. When the soldier cried out his colleagues beat the snake with a stick. It disappeared into the undergrowth but not before leaving one of its fangs embedded in the back of the man's leg.

Cornelius meanwhile grabbed his knife and sank the blade into the bite, sucking blood from the wound. Four or five times he sucked and spat blood and venom into the fire. Then he took the amphora of wine rinsed out his mouth, poured the rest over his wound and collapsed exhausted. The soldier tried to do the same but his bite was in a more awkward position; one of his friends removed the fang.

Marc spoke to Portius.

'Go and fetch the camp doctor. Tell him what's happened. Quick!'

Portius did not need telling twice, he was already on his way. Marc tried to make Cornelius as comfortable as possible, covering him with his cloak and using the leather bag as a rest for his head.

The doctor arrived and his assistants followed bringing blankets, pillows and straw filled mattresses. He ordered that the two victims be kept warm and still so the poison did not have a chance to circulate. He administered small phials of Mithridatum, an antidote to poison that had been brought to Rome by Pompey after he invaded Turkey. Poultices of healing herbs were tied round their wounds and a makeshift tent was erected to protect the patients. The doctor took Marc to one side.

'Can you describe the snake?'

'Yes, I can. It had a brown zigzag band along its back and a dark V-shaped mark on its head.'

'It was definitely a viper then. It's a very dangerous snake, particularly in the evening. It can be quite placid during the day but gets very aggressive at night. How long was it?'

'I would say about a foot and a half, perhaps a bit more.'

'Well, the best we can hope for is that it is still young and not fully grown. I want someone to stay with each of these men at all times and regularly give them a phial of antidote. They are likely to have high fevers. We should know in an hour or two whether they are going to recover.'

Pilate very soon appeared on the scene. For once he was lost for words. His brow furrowed. He looked down at Cornelius, then at Marc and then at the fire. No one dared say what each was thinking.

Marc opened the now discarded leather bag and examined the contents. There were a few small personal items for the trip but there was also a mesh bag that tied loosely at the top; it was empty.

9

-The Man on the Donkey-

Portius sat by Cornelius' side all night and all day, wiping away beads of perspiration from his brow and slipping more phials of the theriac between his master's lips. Thanks to his slave and his own quick actions Cornelius began to improve. Pilate was much relieved, not wishing to lose one of his most important advisers. The soldier also survived. A ceremony was held to thank the gods.

'Portius, did you pack your master's things?' asked Marc.

'Yes sir.'

'Do you remember what was in this mesh bag?'

Portius frowned.

'I'm not sure, sir. The master carries dried figs in one similar to that. It's possible it was left over from his previous trip. If it was screwed up in the bottom of the bag I may not have noticed it.'

Once it was clear the injured men could be moved, Pilate was keen to ride to Jerusalem, so, early in the morning, Marc, Gaius, Justin and Crassus saddled up, together with their escorts. The rest intended to travel more slowly. The road climbed gently at first out of the plain. The riders were moving too fast for any conversation. Marc noticed white-walled villages on the slopes of hills, and open spaces with streams and rocky areas. At Emmaus, where a Roman garrison was stationed, they stopped for refreshments.

About seven miles out of Emmaus the riders reached the summit of a broad plateau. On their right was a ravine beyond which stretched barren hills. Pilate pulled up his horse. In the distance straight in front of them was the city of Jerusalem surrounded by turreted walls. Circular and square towers of palaces and fortresses stood proud, but the most imposing building by far was Herod's majestic Temple Mount.

Everywhere, people were walking, riding, leading animals, laughing, talking, shouting; children were screaming, running, hiding and playing. They rode down towards an encampment covering several acres outside the city wall. On the right a large sunken pool provided water. Marc could see the necessity for more building works. Providing clean water for this number of people needed investment on a large scale. Crassus and Justin left them, thanking Pilate once again; but he was disinterested and irritable.

The remaining men turned left beyond the camp and rather than entering by the western Joppa gate, followed the wall north to enter by the Damascus Gate. This was closest to Antonia Fort, named by Herod in honour of Mark Anthony. The fortress actually formed part of the northern wall of Temple Mount. The gate consisted of three arches, the central one being the largest with two towers at either side. Behind the gate was a plaza, with a high column in the centre.

They galloped the horses down the street to Antonia Fort, dismounted and climbed wide steps into an inner hall. Pilate's chief of staff immediately hailed him to update him on events.

'Ah, sir, I'm glad you're here. I think we might have trouble. There's a lot of unrest. Temple guards are helping us look out for skirmishes. The crowds seem unusually excited.'

'I don't like crowds. They too easily turn nasty. Can't we disperse them?'

'That's easier said than done with this number of people in Jerusalem.'

Pilate turned to his companions.

'Marc, Gaius change your clothes and get out in the streets, ask discreetly, find the troublemakers. Your trip to Herodium can wait.'

They wandered down into the main street with shops on either side. A huge arch formed part of a pedestrian bridge leading to the basilica above with its magnificent façade. Marc had not seen a finer building even in Rome. Hundreds of people were using the overpass; underground entry tunnels with beautifully carved ceilings helped relieve the congestion of worshippers.

A commotion attracted their attention. They climbed up the first steps of the overpass and leaned over the stone balustrade for a better view. A large number of people were approaching, waving palms in the air, shouting and chanting as they walked. In the centre of the group a man straddled a donkey. Cloaks were laid in front of the beast as he proceeded.

Gaius said, 'What's going on? Who is that?'

The donkey paused, confused by the palms, and the followers took the opportunity to hold out their hands to the man, kissing his feet.

'They're almost worshipping him. I don't like it.'

'I agree. Let's get a closer look,' suggested Marc.

They joined the followers and Marc spoke to one of them.

'Who is this man that you admire so much?'

'Where have you been the last few months? He's a great teacher, a rabbi who performs miracles. We've just come from Bethany. I saw him raise a man from the dead who'd been in the tomb nearly four days. Never seen anything like it! I watched him cure a blind man too, down at Siloam Pool. He does some amazing things.'

Marc and Gaius followed the procession into the temple courtyard. It was full of people buying and selling goods from jewellery to birds. The teacher slid off the donkey and stood watching for a while. Suddenly he shouted at the top of his voice.

'This is my father's house. A house of prayer! You have turned it into a den of robbers.'

In anger, he turned over stalls; goods and money flew everywhere rolling into nooks and crannies. Traders screeched at him to stop, falling on their hands and knees trying to recover their coins. Eventually temple guards fetched a member of the senior priests, a Pharisee, who came out to try to smooth the situation. Gaius could not hear and neither could he see because of the crowd.

'What's going on?' he inquired.

'A priest is having a word with our miracle worker, very warily though; it's almost as if he was scared of him. But things do seem to be calming down.'

More people poured into the temple courtyard finding anywhere to sit or stand. Children were lifted onto parents' shoulders. Then the teacher sat on the edge of a stone platform, lifting his hand. The crowd were silent and the man began speaking.

Gaius whispered, 'By Jupiter, he has a lot of power over them. It's uncanny. What's he saying?'

'He's telling a story about an owner who rented out his vineyard while he went travelling. He sends his son to collect the rent but the tenants kill him. I don't understand it but you should see the priests. They've turned their backs on him and huddled together. They keep raising their arms in the air and dropping them heavily onto their sides in exasperation. There's a lot of tension.'

Marc noticed a man standing nearby whose dress was that of a priest. He manoeuvred himself to his side and spoke casually, wondering whether he would even get a reply. Thus when it came, the level of honesty astonished him.

'Who is this preacher?'

'He's called Jesus, originally from Nazareth.'

'Is he a troublemaker?'

'No, I don't think so. He speaks a lot of wisdom but we Pharisees suspect that he's directly criticising us. He calls us hypocrites and I think he's probably right. We pretend to be religious but do we really care about the poor, about the people we teach, or do we care only about our own positions? I suspect the latter. The high priests would like to destroy him but they dare not, he has too much public support.'

Marc wanted to know the priest's name but suspected he would not give it, speaking as he was so openly.

'Do you think he'll lead the people into a rebellion?'

'No. He preaches peace. The kingdom he talks about, where he claims to be king, is not of this world but the next. The trouble is the Jews have been waiting so long for a leader to overthrow their occupiers, they'll grasp at anyone. But this man isn't here to lead an uprising. If the people are expecting that, they'll be disappointed.'

Gaius was fed up with not being able to see anything and had pushed through the crowd nearer to the speaker. He heard someone ask, 'Tell us preacher, should we really be paying taxes to Caesar?' The prophet paused before answering.

'Give me a coin. Now, whose image is this?'

'Caesar's,' someone replied.

'Then give Caesar what is his and give to God what is his.'
Despite himself, Gaius was impressed with the astuteness of the answer. The question had been designed as a trick. He made his way back to Marc.

'I think this chap is all right. I like what he says, but the priests are trying to discredit him.'

'Nevertheless, someone with this amount of influence is bound to be seen as a threat.'

They squeezed out into the street where there were no fewer people; Gaius led the way. As he passed two Roman soldiers, there was a scuffle, a shout and then one of them fell, blood oozed onto the ground. The other, not quite realizing the full extent of what had happened, knelt beside his colleague.

A large man in a brown tunic, still holding a long bloody knife in his hand, started to make his way through the crowd. Ignoring his own safety, Gaius threw his bodyweight at the perpetrator who toppled sideways. The knife flew across the cobbles and Marc pushed forward to pick it up. The man was much bigger than Gaius and managed to wrestle free, but before he had a chance to get to his feet, Marc struck him in the jaw and knocked him out. Within minutes, members of the Temple Guard and another Roman soldier arrived; he was arrested. Marc helped Gaius up.

'Brave, but very foolish,' he said.

'Well, I got my man.'

'Come on, I think we've had enough of this for now, let's go back, hand in this weapon and find out who you captured.'

Pilate, whose bad temper had temporarily dissipated, was impressed by Gaius' quick action and congratulated him and Marc several times. The arrested man was called Barabbas, a well-known troublemaker and leader of the Zealots. The soldier had died from his wounds so the charge was murder, for which the penalty was death by crucifixion. He would be tried within the next few days. Gaius was asked to write a witness statement.

'What else did you find out?' Pilate asked Marc.

'Some of the Jews want to rule themselves again. They see Rome as the enemy and seem to be expecting a leader.'

Pilate sneered. 'Ah yes, that will be their Messiah - their mythical Saviour.'

'Well, they've found one, but I don't think he's what they're expecting. He's a different sort of Messiah, one who is more interested in an after life than this one. I honestly don't think he's a threat to you. Apparently he preaches forgiveness. He even arrived in the city on a donkey. That's not a sign of war; it's more a sign of humility and peace.'
Gaius added.

'And I distinctly heard him tell the people to pay their taxes and support Caesar.'
Pilate replied with gravity in his voice.

'So, if it is just the Zealots we have to fear then maybe arresting Barabbas will be a serious blow to them.'

Marc said, 'Let's hope so! But I think you need to watch the Jewish priests.'

Pontius Pilate looked at him sharply.

'You mean the Pharisees who sit on the Sanhedrin?'

'Yes. They seem to hate the prophet. He tells them some home truths they don't want to hear. They'd get rid of him if they could find a way.'

Pilate said, 'Thanks for your opinions, both of you. My wife will be here soon. We're all staying at Herod's Palace near the west gate. It's a bit more comfortable for Claudia than this fort. By the way, Marc, you may be interested to know that Herod Antipas is in Jerusalem. He's staying at the Hasmonean Palace. It will be a good opportunity for you to speak to him. He's the leader of Galilee, one of Herod's three sons who inherited some of his kingdom after he died. He lived at Herodium while his father was alive and may be of some help. I'll make sure you are introduced.'

'Thank you. That's a good idea. I think I would like to visit Herodium first though.'

'Let's go tomorrow,' said Gaius. 'But right now, I would like a bath. I'm covered in someone else's blood.'

The three of them made their way to the palace to meet the others. It was late in the afternoon and Claudia, Cornelius and the rest of the party had arrived. Cornelius was sweating profusely and the pallor of his face indicated just how much of his energy the journey had taken. Despite her status, Claudia insisted on putting a fresh dressing on the wound in his arm, while Portius continued to administer the antidote. Cornelius said that all he needed now was rest. A room had been prepared for him and he retired soon afterwards. Claudia too looked tired although she made a fuss of her husband and insisted on taking Gaius and Marc to their rooms.

As she escorted them through the cool corridors, she said, 'I love this palace. There is such a peace here that I can't find in Caesarea.'

She paused at an open walkway on the first floor and looked down into the gardens.

'Just look down there, isn't it beautiful?'

Both men had to agree with her. It was truly peaceful despite the disturbances that were still going on outside the walls in the city.

'Have you been to the Temple?' she asked.

'Yes, ma'am,' replied Marc. 'It was full of worshippers.'

'Did you see or hear the young rabbi everyone seems to be talking about?'

Gaius grimaced. 'A bit of both, but not much of either, since I couldn't see a thing. I'm a bit too short. But what I heard was impressive. The priests don't seem to like him though.'

'I wonder why not. You would think that they'd appreciate having some help to get a good message across to all these people.'

Marc said, 'Personally, I don't think they like the message he's giving them. He calls them hypocrites.'

'Well, I must admit I have found the chief priests incredibly pompous when they have visited here.'

'I'm surprised they come at all, knowing how they feel about the Romans,' said Gaius.

'They come quite often. They need Pilate's approval for so many things you see. And they also come to complain to him. Sometimes my husband has to give in, because they can cause so much trouble for him if he doesn't consent to their demands.

'A few years ago our soldiers used to carry standards that had a figure of the Emperor. The Jews objected because they said they were graven images and asked Pilate to remove them. Pilate, of course, refused. The Jewish leaders followed us all the way back to Caesarea and begged him. Pilate threatened them with death if they didn't stop it, but they simply offered themselves as martyrs. Pilate had no choice but to give way. I think he felt humiliated.

'He really does not want any more trouble with them. They won't give in you know. It's quite extraordinary. They have such a strong belief in one God and it seems to give them great confidence, even in the face of Rome.'

'I got that impression earlier today,' said Gaius. 'It's amazing how many pilgrims there are here for their festival, what do they call it, the Passover? What's it all about anyway?'

'It's part of their history. Years ago the Jews were slaves in Egypt. Their leader, Moses, asked Pharaoh to release them, but he wouldn't. Their God said he would kill all the firstborn Egyptian boys, and told Jewish families to spread the blood of a lamb round their doorways so that the spirit of death would pass over them. Pharaoh's own son was killed and he let them go, but later changed his mind and chased them to the Red Sea, where the water parted and let the Jews cross, but Pharaoh's men were all drowned.'

'That's quite a story,' said Marc. 'No wonder the Jews think their God is so powerful. On the other hand, if he is so powerful, why isn't he doing something to break them away from Roman rule?'

'That's why they're expecting a Messiah. He is the one who, like Moses, will lead them in revolt and set them free again.'

'And they think the prophet who has become so popular will do it for them. I think they're mistaken.'

Claudia changed the subject; her eyes twinkled.

'Someone tells me, Gaius, you were very brave today and stopped a murderer.'

Gaius laughed, embarrassed, and excused himself, needing to bathe.

That night Marc lay on his bed, his hands cupped under his head, thinking about the troubles that had happened in such a short time. The task he had been given, to investigate a theft, had quickly turned into something altogether more sinister. And amidst it all was a young rabbi who raised people from the dead. This place was a melting pot waiting to boil over.

10

Rays of sunshine filtered through the shutters, hit a polished silver bowl, reflected off its surface and shone directly onto Marc's face. He was still dreaming that he was with Aurelia and Felix, skimming stones across the surface of a lake. He opened his eyes and closed them quickly against the brightness, turned over and tried again. This was his fourth accommodation since he set foot in Judea and was undoubtedly the most splendid.

He got up feeling stiff but Portius had time to massage his upper back since Cornelius was still sleeping, and by the time he joined Gaius in a sunlit room overlooking the gardens, he was feeling much better. The young man stood up as he entered.

'Good morning! Is it not wonderful to indulge in all this luxury? What a great life! Do you know how Cornelius is today?'

'Portius says he's unlikely to appear; he needs to rest. He didn't look too good yesterday; the journey obviously wore him out. He's very lucky to be alive. There's no doubt that his own actions helped to save his life.'

'Do you think the snake was put in his bag deliberately?' asked Gaius.

'It's difficult to tell. There's no evidence. It could have crawled in while the bag was on the ground. If it was done deliberately, then it's a question of who had the opportunity.'

'I suppose someone could have put it there before we set off.'

'It's possible. They're not very active during the day. There was a mesh bag inside the leather one which could have held a snake, but until Cornelius is better I don't want to worry him. It will have to wait.'

'Someone seems not to like us, what with you nearly being killed by a dagger, the house being burned down, Julius severely injured and now Cornelius bitten by a snake.'

'It does seem that way. But we must be careful not to let it stop us from doing what we came for.'

'Good! What time do you want to go over to Herodium?'

'I suggest the sooner the better.'

'That's fine by me!'

'It's about an hour's ride! I have asked for horses to be saddled. They should be ready by now. We've been provided with some weapons and an escort. Quite apart from the wandering robbers, there are dangerous wild animals on the neighbouring mountains.'

'That sounds like fun! We'll be safe enough if we keep moving. Is anybody expecting us?'

'Pilate has arranged for Silas, the caretaker, to be there. He'll show us round and hopefully answer any questions.'

They walked to the stables and mounted the horses prepared for them. As they left, Gaius pointed out the Hasmonean Palace where Herod Antipas was staying. It was between Herod's Palace and the Temple Mount. Even at this early hour, the streets were crowded with pilgrims making their way to worship or buying daily provisions. They took the road south. On their left was a large pool.

Gaius said, 'That's Siloam Pool, where the blind man was supposed to have been given back his sight. I heard that mud was placed on his eyes; he was told to go and wash and then found he could see. Do you think there's any truth in it?'

'I would like to see it for myself before I pass comment. Look, there's a good hippodrome here. If the theatre is in the west, I wonder where the amphitheatre is.'

'It's in the north of the city, not far from the Damascus Gate. Didn't you see it yesterday?'

'No, I was too busy looking where I was going.'

As they rode south eastwards, a small town called Bethlehem appeared on a slope on their right. White, stepped, flat-roofed buildings with small rectangular windows stood either side of narrow streets. They stopped at a well beside a low wall. A shepherd was fetching water for his flock but he moved to one side when he saw them approaching. By the time they had taken a drink, the shepherd had disappeared into the hills.

Leaving Bethlehem, the east road wound down a rocky slope, through fields of corn and terraced vineyards, until it levelled out into a plain filled with clumps of olive trees. The pasture attracted numerous sheep and goats. Further east, desolate, purple coloured mountains occasionally parted to offer a glimpse of the Dead Sea. But as they came nearer to Herodium, the land turned into a barren desert, so it was all the more surprising that around the palace was an oasis of beautiful trees and plants.

Gaius said, 'Just look at this. I wonder where all the water's coming from.'

'Let's find out!'

The palace building was circular, with three matching round towers, one of which was higher than the others. The central space was open except for covered colonnaded walkways that led from one side to the other.

'Herod certainly had some good architects,' commented Marc. 'Let's hope they've kept the plans.'

They were greeted by a man who seemed to double as the gardener. He bowed low.

'Good morning, sirs. Welcome to Herodium. Allow me to take your horses.'

'Is Silas here?'

'Yes, I'll take you to him. He is waiting for you, although you are earlier than he expected so he is still inside. There are not many of us here, just a skeleton staff. I have been tending the plants until your arrival.'

'The gardens are very beautiful,' said Marc. 'How do you keep them so fresh in this desert?'

'King Herod had an aqueduct built. The water comes all the way from Solomon's Pools. The channels are underground. I don't know whether we'll be able to keep everything so green for much longer though, some of the water supplies have dried up, particularly on this north side. You can see over there where we used to have fountains and a small waterfall, but not any longer.'

Marc judged that Silas was about the same age as himself, a fawning ritualistic kind of individual whose servile gestures would be appreciated by those who required flattery to sustain self-esteem. For those not desirous of such attention, the cringing was distasteful to the point of obnoxiousness. This type always made treacherous enemies who apportioned blame to others and poisoned the minds of weaker leaders. He showed them into the library, a long, high room filled with marble. Refreshments had been provided for them but Marc was keen to see the vaults.

'You'll need a guide, sir,' said Silas. 'I'll come with you.'

The flames of torches barely lit the steep steps and the stones were permeated by a smell of dankness. They went deeper underground, through low passageways. Marc fought against the darkness of spirit that overwhelmed him in enclosed places. He pitied jailers and those who were incarcerated.

'Do you have any prisoners?'

'Not any more, sir. Herod held some prisoners here at one time. The last one was released some years ago. He had gone blind, became a beggar I believe.'

'What had he done?' asked Gaius.

'Don't know, sir, I'd only just been appointed here then.'

They came to the vault. Large wooden doors encased in metal formed the entrance. Silas used two keys to open up. The large doors swung open and they stepped inside. He lit the oil lamps that were fastened to the walls, creating penumbra where the fading light from one lamp hit the darkness before the next. The vault resembled a cavern with a concave roof. It was an irregular shape and the walls were faced with small square-ended stones set diagonally.

'There's nothing here now, of course,' said Silas needlessly. 'Everything was taken to Jerusalem a couple of weeks ago.'

'Is there a record of who the guards were?' asked Marc.

'Yes sir! I am not sure how up-to-date it is. For many years there was an arrangement whereby three soldiers would be chosen at random. When they arrived, they drew lots to see which two would stay on guard duty and who could go. It was designed so that nobody actually knew when he would be here. Also because the soldiers came from all over the place, it was intended that they should not have time to befriend each other, just in case they planned a theft. Mind you, it would be impossible to get through these doors without the keys.'

'How many sets of keys are there?' asked Marc.

'As far as I know, there is only one. It is kept locked in an iron safe and there is only one key to that. The Keeper of the Keys had to carry it with him at all times. There is no need now, not since everything is gone.'

'Gaius, take your torch and start looking at the walls carefully. You start on the left and I'll take this side. If you see anything that looks as though it has been disturbed, let me know. Silas, what's the other side of this vault?'

'I'm not sure. There will be a cell on the right side but there's nothing beyond that back wall as far as I know.'

There must be something, thought Marc, but said nothing. Directing his lighted torch he walked slowly examining every stone, running his hand across the blackened walls feeling for any looseness. He reached a particularly dark corner on the back wall. About two feet from the floor there was a disturbance in the stonewalling. Mortar was missing and some cement lay on the ground. Marc tested it with his finger; it was damp. He was surprised. In the time of Augustus, a type of cement had been developed that hardened in water. It was very strong material.

Marc addressed Silas. 'Have there been any repairs to these walls?'

'No sir! No repairs have ever been necessary. They are very thick.' Marc wondered how he knew.

'Have you seen the plans?'

'No sir, I haven't.'

'Gaius, bring your torch over here, I need some extra light. What do you make of this?'

'It certainly looks as though someone has tried to remove some of the stones, and the area is large enough for a body to climb through.'

'Why was this not noticed before?' Marc asked Silas.

'Sir, we've never really had cause to examine it. Everybody assumed that it was impossible to break through the walls. Herod had the vault built specially. He designed it so that no one could have access to it except through the main doors.'

'We need plans of the vaults. Do you know where we can find them?'

'If we have one, sir, it'll be in the library.'

As they left Silas let the doors swing shut. A loud resonating explosive sound reverberated round the lower floors until the echoes disappeared. The key clunked in the lock, more from habit than necessity, and they climbed back up the steps. Marc was pleased to be able to breathe again. He had suffered from claustrophobia ever since his father had locked him in the cellar for being insolent.

In the library, like the resources at the palace in Caesarea, everything was carefully documented. There were numerous daily records of the names of guards up until the death of Augustus, but they became less detailed after that and there were several missing. Nevertheless, they needed to be studied carefully. They found architects' plans of every floor of the palace except the level where the vault was situated.

'Silas, you said the aqueduct enters the palace below ground, presumably that would be at several different points, would it not?'

'Yes, sir, I suppose it would.'

'Tell me, then, are there any plans of the irrigation system that feeds the palace?'

'I've never seen any, sir. I don't know if the designers of the aqueducts would be different from the people who designed the palace.'

'Where is the water stored?'

'I'm sorry, sir, I don't know exactly. I know there are large cisterns somewhere and they get topped up as the water is used.'
A slave appeared requesting him to come immediately to sort out a problem and he excused himself.

'It's interesting that there are plans of the upper floors but not the lower,' said Gaius, helping himself to some of the juice Silas had provided.

'Herod was too systematic not to have kept the designs and the name of the planner. If the aqueduct started near Jerusalem, the chances are it's someone from the city.'

'But that was nearly forty years ago. The man is probably dead.'

'Perhaps he is, but not necessarily. His business might still be thriving. He may have sons who followed in his profession.'

After sifting through several files Marc found the inventory duly signed and dated from the time of Augustus. He took it with him, failing to mention the fact to Silas who came back later, flushed and apologetic. He was anxious that everything should be put away as it had been.

'Where are Solomon's Pools?' Marc asked him.

'I believe they're almost directly west, maybe more northwest.

The land rises quite sharply and the reservoirs are on top. There are several aqueducts leading from there. One goes to Jerusalem.'

'Is there a road from here?'

'It would be better to go back to Bethlehem and then take the road southwest.'

'Well, I'm not keen to plough through all these lists of names today. There are hundreds of them. Right now, I'd like to find out about the construction of the lower levels of this place.'

They took their leave thanking Silas and indicating they would return.

'It will be a great pleasure to be of service again,' said Silas. Marc got the feeling that he did not mean it.

They arrived at Solomon's Pools about half an hour later. A high wall with access gates and plain square towers concealing pipes and siphons surrounded the main pools. Tunnels driven into the hillsides were clearly visible, with vertical vents that supplied air for the excavators. Aqueducts took off in various directions where the surface water was higher than the ground level. Marc was intrigued.

'It is an interesting feat of engineering. I wonder which of these tunnels takes water to Herodium.'

'Well, we know it will be going southeast. Trouble is the land is so mountainous across that way that it could wind about quite a lot.' Gaius wiped his brow. 'I could do with a beer.'

'Maps, that's what we need. I don't believe there aren't any. I think we'll find that answer back in Jerusalem.'

As they approached one of the southern gates of Jerusalem they could see the full splendour of the Temple rising to their right. At the base were numerous shops, selling clay vessels and oil lamps that the Jewish followers were using in the religious ceremonies and prayers. In front of them was the palatial Hasmonean mansion where Herod Antipas was staying with his wife, and to the left was Herod's palace. Pilate had just returned from Antonia Fort when they rode into the courtyard. He was in ebullient mood.

'Any success?' he inquired.

Marc replied, 'Yes, but there are still some questions.'

'I've seen Herod today. He's happy to welcome you any time. He even mentioned this evening if you wish to go.'

'That's a good idea,' said Marc.

'What about those beers?' Gaius murmured.

'There'll be time for those as well.'

'A meal is being prepared now if you wish to eat first,' said Pilate.

Gaius looked pleased. 'Good! I'm actually quite hungry.'

Pilate spoke to a slave.

'Hurry to Hasmonean palace and inform Herod Antipas that our visitors will be requesting an audience in about two hours. Bring back a message saying whether that is acceptable or not.'

Claudia joined them. She was most anxious to know what they had found at Herodium.

Marc said, 'There are signs of a disturbance in the vault walls, but it's impossible to tell when it was done or even if it's significant.'

'Do you think someone might have got into the vault from the other side?'

'Until we see some plans nobody knows what is on the other side. It is odd that there are plans for each level except that one.'

Pilate offered an opinion.

'It's possible Antipas will be able to help you. He would have been young when Herodium was built but it's surprising what youngsters can pick up from general conversations.'

'I intend to ask him. Do you have any idea who might have been responsible for building the aqueducts at Solomon's Pools?'

'There are one or two architects and surveying firms in Jerusalem. I know one is called Victor's. I don't know who Herod chose to use. He might have brought in experts from Rome, even

Vitruvius himself.'

'Who is he?' asked Gaius.

Pilate almost visibly puffed out his chest with pride.

'He was one of Rome's greatest engineers and architects.'

Marc added, 'He did a lot of work for Augustus and was highly respected. Dead now, of course! But if Augustus paid for the work that Herod did in Jerusalem and Caesarea, it seems possible that Vitruvius would have at least advised him.'

During the meal the slave came back with a message that Herod Antipas and his wife would be pleased to welcome guests at the time suggested.

11

-Herod Antipas-

The bushes and trees in the palace gardens swayed slightly in a gentle evening breeze. It was still light when Marc and Gaius decided to stroll across the city to the Hasmonean Palace. The narrow streets were still filled with people moving in and out of shops selling anything from perfume to young sacrificial lambs. They walked up and down shallow steps, between steep walls and through crowded squares with fountains as their central focus. Pilgrims sat about in groups talking excitedly or simply meditating. But the general atmosphere was one of lively expectation and hope.

When they reached the palace they identified themselves and were kept waiting a few minutes while this was checked. A guard returned to say they were expected and escorted them into a room where Herod and his wife, Herodias, lay, rather than sat, on splendidly upholstered monarchical seats. Herodias was a beautiful woman, although not a little due to the artistry of the makeup that enhanced the porcelain appearance of her skin, and accentuated her eyes and lips. Her long dark hair hung in braids, and gold clothing and jewellery adorned her head, neck and shoulders. She exuded an air of pride and indifference.

Herod, on the other hand, although kingly in his dress, had a degree of hesitancy about him that betrayed insecurity. He had divorced his wife to marry Herodias. She had been married to his half-brother, Philip, but was also the daughter of another half-brother, Aristobulus, and therefore not only his one time sister in law but also his niece. Herod was officially a Jew. He was fully aware of the Jewish view on the sinfulness of his relationship with the woman who sat beside him. He was here to celebrate the Passover, yet he knew his feigned piety would be fooling no one, and that made him uneasy.

A few years ago he had upset his Jewish brothers by founding a new capital in Galilee named after Tiberius. Discovering that it was founded on an old Jewish graveyard caused a great deal of unrest among his people, only Greeks and Romans would enter the new city. Herod Antipas had much reason to feel ill at ease.

Nevertheless, he was gracious and generous in his welcome. He introduced his wife, who nodded to them under sufferance, and invited Marc and Gaius to join them on lavish couches. Wine and fruit was ordered.

'It is always a pleasure to offer hospitality to a guest from Rome. It's some years since I visited the great city although I was educated there as a boy, along with my brothers.'

'Indeed!' said Marc with an element of surprise in his voice. 'I trust you found your learning beneficial to the high office that you now hold.'

Antipas smiled.

'How could a young man from Judea fail to be impressed by so much sophistication in the Empire's greatest city?'

'This morning we visited Herodium, the home of your childhood. It was more than a match for a Roman palace.'

'Ah yes. That's true. My father had infinite respect for Roman architectural accomplishments; he was determined to emulate the grandeur. Nevertheless, it remains a copy, not an original.'

Marc replied, 'Perhaps everything men do are mere copies, or at best small improvements on the ideas of previous generations and cultures. Very little is truly new.'

'I'm sure you are right in your presumption. New ideas grow old, are discarded and reappear as fresh ideas a generation or two later. It is all quite tedious.'

Herodias rather ostentatiously stifled a yawn. Gaius looked

embarrassed, and Antipas, unexpectedly, let out a nervous almost effeminate giggle. A slave topped up their silver goblets.

'I wonder if we could impose on you to tell us something of your life at Herodium. I'm here to investigate the theft of the priceless lapis lazuli jewels that were stored in the vaults, but have very few leads at the moment.'

'Of course, my dear friend, ask anything you like and I will do my best.'

'Who lived at Herodium after the death of your father?'

'We all stayed on for a while. But then Augustus confirmed my appointment as leader of Galilee and Perea. My father's testament had decreed it. My half-brother Philip was sent up north, and Archelaus stayed here. Some of my father's wives continued to live at the palace – he had ten of them you know and fourteen children. I never really got to know the last two of my stepmothers. I'm sure that Pallas continued to live at Herodium with her son, Phasael, and Mariamne's daughters, Cypros and Salampsio. Several others lived at my father's farm in Jericho. I believe one of his last wives, Drusilla, lives there still.'

'Would you mind drawing a family tree for me so I can see who's who?'

'I'd be delighted.'

Antipas ordered writing materials to be brought immediately. Marc decided a direct approach was needed.

'Do you have reason to suspect that any of them would wish to steal the lapis lazuli jewellery?'

Antipas waved his hand flaccidly from the wrist.

'The problem is how many suspects do you want? It was very hazardous living in Herod's household – those of us who survived were lucky to be alive. The two sons of my stepmother, Mariamne, the Hasmoncan, were both put to death because of a rumour that they were plotting against the king. My stepbrother, Antipater, started it. He was the eldest son and at one time had been sole heir, but Herod changed his will so many times, depending on who was in favour and who was out, that we were all suspicious of one another. Then, of course, there were Mariamne's two daughters. Cypros, I am not sure about, but Salampsio actually still lives here in Jerusalem. They may have felt that they should have their mother's jewels as part of their inheritance. My father lived 'til he was seventy-six, even his youngest children were adults by that time. If it's suspects you're looking for, my dear fellow, there are any number of them. All with motive and opportunity, providing they could get hold of the key. That would not have been easy. The least likely suspects are me, Herod Philip and Archelaus. We were the beneficiaries.'

'I understand that your brother Archelaus was exiled?'

'That's true. He had some confrontation with the Jews, didn't handle it well and was sent off to Gaul.'

'Do you know what happened to him?'

'I heard that he died – must be about sixteen years ago now. I don't believe any of us ever saw him again after he left. But if he stole them, I would have thought the jewels would still have been among his final possessions, and we never heard that they were. I am quite sure they would have been returned.'

'Do you remember the name of the Keeper of the Key at the time of your father's death?'

'Yes. He was called Joel – must be well into his sixties or more by now. He stayed on after my father died. I believe he was a very honest sort of chap.'

A scribe arrived and Antipas directed him while he drew the family tree. He included Herod's brothers who were also regular visitors to Herodium.

'Poor old uncle Pheroras actually died for my father, you know, not intentionally, of course. Someone poisoned Herod's wine and his brother drank it by mistake. It was suspected that Antipater was the culprit but nothing was ever proved. I have also written here the names of the towns where I believe some of these relatives live. I don't keep in touch as much now that I am out of the district. I am far too busy.'

Marc thought about his own childhood whose problems were insignificant compared to this family. He looked at Gaius who had been very quiet during this conversation. Marc noticed that he was red in the face. A glance at Herodias told him why. She clearly had a fancy for the handsome young man sitting in front of her and was amusing herself with coy flirtatious looks in his direction. She had removed the golden shawl from her shoulders to reveal her bosom, and, without being too obvious, ran her fingers gently across the cleavage that was exposed sufficiently to be tantalizingly alluring. Gaius was clearly uncomfortable, and Marc decided to keep the rest of the interview short.

'Just one more matter I would like to ask about if I may,' he said to Antipas. 'Do you know what lies beyond the vault at Herodium?' Antipas looked surprised.

'I never had cause to even wonder about it. Never went down there – hate the dark, you know.' The nervous effeminate giggle came again.

'There are plans for all the floors at the palace except that one. Have you any idea where it might be?'

'None at all – it is very curious.'

'Do you know who the architect was or the name of the surveyors who built the water courses for the palace?'

'That, I can help you with. I know the architect and surveyor came from the same firm and it was local – in Jerusalem. My father found out that the main partner in the firm had trained under Vitruvius in Rome and that impressed him. I can't remember the name though.'

'Does Victor mean anything to you?'

'Do you know, I believe it was that – yes, Victor, I remember thinking what an appropriate name it was, seeing as my father was trying to emulate Rome.'

'You and your good wife have been more than generous and most helpful. We won't trouble you any longer this evening. I wonder though if I have any more questions, would it be possible to encroach on your time once more?'

Antipas rose. Using his wrists again, he made a circular movement with both his hands opening up his palms in a gesture of generosity.

'You will be most welcome, both of you. Any friend of Rome is a friend of mine. Send a message first, as you have done today. We shall be here at least two more weeks before returning to Galilee.'

Marc and Gaius both turned towards Herodias and bowed. She smiled, but not at Marc. He picked up the information that Antipas had written down for him. And with that they both left.

When they reached the street Gaius inhaled a long breath of air.

'Phew! I'm glad to be out of there.'

'Yes, I noticed,' said Marc sympathetically.

'Oh dear, did you?' said Gaius in alarm. 'I just hope Herod Antipas didn't notice as well. I'm too young to lose my head.'

'Would that be to Herod or Herodias?'

'It's not funny. Don't joke about that sort of thing.'

'Don't worry! He was too busy answering questions. What a family! I thought these sorts of intrigues were only common to Rome – desire for power obviously corrupts everywhere.'

'Glad I don't have any. Don't want any either. Is there any chance of that beer now?'

Instead of walking back towards Herod's palace, they turned left and headed for Temple Mount climbing steeper steps as the land rose. They entered a small square just near the great overpass where people were walking up to the temple. There was a bakery on the corner and they stopped to look at the circular domed oven. A baker was raking out the embers before putting in another batch of dough. He noticed Marc and Gaius looking at him and turned and smiled.

'If you want unleavened bread for the Passover, it will be another twenty minutes.'

'No thanks,' said Marc. 'We're just enjoying watching you work.'

'Well, you can come and help if you like,' said the baker winking at Gaius. 'I'm rushed off my feet. Don't normally work this late but there's so much demand this week.'

'Strange that the Jews have to eat unleavened bread,' said Gaius. 'What's wrong with putting yeast in it and making it rise? Just one of those food requirements of their religion, I suppose.'

'I can answer that one for you,' said the baker. 'In Jewish law leaven symbolizes error or evil. In the same way that a little yeast can ferment a whole lump of dough, a little sin, if it goes unchecked, can infect everyone and everything around it. That's the theory anyway.'

'Thinking about it, I can see their point,' said Marc.

The baker continued with a twinkle in his eye.

'Of course, it could just have been that they didn't have time to wait for the dough to rise seeing as they were fleeing from the Egyptian Pharaoh.'

Gaius said, 'Funnily enough we were just hearing about that story yesterday. Do you know where we can get a beer?'

The baker laughed.

'I see you're not worried by a little fermentation then? You can have some beer right here, if you like. My wife makes it from an old Egyptian recipe. It used to be an offshoot of bread making, you know. It's very good. There's a seat over there where you can sit and watch as long as you like.'

And Marc and Gaius did just that. It seemed to attract others and before long they were joined by a Greek couple who sat drinking the beer made by the baker's wife - a lovely buxom lady with a raucous laugh.

'Have you come for the Passover feast?' asked the Greek man.

'No. How about you?' said Marc.

'We've come to hear a new teacher. People say he's performed miracles. My wife, well … she has problems. He's up on the mount now. We don't understand much of what he says. I asked one his followers, chap called Philip, if it would be possible to speak to his master. But he said he's far too busy this week. We were just listening to him talking about people walking in the dark and how we must put our trust in the light while we have it. Do you have any idea what he means?'

Gaius said, 'The philosophy is too deep for me. Unless darkness is a sinful life and light means a good one.'

The Greek looked thoughtful.

'That would make sense, but what does he mean by referring to the light while we have it? I don't think I sin very much. I have been married to the same woman for twenty years. I don't steal and I have never killed anyone, so I really can't see that I've done anything wrong.'

'I'm sure most people feel that way,' said Marc. 'But there's a dark side to most of us, things that we are all capable of, that we don't want anyone to know about.'

The man's wife said, 'Well, I would love to see him perform a miracle. Then I could really believe in his special powers.'

'Maybe we will before the week is over,' said her husband.

Marc and Gaius had finished their beers and decided to take a long stroll back to the palace. The light was dwindling and some corners of streets and squares were in darkness. As they turned left into a quiet alleyway, they heard cries of distress and started running towards three men who were attacking a woman. One of them held her down on the ground while another lifted her clothing over her head; the third was preparing to rape her.

The man who was on his feet turned and threw a punch at Marc who crossed his arms, holding them up to block the man's swing, kicking him in the groin as he did so. The man doubled over, Marc pushed down on the back of his arm forcing him to the ground, holding him there with his knee; he groaned in pain as his elbow was twisted in an unnatural position.

Another of the attackers released the woman's skirts and grabbed Gaius' tunic either side of his chest. Using his left hand, Gaius seized the man's right wrist with an underhand grasp and, stepping forward, he looped his right arm under the man's shoulder. By turning his body, leaning forward as he did so, he brought his right foot behind the attacker's leg and levered the man up and over his body. The man fell heavily on his back and lay stunned on the ground. The third man fled.

Gaius said, 'I'll go to the Temple and find a guard. These two need bringing before a magistrate. I assume you can manage.'

The man Marc was holding shouted, 'Why are you protecting her? She is nothing but a prostitute, she asks for it.'

The woman was beginning to smooth her clothes. She was crying gently and shaking.

She said, 'It's not true, sir. It may have been true once but I was forgiven for my wickedness and I have not done it again. Truly, sir, I thank you from the bottom of my heart.'

Marc took a closer look at her face.

'Didn't I see you the other day with the man on the donkey? You were one of those waving palms were you not?'

'Yes sir, I was. My name is Mary. He is my rabbi and I am one of his followers.'

'More likely his loose woman,' said a voice from the ground, his face flattened into the cobbles.

Marc put more pressure on the back of his arm and the man momentarily passed out with the pain.

'That will shut him up for a while. I'm glad for you that you have found a new way of life. But what concerns me now is that these men have committed an offence, regardless of what they may think of you. They have no right of rape.'

Gaius returned shortly with two guards who bound the men when they were sufficiently recovered to stagger to their feet.

'I want these men dealt with appropriately,' said Marc.

One of the guards replied insolently, 'Oh yes, and just who are you?'

Marc showed them his identity documents.

'I'm sorry, sir! We will take them to the jail and make sure they see a magistrate.'

'Good! We are witnesses to this offence. You can reach us at Herod's palace. We are staying with Pontius Pilate.'

The guard turned pale; his cockiness faded into a distant memory.

'Where do you live?' Marc asked Mary.

'It's just a little way down this street.'

'We will walk with you – we are going in that direction.'

'Thank you, sirs! You will be mightily blessed for your kindness.'

Marc looked at her quizzically. Gaius just wished they could have another beer but did not dare mention it. They walked Mary to her door and made their way back to the palace, without realizing the implication of this incident on the investigation.

12

-Rebecca Victor-

Marc finished a letter to his son before going to breakfast. No rays of sun reflected into the room this morning. A dull greyness covered the sky. Marc smoothed out the inventory he had taken from Herodium. It might be useful to find where the rest of the treasure was stored to check nothing else was missing.

Pilate had nearly finished some eggs and cheese and had started on a basket of fruit when Marc sat opposite him.

'Good morning, Commander! I have already had a visitor – the local magistrate – asking about the men you arrested last night. Attempted rape is not treated seriously around here, especially where ladies of dubious character are concerned.'

Marc said, 'I doubt the woman is of dubious character. She is a Jewess and a religious follower.'

Pilate sighed. 'I have had enough trouble with them already. I shall leave it to you and Polybius.'

Marc changed the subject.

'May I examine the artefacts brought back from Herodium? I understand they are stored here.'

'Yes, they are. Stephen, who looks after the archives, will be able to help you. I'll send for him.'

An hour later, Stephen and Marc were checking the inventory in the vaults, which were only one floor below ground level and were considerably more salubrious than those of Herodium. Marc satisfied himself that there was nothing else missing. A fact that he found very surprising! Why take just the jewels? The only answer could be that the thief or thieves were travelling light and knew exactly what they wanted.

On his way back, Marc asked to visit the library. When he returned, Gaius was munching on some grapes.

'Hello!' he said cheerfully. 'Pilate told me you'd gone to the vaults. Is everything all right?'

'Yes! Fine! But we are looking for a considerable number of stones. Chances are most of them were removed from their settings – it would make them more portable and easier to dispose of. I have found out where Victor's is; the firm of architects and surveyors. Thought I might go there. Want to come?'

'Certainly I do.'

Victor's was to be found in the north of the city on the edge of a residential area – a square, symmetrical, two storey stone building with three domes on the roof. The front door opened directly into the street and, above the architrave, was a bronze plaque displaying the name and business of those within. A slave responded to their knock. He looked more like a bodyguard with his powerfully built physique, and long dark hair pulled close against his head and tied at the back.

They were shown through the atrium into a light airy room and invited to sit down at a table. Marc gave him their names and they were politely asked to wait. One wall of the room was filled with bookshelves and Marc as usual was drawn to them.

'There is a complete set of "De Architectura" here, written by Vitruvius. There are ten books altogether. Book 1 is on the principles of town planning; books 3 and 4 on temples; book 5 on public buildings; book 8 is on water supply. These are superb.'

Gaius looked bored. 'It all sounds very tedious to me.'

A few minutes later the door opened and in walked a tall slender elegant woman. Her long fair curly hair was mostly coiffed on top of her head, leaving a few ringlets to trail down the side of her face and back of her neck. Her long dress was made of fine red linen. She looked at Marc and then Gaius and smiled. Her clear blue eyes were intelligent and enquiring. Marc felt an emotional gush that started somewhere in his stomach and definitely finished in his groin. For a moment he could say nothing. It was a long time since a woman had affected him in this way and he could hardly take his eyes off her. She spoke in a soft, gentle and cultured voice, yet had a hint of decisiveness.

'Good morning, gentlemen! My name is Rebecca Victor. How can I help you?'

Gaius noticed his friend's reaction and immediately took the lead.

'Good morning! My name is Gaius and this is Commander Marc Tiro.'

Marc noticed the formality of the introduction, perhaps to detract from his momentary lapse of concentration. It is a good thing we are not all attracted to the same people, he thought.

'I am very pleased to meet you both. Please sit down.'

Marc recovered and became more businesslike than usual.

'We understand that this firm might have been responsible for the architecture of the palace Herodium.'

'Yes, that is true. It was a long time ago – forty or more years – my father was its designer.'

'Is it possible to speak to your father?'

'I'm afraid not. My father died last year.'

'I'm sorry,' said Marc, momentarily thinking of his own father. 'Who has taken over the firm'?

Rebecca hesitated.

'I have.'

'Forgive me for asking, do you employ a qualified architect and surveyor?'

'I am qualified in both disciplines.'

The tone of Rebecca's voice indicated that she had clarified this point before. For a moment Marc felt humbled; he smiled at her but it was obvious she thought him patronizing.

'My father taught me himself and he was tutored by Vitruvius in Rome. Do not allow the fact of my sex to discourage you. My clients receive very thorough work.'

'Forgive me,' said Marc repeating himself. 'I meant no offence.'

'None taken,' she said and smiled at him.

His insides turned to pulp again. He felt thoroughly disgusted with himself. He knew he was behaving like a silly schoolboy, but just at the moment was unable to do anything about it. Gaius asserted himself again.

'Do you know if there are any plans of Herodium?'

'There will be, in our archives. We rarely destroy our plans in case clients wish for alterations.'

'Can I ask if your firm also built the aqueducts from Solomon's Pools to Herodium?'

'Yes, we did.'

'And might there be plans of those also?'

'Almost certainly there will. But may I ask why you are so interested in old workings. Do you not want something new to be built?'

It was Gaius' turn to hesitate, not knowing how much to reveal. Marc intervened.

'Miss Victor,' he ventured, not knowing whether this was her correct form of address. She said nothing so he continued.

'We have been asked to investigate a possible theft from Herodium and we need to know the layout of the lower levels.'

'There will be copies at Herodium, in the library.'

'Unfortunately they seem to be missing. In fact, all the plans are there except the ones we want to see.'

'In that case, I will ask for ours to be brought up so you can look at them.'

Rebecca called the slave who had opened the door.

'Daniel, would you please fetch me the plans of the lower levels of the Herodium palace, and the layout of the waterways from

Solomon's Pools.'

'Miss Rebecca, I don't think they are there. Your brother asked for them several months ago. I found them myself and I know they have not been returned because I always make a note of the dates.' Marc noticed the colour drain from Rebecca's face.

'Thank you,' she said. 'That will be all.'

'Is anything wrong?' asked Marc.

'Are you some sort of magistrates?' she asked. Marc took out his identification and Rebecca looked at it keenly until she was satisfied.

She explained. 'My stepbrother, Anthony Avitus, is a partner in this firm. He is missing. He disappeared four months ago. We have reported the disappearance, of course, but he has not been found. It just occurred to me that it might have something to do with those plans. It is unlike him not to return anything he has borrowed.'

Marc came straight to the point.

'Pardon my asking, but was he in financial difficulties?'

Rebecca was ashen.

'It is believed that he has gone off to live with another woman. His wife let slip some mention of a secret lover. She is not happy I fear. My brother was not of a faithful nature.'

Gaius asked, 'And what do you think?'

'It is unlikely he would leave the firm. He needed the money that it provided for him. His lifestyle is extravagant.'
She hesitated, unwilling to think the unthinkable.

'The theft you mentioned, what was stolen?'

'Jewellery! Very valuable ones!' said Marc.

'Oh dear, I do hope he has not been foolish.'

'Who would your brother contact if he were to come back?'

'He would see his mother, Sabina, who is my stepmother, or his wife, Deborah, or me. My father married Anthony's mother after my mother passed away. We grew up as brother and sister but we are not actually blood relatives. Anthony was very young when his own father died and he was always close to his mother. She owns a tannery, which she inherited from her first husband and decided to keep, even when she married my father. You can't miss it if you take the road to Bethany. I think Sabina would have liked Anthony to take on the tannery but he wasn't interested, so he followed in my father's footsteps instead.'

'Where does his wife live?'

'Deborah has a large house in an enclosure outside the north east edge of the city. It's beyond Gethsemane.'

'Thank you for your help. Can I speak to your slave again please?' said Marc.

Rebecca called Daniel to join them.

'Do you remember if your master had a client with him at the time he asked for the plans of Herodium?'

'I have already looked at my diary, sir. The master had two clients that day, a couple wanting an ossuary for their family remains, the other was Flavius, the chief of staff, wanting a quotation for a new aqueduct. But the request for the plans may have been connected to another client entirely.'

'Your record keeping is excellent,' said Marc.

'Thank you, sir!'

'Miss Victor ....'

'Please call me Rebecca.' Marc looked pleased. He even loved the sound of the name.

'Rebecca, could we encroach on your time to help us locate the waterways to Herodium? We have been out to Solomon's Pools but it's impossible to tell the direction of the underground tunnels. We didn't have much luck seeing where they came into the palace either. In fact, we were told that the water supply has dried up.'

'In that case, we had better start at the Pools rather than the palace, there could be some damage. I will be delighted to help you, particularly if my brother has had some involvement in this.

When would you like me to come out with you?'

'As soon as possible!'

'I have appointments tomorrow, but what about the day after? I could meet you by the gate heading south to Bethlehem at sunrise.'

Marc was very impressed by this woman's resolve. He could not help but admire her.

'Good. In the meantime, we will visit your relatives, with your permission, of course.'

'Please do as you see fit Commander.'

Gaius noted the respectful awe with which she said this and smiled.

As they were walking back through the atrium a young girl came running into the room.

'Allow me to introduce my daughter, Rachel,' said Rebecca.

Marc politely saluted her but inwardly felt disappointed. Where there are children there is usually a husband he thought, it is really time I grew up. With that they took their leave.

'Quite stunning, don't you think?' said Gaius, when they were out of earshot.

'Certainly is.' Marc tried to sound off-hand. Gaius twinkled.

'Well, what do you think? Shall we go and see either or both of these women?'

'Both, and there is no time like the present.'

13

-The Tanner's Wife-

They stopped at Herod's palace to fetch two horses although they did not mount until they had reached the east gate, south of Temple Mount, and took the road to Bethany. They could both smell the tannery long before they saw it nestling amongst some olive trees. Long rows of hides hung on lines, all at various stages of conversion into leather.

They dismounted and watched as the raw animal skins were washed and limed, and loose hair and fat was scraped from the surface before being soaked in a solution of wood and bark. The workers took no notice of their observers. Some were finishing the leather in different colours and textures.

'So, we have visitors!'

A strident voice from behind made them turn round to face a large squat woman wearing leather trousers and tunic, cut so low that it was impossible not to notice the size of her cleavage. Her feet were apart and her arms were folded under her bosom. Her once blonde hair was tinted with silver, and wildly framed her weather beaten face. Gaius' eyes were transfixed. The woman drew her arms closer together so that her breasts heaved, trying to free themselves from their encumbrance.

'Have a good look round,' said the woman, her eyes twinkling at Gaius, who immediately dropped his gaze to his feet. Marc admired the man who had taken this woman to be his wife, and briefly pondered on the nature of their relationship.

'Good day, ma'am! We are looking for Sabina Victor, the mother of Anthony Avitus.'

'You just found her. What can I do for you?'

Marc thought it appropriate to show his identification before asking questions. He took one step towards her. She looked, without moving an inch. Then, with a sideways movement of her head, she invited both men to enter her house. The smell did not improve as they sat in an atrium covered in dust, on chairs covered with old leather skins. Bits that looked like they had been removed from raw skins were floating on the water in the impluvium.

'We had reason to visit your step-daughter, Rebecca Victor, this morning and she is concerned about Anthony, who we understand has been missing for four months.'

'Is she now? Well it's none of her business what Anthony is up to.'

'Have you heard from him in that time?'

'Why should I? He's a grown man – not likely to be contacting his mother now is he? Do you contact yours?'

Marc ignored the question.

'Did your son mention to you that he was planning to go away?'

'No. But he did seem excited about something, I must admit. Mind you, if he found himself a good woman rather than that stuck up cow he married, I wouldn't blame him for taking off.'

She sat bolt upright on the edge of her seat, leaned forward and drew in a deep breath. Marc instinctively sat back in his chair.

'Has he done this sort of thing before?'

'What sort of thing might that be?'

'Disappeared for a period of time?'

'No. But his father did – my first husband. Always dreaming about something he was. He would take off for weeks at a time travelling somewhere. It was always me who ran this place, you know. That's why it was no problem for me when he died. I'd grown really attached to it. I tried living in the city but would always have to come back here, to get back to reality. Some men need to get away, not got the same stamina as women. They need a break from what they're doing – it gets on top of them and they can't cope very well. They're always better when they come back – until the next time that is. It doesn't surprise me that Anthony has gone walkabout for a while – he was probably stressed.'

'Is there any reason why you think he was stressed?'

'Marriage wasn't too good. They wanted children but it didn't happen. He wanted a child by Deborah's maid but she wouldn't hear of it – she's a Jewess – always got to abide by the rules of their forefathers. Mind you, their forefather Abraham sowed his oats with his wife's maidservant didn't he? They never talk about that though.'

'I wonder, ma'am, did Anthony mention to you any project that he was working on?'

'No – although he did say that he'd been offered a big job and was expecting to be well paid. I know he didn't want Rebecca to find out about it.'

'What made you think that?'

'He more or less said so. He cares for Rebecca – don't get me wrong – but I think she's started to take a bigger role in the firm than he likes. I can't blame her, of course, if she's got the talent. But I get the feeling she is taking some of his clients, so he was pleased when he got this offer and wanted to keep it to himself.'

'Ma'am, you have been most helpful. If Anthony gets in touch with you, would you mind sending word to me at Herod's palace in Jerusalem? He has some documents that we would very much like to look at.'

'I'll tell him to contact you, if I see him. Have you spoken to his wife?'

'Not yet, but we aim to do so.'

'Good. She probably knows a thing or two more than me.'

When they left, Sabina appeared deflated compared to the ebullient woman they had first met, as though talking about her son had worried her. She seemed to have been convinced that he was enjoying a bawdy break, but was now confronting the reality of his absence. Not like those of her husband at all, but possibly more sinister.

'Well, what did you think of that?' asked Gaius, as they rode back towards Jerusalem.

'Something certainly doesn't make any sense. Anthony was allegedly excited about a big new project and then promptly disappears. That's the last thing he would do if he wanted to make a success of it.'

'Unless he realized that it was too much for him and he couldn't handle it, and went off in shame somewhere.'

'No, I don't think so. I doubt he would have been willing to admit it, particularly as the job concerned a prestigious place like Herodium.'

'Perhaps he was simply asked to mend the aqueducts. Silas said that the water wasn't getting through like it used to.'

'Is that enough to get a man excited? Do you feel up to another visit, to Deborah this time?'

'It can't be worse than that one!'

They backtracked until they reached a road leading to the north, heading towards Gethsemane and beyond. About quarter of a mile from the city was a small number of substantially built houses, each with its own walled garden. They found the house they were looking for, dismounted and attracted the attention of a slave girl.

'May we speak to your mistress?' said Marc.

'I'll see if she's at home, sir. Whom shall I say is calling?'

'My name is Commander Marc Tiro. Tell her it's about her husband, Anthony.'

The girl disappeared and when she returned she asked if they would mind sitting in the garden, until her mistress was ready. They were kept waiting at least half an hour. When Deborah approached, she was unsteady; her words were slurred and her tone aggressive. Marc rose and showed his identity documents again.

'What do you want?' said Deborah.

"Ma'am, we are investigating the disappearance of your husband Anthony. May we ask if you have seen him in the last four months?'

'He comes and goes as he pleases. He is my husband, not my child. I make no checks on him.'

'I understand that, ma'am. But have you seen him recently?' Marc was dissatisfied with the vagueness of her answer. Deborah swayed and sat down with as much dignity as she could.

'I saw him last week. He came and stayed with me for a few days, but said he had important work to do elsewhere and would be back soon.'

'Did he say where he was working?'

'No. But my husband is an important man. He is senior partner in a firm of architects, so naturally he would not tell me, a mere woman, about the nature of his work. I couldn't possibly understand it anyway.'

'I'm sorry to press you on this matter, but can you be more specific about when he stayed with you?'

'I said last week. Must have been at the beginning of the week – he stayed two nights. We are trying to have a child, so he wouldn't stay away from me too long.'

Deborah stood up, clearly distressed by the interview.

'I'm answering no more of your questions. I need to rest. I shall ask Sarah to show you to the gate.'

'Obviously lying!' said Gaius, when she had left.

'Yes, a very sad and unhappy woman! But then I suppose if you think your husband has left you for another because you can't give him a child, you are not likely to say so.'

The young slave girl, Sarah, returned to show them out. As they strolled towards the gate Marc took the opportunity to talk to her.

'Have you seen your master recently?'

The girl looked alarmed then decided to answer.

'No sir! He has not been here for several months. Certainly not since the weather was cold.'

'Do you know if he had any visitors to the house before he left?'

'Well sir, he was a bit of a one with the ladies.'

She looked furtively behind her to make sure Deborah was not within earshot.

'Once, the lady was married and her husband came and demanded money from him – compensation I think he called it, but the master said it was extortion.'

Marc repeated his question. 'Did he have any visitors before he left?'

'Oh sir, I'm not sure I should be saying anything but two men did come. Their first visit was last summer; they came late when it was getting dark. I couldn't see their faces when they arrived; they were covered. I showed them into the living room. Mistress was in bed, resting. The master told me to go about my work, but you know it doesn't stop us hearing things. I was in the next room. People always think we slaves are deaf and dumb.'

'What were they talking about?'

'I couldn't hear everything, of course. I heard them mention Herodium palace. One of them said there were some things there that belonged to him and his folk, and that he would pay handsomely for the master's help. The men who arrived were very bothered about being seen though; I heard them say they were seen several times, but I don't think anybody could have seen them, their faces were covered and, as I said, it was getting dark. Besides, what difference would it have made?'

'Did your master agree to help them?'

'I think so because he seemed interested in what they were saying. They didn't argue or anything. And the master was quite excited after one of their visits.'

'Did you hear what your master was expected to do?'

'No sir, but it wasn't until sometime later that he didn't return home. As I said, the winter had come. But the mistress didn't worry about it because …. well …. I think she thought he was spending time with one of his …. other ladies.'

'How did she feel about him spending time with other ladies?'

'After the last time, they had a terrible row. She said she would kill him if he did it again.'

'Do you think your mistress is capable of murder?'

'I think anybody is capable of murder if they are angry enough.'

'On the day that he didn't return, did you see him leave in the morning?'

'I can't remember, sir. But I don't always see him go. I leave breakfast ready and clear away later, but he doesn't always stop to eat.'

The girl hesitated then added, 'One thing happened not long ago – I don't know if it is important – we were burgled. The burglar took all the gold in the house – there was quite a lot. He knew just where to look. I think that's why mistress is so distressed. She needs her husband to come back to protect her.'

They had reached the gate and Marc was careful to ask no more questions in case Deborah was watching. He thanked the girl for her help.

When they were away from the house Gaius said, 'Deborah may be lying because she killed her husband. Not every woman is happy for her man to have affairs.'

Marc was non-committal. 'Possible! One thing is for certain - we seem to be digging up more than a pile of old stones.'

14

-Marcellus and Aemilia-

The following morning was dull but still. Marc was pleased to see Cornelius. He had lost weight and was pale but nevertheless ebullient.

'Good morning!' Cornelius greeted him.

'Good morning! It's very good to see you looking so well – how are you feeling?'

'I'm much better, thank you. But I'm so bored doing nothing; I must be improving. I've been told not to overdue things at first. There's plenty of time. How are your investigations going?'

'We have been to Herodium and to Victor's, the firm of architects, and I spoke to Herod Antipas. The plan I need most is missing as is Victor's stepson, Anthony, who took over the business.'

'Did you look at the vaults?'

'Yes.'

'Any indication of how the thieves may have got in?'

'There has been some disturbance of the mortar in the stonework but I would like to know what is on the other side.'

Pilate entered the room and greeted Cornelius. The three men enjoyed pleasantries.

Pilate said, 'Marc, I shall be divesting you of the services of Gaius today. I need him to update some administrative files for me. I trust that will not inconvenience you too much.'

'I'm sure I shall manage without him for one day. But can I ask for his services again tomorrow, if you can spare him?'

'Yes, by all means! Those two men you arrested the other night, they're in custody, but the magistrate has asked if he can speak to you since you are a key witness. He suggested this morning.'

An hour later Marc walked to the Antonia Fort to find the judge. He rose in welcome as Marc approached.

'Morning Commander! Good of you to come. I'm Tribune Polybius. We arrested two men at your behest two nights ago but it looks as though rape is only one of their crimes. They broke into the villa of Marcellus, a Roman citizen living in Jerusalem. They severely beat two of his slaves, one of whom has died, raped his stepdaughter and stole valuable jewellery. Before they left the house, they plied themselves with wine and then got careless. A member of Marcellus' household has already identified the men. But I would like a statement from you and a description of the third man if possible. His comrades have given us a name but he is not from these parts and we have not been able to find him so far.'

'I can do that for you. What's their sentence?'

'It will be death by crucifixion, probably the day after tomorrow. I have already made out the order. I am due in Jericho so no time to waste. I have a large circuit to deal with.'

Polybius demonstrated the extent of his responsibilities by stretching out his hands level with his head, and drawing an arc with his arms. He continued.

'Marcellus would like to meet you, by the way. He wants to thank you personally for arresting the offenders, and also because you are a fellow Roman. He told me to tell you that you are welcome at his house any time.'

'That's very gracious of him and I accept. I'll go today.'

'That will please him, I'm sure. His wife would like to convey her thanks to you as well. She is delighted that her jewels will be returned. In fact, would you mind taking them with you? It will save me a job. I need to be moving on. I will send one of our guards with you.'

The tribune brought out an iron box, unlocked it and placed the jewels on a table. Marc picked up a startling blue necklace and examined it closely. It was instantly recognisable. Its design was like the one he had seen on the picture of Cleopatra at Herod's palace in Caesarea.

Marc said, 'I'm afraid I shall have to ask you to come with me to see Marcellus. I'm in Jerusalem on the authority of Pilate looking into the theft of jewellery that once belonged to Herod's wife, Mariamne. Jewels made of lapis lazuli. This necklace is similar to one that was among the collection. I shall have to impound it.'

Polybius looked annoyed.

'Well, yes, I understand. But surely you cannot suspect one of our most prominent citizens of stealing a necklace?'

'I must reserve judgement, naturally, and I am accusing no one. But I need to ask him where he obtained it and how long it has been in his possession. I also need to get it valued – it may simply be a copy.'

'That must be it!' Polybius sounded relieved. Flogging and crucifixion was one thing. Having to accuse a man whose support he might need in the future was quite another.

'All right, I'll come with you. Marcellus lives in the north outside the gate.'

The villa was of typical Roman design, a large central square courtyard with a colonnaded walkway leading to various living quarters built of brick with red tiles. The entrance was impressive and palm trees and fountains gave an air of tranquillity, despite recent traumatic events.

Marcellus was out but his wife, Aemilia, received the two men assuring them that her husband would not be long. Polybius introduced Commander Marc Tiro, which elicited an immediate effusive response. She fussed over her guests and insisted on waiting on them herself.

'Have you got my jewels?' she asked.

'Yes ma'am,' said Polybius.

'Wonderful! Can I have them?'

'I think we can give most of them back to you but there may be a delay over the lapis lazuli necklace.'

Aemilia screeched.

'Oh no, it has been damaged hasn't it? I knew it. I knew the gods would take it away from me. Whenever I have anything beautiful I am never allowed to keep it.'

Marc spoke in a calming, sympathetic voice.

'No, it has not been damaged. It is perfectly intact. I can see why the theft would be such a loss to you. The lapis lazuli necklace is of particular beauty.' His words had immediate effect.

'I do enjoy wearing it, although I have so few chances. My husband is mindful of its value and won't allow me to wear it outside this house.'

'So it's unlikely that the thieves knew it was here?' said Polybius.

'I can't imagine anyone would have seen it. I have very strict instructions to keep it locked away. But I get it out every now and then, and put it on. I love it.'

'May I ask where you got it from?'

'My husband gave it to me. He has such an eye for colour and form. Oh look! Here he is.'

Marcellus walked towards them and smiled as he saw Tribune Polybius. He was of middling height, overweight with puffy cheeks, hooded lids and a large double chin. Marc guessed he was in his sixties.

'Darling, this is Commander Tiro who arrested the two thieves. They have brought back the jewels. I was just saying what a good eye you have for choosing jewellery, particularly my blue necklace.'

Marcellus looked pleased, his ego visibly imbibing the flattery in front of the two visitors.

'I selected it personally, of course,' said Marcellus.

'Can you remember where you got it, darling?'

'I bought it from a jeweller in ……… oh dear, I can't

remember.'

'My husband travels such a lot you see.'

Marc asked, 'Have you had it long?'

A look of wariness passed fleetingly over Marcellus' face but Marc did not miss seeing it. His wife saw it too. She opened her mouth to speak but shut it again.

'Several years – I can't remember.'

'I'm sorry to have to tell you that the necklace closely resembles one that was part of a collection that has been stolen from the vaults of Herodium. For the moment I need to keep it. It will of course be returned to you as soon as possible.'

Aemilia screeched again.

'You surely can't think that we stole it! We had no idea ......'

Her husband raised his hand to silence his wife.

'If it is stolen, it was not stolen by me. I bought it in innocence and good faith.'

'Of course,' said Polybius. 'That is what must have happened. But it would be helpful if you could remember where you bought it and when.'

'Well I can't!' There was a note of agitation or perhaps panic in Marcellus' voice. 'It was probably from Damascus. I go there a lot on business.'

'There may be another simple explanation,' said Marc. 'It may be a copy.'

Marcellus turned pale. His eyes moved from side to side in rapid succession. He put his hand to his face and squeezed his mouth into a pout.

'I'm sure this is not a copy,' he said in a tone indicating he had been insulted.

'Perhaps it is the original then?' said Marc.

Marcellus realized the trap.

'Well maybe it is a copy. Who knows? My wife likes it, that's the main thing.'

'Oh yes, I do. I love it. Please bring it back soon.'

Marc smiled at her.

'I will get it back to you as soon as I possibly can.'

Aemilia was persuaded, for the time being. Polybius changed the subject and he inquired after their stepdaughter.

Marcellus answered, 'She is still feeling unwell. My wife and I shall do all we can to protect and care for her. She is not actually related by blood to either of us, you understand, so we are under no obligation. She is the daughter of my second wife by her first husband. Both of them have since died so we gave her a home.'

Despite the nature of the words, Marc detected a definite lack of concern for the woman who had been raped. He was beginning to feel irritated by this self-centred couple and was now anxious to leave. Marcellus seemed to have recovered his equilibrium and was concerned he may have appeared rude earlier.

He said, 'Please call in any time. I would love the opportunity to speak to you about Rome, Commander. We are planning a banquet in the next month or so. You are both cordially invited.'

His wife added, 'By that time, I shall have my necklace back. Perhaps I may even be allowed to wear it.'

Marc thought he would prefer to endure another storm at sea. He did not trust these two people and had a bad feeling about both of them.

15

-Joel and Anna-

'Can you recommend a good jeweller in the city?' Marc asked Polybius, as they rode back to Antonia fort. 'I need to know whether the necklace is genuine.'

'The one with the best reputation is called Theo. I will get a guard to go with you to provide some protection. The last thing we want is for it to be stolen while it is in our care.'

Theo's shop nestled underneath the main archway leading up to the Temple Mount. An opening in the door slid back as Marc knocked and he was asked to identify himself. The jeweller was elderly and slightly stooped. His long grey hair was streaked with black indicating a richness of an earlier age.

'I am sorry about the precautions. But I have been robbed twice. People often leave valuables with me for mending. I have to tell them now that it is at their own risk. What can I do for you?'

'I have a necklace that I would like you to value and also tell me if you have seen it before.' Marc removed the leather purse that was tied round his waist under his outer tunic and cloak.

'My, my, where did you come by this?'

'Do you recognize it?'

'Most jewellers would. It was said to be one of the most beautiful pieces ever to come out of Ugarit. It's a royal necklace, made for a princess on her wedding day many hundreds of years ago. The lapis lazuli was mined in northern Afghanistan – they are some of the rarest stones in the world.'

'Do you have any idea as to its value?'

Theo disappeared into the back of his shop and shuffled back a few minutes later.

'The original would be worth a great deal. But this is a copy. The stones are not lapis lazuli. Its only value would be as a decorative piece. It has been very well made though, done by someone who knows what he is doing. It would need a person more skilled than me.'

'Can you suggest anyone who might have made it?'

'Damascus is the place to go. Precious and semi-precious stones were sold in Ugarit from the mines in the east and sent down to Damascus for setting. The design can be as important as the gems themselves. But in this case most of the value would be in the quality of the stones.'

'Thank you very much. That has been very helpful.'

Marc spoke to the soldier who accompanied him.

'Go back to Tribune Polybius. Tell him the necklace is not valuable but I wish to keep it longer for investigation. Please ask him to inform Marcellus.'

To say he was disappointed was an understatement. Marc had hoped for a lead in this mystery, and the necklace seemed to provide it. He had no reason to believe now that Marcellus was not telling the truth and that he had bought it in Damascus. He wondered how much Marcellus had paid for it.

Looking up, he was surprised to see Claudia descending the steps from the Temple. Her cloak covered her head and face so he did not recognize her at first but something in her stance and gait caught his attention. It is strange how we identify people as much by their movement as by their facial features, he thought. Marc called out to her and she turned to look at him.

'Hello, what are you doing here?'

'I could ask the same of you,' he said.

'To be honest, I have just been up to the Women's Court at the Temple. They sit and pray for hours. You can also hear the young preacher. I love to listen to him but I would appreciate it if you wouldn't tell my husband. I'm not sure he would approve.'

'Would you like a drink?'

'Marc! I have never done such a thing. People will think I'm a prostitute.'

'We're not going to a bawdy tavern, Claudia. There is a rather unusual place not far from here. It's actually a bakery. The baker leaves benches outside so people who are waiting for the bread and pastries can sit down. Some people stop there and eat while his wife serves drinks. She actually makes very good home made beer but there is juice as well.'

Marc walked Claudia to the place where he had sat with Gaius. The baker's wife recognized him and smiled broadly. He ordered a drink for them both.

'Claudia, do you remember a man called Joel? He used to be the Keeper of the Key at Herodium. It was a long time ago.'

'I do remember him, yes. He retired about seven years ago. I knew his wife, Anna, as well. They sometimes came to the palace with reference documents. He seemed very sad to me, as though there were something on his mind. Never saw him smile much.'

'Do you know where they live?'

'Yes, I do. If they still live in the same street. They were very kind to me when Pilate and I first moved here. He had retired from Herodium but worked in the palace in Jerusalem for a year or two. I liked to read and Joel introduced me to the library. His wife, like me, reads a lot, and sometimes we would compare books and tracts. I'm not sure if they are both alive. Do you want to visit them?'

'Yes, I would. Will you come with me?'

'Yes, of course! I would love to see them again.'

'What can you tell me about them so I'm prepared?'

'Not a lot really! Joel once told me that he was about thirty when he went to work at Herodium. He's Jewish and so is his wife, Hasmonean, I think he once said, but I'm not sure how different that is from the ordinary Jews. They observed all the rituals and were always busy writing – a very literary couple.'

'As I understand it, from a history lesson I once received in Caesarea, the Hasmoneans were a Jewish group who ruled Judea before the Romans. They disliked Herod's variety of Jewish observance, so he married Mariamne, a Hasmonean, as a kind of peace offering.'

'Maybe Joel wanted to work close to Herod to support Mariamne. It is the sort of thing he might do - perhaps he saw himself as the protector of her faith. Herod executed her for adultery but Joel never believed she was guilty.'

When they finished their drinks, Claudia led Marc through a maze of narrow streets in the southern part of the city until they found the house she was looking for. It took a long time before the door was opened in response to their knock. An elderly woman, barely able to walk, appeared just as they were about to leave.

'Anna, it's me, Claudia.'
The eyes lit up and then became watery.

'Claudia, my dear, how good to see you. I thought you must have forgotten all about me. Please come in and bring your friend.'

'Anna, let me introduce Marc to you. He is staying with us for a while and would like to speak to you.'

'Really, I can't imagine anyone would wish to speak to me but do sit down. First, let me look at you. How fine you are and you look happy – that is good. How is that husband of yours?'

'He's well Anna thank you. But how are you – are your aches and pains more troublesome?'

'Yes. And I find it more and more difficult now my beloved Joel is gone.'

'Oh Anna, I'm so sorry to hear it. When did it happen?'

'Only a few months ago, some men brought his body to the door and said they had found him hanging in a field. They also brought a brief note they said Joel had written, saying that he could not live with what he had done any longer and deserved to die. But Claudia, I don't believe it. I don't believe that Joel would take his own life. It's a sin and against our faith.'

Marc asked, 'Are you saying you think someone murdered him?'

'Yes, I am. But I don't know who.'

'Do you still have the note?'

Anna rose painfully to her feet and fetched a piece of papyrus from a wooden box on the floor. She gave it to Marc. It read:

I cannot live with my guilt any longer. Please forgive me.

'It isn't even his writing. I would know it anywhere, we wrote together so much. The men who brought him to me probably wouldn't suspect that. It is unusual for an old woman to know how to read and write. They think they can tell me lies and get away with it. My legs and feet do not work anymore but my eyes and my brain still work fine.'

'What is it that you and Joel used to write about, Anna?' asked Claudia.

'We are writing a history of our times and our religion. We're Essene, a group who support the ways of the early Hasmoneans. We despise the corrupt heretical ways of the Jewish groups that succeeded them, such as the Pharisees. We need to be in a constant state of readiness for our Messiah. God has a pre-determined plan to deliver us. That is why I know Joel would not take his own life.'

'Are the Essenes a large group of people or is there just a few of you?' asked Marc.

'Only a few of us are married and live in the general population, like Joel and me. Most of us live in separate communities. The nearest one to Jerusalem is at Qumran, on the northern shore of the Dead Sea. There is another at Damascus. They spend their time in prayer, leading a simple and celibate life. They study the ancient scripts and are dedicated to writing down our traditions.'

'The men who brought Joel's body home, do you have any idea who they were?'

'None at all, I had never seen them before. It all happened so quickly. I couldn't leave Joel's body here – I had to arrange for a burial. My friends and neighbours helped me.'

'Is there anything we can do for you?' said Claudia.

'No, my dear, there's nothing, unless you can find out who murdered my husband and accused him of committing suicide.' Her lips quivered and her eyes questioned.

Claudia looked at Marc. He said, 'Forgive me for asking you this, Anna, but is it possible that Joel had done something in his life that he regretted?'

Anna hesitated.

'To be honest, I think he had done something wrong at some time. But remember that our faith defines 'wrong' in different ways to this Roman society or even some Jewish ones. Anything that puts a barrier between God and us is a sin. We do not have to kill or commit adultery to be sinners. So it is not possible for me to say how serious my husband's offence might have been. I know he had many nightmares and would get on his knees and ask for forgiveness. If he did anything really bad I think it would have been for the best of motives, even if it proved to be misguided. I could never persuade him to talk to me about it. He would always say that it was between him and God, and simply adding to my worries would do nothing to improve matters.'

Anna began to sob. Claudia put her arm round her shoulders and together they rocked gently to and fro.

Marc, with elbows on knees, sat resting his chin on his fists. Something Anna had said triggered a memory but he could not remember what it was – something he'd heard recently. He gave the problem to his brain and quietly allowed it to cogitate.

16

As they left Anna's house Marc looked at Claudia. Her eyes were red and swollen. There was a hint of despair in her voice.

'Do you think there is anything we can do to help her?'

'I don't know. Only by solving this crime I suspect.'

Marc decided to take Claudia into his confidence and found a quiet corner where they could sit down.

'You know, don't you, that your husband has commissioned me to find lapis lazuli jewellery missing from Herod's vaults after his death?'

'Yes, yes, I know. And around the time of the first inventory Joel was Keeper of the Key. Do you think he had anything to do with it? Is that his great secret that he couldn't tell Anna?'

'I don't know, but I have remembered something that might be important. The surveyor who designed Herodium and the waterways leading to it is dead. But a few months ago his stepson, Anthony, who carried on the business, disappeared. We know that he had a couple of visitors at his house a few months before. A young slave overheard some of their conversation. They discussed Herodium palace and one of the men said there was something there that rightfully belonged to them. She also said they were very concerned about being seen, which she couldn't understand, but supposing they were saying, "We're Essene."'

Claudia took a sharp intake of breath. She realized the implication immediately.

'The Essenes may feel that they have a right to Mariamne's jewellery since she was Hasmonean.'

'That's right! The jewellery was originally given to the Hasmoneans by Cleopatra to support their fight against the Romans. It would also explain why the stones were the only valuables missing from the vault. Nothing else was stolen.'

'But if all this took place only a few months ago, that would make the theft quite recent. That means that Joel had nothing to do with it, he wasn't even there.'

'Correct! So, why was he murdered?'

'As you say, if we could solve the crime, maybe we could find the reason.'

'Claudia, do you know a man called Marcellus and his wife Aemilia?'

'Yes. They are not exactly friends but we have to mix socially with them since they are Roman citizens living in Jerusalem.'

'Some thieves broke into their villa two nights ago and stole some jewels. Among the recovered pieces was a copy of a necklace that was part of Mariamne's inheritance. Have you ever seen Aemilia wearing it?'

'A necklace made of lapis lazuli, no, never. She hasn't even mentioned it.'

'She told me and Tribune Polybius earlier today that her husband thought it was so valuable that he did not allow her to remove it from the villa, or wear it in public.'

'He must believe then that it is worth a great deal.'

'One would assume so. But I have just had it valued and was assured it is a mere copy of the original and practically worthless.'

Claudia's eyes opened wide and her lips parted.

'Have you told him that it's a fake?'

'I have told Polybius so it will not be long before Marcellus knows.'

'But surely if he bought it and paid a lot of money for it, he would have had it valued at the time?'

'You would think so. He said that he bought it, although he was less clear from where – Damascus he suggested.'

'Well – I don't believe him. I have written proof of good title to all my jewels and value at time of purchase.'

'I thought that would be the case. So if he did not buy it, he either stole it or someone must have given it to him.'

'And made him believe that it was original - that would account for why he doesn't want his wife to be seen wearing it.'

'If he believed it was stolen, it would also account for why he has never had it valued.'

Claudia hesitated.

'There is another possibility. Perhaps he knew it was a copy but wanted his wife to believe it was real. You know the sort of thing, to show her how much he loved her. And she would not know any better.'

'Now it takes a woman to think of that,' said Marc with a grin. 'You are a suspicious lot.'

'Perhaps we have to be,' said Claudia. She laughed too and her face brightened a little.

Marc said, 'One more secret, I have still got the necklace and there is someone I would like to show it to. Herod Antipas said that Mariamne's daughters were still living in Jerusalem or at least one of them is, a woman called Salampsio. Have you ever met her?'

'No. I understand she is never seen in society. She became a recluse. Not surprising when you think about how many of his own family Herod had executed.'

'Feel up to another visit?'

'Yes, of course, do you know where she lives?'

'Not far as it happens, quite close to the Hasmonean palace.'

Claudia and Marc stood in front of a tall three-storey house – immaculately maintained with no access either side. The only means of entry was a double fronted door that resembled that on a vault. There was a small wrought iron window in the door. The wood behind it slid back and the face of an elderly man appeared.

'Who is it?' he said.

'My name is Commander Marc Tiro and this is my companion Claudia. We would like to speak to Princess Salampsio. We have some information regarding jewels that once belonged to her mother, and have authority from her brother, Herod Antipas, to visit her.' Marc suspected anything less would not get them through the door.

'Wait here.' The slide was put back in place.

Several minutes passed before anyone reappeared. Several bolts were thrust back and the door opened – just enough to allow them to squeeze through. They were guided to the back of the house, up some stone steps and onto a veranda where sat a lady with silver hair, clothed in purple. She had an altogether more regal presence than Herod Antipas. Her steely blue eyes missed nothing. Marc and Claudia were formally introduced. She asked to see his documents. Waving her hand at two chairs, she indicated that they could sit down.

'You have some information regarding some jewels?'

Marc took out the leather purse.

'Ma'am, I'm investigating the theft of jewellery from the vaults of Herodium palace. Have you ever seen this before?'

Salampsio took it and laid it on the table in front of her. She stared at it for a long time. Marc noticed her blinking rapidly. Then she picked it up and examined it closely.

'Yes. My mother wore it. There was a matching bracelet and anklet.'

Now she could hold back the tears no longer and drops fell onto her cheeks.

She said, 'Excuse me! This is an emotional moment. I have not seen this for years. I wondered what had happened to it.'

'I'm afraid this is not the original.'

Salampsio looked up at him and held her gaze for a few moments.

'I can assure you Commander Tiro, it is the original.'

Now it was Marc's turn to be surprised.

'I took it to be valued just this morning. The jewels are not lapis lazuli.'

'Well, someone has made a mistake. There is a tiny mark in the silver where it had to be mended. My mother was preparing to wear her necklace for a state function. I was in her room. It was always a very exciting time – everyone dressing in fine clothes. She allowed me to put it on and I was pretending to be a queen. My brother, Alexander, came into the room wielding a sword; he was pretending to be fighting a battle and lashed out to frighten me, but accidentally caught my neck.'

She removed a silk scarf just far enough to reveal a scar under her left ear.

'The sword also caught the necklace and it broke and fell to the ground. I shall never forget it. My mother was distraught. We were both severely punished. It was given to a trusted silversmith to be mended. He did a very good job but the join is still visible, if you know what to look for.'

Salampsio held out the necklace for Marc to see and showed him a small flaw in the back of the setting.

'If this is a copy then the jeweller must have been very clever indeed to imitate the flaws. But why bother? There would be no point.'

She continued to caress the jewels; lost for a few moments in her own memories.

Marc and Claudia sat silently pondering this shattering revelation. There were three possibilities. Either the artist who copied the original did so in every detail, or Theo was mistaken, or the necklace never did have real value and these blue stones never were true lapis lazuli. Marc looked at Claudia's frowning and bewildered expression. He felt the same.

'Ma'am, we know that your mother's jewels were in the vault at

Herodium after your father's death. Emperor Augustus made an inventory. We also know that from then onwards there was a constant Roman guard. Can you recall anything unusual that may have happened to cause the theft or disappearance of the jewellery?'

'I continued to live at Herodium after Herod, my father, died. My sister Cypros was there and also Pallas, my stepmother and Phasael her son. There were others, two more of Herod's wives whom I really did not know. They did not stay long and they had no children. I think they remarried. We were there because my stepbrother, Herod Archelaus, allowed us to be. He used the palace when he inherited Judea from his father. He was a disaster for the people and was removed from office. But by that time there were very few of us left. Then the Romans came and used the place just as they liked. It was a distressing time for all of us – seeing our home taken from us. We were Princes and Princesses.

'People assume that because we were born of a king that our life must be easy. They know little of the plots and schemes that often threatened us; that's why I live here, alone, away from everyone. There's just me and my dogs and slaves! It suits me fine. My sister stayed with me until she died.'

Marc let her muse a little longer before reminding her about the theft.

'Oh yes, that. Well, I suppose there were one or two strange happenings. I wanted my mother's jewels. Not because of their value but because of sentiment. I felt they should have belonged to my sister and me. They were given to my mother not to Herod and he had stolen them from her. A man named Joel was Keeper of the Key. I used to ask him if I could fetch the jewels from the vault, just to see them, to wear them and to remember my mother. But he would never allow it. He told me that they had never really belonged to my mother anyway, that they were given to John Hyrcanus by Queen Cleopatra for a good cause and should be used to benefit that cause, not to adorn women. He was wrong, of course. They did not belong to any of us. They belonged to Augustus. Herod had used them as collateral to build Jerusalem, to give the Jews back their precious Temple Mount.'

Salampsio paused to allow the anger that had momentarily risen inside her to subside.

'Nevertheless, it was cruel to say such things. My mother died as a result of being married to Herod. She had given her life and we were left with nothing.

'One day something happened down at the vaults. It was hushed up so I never really knew the truth. It was a year or two after the death of my father. I was told that a guard was suspected of breaking in. He had been overwhelmed and thrown into the dungeon in the very lowest level. It gave me nightmares. The lowest level is a terrible place, damp, dark and full of rats. Nobody could survive down there for very long. Some said the man had his tongue slashed as punishment and could no longer speak.'

She stopped as her voice quivered, barely able to continue thinking of the horror. Marc remembered that Silas had told them a prisoner had been held in the dungeon but had been released a few years ago. Could it be the same man?

'Did you ever hear what happened to him?'

'No. I presume he died. He was Greek not Roman. Many of them were. Augustus sent only a small contingent of his own people to guard the vault. Others were recruited locally; some came from Syria and even further away than that. The decree from Rome was that they should not be allowed to befriend each other in case they plotted to somehow steal the treasures. I don't know how they would have done it without the co-operation of the Key Keeper though. Not even Archelaus was allowed to enter the vaults. As I said, he did not own what was there, Augustus did, and then presumably Tiberius, after his death. As for the prisoner, well it is anybody's guess. One thing I do remember though, his family lived in Capernaum, a small town on the Sea of Galilee. Joel told me he was going to see the man's wife to tell her what had happened.'

Marc took the necklace from the table.

'I would like to thank you ma'am for being so honest with us.'

'One thing before you go, Commander. You haven't told me where you got my mother's necklace, or who now owns it.'

'Just at the moment I prefer to say nothing.'

'Could I ask one favour?'

'Yes, if I can be of service.'

'If the necklace proves to be of no real value, and nobody wants it, may I have it?'

'Ma'am if that is at all possible I promise I will see to it. At the moment though, it is not within my power.'

'That is all I can expect.'

Once in the street, Claudia was full of questions, none of which Marc could answer satisfactorily. If this necklace was original and the valuation was correct, then someone had gone to a lot of trouble for nothing. He was not releasing it to Marcellus and Aemilia until he knew for sure. They walked slowly back to the palace trying to make sense of what they had heard. Marc asked Stephen to place the necklace in the vault. It was evidence.

Gaius was keen to hear about the events of the day and Marc gave him the briefest outline, preferring to be alone to think. He spent the evening writing, in shorthand, a full account of what he had learned so far with details of the conversations. Tomorrow he was meeting Rebecca to try and find the waterway into Herodium. A stab of excitement pierced him. Despite the disdain he felt for his emotional behaviour, he was looking forward to seeing her again.

17

At dawn the next morning Marc rode with Gaius to the southern gate that opened onto the road to Solomon's Pools. He had made arrangements for Silas to expect their party so that they had access to the grounds of the palace.

Rebecca was already waiting, sitting astride her horse. She was dressed in leather boots and trousers covered by a leather tunic with a hint of white linen at the neck and cuffs. Her hair fell down her back and was loosely tied with a red ribbon. She smiled radiantly when she saw them both. Next to her was Daniel, her guardian and protector. Marc wondered how long he had been in love with his mistress. He was surprised to see Rachel, Rebecca's daughter. She looked very much like her mother and was similarly dressed in leather. No doubt courtesy of Sabina.

Rebecca sensed Marc's hesitation about the wisdom of taking a young girl along.

She said, 'Rachel has a remarkable skill of water divining. All the surveying techniques and instruments in the world cannot compete with her abilities. If it is water we are looking for, then Rachel will find it.'

The girl looked down at her hands, embarrassed. She glanced slyly at Gaius, who was quite dashing this morning, but he was too busy tightening his girth strap to notice. They rode at a steady canter and the sun was still low and dazzling when they reached the Pools. Daniel dismounted and erected a portable sundial from instruments that he was carrying in his saddlebags, to establish the orientation of Herodium in the south east.

Marc watched Rebecca working. He loved the way she used the back of her hand to push away the tiny curls that fell across her forehead. Pull yourself together he told himself; this is not the time to be romancing over a married woman.

Eventually she selected the most likely direction an underground aqueduct would have taken, and started to look for vertical vents that had been inserted to supply air for workmen during the excavation. Some of these now formed inspection chambers to allow for cleaning; they checked each shaft as they found them. Because of the terrain, the tunnel often moved north before turning south, sometimes forming a huge loop. When they lost track of it, Rachel used her divining skills. She had a hazel twig in the shape of a 'Y.' With upturned palms, she lightly held the two equal sides in each hand and walked slowly, until the longer one started to vibrate. She was always correct.

It was nearly noon when Herodium came into sight. Its grand towers appeared first. From a high vantage point Marc could see how vast the palace and gardens were, covering an area the size of a small town. Many branches of the aqueduct would be required to irrigate this amount of land. Rebecca was puzzled.

'There are no problems with the supply from the Pools; no cracks or breakages. The system is simple, and if there was a substantial blockage causing the water to build up, it would overflow into other channels.'

The next inspection chamber that they came across was deep, but the iron ladder seemed intact. Gaius offered to go down since he was the shortest of the three men. The descent was difficult; some of the rungs gave way beneath his weight, causing him to slip, leaving him suspended from one arm, since he was holding a torch, until he could find a foothold. His technique improved as he became more cautious, and eventually he reached the bottom safely. He was able to stand upright in the chamber.

Gaius shouted from below, 'The water divides into three

channels at this point; it's flowing freely but it's deep. I'm coming back up.'

Gaius emerged, soaked to his waist. He wiped grimy hands over his tunic, staining the material with black stripes. A drop of blood fell from a cut in his chin and veins of rust streaked across his face.

He said, 'I'm no expert but I think the water in the middle channel is not flowing downwards properly; it appears to be siphoning off into the other two.'

Rachel used her divining skills once again. She followed the line of the water until it dried up; nearby was another inspection cover. This time Marc insisted in climbing down with Gaius as they would need to follow the channel underground. Marc went first. When they reached the bottom it was clear why no water was flowing into this section, the tunnel was completely blocked – with concrete.

'It would take at least two men to do this,' said Marc. 'There must be quite a weight of water behind that wall.'

'How do you feel about walking down there?' asked Gaius. 'You'll need to stoop.'

'I'll manage. I'll let the others know what we're proposing to do.'

Marc shouted to the surface what their plan was. Rebecca said they would try to find the next chamber and remove the cover to let some light in from above. She warned them that they might come to yet more divisions in the tunnel, but to keep as straight as possible. Secretly Marc was already fighting his phobia but knew it had to be done. The torches, made of skins soaked in oil, cast weird shadows over the rounded walls. Rats lined up either side of them but ran off into the distance, disliking the light.

'Imagine what it must have been like building these things,' said Gaius.

The air was becoming thin, and Marc was beginning to notice tightness in his chest when thankfully they reached the next shaft. Rebecca had taken the cover off allowing a draught of fresh air to enter the chamber. It was not so deep underground as some of the others and they could converse without shouting. Rebecca called to them.

'The next vent won't be easy to find because of the trees and foliage inside the gardens, so if we don't see you again, we'll wait here for you. May the gods keep you safe!'

'Thanks!' said Gaius.

They continued their odious journey through interconnected ducts. There was a distinct smell of foul water and the number of rats was increasing. The next stretch seemed endless. Beads of perspiration dropped from Marc's brow. Waves of panic came over him in floods and he forced his mind to focus on something other than his surroundings. But words of poetry provided little comfort. His hair was coated in green slime where his head touched the roof of the tunnel. He could not breathe and, whilst air entered his throat, it never seemed to reach his lungs. He began to feel light headed; his limbs were heavy.

They came to another chamber where they stood and stretched, but the ladder had broken off half way up so they were unable to reach the surface, and the cover had not been removed, presumably too well hidden for Rebecca to find it. They continued their trudge through muddy pools of stagnant water. Bolder rats attacked their boots; continuous kicking made walking uncomfortable and slow.

Without warning Gaius stopped, immobilized by horror.

'What on earth is this?' he said. 'My gods!'

Marc, who was stooped over so far that he could only see his own feet, bumped into him. But the diameter of the tunnel had increased and the height easily enabled them to stand. They looked over the edge of a huge cavern, the water's resting place - a cistern the size of a throne room, except that it was empty.

Gaius' stomach heaved; if there had been food in his belly, he would have been sick. Then Marc saw it too – the rat eaten remains of a body. It was lying on its side, the left hip taking the burden of the weight and the right leg bent out backwards in support of the frame. The left arm was crushed beneath, and the fingers of the right hand were splayed in a crab like fashion, clawing at some invisible assistance.

Marc knelt down beside what was little more than a skeleton. As he gently lifted the skull, he saw where it had been smashed open from behind. He was startled by a rat leaping from the gaping hole, plump from feeding on what remained of the brains. The flesh of the face and the eyes had been stripped away; the mouth lay wide open as if in surprise or anguish or both. Marc only hoped that this man was dead before these disgusting rodents had time to attack his injured defenceless body.

A cold icy chill ran down his spine and caused him to shiver. On what remained of the middle finger of the right hand was a ring with a central seal. Marc removed it as carefully as he could. A large leather pouch, remarkably untouched considering the condition of the clothes and corpse, was attached to the dead man's belt. Marc took it off and then examined the buckle - it had a distinctive design. He opened the pouch, inside which were some documents. A cursory glance revealed a map and a copy of what looked like the missing plans. He placed the buckle and the ring in the pouch and tied it to his own belt.

Marc looked up at Gaius.

'I fear this may be the body of Rebecca's brother. The seal has a "V" in the centre. This is not going to be easy. Are you feeling better?'

'Yes! I am sorry. Not used to seeing sights like that – I'm not a soldier.'

'Death is never pretty. Can you climb down?'

'A dead body will not stop me doing that.'

A long ladder stretched downwards to the floor of the cistern. The wall opposite was curved towards them like the end of a huge pillar and it disappeared round to the right, from where shafts of light were entering the cavern. Marc climbed down. The water on this side of the floor covered his feet so he was obliged to wade until he was standing on a bank of sand and cement on the other side. Gaius followed. There were two smaller tunnels leading from the cistern at floor level, obviously feeding some other parts of the palace.

Marc said, 'I would like to have a closer look at the wall on this side. Let's bring the ladder across.'

It did not take long for him to find where the surface layer had come off, revealing an area of stone blocks beneath that had the appearance of being disturbed. Marc descended and Gaius climbed up to examine the damage.

'Got any thoughts?' said Marc.

'I think that the vault could be the other side of this wall.'

They carried the ladder back to the tunnel from which they had first emerged, and began the ascent. Marc had reached the top and climbed onto the ledge when they heard a loud roar. A lump of concrete came down the channel, moving at great speed, carried by a slide of slime and pushed from behind by the force of a surge of water. Gaius was just pulling his body over the edge when the missile clouted his right leg causing him to fall backwards. He gasped in pain and his lungs filled with the water that temporarily submerged them both.

Marc threw himself on the tunnel floor and grasped Gaius' right arm with his own. Searing pain swept through the shoulder permanently damaged by Sejanus' knife, but he clung on, knowing that his hold was the only thing stopping his companion from a forty-foot fall. When the initial rush of water subsided, Marc crossed his left arm over his right.

'Give me your hand.'

Gaius lifted up his arm and grabbed Marc's hand. Most of the rats had been swept over the edge; those who survived let out piercing squeals in the bottom of the cistern. Marc had difficulty maintaining his stability because of the slipperiness. The ladder had miraculously stayed in place.

'Try to find a rung,' shouted Marc.

Although Gaius was choking for air, he had the presence of mind to follow orders. His left leg flailed about for several seconds until his foot found a resting place. Marc felt the weight lessen on his arms. He carefully manoeuvred the other man into a position from which he was able to haul him up. Gaius turned over and lay on his back coughing until the water cleared from his lungs and he was able to breathe. He lifted himself sideways onto his elbow, gasping, until he recovered.

The water was now a continuous flowing stream several inches deep having found its own natural level. The body had gone – swept with the rats into the cistern – its brittle bones smashed on the stones beneath.

'My gods, that was close,' said Gaius. 'Thanks Marc, you saved my life.'

The only light now came from the shafts in the cistern to the right. Both men had lost their torches. The concrete block had struck below the knee; skin and flesh had been gouged away leaving the bone exposed.

'That leg needs urgent attention. Can you put your weight on it?' said Marc.

'Yes, with help.'

Marc placed Gaius' arm round his neck and put his own round the other's waist. Together, slowly, very painfully and in darkness they made their way back to the open chamber where they had last spoken to Rebecca. She now went to find Silas to explain their plight. Gaius could not bend his leg but insisted on climbing the ladder, hauling himself up by his arms and resting the uninjured foot on each rung. A litter was sent to carry him to a room where he could rest. He had lost a lot of blood and was feeling weak. A slave trained in medical matters cleansed the wound and bound it with poultices of healing herbs and fresh linen. He also administered a painkilling drug. Eventually Gaius slept.

Marc found a moment to speak to Rebecca who wept at the sight of the ring and immediately identified it as that of her brother, Anthony. She recognized the buckle as one given to him as a gift from his wife, Deborah. Her first reaction was wishing to see the body; Marc explained the impossibility of doing so.

Next he spoke to Silas.

'The aqueduct was blocked; at least one of your cisterns was completely empty but the water has now broken through. We found the remains of a body in the tunnel so you can expect a visit from the military police. I would appreciate it if you could take charge.'

Silas frowned.

'I'll do my best, sir. But why would someone block our water and commit murder?'

Marc said, 'I don't know whether there has been a murder; it might have been an accident.'

'Oh, I beg your pardon, sir, I misunderstood you.'
Silas cupped his hands in front of him and held one beneath the other, adopting a pious stance.

'One other thing, Silas, I would like the name of the man who was imprisoned here. Could you search the records? You may find that he was arrested for attempting to break into the vault. It happened a year of two after Herod's death.'

'You don't think it is his bones down there, do you?'

Marc sensed slight sarcasm in the comment.

'No, I don't. The prisoner came from Capernaum. See what you can find out, will you?'

'Yes sir!'

It was evening when they headed back towards Jerusalem. A carriage and mule was provided for Gaius. They rode in silence, quite different from the optimistic group that had set out from

Solomon's Pools a few hours earlier. Rebecca's tears had stopped but consternation showed on her face. Rachel was very tired and Daniel had nothing else on his mind except concern for his mistress and her daughter.

Marc offered to visit Sabina and Deborah. Rebecca was grateful. As they said goodbye on entering the southern gate, they promised to keep in contact.

18

-Gethsemane-

On reaching Herod's Palace the first priority was to attend to Gaius. Claudia took charge and a surgeon was summoned. Pilate and Cornelius asked for an explanation.

Marc said, 'An underground aqueduct was deliberately blocked, diverting the water and leaving one of the main cisterns drained.'

'Are you suggesting that this enabled access to the vaults?' said Cornelius, interrupting him.

'I don't know until I've looked at some plans, but it's possible.'

'That is good,' said Pilate enthusiastically. 'This could change everything for me.'

Marc described how Gaius had sustained his injuries and the finding of the body who, they assumed, was that of Anthony Avitus. Pilate proposed a summary investigation.

It was the night of the feast of the Passover and the city was relatively silent. People were inside taking their evening meal. Marc rode eastwards across the Kidron Valley out towards the tannery. It was dark by the time he arrived. Sabina had finished work for the day and was busy preparing a meal. She recognized him and invited him in. He showed her the ring he had removed from the dead man's hand. She held it between her fingers and moved it back and forth thoughtfully.

She said, 'This is my son's seal, where did you find this'?

'Sabina,' he said gently, 'I'm afraid we removed this from the body of a dead man out at Herodium.'

Sabina said nothing for several minutes trying to take in what she had been told.

'You must have made a mistake. Why would my son be dead? Maybe this man stole Anthony's ring.'

Marc knew that she was right although he did not support her analysis.

'I accept that. But there was a plan of Herodium's watercourses on the body. We know that Anthony was the last person to ask for it and it has not been returned.'

'That's pure speculation. My son will turn up soon, you see. He is enjoying himself in the arms of one of his lovers. You'll see, you'll see, he will come back.'

'I'm afraid I must take the ring for the time being until we are sure.'

'Yes, yes, of course. You can give it to him when he returns.'
On saying this she turned her back and continued preparing her meal. He quietly left.

He followed the road back towards Jerusalem, turned right and travelled north towards Deborah's house. Deborah was dressed ready for bed and at first refused to see him but Marc insisted, and after keeping him waiting for some time, as she had done previously, she finally made an appearance.

Marc showed her the ring and explained, as best he could when breaking bad news, that her husband was probably dead. Deborah's reaction was quite different to Sabina's. She became hysterical, threw herself on a couch, wept uncontrollably, tore her clothes, and finally collapsed onto the floor.

Sarah came running into the room to help her mistress but was unable to get near to her, since Deborah was thrashing about and her arms were flailing. The young slave ran to fetch a sleeping draught to calm her down; eventually she was under control, although this took a considerable length of time. Marc was unaccustomed to such excessive outpourings of grief and was grateful for Sarah's intervention.

Sarah said, 'Please do not worry, sir, I have had to deal with similar outbursts before; I am quite able to cope with the situation. I suggest you leave and come back in a couple of days when she is calmer.'

He felt a certain degree of guilt about leaving Sarah alone with Deborah, so he stayed for a while, sitting in the darkness under the trees, lit only by the moon and the warm glow emanating from within the house. When all was still, he departed, walking his horse back to the road. He was in no hurry; the cool twilight soothed the emotions engendered by the events of the day.

He was approaching Gethsemane when he heard raised voices. A detachment of soldiers had arrived carrying torches, lanterns and weapons and were entering a gated garden. The torchlight reflected upwards through the trees, and the new leaves shone like pieces of transparent gold. Marc walked closer to observe the scene.

The preacher whom he had seen and heard in the Temple earlier in the week appeared to have been kneeling as if in prayer. Several men were with him a short distance away. As he rose, a man stepped forwards and kissed him on the cheek. The prophet spoke quietly to the man and then more loudly he asked, 'Who is it you want?'

'Jesus of Nazareth,' someone replied.

'Then I am the one.'

At this point Marc observed that the soldiers seemed to step back as though uncertain of what they should do next.

The prophet continued, 'Do you think I'm leading a rebellion? Have you come with swords to capture me? You've seen me every day in the Temple peacefully teaching. You didn't arrest me then. But you have come now because it's time for the prophecies to be fulfilled. It is me you want. Let these men go.'

That seemed to stimulate them into action and they grabbed his arms and bound him. His followers fled in fright.

The gathering followed the road past the eastern gate and

stopped by the southern part of the wall of Jerusalem near an imposing house.

'Take him to the high priest, Caiaphas,' ordered their leader.

'Why have you arrested this man?' Marc asked him.

'He is guilty of blasphemy – been claiming to be the Son of God. The Jews won't stand for it.'

'If you have arrested him, he should be taken immediately into custody and kept safe by the authorities until he can be properly interrogated. If you have not arrested him, then he is free to go. What right do you have to bind him, then march him about visiting high priests at this time of night?'

The soldier looked down then tossed his head.

'I have my orders and I am following them.'

When they had disappeared into the house, Marc rode back to Herod's Palace. Pilate was enjoying some refreshments with Claudia by a fireside. On their invitation, Marc joined them.

'I thought you might be interested to know I have just witnessed the arrest of the Nazarene prophet in the Garden of Gethsemane. He has been bound and taken to the house of the high priest.'

Pilate groaned. 'I thought something like this would happen. The Jews do insist on doing things their way. There is going to be trouble now and it will end up in my lap, you see.'

It was not long before a servant entered and announced that there was a senior member of the Sanhedrin waiting to see him.

'Confound him,' said Pilate.

'Sir, he gives his most profound apologies, but says it is of the utmost importance that he speaks to you.'

Pilate got up and invited Marc to join him, making it clear that he was seriously displeased at being disturbed at such a late hour.

'Sir, a thousand apologies, but we have tonight arrested a prophet called Jesus of Nazareth. Our chief priest, Caiaphas, is severely upset. He has just interviewed the Nazarene before the whole Sanhedrin. He is guilty of a serious breach of our religious code – he claims to be the Son of God – and deserves the maximum penalty. Sir, may I impose upon you to put this prophet on trial first thing in the morning, so that you may be able to ratify the death sentence before sundown tomorrow.'

Pilate was indignant, 'No, certainly, not! You do not have any authority for that. The man is entitled to have a properly conducted trial. We need witnesses.'

'Sir, I would agree with you, except that there have been many witnesses to what he has said. Caiaphas has already advised us that it would be good if one man died for the people. They like their martyrs; it keeps them satisfied for a while because it gives them something to focus on other than …. well …. their occupation by foreigners.'

Marc failed to see the logic of this argument but Pilate did not challenge it.

'Sir, you would be well advised to do as Caiaphas suggests.'

'Are you threatening me?' roared Pilate.

'No, no, of course I'm not, sir! We both have the same aim do we not? To maintain and keep order! It will not be of benefit to any of us should things be otherwise.'

'All right, all right, bring him before me first thing in the morning and I'll see what I can do, but I am promising nothing.'

Claudia was anxious to know what conversation had taken place. Marc knew why, but that was her secret from her husband. Pilate invited Marc to join him in the morning, just so that he could see how difficult these Jews were to govern.

In the stillness of his room, he looked more closely at the documents he had retrieved from the corpse in the aqueduct. There was a plan of the lower level of Herodium and the tunnels. It was certain that the vault had been situated next to the cistern that had been deliberately drained. That being the case, access would have been relatively recent, not thirty years ago.

He took a look at the map. It showed a mountain range and

then low land beside the Dead Sea and the name of Qumran. Written at the edge of the map in Latin and Hebrew was a mixture of numbers and quotations.

III XL CXXXV:
'The angels have climbed up and down the steps to heaven.'
'Give them fresh bread, curds, milk and best veal.'

Beneath was a statement that looked like a line from a piece of poetry.

'Man's greatest friend and worst enemy'

Was this some kind of clue? If so, who had written it? Was it Anthony, trying to tell them who had killed him? No, that made no sense. Nothing made any sense. It was imperative to decipher what this meant. The problem was how.

19

-The Trial-

'What has he done?'

Pilate was gruff and ill tempered as he addressed his chief of staff on arriving at Antonia Fort the following morning.

'They say he has committed blasphemy, sir. He claims to be the King of the Jews. I am sorry, sir, but representatives of the Sanhedrin are outside and most insistent that they see you.'

'Invite them in. I will hear what they have to say.'

'Pilate, I am sorry, sir, but we must go out to them. It is the feast of the Passover and they will be defiled if they enter the palace.'

Pilate looked at Marc.

'See what I mean. Totally mad! We are the unclean ones!'

The two men followed Pilate outside to where three high priests stood.

'What charges are you bringing against this man?' asked Pilate.

'If he were not a criminal, we would not be handing him over to you.'

'Take him yourselves and judge him by your own law.'

'Pilate, we have no right to execute anyone.'

Pilate was exasperated. He knew that under the law of Roman occupation, only he, as Governor, could give that authority, but at the moment he could see no need for it.

'Bring him here, let me question him.'

Marc watched as a thin figure, slow but upright walked towards them. He looked into the man's face. He was certainly not the usual kind of prisoner that Marc had dealt with many times in

Rome. He looked peaceful as though he knew what was about to happen and was compliant. It is almost as though he expected to be here, thought Marc.

'Are you the King of the Jews?' asked Pilate.

'Yes. But my kingdom is not of this world.'

'You are a king, then!'

'You are right. I am a king. In fact, it was for this reason I was born, to testify to the truth. Everyone who wants to hear the truth listens to me.'

'What is the truth?'

No reply came. There was a long silence as Pilate simply looked at him. At last he gave a long sigh.

'I find no basis to charge him.'

'But sir, he tells us not to pay our taxes to Caesar. He stirs up all the people in Judea with his teaching. He started in Galilee and has come all the way here.'

Marc wanted to protest loudly over this deliberate lie, but for some reason he said nothing. Perhaps it was the presence of the man himself. What had he said in the garden at Gethsemane? 'It's time for the prophecies to be fulfilled.' Marc was longing to ask him what he meant by that.

'Is the man a Galilean?' asked Pilate.

'Yes, he is sir!'

Pilate blew out his breath between his lips.

'Well then, he must be taken to the ruler of Galilee – Herod Antipas – he's at the Hasmonean palace. Take him away. Let Herod deal with him.' Pilate allowed himself a small smirk.

'I'm off the hook,' he murmured quietly.

He sat down heavily in his judge's seat and ordered some refreshment.

'Well, I'm the governor of Judea, not Galilee – the man has nothing to do with me.'

He went about other business but was interrupted by a

messenger sent by his wife.

'Look at this, Marc. Claudia says she has had a restless night dreaming about this prophet. She tells me to have nothing to do with this innocent man. What do you make of that, eh? She has more sense than the whole of the Sanhedrin put together.'

Before long the chief priests returned with Jesus – Herod had dressed him mockingly in an elegant robe.

Pilate said, 'Well, did Herod find any fault with him?'

'None,' replied his chief of staff.

'Then I don't either. He's done nothing to deserve death. Take him out and flog him. That'll wake him up.'

Marc observed the flogging from a balcony that overlooked the courtyard where the soldiers were using leather thongs embedded with small metal spikes. These dug into flesh and ripped it as the thong was pulled off the back. He had witnessed this procedure many times. Roman justice was cruel; torture, branding, mutilation, decapitation, burning alive, drowning in a sack and throwing to wild animals for public entertainment were all part of its repertoire.

He was quite sure he was immune to it all, but this time he was feeling very uneasy. The prisoner did not shout out, or scream abuse or wail his innocence. Despite the pain, he made no sound. Neither did he object when the soldiers made a twisted crown of thorns and forced the sharp needles into his scalp, so that blood ran down his face. Marc wondered why the soldiers were demonstrating such hatred towards this unassuming person.

Pilate had the prisoner brought back. Marc observed Pilate's extreme agitation.

'Look, here he is, I'm bringing him out to let you know that I cannot find any crime to charge him with.'

But the priests vehemently demanded the man's death by crucifixion. Pilate was hot and uncomfortable. He had already displeased Tiberius. If he went against these powerful Jews they might complain to Rome and have him removed. Would he stay with his own convictions or would he bow to the pressure? Marc thought he already knew the answer to that one.

Pilate went back to speak to the man again.

'Why don't you defend yourself? Don't you realize I have power either to free you or to crucify you?'

Then the man said something that astonished Marc.

'You would have no power over me if it were not given to you from a higher authority.'

Pilate brought his shoulders up to his ears, pushed them back and let them drop.

One of the priests said to him, 'If you let this man go, you are no friend of Caesar. Anyone who claims to be a king opposes Caesar.'

There was a long pause. Then Pilate turned to his assistant standing next to him.

'Tell me, isn't there an old custom that at the time of Passover we can be generous and release a prisoner.'

'Yes, there is sir.'

'Let the people decide then between our two prisoners. Bring out the one called Barabbas.'

The two prisoners were brought out onto a platform, one on the left and the other on the right of Pilate. He asked the crowd which of the two they would like him to release. The crowd shouted continuously,

'Barabbas! Barabbas!'

Pilate narrowed his eyes and shook his head. He called for a bowl of water and washed his hands in front of the crowd.

'I am innocent of this man's blood. It is your responsibility.'

Some in the crowd actually shouted back at him.

'Let his blood be on us and on our children.'

Marc agreed with Pilate, there was no justice in this city. There was no delay between the charge and the execution as Roman law normally demanded. The convicted man was given a cross limb of a crucifix to carry to Golgotha just outside the city gates to the west. He was weak and suffering from loss of blood. His hands had been tied for several hours and he was exhausted.

Marc uncharacteristically watched the bizarre procession move along narrow streets, up and down stone steps. The man struggled under the weight of the wood and the crowds jeered. Yet not everybody, there were women in the crowd, weeping and groaning. Some were distraught beyond measure and many were simply bewildered. Marc thought he spotted Justin but the young man disappeared out of sight. The prisoner looked directly at Marc as he walked by and then he fell. No amount of whipping could get him back on his feet. A black African was dragged from the crowd and told to help him.

When they arrived at Golgotha, the soldiers laid his body on the beam and drove large rusty nails through his flesh into the wood. As they hauled him up, the man was hanging by his arms and his swinging body jolted as the beam dropped into place. He gasped. The soldiers drove more spikes through his feet but he did not say a word. On either side of him, also being crucified, Marc recognized the two thieves he and Gaius had apprehended. A soldier climbed up the back of the cross and nailed on a small board by order of Pilate. The words on it said, 'King of the Jews'. A woman who looked like the preacher's mother stood near the foot of the crucifix, being comforted by others. Marc recognized one of them as Mary whom he and Gaius had saved from rape by the thieves.

He could not understand the fascination that made him stay. This was so different from the other executions he had witnessed. Perhaps it was the peaceful look on the prisoner's face. He heard him say, 'Father forgive them.' The soldiers were fighting amongst themselves who should take a seamless garment that they had removed from him.

'Let's not tear it,' one of them said to the others. 'Let's decide by lots who will take it.'

There was one centurion though who was not joining in. He removed his helmet and wiped his brow, frowned and shook his head from one side to the other.

In the middle of the afternoon, without warning, the sky blackened and the sunlight died. Lightening struck the earth and the thunder was deafening. Torrential rain fell on the pathetic crucified figure and formed streams of diluted blood in the mud. Marc knew the man was dead.

Marc had waited until a soldier came to break the legs of the two thieves; they instantly suffocated without the essential support. When the soldier had looked up at the preacher, he decided he was already dead, but had pierced his side with a sword just to make sure.

'This untidy lot has got to be taken down – the Jewish Sabbath begins in a few hours – they can't be left up there overnight and all tomorrow,' he had commented to his colleague.

Marc had watched as the weeping women laid the lifeless body on the ground – they were inconsolable. The rain had driven away most of the onlookers. Marc too had walked slowly away, soaked as he was, and headed back to the palace. Although it was the middle of the afternoon, it was very dark.

When he arrived he was surprised to see a man he knew. It was the priest he had met at the Temple Mount when first he arrived in Jerusalem, the one who had spoken so openly. He introduced himself as Nicodemus; with him was a wealthy merchant called Joseph of Aramathea. They were asking Pilate if they could have the body of the Nazarene preacher to place in a new tomb nearby, which belonged to the merchant. Pilate was in agreement. He saw Marc approaching and spoke to him.

'I am glad it's over, but I'm not happy about the proceedings. In fact, I am quite disturbed about them. I hate the feeling of being manipulated into doing something I don't want to do, particularly releasing Barabbas. It's entirely against my principles to release a man who murdered one of my own guards. All I can hope is that there will be no repercussions, that it will be the last I hear from these trouble making Jewish priests for a while.'

Marc restrained from saying that he thought 'it' was far from over – but he was not sure what 'it' was. He bathed, changed and went to visit Gaius.

'What has been going on? I hate lying here like this – the doctor says my leg is not broken – but I have very little muscle left in my calf and it will take time to heal, I could be here some time.'

'Look on the bright side, you could be dead.'

'True! But, thanks to you, I am not. But I am no use either at the moment. Have you been to see Deborah and Sabina?'

'Yes. They had very different responses. Sabina is in denial and Deborah had hysterics. It took a long time before I felt I could leave. Sarah gave her something to calm her down.'

'Not the response I would have expected from her. Maybe she really did love her husband.'

'As I passed the Garden at Gethsemane on the way back, I saw that preacher being arrested. He was crucified earlier today, along with the two thieves we caught the other night.'

'What on earth had he done?'

'We were right about the high priests. They couldn't wait to get rid of him. They accused him of blasphemy. Pilate gave the people the choice of releasing Jesus or Barabbas, and they chose Barabbas.'

'But I saw him murder a Roman soldier,' said Gaius incredulously. 'I even jumped on him and you hit him.'

'I know. Justice has not been done. The preacher's behaviour was strange. It was almost as if he was expecting what happened to him, as though he was fulfilling a prophecy. At the point of his death the sky went black, and there was a terrible storm with torrential rain.'

'Yes, I heard that this afternoon – felt like the Empire was about to be destroyed by the gods. I hope Pilate knows what he's doing; he's in enough trouble already with Tiberius. Jerusalem has always been a hot bed of discontent – anything can happen here. By the way, have you seen Rebecca again?'

'I intend to visit her tomorrow. I'd like to know if she recognizes this handwriting. What do you make of it?'
Marc showed Gaius the map he had removed from Anthony's body.

'It looks like a map of caves – there are plenty of those out in the Judean Wilderness. I have never ventured there before, never had the need to.'

'Apparently there is a group of Essenes living and writing in Qumran – near the Dead Sea.'

'A group of Essenes?'

'They are descendants of the Hasmoneans. Joel, who was Keeper of the Key at the time of Herod's death and some twenty years after, until Silas was appointed, was a member of the sect. He was found hanging from a tree not long ago. Suicide was presumed.'

Some inner sense kept Marc from telling Gaius about Anna's suspicions concerning her husband's murder. The official view would do for the time being.

'Why would an old man like that want to commit suicide? Do you think he knew something?'

'Perhaps he had a guilty conscience. Look at the writing on the edge of the map – any ideas as to what it might mean?'

Gaius looked carefully and reiterated what it said.

'Three, forty, one hundred and thirty five, the angels have climbed up and down the steps to heaven. Give them fresh bread, curds, milk and best veal. That makes absolutely no sense whatsoever.'

'What puzzles me is who wrote it. I thought it might be

Anthony himself at first, but the map could have belonged to someone else who gave it to him. The line beneath is even more curious. "Man's greatest friend and worst enemy." What do you make of that?'

'I suppose it could mean money or a dog,' suggested Gaius.

'It could of course be totally irrelevant. I intend to find out.'

'What are you going to do?'

'I'm going to Qumran.'

'Wish I could come. You will need a guide.'

'You rest and get yourself fit. I'll keep you informed.'

'Somehow, that's not very comforting.'

The following day was the Sabbath and the city was quiet. Marc spent the morning writing notes of the recent events in shorthand and drafted a letter to Felix. In the afternoon he strode out towards Victor's to visit Rebecca.

Daniel opened the door and was clearly delighted to welcome him. He guided Marc into the rear garden where Rebecca was reading in an arbour of palm trees. She was as beautiful as ever but had lost some of her radiance; her hair was tied back as it had been the day before yesterday. Rachel sat with her and smiled broadly.

'How are you?' Marc began.

'I'm devastated! I have been trying to understand what has happened, but can find no answer. Did you see Sabina and Deborah?'

'Yes, they did not take the news well, as to be expected. Deborah was quite hysterical.'

'I shall visit them tomorrow. Anthony meant everything to his mother. And I think Deborah really loved him – it's just that he didn't make himself very loveable to her. I don't suppose there could have been a mistake and the body was of someone other than my brother?'

'Anything is possible. I'm afraid the corpse was not identifiable.

Items have been planted on bodies before to disguise the truth.'

Rebecca sighed.

'It will be hard to continue the business. I feel I have lost nearly all the men in my life. First my husband, then my father and now Anthony, but somehow I must keep going.'

Marc noted what she had just said with mixed feelings. He gently folded his hand over hers.

She said, 'Do you trust me enough to tell me what all this is about now, or are you leaving me to guess?'

Rebecca's tone intimated hurt. Marc looked at her. She had lost a brother and had a right to know why, no matter how painful the truth was.

'It seems that the theft of jewels from Herodium might have been achieved by entry into the vaults from a cistern, emptied of water by blocking up the aqueduct.'

'And you think whoever did it went to my brother to obtain the plans and ask for his help?'

'It certainly has been made to look that way. Anthony had a map in his leather pouch that looks like Qumran. There's some writing on it and I wondered if you would have a look at it – to see if you can identify it.'

'How come this has survived when you said everything else had deteriorated so badly?' she said.

'That is a very good question.' Marc was impressed by her observation as well as being a bit in love.

She attempted to answer her own question. 'I suppose it could have been more hardwearing. Sabina's leather clothes seem to last forever.'

Rebecca pondered over the letters and numbers.

'It's difficult to judge but I would say that none of this was written by Anthony. The numerals are Roman as is the last quotation. The other two are Hebrew and Anthony usually made his notations in Aramaic. I'm not an expert but I think this has been written by two different people.'

'Do you recognize the plan as that of Victor's?'

'Yes, it's ours. We always put our symbol – V - in the corner.'

'Your brother had two visitors at his house. It's possible they were from the Essene community. These numbers and notes must have a meaning and I'm hoping I can find the answer at Qumran. That's where I intend to go tomorrow.'

Rebecca frowned.

'Marc, if you are not familiar with the wilderness, you need a guide. Daniel has a friend called Daleel; he knows the country very well, his name actually means guide. I insist you take him with you. You can easily get lost.'

Rebecca called Daniel.

'Please find your friend Daleel and tell him we need his services as a guide, to take Marc to Qumran, tomorrow if possible.'

'I'll try,' said Daniel. 'It depends if he's about, but if he is here I know where to look for him.'

An hour later, Daniel approached a small settlement on the way to Emmaus. He greeted an elderly man, bent over, feeding some pigs.

'Hello, sir, is Daleel around?'

The man looked up unsmiling, bedraggled; he pulled himself up by a rail of the pen but remained painfully stooped from the waist.

'Hello Daniel! He's up there, minding the lambs.'

The man nodded his head towards the hills.

'Is he planning to stay?'

'You know Daleel, he never stays long.'

Daniel rode up the steep rocky bank in the direction indicated and spotted a man seated on a rock overlooking a valley. Lambs were gambolling nearby in the sheer joy of living. The man was on his feet in a trice, tall and thin, one arm behind his back. Daleel relaxed and smiled when he saw who it was; his face was kindly and he had an air not of this world.

'It's good to see you. How are you? Are you still looking after Rebecca and Rachel?'

'What else?' Daniel replied. The two men embraced heartily.

'You're needed, Daleel, an assignment to take an investigator to Qumran. His name's Marc Tiro. He's all right.'

'If you say so, that's all I need. What's he going for?'

'He wants to talk to someone at the community.'

Daleel grimaced.

'He'll be lucky to get anything out of them. All they do is to write and pray.'

'He wants to try – it's important to Rebecca, her brother's been murdered. He may have been involved in a theft and she wants to clear his name.'

'When does he want to go?'

'Tomorrow!'

'I can't go 'til afternoon – promised to do a job for my uncle – can't let him down, I owe him. Tell Marc Tiro I'll meet him at your place, about the eighth hour. We will need to camp out overnight, so tell him to come prepared.'

He turned to look back at the sheep, revealing very long, thick, shiny black hair and exposing the hilt of a dagger stuffed into the back of his trousers. He sat down and Daniel sat beside him. The two friends, similar in character yet different in build, watched the sun disappearing behind the hills.

20

-Resurrection-

Early next morning Marc was preparing for the journey when he heard a commotion from the floor below. He stood at the top of the stairs of the great hall and listened. Two men had called to see Pilate.

'Sir,' said a disembodied voice, 'we have bad news. The body of the prophet, Jesus, it has disappeared.'

'What do you mean … disappeared? I put a guard on the tomb to keep watch.'

'We know, sir, but the stone in front of the tomb has been moved in the night and the body has gone.'

'What incompetence beyond measure! I want to know who was on guard duty; I'll have them flogged for sleeping on watch.'

'The high priests are anxious that the body has gone. The prophet predicted that he would rise from the dead and they are concerned that people may believe he has done just that.'

'What nonsense! It is obvious his followers have taken him. They have probably hidden the body to make it look as though he has risen from the dead.'

'Well, yes, of course sir.'

'So, go and find them. Find out what they have done with it. I don't want to hear any more of this "risen from the dead" rubbish.'

'We can't find his followers, sir. They have gone into hiding.'

'Enough! I'm sick of your whining excuses. Get out of my sight. I don't want to hear any more. Deal with it yourselves. Do what you are paid for, and you had better do it quick and soon else you will suffer for your incompetence.'

Marc descended the stairs. Pilate was pacing up and down baring his teeth, with arms akimbo.

'Did you hear that, Marc? The body of the Nazarene preacher has been taken away during the night. I can't trust anyone to do a proper job for me. It's obvious what has happened. His followers want to make it look as though he's the Messiah, the risen King.'

Marc rubbed his chin. He looked at Pilate from under his brows.

'It would not make much sense for them to do that. Nobody will believe he has risen just because of a disappearing body. People want proof. They will ask to see and touch him and hear him again. So what would it benefit his followers to take the body when it was already entombed nearby and could easily be attended? Nicodemus and Joseph of Aramathea came to ask for it to be released to them, did they not?'

'Well, who then, who would have taken it? I haven't time to deal with it. I don't want any more trouble from the Sanhedrin.'

'I'm leaving this afternoon for a day or two but I will see what I can find out.'

'Thank you, thank you, I would be most grateful.'

Marc knew where he was going. Having completed his preparations, he walked to the house of the woman called Mary. A knock elicited a voice from within asking who was there.

'It's Marc Tiro. We met the other night.'

A bolt at the top and bottom of the door was drawn back and partially opened.

'What do you want?'

'I want to know more about the prophet.'

The door was fully opened and from the threshold he caught a glimpse of a tableau of four chairs in a circular formation, three of which were occupied by women whose hair and faces were covered. Stirred by fear, they moved with alacrity into an inner room.

'I hear that your Messiah's body has been removed.'

'Yes, it's true.'

'Do you know who has taken it?'

'No. I went to the tomb this morning to embalm the body and the stone had been moved.'

'What do you think has happened?'

'Sir, you have been very kind to me and I shall never forget, but you will not believe me if I tell you.'

Her hesitancy revealed the sadness and disappointment of one for whom disbelief was a commonly received response.

'Try me!'

'He has risen. He said he would and he has done it.'

Marc was taken aback. She was correct in her presumption; he did not believe it and was seeking a more rational explanation.

'What makes you think that?'

'I have spoken to him.'

'Then perhaps he was never dead.'

'He was certainly dead, sir. There was no breath in his body when we took him down. It's easy to pretend to be still but impossible to stop breathing unless you are dead. In any case, a single person could not have moved the stone alone from the inside or outside, and there were guards on duty all night. This morning there was a man dressed like a gardener near the tomb. He knew my name. He called me Mary and then I recognized him. His body did not seem fully formed at first and he told me not to touch him but to go and tell the others.'

'And did you?'

'Yes, but they didn't believe me either. They think I'm distraught over his death, as they are. It's true that I was, but now that I've seen him, I'm really happy. He said he would rise, and why shouldn't he raise himself from the dead? He has raised others, Lazarus, and the daughter of Jairus. He has overcome death and fulfilled what he came here to do. He said he was the Son of

God. He was so wise, brave, kind and powerful that he must have been telling the truth. Why would he lie?'

Marc remained unconvinced but what interested him was that this woman, one of his close followers, had no knowledge of the body being taken. So if it was not the followers, who was it? It certainly was not the Roman guard. They had strict instructions to make sure it was not taken. The last thing Pilate wants at the moment is an uprising due to the arrival of a Messiah. The high priests would not benefit either. They wanted Jesus dead and as far as they were concerned that had been achieved. His mouth twitched at the corners as he considered these possibilities. He realized there was no point in delaying further.

'Thank you for your help, Mary! I trust you will see him again.'

'I undoubtedly will,' she said. 'And so will many others.'

She smiled and her complete happiness was evident.

Marc decided there was one person who was open enough to tell him honestly what he thought, Nicodemus.

'Do you know where I can find Nicodemus?'

'The Pharisee,' Mary asked in some surprise, 'certainly, I can tell you where he lives.'

Marc left and walked to the house of Nicodemus near Temple Mount. He was becoming very familiar with the city by this time, walking was the best way to get to know a place. Nicodemus was not expecting visitors but welcomed him with enthusiasm.

'Please come in. I believe I may know why you are here.'

A perfume redolent of incense struck his nostrils as Marc passed into the atrium.

'There has been some unsettling news this morning. Pilate is deeply disturbed, as I believe are the high priests. As an open and honest man I thought you might be able to enlighten me.'

Nicodemus smiled. 'Yes, I can enlighten you as Jesus has enlightened me.'

'You don't believe he has risen do you?'

'Yes. I do. I went to see Jesus in secret. He performed many miracles that can have been ordained only by God. He told me that he must be raised up, so that everyone who believes in him may have eternal life.'

'These concepts are too difficult for me to comprehend,' said Marc.

'It's true, they are difficult. It is all quite plain to me now, though I didn't understand at the time. He died as a sacrifice for all of us, to save us from our sins, and now he has risen he has overcome death so that we may live forever.'

Marc still felt intuitively that there was a simpler answer.

'Is it possible his followers absconded with the body?' he asked. Nicodemus answered without hesitation.

'They could achieve nothing by doing so. They were devastated by his death. They didn't expect it, nor did they understand it. The true believers may very well go on to die for him themselves now; and they will do it gladly, as did his cousin, John the Baptist.'

'What happened to him?'

'He was beheaded by Herod Antipas.'

'Why?'

'John criticised his marriage to Herodias. She hated him. One night her daughter Salome pleased Herod by dancing for him. He offered her whatever she wanted. Her mother told her to ask for the head of John the Baptist and it was done.'

'What will you do now?'

'I don't know yet. The Sanhedrin will certainly vote me off the council if they learn of my views, but it will be hard to keep them secret any longer.'

'I wish you well,' said Marc with genuine feeling.

'Thank you! And may God go with you!'

Marc avoided Pilate on returning to the palace, not wishing to disclose his findings from two of the followers of Jesus, but more than that, the slightest self-derisive analysis revealed his confusion, his inability to speak any longer with conviction. His belief in the gods, in Roman justice and his own moral integrity were severely challenged. He was glad of the opportunity to focus his attention on the case in hand. He had no desire to explore those dark recesses of doubt. Yet he could not deny the burden he felt to throw light on the truth, whatever discomfiture may arise as a result. But for now, there were more pressing matters. He walked his horse to Victor's where the guide was already waiting.

21

-Qumran-

Daleel had packed a mule with essential gear for their journey overnight. A short conversation brought an instant rapport between the two men, although there were no mutual factors in their backgrounds that could give them common ground, except a propensity for independence, nurtured by confident self-reliance. Each had different strengths for which they would come to respect the other.

They left the city by the eastern gate and followed the Valley of Kidron. Trees found soil suitable for their roots along its banks. But before long, the land became arid and barren. The men walked along a narrow ledge above the gorge of the river some twelve hundred feet below. Perpendicular walls of rock moved apart and came together revealing a labyrinth of caves and murky passages within. The desolate landscape was reminiscent of a giant quake, as though the earth, tired of the weight of the cliffs, took a deep breath, lifting its belly, causing them to break up, and as the breath expired they folded back into place in uneven disarray. The Wilderness of Judea was an extraordinary place.

Evening was approaching. The bottom of the ravine along which they now walked was barely wide enough for a packed mule. Sets of two feet and four weaved in and out between huge boulders. Marc looked up at the overhang as the rock on his right leaned towards that on his left, meeting somewhere far above. When a gap came, he caught a brief glimpse of the moon already brilliant, though the sky was still blue.

'We will camp when we are through this pass,' said Daleel.

He was a man of few words, which suited Marc who was grateful for the spiritual and physical uplift that this bold desolation was instilling into his body.

They reached a clearing with the mountains behind them. In front, a myriad of giant white flat-topped mounds of varying height replaced the precipitous rocks. Dried up torrents of water had gouged out furrows creating innumerable horizontal layers in the malleable chalk. These incredible, individually designed shapes rose from fifty to a hundred feet. Nearby, defying all the odds was a small clump of palm trees and a fresh water spring arising from a cleft.

Daleel said, 'This is a good place. There's a lot of protection here.'

The two men worked in harmony erecting a black tent, fetching kindling and lighting a fire. As their meat began to roast, the howling of jackals echoed and reverberated through the labyrinth of passages they had just left.

Marc asked, 'What do you know about the Essene community at Qumran?'

'Nearly everything, I was brought up there. My grandfather was from a proud nomadic tribe, descended from the Ishmaelites. He was wandering these parts some sixty years ago when an earthquake struck. The Qumran community was devastated, but my grandfather saved many of their lives by bringing them out of the rubble – in particular he saved the Maskil or Chief Instructor. It took time for them to re-establish themselves, but when they did they offered to take me in, to train and teach me as a reward. The men who live there do not marry, but others, who live throughout the region in the towns and cities, they do marry and have children. Often the boys are brought there to be taught properly.'

Daleel threw another log on the fire and continued.

'My father was hesitant at first. The Essenes are descendants of the Jews. They come from a different branch of our ancestors.

Abraham, one of our forefathers, had two sons. His God had promised him a son by his wife Sarah, but she grew old and barren and Abraham despaired that he would ever produce, so Sarah agreed to him bearing a child with her maidservant, Hagar. A boy called Ishmael was born. But God did fulfil his promise to Abraham, and Sarah gave birth to a son called Isaac. Ishmael and his mother were then cast out into the desert, but God was good to them and protected them. He told Hagar that he would make a great nation from the offspring of Ishmael, and he kept his word. So although we have common ancestry we are different to the Jewish bloodline. They consider us to be heathens and it was unusual for them to offer to teach a boy such as myself. I learned a great deal and mastered the languages of all the great nations, Hebrew, Aramaic, Greek and Latin. A man named Jerome was my special mentor. These mountains were my playground.'

'The Essenes will not welcome a Roman. How do you intend to introduce me?'

'You are right about that. They hate the occupation. They rarely accept strangers and are unwilling to tell them anything about their beliefs. But I shall have access and will help all I can, particularly if it is to benefit Rebecca and Daniel. Just tell me what you want to know and I will endeavour to find out. I am afraid you will have to pretend to be Hebrew and believe in one God. I shall say you are my friend and need time to pray and contemplate – but getting information may take some time.'

'I need to find out if the Essenes have had anything to do with Anthony's death and also the theft of lapis lazuli jewellery from Herodian Palace.'

'I cannot think any of them would steal what does not belong to them.'

'This may be different. The jewels originally belonged to John Hyrcanus, the Hasmonean, to be used to fight the Romans. Some Essenes may feel they have a right to them. We suspect that two of them visited Anthony just before he disappeared.'

Daleel dropped his head and brought his lower lip over his top.

'There is a scroll – made of copper – that I have seen them working on. It contains a list of all the valuable artefacts belonging to the Jewish community, particularly those in the Temple. I know that some of the wealth has already been hidden in places all over the country.'

'Is it possible you could look at it?'

'Yes, I can try. Jerome trusts me. I don't feel that I am betraying that trust in a situation like this.'

Marc took the map from his bag and showed it to Daleel.

'All I have to go on is this - a map of caves, some quotes and a number in Latin. I wondered if it was a reference.'

'It could be. I'll bear it in mind - anything else?'

'Is it possible that this community is not as peaceable as it seems. Might they be planning war against the people they see as oppressors?'

'There is something called The War Scroll but I always took it to mean spiritual war. The Essenes are very much against the Pharisees whom they see as moving away from God's sovereignty. The Essenes deny human freedom and believe that God controls everything, whereas the Pharisees believe that humans have control also.'

'What else do they believe?'

'That righteous people will receive the reward of an eternal life. The flesh will be resurrected and will never perish.'

'Do they believe in a Messiah? '

'Yes. But some say the Messiah has already come in the form of the Teacher of Righteousness who was there at the establishment of the community. He will come again when God judges the world and will overcome the Angel of Darkness.'

'And what do you believe?'

Daleel looked at him briefly without speaking.

'Me? I believe it is time we slept. We need to keep watch – I will take the first.'

Daleel was tireless climbing higher to oversee the small camp they had built. Marc lay under the stars, which shone with a deep penetrating light. He could see the dark figure of Daleel against the sky and sleep was enveloping him when a movement stirred his instinct; he sat up. He was sure Daleel was not alone – a ghostly figure had surreptitiously crept beside him. Fearing for the safety of his guide, Marc was instantly on his feet but Daleel turned and faced the apparition – the two seemed to briefly merge as one. Marc's natural adrenalin and curiosity forced him fully awake, but the phantom disappeared with as much stealth as when it arrived.

Marc saw no more of the night visitor and he said nothing to Daleel. The eerie howls continued – some with a more distinctive note than the others. As one used to military campaigns, Marc assessed that they were being watched. Yet he could not determine by whom or where they were positioned. This place was spiritually disturbing – and he waited for the sun to display its rays from behind the mountains of Moab.

'We will be there in less than three hours,' said Daleel, as he packed the mule the next morning. He looked as fresh as when Marc had met him the previous day.

The descent was now gentler. A marshy area of dense reeds nearly ten feet high replaced the rocks. The men were hacking a way through when Daleel raised his arm for Marc to stop. They were in a small clearing. Broken reeds had been deliberately laid across one another, lifted off the ground and caught in the surrounding brake forming a roof a few feet high. A pointed snout appeared at the entrance to this makeshift home, disturbed by the noise of the two-legged creatures invading her space. The only time Marc had previously seen a head like this was on a feast plate in Rome – a large wild boar bared its teeth and pawed the thin soil.

Daleel waved his hand slowly to Marc indicating that he wished him to retreat. Meanwhile, he quietly took the knife from his back and held it in his right hand by his side. Resting on one knee, turned slightly away from the boar, he dropped his head so that he was not looking directly at the animal's eyes yet keeping her within purview. The only movement was that of his chest rising and falling as he breathed. Marc was reminded of the comment made by Mary the previous morning, about the impossibility of remaining completely still because of the inevitability of breath.

The animal looked bewildered for a minute or two – not knowing what to make of this being she had never seen before. Its lack of aggression seemed to reassure her. Squeals at the rear of her home reminded her of her duties and she gave one final snort, baring her teeth one last time as she did so and took two steps towards the crouched figure. Daleel moved his eyes without disturbing the position of his head. His grip tightened on the knife but there was no perceptible movement of his arm.

Quite unexpectedly the boar sat on its haunches and dropped its head to one side mirroring Daleel's behaviour. Then after a minute or two in this standoff position, she turned and walked back inside. The guide slowly stood up, and the slightest movement of his fingers indicated to Marc that it was safe to proceed. Marc marvelled at this true huntsman who killed only when necessary, not as a sport or an instinctive aggressive reaction as the Roman army was minded to do.

When they emerged from the thicket the sun was high and hot. A crawling sensation ran across Marc's skin, as old and new sweat combined with the skin's natural oils and dust from the marsh grasses. They had reached the shores of the Dead Sea. Vegetation ceased; no living matter could survive the bitter salt waters that washed over these beaches. Petrified skeletons of trees and animals glistened and hurt the retina like sharp crystal. This saline sea would not and could not support life, yet it sprayed deposits over all that reached its path and encrusted them for eternal preservation.

The desolate flatness of the northern shore was shamed by the towering cliffs of the mountains of Moab in the east, diving steeply into the sea. The sun's reflections on its ridges changed colour from pink to orange to deep red and purple, as if those stately precipices had magical qualities. The long view to the south across the waters, deep blue with white frothy crests, was no less grand, and panning round to the western shore the mountains, though not as high as those of Moab, had a striking, irregular, wild beauty.

Marc was awed by the majesty of this land. Daleel watched his face and smiled.

'It gets everyone that way, first time. We want to go this way though.' He pointed northwards.

In the distance, shimmering in the sun like a mirage was the outline of the walls of a small community. Beyond, the mouth of the river Jordan entered the salt sea, the living matter within it unaware of the approaching inevitability of death. As they came nearer, the buildings were bigger than they had first appeared. They passed through a narrow arched gateway into a courtyard of what was to prove to be an intricate complex. The tallest building had a square tower-like top. Most of the other roofs were flat. An aqueduct brought fresh water from the river Jordan. Steps led to lower and upper levels and there were numerous small rooms, storehouses, baths, communal eating areas and libraries.

Daleel was greeted warmly and he asked to see Jerome whom he was told was in the scriptorium. The guide knew the way. Jerome was an elderly man with grey wiry hair and beard. The scriptorium was an oblong shape with workbenches on either side. Stools were placed at intervals down the centre so that scribes sat side-by-side facing the wall and with their backs turned to those seated at the other table. But for the moment, Jerome was alone and the stools stood unoccupied. The benches were covered with scrolls of leather, papyrus and parchment; some lay propped open while others were rolled from either end, the cylinders meeting in the middle. Pens and copper inkwells were neatly placed until the users returned.

'My friend, how good to see you,' said Jerome embracing Daleel. 'It has been too many months since you came to visit us. I hope you will stay a few days this time.'

'Yes, I think I shall. Where is everybody?'

'They're at the first meal of the day! You know the routine – reciting prayers before dawn and then working until mid morning – some minding the farms, some shepherding and others bee-keeping. As for me, I have very little appetite. I prefer to keep writing – I have such a short time left and there is so much to do.'

'Don't say such things.'

'Alas, my son, it is true. My days are short. I have no regrets but I need to finish what God has sent me here to do.'

'I have brought someone to meet you, Jerome. This is Marc Tiro. He would like to take some time to pray and study if that is all right?'

'If he is your friend, then he is mine.'

Jerome placed a hand of hospitality on Marc's shoulder.

'I trust you will find what you are seeking my friend.'

Marc had a strange sensation of guilt, knowing that what he was seeking was not of a spiritual nature. And yet he felt pleased to be spending some time in this place of solitude and quiet.

'I will see to it that you have rooms. Please bathe and take fresh clothing while your own is washed. Take your meals at the same time as us, but I'm afraid you will have to sit separately because of the need for ritual cleansing. Pray with us though if you wish, take walks, read and contemplate, and if you want to talk, you will always find me willing, although I cannot say the same of the rest of the brothers. Many will ignore you or may even appear hostile.'

'You were always very kind,' said Daleel. 'That has not changed.'

When Marc returned to his simply furnished room after bathing, he found a fresh white linen garment on the bed. Reading material in Hebrew and Aramaic was left on a low table. But there was no sign of his personal possessions.

A shuttered window opened to the south revealing the mountains on the western shore that they had just crossed. Marc gazed at the contours of those strange shapes that resembled enormous beehives or potters' kilns. Then a not too distant memory told him he had seen this somewhere before. Whoever had been the cartographer of Anthony's map had been standing not far from this very place.

22

-The Copper Scroll-

Marc was keenly aware that not every man in this community would have the gentleness and kindness of Jerome. There were some whose motives enabled them to justify murder. He was reliant on Daleel and his relationship with his elderly mentor to progress the investigation. He was here under sufferance and had no access to the scriptorium or even the libraries. During the working times, he had been allocated a job in the pottery on the eastern side making everything from domestic cups to tall jars. The work was unbearably hot, yet the repetitiveness of the tasks and the satisfaction of seeing the final product brought him an inner peace. He did once venture to ask what the tall jars were used for.

'Storage,' was the single reply.

Meanwhile, he failed to understand the desire within him to read the ancient Hebrew texts that the scribes had so carefully copied for posterity. He had always enjoyed learning for its own sake - seeing it as an end in itself – but his reading had never before consisted of Jewish scriptures, plays and poetry maybe, but not this. Nevertheless, he had been reading avidly for three days. So much so that he was left in relative peace and no one challenged his presence. He busied himself making notes, using the invaluable shorthand. Some quotes he found deeply disturbing because he had either heard or witnessed them. This morning he took up his notebook and contemplated some verses he had copied.

Zechariah :   *Rejoice greatly, O daughter of Zion! Shout, Daughter of Jerusalem! See, your king comes to you, righteous and having salvation, gentle and riding on a donkey.' [i]*

Jeremiah : *'Has this house which bears my Name, become a den of robbers to you?' [ii]*

Isaiah : *'He was despised and rejected by men, a man of sorrows, and familiar with suffering . . . . he was pierced for our transgressions . . . . he was oppressed and afflicted yet he did not open his mouth; He was led like a lamb to the slaughter . . . . though he had done no violence, nor was any deceit in his mouth.' [iii]*

Psalms: *'I am poured out like water, and all my bones are out of joint . . . . Dogs have surrounded me; a band of evil men has encircled me, they have pierced my hands and my feet. I can count all my bones; people stare and gloat over me. They divide my garments among them and cast lots for my clothing.' [iv]*

Zechariah: *'They will look on me, the one they have pierced, and they will mourn for him as one mourns for an only child . . . . on that day the weeping in Jerusalem will be great.' [v]*

Psalms: *'.. but the Lord delivers him from them all; he protects all his bones, not one of them will be broken.' [vi]*

These scriptures had been written hundreds of year ago. Were these the prophecies he had heard Jesus talk of in the Garden of Gethsemane? Marc had always found a scientific, legal or academic answer to a problem – this required something more of him and subconsciously he was fighting against it – whatever it was.

Daleel meanwhile had been equally busy in the scriptorium. He was copying parts of Genesis onto leather in Aramaic whilst waiting for an opportunity to ask pertinent questions. When the scripts were finished, they were taken into an adjoining storeroom and placed in tall earthenware jars. He was rarely alone with his mentor and the other scribes would permit no talking whilst working. This morning, however, his opportunity came. In a low voice he asked,

'Would you take a look at my work, father, just to see that it is of an adequate standard?'

'I have already done so, my son, you learned your lessons well as a youngster and you have not forgotten.'

'What will happen to this leather scroll when I have finished? The storeroom is nearly full.'

'It will be buried in caves not far from here with the others – many have been placed there already. They will be safe from our enemies and will survive many hundreds of years. I have seen a vision of a young man, maybe over a thousand years hence, who will one day break a jar with a stone, climb into the caves and the world will be exposed to the many spiritual secrets that are hidden within our scrolls. This is valuable work that you are doing Daleel.'

'I would like to think of my work surviving beyond my own life for a future purpose. How will I know which jar and cave it will be in?'

Daleel tried to sound nonchalant and keen at the same time. He could only hope he had succeeded, but Jerome's slight hesitation was not lost on him.

'The caves are numbered; the one closest to the community is the first. When your scroll is finished it will be placed in a jar, which will be given a number like the others in the storeroom and then placed in a cave. The first three caves are full and the fourth nearly so, perhaps yours will be put in the fifth.'

'I shall cherish the memory of that happening. Thank you, father for the privilege.'

Jerome relaxed and seemed satisfied. He laid his hand on Daleel's shoulder.

'May God bless you!' he said.

Daleel had no opportunity to ask about the copper scroll, but he knew he had seen someone working on it when he had last visited the community. The storeroom was kept constantly locked but if he could finish his scroll, he might be given the chance to investigate further.

His fingers became sore with the laborious work; some of his letters were not as clear as they should be and he had to go over certain lines again. Soon I shall know this off by heart, he thought. His access to Marc was severely restricted. They saw one another only at mealtimes and then speaking was not permitted. They were observed at all times.

Daleel had forgotten how hard this regime had been, and realized that his instinctive desire for solitude and independence had been nurtured in this place. His previous visits had been fleeting but now he had been here nearly a week. One morning, when once again he had a brief opportunity to speak to Jerome alone, he made a suggestion.

'Master, I want to finish these scripts but I am concerned that I may not have time. My friend who came here with me is educated in Hebrew and Aramaic, would it be too much to ask if he could help me. He is trustworthy, and between us we could finish this translation.'

Jerome said nothing and Daleel thought he had overstepped the mark but after a while Jerome said,

'It does seem a shame to keep an educated man in the pottery when there is so much to be done. Ask your friend to come and help us.'

Later that day Marc sat at a stool in the scriptorium. He and Daleel divided the remaining work between them. Daleel was translating the story he had recounted to Marc about Abraham's son Ishmael, the founder of his tribe, and the prophecy about Isaac. Marc's section concerned Isaac's sons, Jacob and Esau. Communication, however, was forbidden.

Another week passed and the assigned work was completed.

Jerome asked Daleel to take the scripts to the storeroom and file them in the cylindrical jars that Marc had been producing only a week previously, and to add to the numbers that were already there. This was his first visit to the room – he had never had cause or desire to enter before. On each jar lightly written in chalk was the number of the cave, the number of the jar, followed by a reference to the lines of engrained scriptures. He searched in each jar for the copper scroll but it was nowhere to be seen.

'What do you think you are doing?' A deep and stern voice sounded from the doorway from one of the scribes.

Daleel stood up and smiled.

'I'm looking for some empty pots,' he said calmly.

'They are over there.'

A finger pointed to a corner. Daleel's search was frustrated, yet he had gained valuable information.

The next day the two men took their leave. Jerome was sorry to lose his protégé again.

'Each time you go, I wonder if I shall see you again, my friend. One day you may come and I shall not be here. Do not forget to live by what you have learned and I shall meet you in the next life. There will be much more for us both to learn there and my body will be young again as yours is. We will have an eternity – time will not be restricted as it is now.'

Soon they were heading across the barren coast and black beach with its sulphurous smells, and rode into a cleft in the high kiln shaped limestone rocks until they were out of sight of the community. They dismounted, able to talk freely for the first time in two weeks and Marc withdrew the map from his possessions, which had been confiscated during his stay. Daleel told him about the referencing system for the scrolls.

'So we need to find cave three and jar number forty and find reference one hundred and thirty five. Thank you, Daleel. That is really good investigative work. I could not possibly have done this without your help. I wonder about these quotes – are they clues to hiding places?'

Marc read once again what was written on the edge of the map.

'This says, "The angels have climbed up and down the steps to heaven." I was translating a section of the story of Jacob where he had a dream about angels ascending and descending a ladder to heaven, and the next morning he erected a pillar where his head had laid – he called the place Bethel.'

'I know it,' said Daleel. 'It's north of here. Remind me of the other quote.'

'Give them fresh bread, curds, milk and best veal.'

'There is a passage where Abraham has three visiting angels who tell him that his wife will give birth. He offers them a meal as described, and while they are eating he stands under a tree. It is said to be one of the great Syrian oaks – known as Abraham's Oak – it is in a grove at Mamre near Hebron. My people settle there regularly; the pasture is good. I was intending to go and visit them once we had finished this assignment.'

Marc looked at Daleel from under a furrowed brow.

'I need to get into cave number three. Will you help me?'

'Yes, of course! We should do it now. The pale colour of our clothes will give us camouflage against these rocks. If we wait until dark we'll need torches and they can be seen. There's a plateau joining this particular range of rocks. I suggest we climb up from the back and reach the cave from the top.'

The climb was hot and arduous. Daleel went first and roped himself and Marc together. They were helped by the horizontal ridges that the weather had forged in the soft rock but it was often reduced to gravel under foot and gave way, covering Marc with dust and stones. Once at the top Marc lost his bearings and was unable to visualise the map from this angle. Not so Daleel, he knew exactly where they were and selected the gully he was looking for.

They hurled themselves off the top, landing with feet together and allowed the natural movement of the loose rock to catapult downwards towards the ledge outside the cave. At the entrance was a system of ropes and pulleys. Below was a wooden platform, built to haul up the tall cylindrical containers.

The opening was narrow and both men had to turn sideways to enter. It took sometime for their eyes to dilate to enable them to focus on the scene before them – dozens of pots half buried in the soft earth. An aperture in the rock towards the back of the cave provided a narrow and intense source of illumination casting white light on the floor and walls.

The scrolls were surprisingly well filed and they soon found what they were looking for. Daleel lifted off the lid and there, neatly coiled, was a scroll of copper. They carefully lifted it out and unwound it until they found the reference and there a hand had neatly scripted,

'Lapis lazuli x 2'

So the Essenes had received some of the Herodian stones. But there were hundreds of entries listed; surely this had not been added recently. Whose hand had made this entry and when?

Voices drifted up from below. Daleel looked out. A horse and cart had arrived filled with jars. Three men were arguing about which jars should go where.

'This cave is full,' said Daleel softly. 'Jerome told me so. It will take time to climb back up and we will be seen. I suggest we wait. But I should warn you, they will kill us if we are found.'

'Not if we get them first.'

They moved into the shadows at the back of the cave and waited what seemed like an interminable length of time. Eventually the rope and pulley outside cave number three began to move and the sunlight was blocked by a figure standing on the ledge outside. Marc and Daleel instinctively wrapped a fist round their daggers.

The figure stooped and looked inside but before his eyes had time to adjust a shout came from below.

'I told you not that one. It's full already. You want cave four. Move across and stop wasting time, we'll miss our meal.'

The face issued an expletive unbecoming of a Godly man, but moved away and sent the jars back down to be placed on the next platform. Marc and Daleel began to breathe easier but the whole process took so long that the sun had disappeared behind the mountains before they were able to move. The air in the cave was thin and Marc felt the plague of claustrophobia coming upon him.

They waited until the men were out of sight before venturing outside. Daleel jumped from the ledge onto the scree. Going up was infinitely more difficult than coming down and every step upwards was followed by slippage back, progress was slow and gradual. The sound of a bird of prey came from somewhere over their heads. Daleel stopped, cupped his hands over his lips and replied. A figure stood on the summit, his outline shadowy against the skyline. A rope fell beside Marc.

'Take it,' said Daleel. 'It will help you get over the top.'

Both men rested after their exertions. Daleel briefly hugged the man who had helped them and introduced him.

'My brother, Nadeem,' he said. 'I knew he would not be far away.'

'So you are the ghost,' said Marc.

'One of them' replied Nadeem. 'There are a lot of us. We protect one another. Come on, we need to get away as soon as possible. I have a camp in a nearby cave.'

Daleel said, 'Good! And tomorrow we are going to Mamre.'

23

-Abraham's Oak-

The next morning the three men headed south again towards Hebron – a day's ride. There was no defined track and the way wound in and out of rocks and boggy regions with the same massively irregular grey mountains on either side, barren and without trees or vegetation. After hours of depressing landscape they finally reached a lush valley of fruit and vineyards, some of which were fenced to protect the wine producing equipment. This was the plain of Mamre; the natural stone built constructions of Hebron could be seen in a valley in the distance.

The plain was decorated with pitched tents interspersed among the trees. Men sat crossed legged talking, laughing, eating and drinking in the evening sun. Older girls wearing colourful long dresses and scarves round their heads were ushering goats and sheep into pens for the night and securing the camels. Women sat hand spinning goat hair or weaving the spun thread into cloth, while others sewed strips together to make panels for dividing the very large tents into separate rooms, catering for the extended families.

'These are my people,' said Daleel, not without a hint of pride.

Long before they actually reached the tents a young woman, Marc guessed she was eighteen or nineteen, gave a loud cry of delight, lifted up her skirts and ran towards them.

'Big D, it's big D,' she shouted to the others who stood up and waved at the men.

Daleel jumped from his horse and lifted up the girl in his arms. She wrapped her bare legs round his waist and hugged him before leaning back to look at him, dependent on his hands looped under her shoulders to stop her from falling.

'You said you wouldn't stay away so long this time,' she scolded him.

'I'm sorry my little sister, I had business to attend to, but you know you are always with me wherever I go.'

The young woman gave a dissatisfied sigh, unwrapped her legs from his body and jumped to the ground. She turned to welcome her other brother and then looked towards Marc, shyly at first.

'Let me introduce you to my friend, Marc. This is my sister Keren. Actually she is the Royal Princess Keren, married to a Prince of a neighbouring tribe but you would hardly think so, the way she behaves.'

Keren took a swipe at his cheek. She laughed gaily and Marc thought he had never before seen someone exude such happiness; her smile was wide and white; her eyes dark brown under lengthy lashes; her hair was long, straight, black and shiny. She lifted the spirits with her energy. She took hold of Daleel's hand and pulled him towards the encampment. Daleel's family were no less hospitable. The water and pasturage in this lowland area was enough to support their largely nomadic lifestyle for several months.

A large man with wild grey hair strode out to greet them, his arms flung wide and his red and brown cloak billowing like a great eagle contemplating a landing.

'My son, it has been nearly a year this time. I have forgotten what you look like. I have made another son since you left.'
He chortled loudly and bear hugged his firstborn.

'You haven't missed me too much then, father.' said Daleel.

'I have to keep my wives happy.' He laughed again. 'But you … you are my first son, always with a special place in my heart. So, who is this? We have a guest?'

'This is Marc Tiro, father, from Rome. We have been carrying out an assignment that has strangely led me back to you. Marc, this is my father, Aziz.'

'I have nothing against the Romans, they do not affect my lifestyle; they leave me alone. It is no worse than living under the Jewish regimes – in fact, I think I prefer it. I understand ruthlessness but pious pretence lacks honesty; it is vulgar.'

He put great emphasis on the first syllable and his top lip curled and his nose wrinkled as though a bad smell had offended his nostrils. His teeth flashed with pieces of gold where they had been repaired.

'Come, Marc Tiro, you shall experience some ancient Ishmaelite hospitality. We shall feast tonight.'

His voice grew louder so that his wives could hear what he was saying. When they appeared not to respond he held his arms level with his head and clapped his hands. The women briefly ceased their conversation and looked languidly his way before resuming it and eventually, but clearly in their own time, rose to accord to their husband's request.

'It is time you took a wife Daleel, more than one. We need our numbers to grow. I am doing my best but I am getting older and need help. And you, my Roman friend, do you have a wife?'

'No! I'm afraid not!'
Aziz retaliated with gusto.

'In that case I will get you one. What is the matter with you men? I blame education and reading. A man should keep his brain in his seat – it is better for his lovers and better for fighting his enemies. Now indulge yourselves for an hour. I shall send my slaves to attend to you – and when you are refreshed you shall tell me about your adventures.'

He turned to face his daughter.

'Keren, my daughter, you look like a boy. Your husband will return tonight. He will want to make love to a woman – go, make yourself look worthy of a princess.'

Marc found it extremely difficult to determine who belonged to whom. The tents were enormous with many divisions sumptuously draped with furs and silk. Aziz might be a nomad but he was far from being barbaric. Artefacts of gold and silver were much in evidence. Evocative smells drifted from ceremonial bronze incense burners and hung heavily in the air. Statues and figurines stood on the ground or on low tables. The regalia worn by the men and women were varied and colourful, decorated with medallions, chains and bejewelled headbands. Before the eating began, there was music from stringed instruments, flutes and tambourines.

Marc sat well scrubbed outside the tent of Aziz wearing a new rustic red robe. His hair was growing longer and returning to its unruliness. Fires burned roasting pigs and goats, and the wine flowed generously. Young women moved rhythmically in exotic semi transparent dresses, whilst young men displayed their acrobatic skills.

The slave woman who had helped him bathe had nerve enough to playfully unravel his curls; she delighted in watching them spring back into place. Marc was too relaxed to care. She leapt deftly to one side, giggling, as he pretended to swot her away. He noted that Daleel and Nadeem were receiving equally attentive treatment.

'You see, we are civilized. We live as we wish. I am a powerful man. My name means powerful. My children make good allegiances with other tribes who desire my protection, but that just makes me stronger. I have many wives, slaves, sheep, goats, calves, camels and horses. What do you say man of Rome?'

'I say that your gods have blessed you richly.'

'Good answer! Even Abraham himself has blessed me.'

Before Marc had a chance to reply, there was a pause in the music. Princess Keren had emerged with her husband, Prince Harim, and many were paying homage to the couple. The change in Keren was quite remarkable. The boyish charm and verve had been replaced by dignity and sophistication, the jolly linen dress by a long flowing gown. But the feature that interested Marc most was the crown adorning her beautiful black hair - an exquisite diadem of deep blue stones.

When courtesy allowed it, Marc asked Daleel if he knew the origin of the diadem. He said he could not remember seeing it before, but his sister had married only three months ago. Daleel undertook to ask his father about it.

The opportunity came sooner than expected. Already Aziz was drunk, each goblet increasing the lasciviousness with which he launched himself at the flesh of his wives and concubines, although all but the very youngest skilfully foiled his thrusts.

'That's a magnificent crown Keren is wearing,' ventured Daleel. 'I don't remember seeing anything so splendid.'

'That was Abraham's special present to me,' replied Aziz, 'and now my wedding present to her.'

'Where did it come from, father?'

'It came from the great oak. I was waiting for the birth of Jonathan, lying under the tree and watching the birds. They had made a nest near the top. I was younger then and climbed up to see the little ones. There was a hollow gap in the branch and inside was a leather purse; it held the crown you see. I kept it hidden for many years – knowing that I would give it to my daughter on her wedding day. I now have twelve sons and only one daughter.'

The three men simultaneously looked towards Keren who smiled, blushed and looked down. It would have been no good trying to explain to Aziz in his present condition that it probably did not belong to him.

'Will you show us tomorrow where you found it?' said Daleel.

'Yes! We shall go to the oaks, my favourite spot for relaxation and meditation.'

'How old is Jonathan?' Marc asked Daleel.

'He is fifteen.'

Marc sat pondering the implication of this but he felt addlepated. Later that night as he lay in his tent on his side, asleep, the cold draught of someone lifting his sheepskin cover awakened him. A body pressed against his back, warm and comforting. An arm slipped over his chest and held his hand. He let it remain.

The great Syrian oaks were less than half an hour's walk from the encampment, the last surviving grove from the time of the great patriarchs. Abraham's Oak was the most magnificent and of a very great age. Marc estimated it was approximately twenty-five feet round its trunk and some of its branches were up to ninety feet wide.

'This is where Abraham received his visitation from the angels over a thousand years ago and was told to expect a son. I sit here too, and it was here I was waiting for my son to be born.'

Aziz pointed vaguely in the direction of the branch where he had made his find. Marc and Daleel spent an hour scouring its limbs and trunk for hidden openings, many of the secretive places had holes too small to reach inside and the larger ones were empty. Daleel began hesitantly, expecting a difficult conversation.

'Father, we have been seeking some precious jewellery that was once owned by dead King Herod and was willed to Emperor Augustus and now belongs to Emperor Tiberius. It consisted of necklaces, diadems, anklets, rings and bracelets made with lapis lazuli stones. The jewellery was stolen from Herod's vault at the palace of Herodium. We are unsure when the theft took place but it could have been a long time ago. Already we believe two men have been murdered for the sake of this secret. On the body of one of the men was a map of Qumran and a clue to the whereabouts of the stolen jewels. One of the clues referred to the place where the angels were given a meal, just like the one Abraham gave to the visiting angels while he stood under this tree. It is probable that the crown is part of the stolen jewellery and rightfully belongs to Rome.'

'Ridiculous! I expected better of you Daleel than to tell me such a pack of lies.'

Marc said, 'Sir, Daleel is not lying. It is why I have been sent from Rome to Judea. Have you had the crown valued?'

'No! There is no need. It is beautiful, that is all I need to know.'

'I would like to find out more about the diadem. I am asking if I might borrow it. I promise to take care of it. If at all possible it will be returned to you.'

Aziz paced up and down, scowling deeply. At last he said,

'No, you will not have it, either of you.'

With that he walked away waving his arm out to one side as if to tell them to go away.

'Give him time,' said Daleel. 'He may change his mind.'

They stayed another couple of days. Jonathan proved to be a well-built young man of middling height; dark curls fell across his forehead to the right, irritating his eye and obliging him to run his hand through his hair to push it back. The broad white easy smile, like that of his sister, and the glint in his eyes exposed a mischievous character.

Jonathan was anxious that the illustrious Roman should like him; he showed him precise drawings, the drafting of which took meticulous care of perspective, angles and lighting. He impressed Marc with his knowledge, intelligence, wide reading and mastery of the main languages, a talent that Daleel had carefully nurtured in his younger brother.

Aziz, like Cornelius, was proud of his Arabian stallions.

'Come, let Jonathan show you what my magnificent beasts can do,' he said proudly.

To one side of the encampment, shielded by palm trees, was a makeshift hippodrome. Four black horses were already lined up and waiting restlessly, tossing their heads, snorting into the air and pawing the ground. Jonathan stood on the platform of his wooden chariot dressed in a simple sleeveless tunic. The muscles of his tanned bare arms stood proud as he used his strength to restrain the animals.

The horses were harnessed together in pairs so he had only two leather reins in his hands wrapped round his wrists. The boy hesitated until he was sure he had the full attention of his observers, then, leaning forward he let the horses go. Clouds of dust rose into the air as eight pairs of hooves broke instantly into a gallop, barely slowing as they approached the tight corners in perfect harmony under the control of their charioteer.

After twelve laps Jonathan drew the steeds to a halt and leapt from his chariot as if he had been out for a stroll. Marc could see so much of himself in this young man, but that was a long time ago.

'Well done!' he said raising his voice.

'You want to see me do it again Master Marc?'

But Marc had seen enough to recognize the boy's ability and his affinity for the horses he loved and cared for.

'You see, I told you they were magnificent,' said Aziz, waving his hands flamboyantly.

'Yes, but only as good as the charioteer.'

'Of course, yes, and my son – he knows how to do that. When you take him with you, I would like you to provide him with a chance to compete in the Hippodrome of Rome.'

Marc looked askance at Aziz.

'What do you mean?'

'I have decided to do you a big favour. You shall have the crown. I have a condition – that my son Jonathan goes with you and you find him training and teaching. Take Daleel here – I made sure he was well taught by the holy men at Qumran even though I did not follow their religion, and what does he do – he is a guide – the teaching was for nothing.'

Daleel opened his mouth to protest but closed it again realizing this was not the time.

'My son Jonathan, he is not like the others. He has no interest in herding and breeding animals. All he does is read. He marvels at the Roman buildings, their aqueducts and monuments. Daleel has spoken to me of his friends in Jerusalem who know about architecture and building; I want you to find a position for Jonathan. If necessary you must take him to Rome. But he must have his chance. This is my condition, take it or leave it.'

Marc pondered this suggestion for a while; then looked at Aziz without fully lifting his head. He cast a glance at Daleel who was clearly thinking about Rebecca and Daniel and whether his father's request was reasonable.

'I cannot in all honesty promise this. I can promise that I will do all I can to find him a position, but I am new to this country, I know very few people and I do not yet know when or if I shall return to Rome permanently.'

'Do you promise to try?'

'Yes. I will do everything within my power.'

'Daleel, do you promise me also that you will do your best for your brother?'

'You know I will father.'

'Good, then that is decided. But I want to know what is happening before the moon is full again. Daleel, do not stay away too long this time.'

24

-Bethel-

Although the way across the wilderness from east to west had been difficult, the road back to Jerusalem from Hebron via Bethlehem had concrete form, making the ride much easier. They headed down the valley, the gentle rolling hills of Judah on either side, and picked up the route north. Jonathan was to ride with them back to Jerusalem, where he would stay with his father's brother on his farm near Emmaus until a position was found.

The sight of the spires of Jerusalem produced an odd feeling in Marc – it was that of coming home, a sense of belonging. Yet intellectually he knew he was not part of it – maybe any civilised city felt comfortable after several weeks in the wilderness. They arranged to meet outside the western gate the following morning to ride to Bethel to search for Jacob's pillar.

Herod's palace seemed a little less grand. The late afternoon sun revealed bits of crumbling facia, and woodwork that needed a carpenter's attention. Its self-conscious pretentiousness seemed less worthy, almost pointless, a tribute to the mere flawed mortal who built it – none of it was lasting and sometime soon it would be nothing more than an archaeological curiosity. A light-headed feeling enveloped Marc as though nothing was real; he was living between worlds, firmly placed on earth yet somehow not part of it.

He knew that this mystical experience would not find any credence or sympathy from within the palace walls, except perhaps from Claudia, and resolved to force his mind to readjust to this stone reality. The noise of clattering hooves on the cobbles was reassuring as were the slaves that came running to greet him.

The first person he met was Cornelius, now fit and well. He appeared to be delighted to see Marc and greeted him with a semblance of warmth that did not come from anywhere near his inner being. Perhaps, thought Marc, as he returned the greeting, watching himself through a cloudy mist of the mind, the soul remains within the body but is concealed by a dark screen made increasingly impenetrable by life's blows and evil deeds; only smashing it will let in the light.

He felt an overwhelming desire for the light. The heart of darkness that he had detected in Cornelius and men like him that previously he accepted as part of the outcome of power and ambition, now made him feel deeply depressed. He wanted to find solace in solitude. A figure came into view from a bower on his left. It was Marcellus. Marc was surprised; Marcellus was gushing.

'My dear chap, you look dreadful, but we are all dying to hear about your adventures. I shall be entertaining the very best of Jerusalem's society tomorrow evening at my house and I absolutely insist that you come. Remember we spoke of it when we last met?'

He could protest, refuse to go, give an excuse, but Cornelius added his support to the suggestion, pointing out that Pilate would be there and it would give them all the opportunity to celebrate his return. So, taking the least line of resistance, he accepted.

He raised his left hand in assent, excused himself and hurried inside. He quickly bathed and changed and went in search of Gaius who was resting his injured leg, sitting under some palms, in the garden. The gentle sound of running water from a nearby fountain had encouraged him to doze. He awoke with a start as Marc approached.

'How are you?'

'The gods be praised! I'm doing well, thanks. I have been walking a little each day to build up what is left of the muscle. I feared you were dead, but then a message came from Rebecca that you were all right. Your guide's brother was keeping her informed.

Where have you been all this time?'

'Mostly I've been at Qumran, copying ancient Hebrew scripts for posterity! Do you remember the quotations that were written on the map we found on Anthony's body?'

'Of course I do. I've been puzzling over them since you left. I even asked Stephen to take me to the library and spent several days looking up possible references – didn't get anywhere though.'

'At least two of the references are from the book of Genesis, one of the five oldest scriptures, written well over a thousand years ago. Quotations from them are used as clues to the whereabouts of valuable artefacts, including those in the Temple, owned by the Jews. The scribes at Qumran have listed them on a copper scroll. We found an entry referring to two items of lapis lazuli.'

'So it looks as though Essenes were involved with the theft – brought the jewels back and hid them.'

'One clue referred to a large old oak tree in Mamre.'

'And was anything hidden there?'

Marc decided to be circumspect.

'We came across a diadem.'

'That's exciting. Are you going to follow up the other clue?'

'Yes. It refers to a stone pillar near Bethel, a few miles north.'

'There was a third clue wasn't there – something about being man's best friend and worst enemy?'

'I haven't got anywhere on that one yet.'

As he walked away Marc felt uneasy. If someone had left the clues intending him to find some pieces of jewellery, then surely whatever was hidden at Bethel would still be there. Pilate was a political animal. Had he planned this situation so he could blame the radical Jewish community and use it as a reason to rout them and put them to death? The Sanhedrin and Pharisees would certainly not object. They may even look on Pilate with favour. If the items were then found to be of no value, like Marcellus' necklace, Pilate would certainly be forgiven, if not totally vindicated. The blame would fall on Herod for having duped Augustus all those years ago. Either way Pilate could not lose. It would secure his position with Tiberius. Marc decided not to wait.

The sun was setting as he approached Bethel – the small town was completely still and quiet except for the occasional squawk of night birds. The ride had been hard, requiring constant concentration at the speed he was travelling, the terrain was hilly. White sweat foamed on his horse's neck and steam exuded a distinctive aroma. He was looking for the landmark established by Jacob hundreds of years ago – a tribute to his dream and to his God. His horse was finding it difficult to walk and stumbled on stones that lay in disarray, the remains of some ancient ruins. And then he spotted it, a pillar standing erect on a round plinth, perched on a low stone circular wall.

He dismounted and started towards the monument. He heard the slight scuffle too late to avoid the sharp, hard implement that hit him from behind. He became aware of falling through the air, then pain in his back and then nothing.

'Be careful, something may be broken.'
A voice sounded in the distance above.

'Don't worry! I can do it.'
As he submitted his body he heard a voice much closer, breath on his face, an aching in his body, an awareness that drifted in and out of consciousness, memories not quite there, reality struggling to take control.

'That's it,' said a vaguely familiar voice. 'We'll soon get you back up Master Marc.'
Visions of galloping horses struck the inner mind, trees and tents. The cloud lifted briefly.

'Jonathan, what are you doing here?'

'Keep still, master. There isn't much room on this ledge. Let me do all the work.'

The young voice was authoritative and determined. Marc did as he was asked. He felt the ropes tighten under his arms and round his back and was aware of being lifted; his body stayed close to a rocky face. Jagged pieces caught his arms and legs – he moved instinctively. He was hauled onto a flat surface as he reached the top and lay on his back, breathing heavily, whilst the figure towering over him released the rope and threw it back over the edge. The outline of his rescuer appeared over the top. Marc watched his dark form against the sky as he hauled himself up by his elbows. His face came level with Marc's as he lay on the ground. Marc smiled weakly then blacked out.

When he woke he was lying on his side, a few feet from a smouldering fire. It was light; dawn was breaking. Daleel sat on his haunches watching him.

'You gave us quite a fright last night. We thought you were dead.'

'You mean I wasn't?'

'Ah, I see you are feeling better.'

Marc struggled to sit up and Daleel moved quickly to help him. Congealed blood covered his hand as he tried to massage his head and neck.

Daleel said, 'You were lucky. The wound looks worse than it is. I bet you've got a headache though.'

Marc thought that was putting it mildly. It felt as though sharp knives were stabbing his head. His back was also very sore. Jonathan was rousing from his slumber on the other side of the fire.

'Thank you for what you did last night. How did you know where I was?'

Daleel said, 'We decided to come back into the city and saw you riding away from the west gate. Jonathan recognized you even at a distance. I guessed where you were going, though I don't know what was so important that it couldn't have waited 'til morning.

Did you know you were being followed?'

'No, I didn't. I just knew I had to get here quickly although I can't remember why, must be that blow to the head.'

'Someone tried to kill you! There's a steep edge just here. You fell onto a ledge, otherwise you could be dead.'

'So I owe you both my life.'

'You would have done the same for us.'

'I came to examine the pillar - to find if the jewels were here. I didn't get a chance.'

'We'll do it now. You rest. Jonathan and I can look.'

Sand had silted up against the base. Jonathan scrabbled fast revealing the lower layers, closely examining the small rocks that had been skilfully placed on top of one another. As he tugged at one of the stones it came out easily without displacing any of the others. He took away the next and the next and the ones above until a small cavity was exposed – inside the hiding place lay an old leather pouch. He took it out and shouted to his brother. Daleel opened it, finding an exquisite blue anklet.

'So, it's still here. Whoever followed you, clearly didn't want to steal it, or saw us coming and took flight.'

'I think it was the latter,' said Jonathan.

'So what was so important that it couldn't wait until this morning?'

'I had been talking to Gaius.'

Marc frowned and pushed his fist against his chin.

'I can remember thinking that if there had been a real theft the jewels would be missing. If I had been set up, they would be where the clues indicated.'

'Presumably if this is part of the original collection, it will be valuable, and if it is part of a plot it will be worthless,' said Daleel.

'I'm not even sure about that,' said Marc. 'A stolen necklace was identified as an original by Herod's daughter, but that was worthless as well.'

'Perhaps the originals were fakes.'

Marc's head was pounding. He poured water over the congealed blood on the back of his neck.

Jonathan jumped up and carefully washed them for him.

'Sorry, we didn't dare touch your wounds last night; we couldn't determine how serious they were.'

Marc felt more comfortable by the time he had finished.

Jonathan said thoughtfully, 'There's something else though. If blocking up the cistern was a diversion, it still means that someone, at some time, took all the jewels. So where are they?'

'That is perceptive of you, my little brother.'

'Don't call me that.'

'But it goes straight to the heart of the problem,' added Marc. 'If we ignore the idea of a genuine recent theft, it opens up the list of suspects.'

'So the hunt goes on,' said Daleel. 'All I know is that someone tried to kill you last night. You really have got someone worked up. But if there is a plot, why kill you before you have had time to report back to Tiberius?'

'Unless they suspect I have guessed. I intend to find out the truth. I'm feeling much better now. Let's get back. My reappearance will be extremely irritating for someone.'

As they rode slowly towards Jerusalem, the sun was climbing higher, highlighting the detailed pinnacles of the temple mount. Its beams settled on the place where the prophet Jesus and the two thieves, reprehended by Marc and Gaius, had been crucified. Vultures circled black and ominous against the sky, scavenging any unburied forlorn bodies. When they were closer, Marc saw a figure he recognized walking from the encampment, buckets on either arm, towards the pilgrims' water supply. Crassus looked up as he heard his name and he beamed with pleasure.

'It's good to see you again, sir,' he said to Marc. 'We were hoping you would come to another of our plays.'

'I was hoping so too, but work has rather got in the way. Are you still performing?'

'We finished last night. Pilate and his wife came to watch us, but today we shall be packing up. Sadly, Justin will be leaving us at the end of our next tour.'

'Why? I thought he was so keen on acting.'

'Yes, he was. But something came over him after he witnessed the crucifixion of the man they called King of the Jews. He could not concentrate. He spent time discussing it with others. Then two men came by here one evening. They claimed to have talked to the prophet, alive after his crucifixion, on the road to Emmaus. Justin spent nearly all night listening to their stories. He said that Jerusalem had become too dangerous and he would be moving to Damascus. I don't understand it, but it's his life. I shall miss him.'

'Don't worry about him, Crassus. He's in good hands, I'm sure. Perhaps he has found what it was he was looking for.'

'Well, if he hasn't he will always have a place with us.'

'Will you be returning to Greece?'

'Not just yet, we have more bookings in Sebaste and then we go back to Caesarea. It has become quite a centre of culture. It doesn't have the same religious restrictions as those imposed by the Jewish sects in this city. People are more open to ideas.'

'I wish you luck. I shall be returning to Caesarea at some point so maybe we will meet again.'

'I hope so, sir. And good luck to you.'

Marc felt sure he was going to need it.

25

Marc looked for any signs of surprise or annoyance at his presence. He detected none in Cornelius, Pilate or Gaius, all of whom he joined at the first meal of the day. No one mentioned seeing him leave and all presumed he had slept in his bed like everyone else. Gaius commented that he had seen healthier looking corpses, but attributed this to Marc's time in the wilderness – known for its tests of endurance.

'I shall have a report for you soon,' said Marc to Pilate.

'Excellent!'

His mouth was full of bread, and morsels showered over the table. He quickly applied his hand to his face.

'I shall look forward to it. I had no idea the investigative experience would be so arduous.'

Cornelius said, 'I assume your findings will have something to do with the blocked cistern at Herodium. The finding of the body of Anthony Avitus and its subsequent loss must have been distressing for his family.'

Marc observed Cornelius as he made these appropriate remarks of empathy. There was no apparent sign of cynicism. Reactions to death fell into three categories for those familiar with its impact. The first was reserved for the enemy, the second for that of unknown colleagues and the third for that of friends or family. Marc assessed the intonation of the words suited the second.

Pilate decided to talk of something less morbid.

'You missed a good performance last night, Marc. I take it we are all going to the house of Marcellus this evening. The elite of

Jerusalem will be present, and they are all anxious to meet our famous investigator from Rome. You must admit you have had an exciting time since you came – stories of your exploits are already spreading, including the capturing of Barabbas. Not that I was able to accomplish his end.'

Pilate paused and grimaced as he thought of his distasteful experience of offering the crowd Barabbas or Jesus. He continued.

'Then you and Gaius caught the two thieves, inadvertently regaining Marcellus' stolen goods – not that he has had them returned yet – he whittles about it constantly. You saved Gaius from being killed down an aqueduct, and then disappeared into the wilderness for so long we thought you had at least been torn to shreds by some wild beast. That is quite a catalogue of events considering we are living in a time of relative peace.'

'Not to mention nearly getting yourself killed in my house and having it burned down around you,' added Cornelius, oddly without a shred of bitterness or resentment.

'All the ladies are dying to meet Commander Tiro,' said Gaius. 'They will swarm round you like bees in a hive. I would like to have been there to see it.'

None of this banter made him easier in his mind. Marc was not looking forward to the feast, yet he knew he would be going despite his mild concussion and aching back. He instinctively did not trust Marcellus but was keen to meet some of his associates.

His first visit of the day was to Theo. Marc showed him the anklet and the crown.

'The designs are beautiful and the stones are most attractive but not genuine,' Theo said with gravity.

'Would you put this in writing for me? Please include your assessment of the necklace as well, but separately.'

Marc waited patiently while the jeweller disappeared to formalise his thoughts on parchment, complete with his signature and the qualifications that gave him the right to pass judgment.

He spent the day writing a standard report for Pilate, outlining what he felt he was probably meant to find, recording only what he and Gaius had witnessed. The report stated that the theft had most likely taken place within the last few months, by way of breaking through the walls of the vault after blocking the adjoining cistern, the plan having been formulated by a small Jewish sect who were plotting an outrage against Roman control. The jewels recovered as a result of following clues found on the body of Anthony Avitus were of little value, since the stones were not genuine. He included the statement from the jeweller.

A commentary indicated that it seemed Rome had been deceived as to the value of Herod's collection, that no blame could be attributed to the guards and the only real negligence had been Herod's failure to be truthful to Augustus – if indeed the king had even known that his wife's inheritance was faked.

Marc knew that this would please Pilate. After some moderate reproof the whole affair would be forgotten, attributed to bizarre Jewish ranting. He had no way of knowing at present whether or not Pilate had orchestrated the plan, but he was determined to find the truth even if it was never exposed. There had been too much bloodshed, too many attempted murders and injuries, but above all, he did not believe the report he had just written.

In conclusion, he asked for permission to continue his investigation for a further two weeks, wishing to visit Damascus to discover more about the origin of the jewels, how they came to be fake, and hopefully to obtain information about the remainder of the collection. He omitted to say that he also wanted a second opinion of the valuation, by a jeweller of his choice who had no chance of being corrupted by Jerusalem's society. Pilate could surely have no objection. Should he be innocent, he would appreciate knowing where the jewels were. If guilty, he already had a written report to send to Tiberius and had nothing to fear.

Marc wondered whether he would have pursued this search if

he had not been so attracted to Rebecca. Was he doing this for her alone, to find some exoneration for her brother? Would he have normally been on the first boat back to Rome by now? Or perhaps it was just the complete mystery that challenged his intellect.

He thought carefully about these questions and decided there was something else that was driving him on – he was no longer satisfied by half-truths and lies to satisfy the ambitions of the powerful. He was tired of negotiating deals to soothe political egos. He had spent too long in Rome doing just that – he was good at it, he knew that, but he remembered what he had felt when he stood on board the ship as it docked into Caesarea – a freedom; he was not going to throw that away.

Marc took a walk to the house of Salampsio. She greeted him like a long lost friend. Clearly she had few visitors.

'Come and sit by me and tell me what you have been doing since I saw you last.'

She laid her hand on his sleeve. Marc smiled at her.

'There is almost too much to tell. I have brought some other pieces from your mother's collection, or at least I believe them to be. Would you mind taking a look and telling me what you think?'

'Any reminder of my mother is a pleasure to me – let me see.'

Marc noticed the twitching at the edges of her mouth as she gazed on them.

'She loved this crown best of all – it has a very distinctive centrepiece that looks like an eagle. This was her favourite.'

'So there were several of them?'

'Oh yes. And there were several of these anklets. Each one had a matching bracelet, necklace, belt and hair pins.

'Do you know if she ever had her jewels valued?'

'I don't know about all of them, but I do remember one piece – a huge brooch, one large stone surrounded by others of a smaller size. My stepmothers – one of them still lives in Jericho, she was very young when my father married her - were envious and took bets as to its value so my mother obliged them. Even the highest guess was nowhere near the mark. I remember it because the jeweller's assistant delivered the letter. He was handsome and I kept glancing at him only to find he was glancing back at me. It was very exciting for a girl of eleven.'

The old lady giggled and it occurred to Marc that age is no barrier to sexual attraction – it was not something reserved for the young alone.

He asked her, 'Do you think that Herod would have made a gift of the jewels to a trusted servant?'

'No! That is very unlikely knowing father. He might give to a wife, but never outside the family.'

'I don't know if I shall be able to recover any of these for you, but if I do, you shall have them,' said Marc.

Salampsio replied, 'You are such a kind man. And not unattractive either – do you have a wife?'

'Not at present! But you never know.'

'Well if I were only a few years younger my dear and thought there was the slightest chance of reciprocation, I should most definitely want you to make love to me.'

Marc was taken aback but laughed with her and squeezed her hand.

'Tell me, your stepmother living in Jericho, is her name Drusilla?'

'Yes, she is barely older than me. She lives at the farm that once belonged to my father.'

'I think I shall pay her a visit. I'm afraid I must go now. There's a society dinner tonight, which I have no desire to attend.'

'I know that feeling. Fortunately, nobody invites me any more so I don't have the problem. Goodbye my dear, I hope we shall meet again.'

'And so do I,' said Marc and he meant it.

Marcellus' house was full of people, chattering and drinking and touching and laughing loudly. The banqueting hall was filled with couches and low tables. Slaves, both male and female, ran hither and thither, filling gold and silver wine goblets from matching jugs.

Marc was given a seat of honour near his host. He thought he noticed a short hesitation by Marcellus, but it was Aemilia who looked icily at the Commander who had so deftly divested her of her necklace. She made no attempt to conceal her extreme dislike of him. No doubt she had heard about the valuation.

'You are not looking well this evening Commander.'

'I feel fine thank you ma'am.'

'I intended to wear my necklace tonight. My evening is quite ruined.'

Marc doubted the truth of this statement.

'I apologise for the inconvenience ma'am. It has been a useful piece of evidence. I assure you it is safe, and I shall ensure it is returned to you.'

She looked at him as if she wished him dead. She replied angrily.

'Why would I want it back now you have defiled and devalued it?' She walked away before he could reply.

Glamorous women and sartorially dressed men were eager to meet him. Marc slipped into formality mode. He had attended many such gatherings during his years in the higher echelons of Rome. Once he had enjoyed them, but now he felt disdain for his own participation. A slave brought him a goblet of red wine. He was determined to drink only that which symbolised sociability and no more. He still felt the after-effects of his blow to the head and had no desire to pass out in front of Jerusalem's most illustrious citizens.

Tribune Polybius approached him.

'Ah …. Commander … it's good to see you alive. I hear you have been charging around our countryside causing quite a stir.'

'Is that so? I can't understand why people would think that.'

'The population is suspicious of anyone new; they are watched carefully. There has been too much trouble over the years – the history of this place spells disaster – individuals will think nothing of stabbing you in the back if they suspect you are likely to upset their cosy lifestyles.'

'Are you referring to anyone in particular?'

Polybius rubbed his nose and sniffed loudly.

'All I am saying is that there are secrets. The elite close ranks, support one another to protect their privacy.'

Marc looked down then gave Polybius one of his incisive sideways glances.

'That all sounds familiar. There's nothing new about that!'

'All right, just as you wish, but I am warning you, watch your back.'

When the eating and drinking was into its finale, the entertainment began. Jugglers and acrobats delighted the audience while musicians played flutes and lyres, trumpets and drums. A roll from one of the musicians had Marcellus on his feet. Everybody was invited to top up their goblets, an event that proved compulsory, and then a number of toasts were made each followed by a swig of wine.

He then announced that his young granddaughter, Sydonie, would delight the assembled company. A hush came over the room as a girl danced into view, barely developed into womanhood yet her nubile breasts clearly visible beneath the open weave of her necklace. A sparkling belt hung from her hips and pink diaphanous fabric wafted round her brown legs. She held a long veil in her hands which she used to effect as her body swayed seductively. The audience were entranced and clapped as she danced round the couches. When she reached Marc she paid him special attention.

The young dancer lightly brushed the veil across her breasts stimulating her own unformed sense of sexual excitement. As she came close she threw back her head so that her long hair fell down her back. Then she thrust her neck forward and the hair enveloped his head. He could smell the exotic perfumes of the tresses as they brushed across his face, intoxicating and numbing his senses. She brought her breasts close to his mouth almost willing him to touch them with his lips.

She was old enough to understand the sexual power of her body and to appreciate the strange delightful unfulfilled sensation of a light silken touch on her firm nipples, yet she was too young to understand the full force and pain of the fury she was capable of unleashing with her dalliances.

Marc could not move. Panic swept over him. He was helpless, in the same instant realizing that his drink had been spiked with an aphrodisiac, an immobilising drug. A strong sense of desire filled his being and he was unable to stop it. He sat firmly on the edge of his couch, feet planted on the floor and hands supporting him at his sides. Perspiration ran down the side of his face and into the nape of his neck.

Raising her arms over her head, she leaned her body backwards from the waist and lifted her leg until her small bare foot, unseen, moved into the folds of his garment between his legs. Her toes deftly and gently massaged his groin. Marc began to hallucinate. He imagined lifting her onto his knees, her legs wrapped round his waist, his hands holding her buttocks and ………..Oh God, what am I thinking of?

His intelligence told him that this was a trap. Any inappropriate touch he made to the granddaughter of his host would discredit him. He also knew that this was the intention. Yet he was unable to control the situation any more. In his heart and his soul he cried out for help. He knew to whom he was speaking – the Hebrew God. Words from the old texts came flooding into his mind:

'Do not let me be put to shame, nor let my enemies triumph over me.' [vii]

Without warning it was as though a glass bowl had been placed over his head, blurring his senses, making him less aware of the events and noises around him. Fleetingly he saw the face of the prophet who had hung on the cross. Then he heard a voice. It was not audible as from his ears. It somehow reached deep within, from the inside out, rather than outside in. The words were spoken softly but were unfaltering.

'I shall not allow you to be tempted beyond what you can bear.' [viii]

His mind was entirely focused on the voice and the recollection of the face. His lust disappeared; he was in full control again. He felt nothing but disgust for what he had even been thinking and this made him ashamed, yet thankful. He smiled at the young dancer. She was hardly older than Felix, his son.

'Thank you, you have danced well. But I am sure there are others who would also appreciate your attention.'

He stood up, bowed slightly towards her in recognition of her gracefulness and walked away, not before noticing the glance of disdain that emanated from her eyes. She had been slighted.

He walked out into the garden and felt the coolness of the air refresh him, the influence of the drug completely gone. He lay down on a bench under some trees beside water tumbling over rocks gently falling into a pond. It was restful and briefly but deeply, he slept. He awoke feeling completely renewed. His mind was clear and his body no longer ached. He lifted his hand to the back of his head. There was no sign of the wound. He closed his eyes, enjoying for a little longer the complete peace of the moment.

From a pillared walkway to his right he heard muted voices. One was furious, the other conciliatory. The sound of a disturbed Marcellus was unmistakable, the other he was less sure about, the occasional intonation sounded like Cornelius. But why would Marcellus be angry with Cornelius?

26

-The Cell-

The next morning, filled with new energy, Marc decided it was time to pay another visit to Herodium. As he was preparing for the journey a servant, bowing from the waist, respectfully asked if he would see Pilate in his offices.

Pilate was filled with bonhomie, delighted with the findings of the report.

'Marc! What a splendid official account of your investigation! I am sorry you have been put to so much inconvenience and harassment during your stay with us. Nevertheless, I thank you.'

'Not at all,' said Marc slipping into legalistic mode. 'I am only too pleased to help.'

'I see you would like to have more time to investigate the whereabouts of the rest of the jewels. I think that is a splendid idea. It does rather look as though Herod duped the Emperor Augustus, deceiving him as to the value of his so called treasures. You can have as much time as you please with my full authority. I have spoken to Tribune Polybius. I hope you find the dastardly people who perpetrated this crime.'

Marc wanted to laugh. He pursed his lips but was unable to control the slight upward movements at the side of his mouth. Pilate was so stereotypical of every administrator he had ever met. He had not quite realized how the actions and language were worn like a uniform. He speculated on the extent to which he still wore the same cloak.

'I have one request, though,' continued Pilate. 'Gaius is nearly recovered from his accident. He has the highest regard for you and would like to join you once again. It would please me greatly if you would adopt him as your colleague.'

'By all means – he is entitled to see this through to the end. He has been extremely brave and his help has been invaluable.'

Marc had expected this demand, which he suspected would be a pre-requisite of Pilate's approval to continue. The governor looked satisfied. He was already organising a copy of the report to be forwarded to Tiberius, aware that he would now need to find alternative means of financing his projects. But there was always the Temple Mount with its extensive collection of golden artefacts.

Silas was clearly not pleased to see Marc but was as obsequious as ever, and led him to the library where the old records were kept.

'Did you ever find the name of the man who was imprisoned here, Silas? Do you remember I asked you to look for it when I was here last? It was the day we found the body.'

'Alas, sir, it had gone completely from my mind. There has been so much to attend to what with the investigation and then the repairs to the aqueduct.'

Marc was undeterred. He looked for the scrolls that contained lists of guard duties and recorded incidents over the last thirty years, removed them from their resting places and put them on a long table. He knew this would be a long and arduous job. He rebuked himself for not having been more thorough earlier, but then this elementary form of investigative work had been overtaken by events.

He worked backwards chronologically. Many of the later records were missing or simply not completed. However, those up to the time of the death of Augustus were scrupulous – doubtless because it was by his orders that the system was put in place.

The guards came in groups of three. One of the names had a small 'X' beside it in brackets. Marc remembered Silas telling him that three soldiers would be sent for guard duty and would then draw lots to see who would be sent away. Only the guard's first name appeared and where there was more than one with the same name, they had been numbered. Nearly all the commonly known names were listed, including Marcus.

He was most interested in the records that were fifteen or more years old. Aziz claimed to have found the crown on Jonathan's birthday so at least some of the treasures had been stolen by that time. There was no sign of any deletions or interference. He was obliged to move back another ten years. Joel had been Herod's trusted Keeper of the Key. He would have been a young man, known for his staunch religious fervour and honesty. It was easy to forget that Herod was also a Jew, even though he was a supporter of Rome.

He found himself quietly asking for help and guidance as he ploughed through pages of names. Stiffness crept into his neck after hours of searching poised at an unnatural angle. He rubbed his shoulder and stood up and walked across to the window where the shutter was open. Herod himself must have stood on this same spot and regarded his lands. As one of the most revered and feared leaders of the time, nobody would have dared to interfere with his possessions whilst he was alive.

But, who would have known about the inventory taken just after his death? Marc thought. Who would have known about the contents of the vault and their alleged value? A trusted servant would have taken the news to Augustus in Rome and it was most probable that Archelaus, the son who ruled Judea after his father's death, would also be told. But he was exiled and Herod Antipas said that he had died about sixteen years ago, and there were no lapis lazuli jewels amongst his final estate.

Marc walked back to the records and concentrated on those that were more than twenty five years old. It was in the second year after Herod's death where he detected some scuffing on the page. On one of the shifts the names of the three guards had been effaced. He took the papyrus to the window and held it up to the light. The fabric was undoubtedly thinner and the surface was scratched. It had been done very carefully and cleverly with a fine point so it appeared the amount of ink used at the time had been insufficient, leaving out essential letters, age having completed the rest of the job of obliteration.

The cross beside one of the names remained. There had not been so much destruction here and it was possible to determine part of the first letter. The first stroke was straight but there were signs of the beginnings of what appeared to be slightly curved lines at the top and bottom, making it possibly a 'D' or a 'B.' If the curves were mere hand movements of the scribe, then an 'E' could be added to the list of possibilities. From the length of the space Marc estimated the maximum number of letters to be around six. A small letter 'i' was also evident somewhere in the middle. Presumably it was less urgent to remove this name since the person would have had to leave and not get involved.

The light was fading and Marc asked Silas to make him up a bed to stay the night. Whilst the servants prepared a meal he walked in the grounds, acres of magnificent gardens, the fountains and waterfalls now fully functional. He pondered on the poverty he had seen riding from Caesarea to Jerusalem, people eking out a meagre living on the land, and the social system of slavery that enabled a few people to indulge in so much wealth whilst others could starve. He thought of his own plantations on the outskirts of Rome, the gold that would keep mounting up even while he sojourned in Judea, allowing others to create it on his behalf, slaves working for nothing more than somewhere to sleep and eat under the protection of a master. When he returned to Rome no man, woman or child would work for him as a slave – they would all be given their freedom to choose where they wished to be, and if they chose to stay, they would be paid a proper wage.

The night passed fitfully. Marc dreamed once again of his

youthful wife, Aurelia, of the runaway horse that he had been unable to stop before she was trampled to death. He woke in a cold sweat. His immediate instinct was to get out of bed and kneel beside it. He began to pray to a God that he now knew was increasingly his, asking for forgiveness, guidance and wisdom. Soon he was flat on his face. Somehow the floor was not low enough – he wished it would open up and swallow him like a worm. He eschewed the life he had led so far with its pomposity and aggression, he wanted above all else a fresh start. He awoke to find himself still prostrate yet warm and invigorated.

Silas was in the room reserved for dining. The Great Hall was closed and the furniture covered.

'I would like to go to the lower levels this morning, Silas. If you could oblige me with a torch and keys I will go alone. I know the way.'

Silas protested but gave in since he had duties to attend to, and did not wish to be subjected to more questioning than absolutely necessary.

Marc opened the wide door at the top of the stone steps that soon twisted out of sight. He drew a deep breath. Oddly, none of the old claustrophobia was in evidence. The walls seemed to close in the further down he went. The steps were well worn and he thought of all the feet of the guards and prisoners that would have passed this way. How many souls had descended never to return? The dank smell of damp rose to his nostrils, the air became thinner, yet he felt well and relaxed. But one thing he did feel that he had never felt before was an overpowering sense of evil. He quietly prayed for protection and it came.

Lighting the oil lamps along his path he eventually reached the vault and the corridor straightened. But he was not interested in the vault. He walked further along to the dungeons. He entered each one and carefully examined the walls. The smell of death was prevalent but somehow he felt safe.

The third cell in the row was difficult to open. The lock had rusted, although unlike several of the others the small hatch in the bottom of the door lifted easily as the wood was smooth. The key turned with a sharp crack and the iron door swung open. He stepped inside to unimaginable horror. Pools of water rested in indentations on the floor and drips clung to the vaulted ceiling. Iron hooks and chains hung from the walls and the stench made him want to retch.

He did as he had done with the others, slowly examining any marks in the walls. Beside the chains was carved a name – Dimitri – together with hundreds of small marks, presumably representing days, which could be determined only by the delivery of food. Further along the wall was the phrase:

'God have mercy.'

But the letters crossed one another and were at different angles.

A cry from within, thought Marc. The engraved name fascinated him. Was this the name someone had attempted to remove from the records? Had the man seen something that brought about his demise? Or was he speculating a little too far? He stayed for some time in that dismal place, putting himself in the place of the prisoner who had sat here year after year with no light, little food and no communication. What did he feel about his God that had forsaken him?

He stood up aware of a slight change in the degree of light entering the cell. The door was closing. He yelled out and rushed towards the entrance, dropping the torch that extinguished in the pools, but too late to place his booted foot on the threshold – the closure resounded round the stones of the small stone cell with a roar. For a brief moment Marc experienced the deepest pit of despair and fear engendered by total darkness in an enclosed disgusting, loathsome place, the senses stimulated only by hideous odours.

He heard someone wrestling with the encrusted key as he had

done, giving him a vital few moments. With the full force of his body he hurled his shoulder against the cold metal. At first there was no response but on the second attempt the door gave way and swung open violently, crashing against the outer wall.

Silas lay sprawled on the floor on his back, and made rapid movement with his heels and elbows to retreat from Marc's advancing frame.

'Please, please, I am sorry sir. I did not realize you were there.'

Marc was raising his voice. 'What are you up to? It was obvious I was there. You would have seen my light and could not have missed my shout. Besides the key was still in the lock and the door was open.'

Silas struggled to his feet. All he could do was to repeat that he was sorry.

'I don't believe you. You know something that you don't want me to find out. Who was it who was imprisoned in this cell?'

'I don't know.'

'Who was imprisoned in this cell?' he repeated. 'Was he the last prisoner at Herodium?'

'Honestly, sir, I don't know. But I believe he was.'

'How long had he been here?'

'Many years – nearly twenty, I think.'

'Was he still alive?' asked Marc incredulously.

'Yes sir! But he was in a poor state. He was blind and dumb and his skin was diseased.'

Marc hesitated for a moment overcome with pity for the man who had spent so long in that terrible dungeon.

'When was he released?'

'I'm not sure. I think it was about the time I came here. I would say about seven years ago.'

'Was he once a guard?'

'Rumour has it that he had been guarding the vault and tried to break in. But it is only a rumour.'

'And who else was involved.'

'No one that I know of, sir!'

'What was his name?'

'I don't know that. There are no records. Please, Commander, I would appreciate it if you would say nothing of this…..accident to the chief administrator or Pilate.'

'Would they disapprove of your failure?' asked Marc, not without a hint of sarcasm.

Silas was silent. They walked back through those desperate corridors of misery to the main living area – Silas leading the way. Marc did not allow his mind to dwell on the horror that might have been afforded him had he been unable to prevent his internment. But he did not trust Silas. Neither did he trust those who gave him their orders. How easy it would have been to quietly dispose of him in that place. An assumption about marauding gangs on the way back to Jerusalem, robbery, thrown to the bottom of a ravine – that had already been tried once. He wondered how such a warm invitation to the Promised Land by Cornelius could have turned into such a horrifying drama.

He had stayed at Herodium long enough. Salampsio had told him that she remembered an incident after the death of her father about a treacherous guard who had been thrown into the dungeon at the lowest level; she said it had given her nightmares. His family had lived in Capernaum, on the Sea of Galilee. Joel had gone to inform the prisoner's wife. She also said that she could not understand how a burglary could have been achieved without the aid of the Keeper of the Key – Joel. Were they co-conspirators? Is that why he went personally to see the family? Was it continued guilt that led to his suicide? Marc noticed that every time he learned a new piece of information there were more questions than answers. A trip to Capernaum was inevitable.

As he rode through the Jerusalem gates once again he realized how long it had been since seeing Rebecca. Events were constantly getting in the way. He now longed to see and speak to her.

Daniel opened the door and was as pleased to see Marc Tiro as he was to see him. Despite their relative status, they hugged each other slapping one another on the back as they did so. Rachel, hearing the exclamations, came running into the atrium and Marc lifted her up over his head as she squealed with delight. How quickly and easily this group had become part of him, as though they were family.

Rebecca's tall, elegant body emerged from within, the fair long curly hair flowing loosely down her back. Marc's heart surged. He knew that he was falling in love with the part of her he knew already, the elegance, the beauty, the gentleness, the intelligence and the fortitude. One glance at Daniel however and he was reminded that he was not alone in that emotion, the slave who had become protector, friend and loving admirer.

She threw her arms around his neck and kissed his cheek and Marc felt himself flush from his chest upwards. He gave her a chaste squeeze and released her quickly.

'We were worried about you. It was several days before we heard from Daleel's brother, Nadeem. We did not expect you to be so long.'

Marc and Rebecca sat in the bower once again while Daniel prepared some refreshments and Rachel went off to rejoin a visiting friend.

'There was no opportunity for messages while we were at Qumran. In fact, Daleel and I were not allowed to communicate with one another, even when we worked together on translations of the Hebrew scripture.'

'That sounds interesting. How clever you both are to be able to do that. And what a perfect cover while you were investigating.'

'It was not quite as easy as it sounds. I still think there were some who suspected us, particularly me. But we did manage to decipher the code on the map found in Anthony's pouch. We only recognized the references because we were working on those very same pieces of script – it was pure chance – someone was watching over us.'

Rebecca smiled, not realizing that for Marc his statement felt as though it had an element of truth.

'So, you found some pieces of jewellery.'

'Yes, and I have had them valued by the local jeweller. Neither of them it seems is genuine, if he is to be believed. Either someone has been very busy making copies over the years or they never were as valuable as supposed.'

'I find that hard to believe.'

'So do I, but the facts indicate that it's a possibility.'

'Has Pontius Pilate made any comment on your findings?'

'He was delighted. Everything points to the theft being recent, unfortunately involving your brother, though the extent of that is indeterminate. He might have been murdered because he uncovered the plot and was going to reveal all to the authorities.'

Rebecca looked down at her hands and without moving her head she spoke with sadness.

'I would like to think that was the case. I certainly think it's the version that must be told to his wife, Deborah, and mother, Sabina. Neither of them would accept any other and we will never know the truth now, so it hardly matters.'

Marc had an overwhelming desire to hold her in his arms, to kiss her lips, touch her hair and tell her everything would be all right. But he didn't. Instead he told her how impressed he had been with Daleel's younger brother, Jonathan.

'Daleel would like me to employ him. But with Anthony gone our income is limited.'

'If you are prepared to do it, I will pay for all costs for his keep and his training. Daleel and Nathan saved my life the other night.'

Marc lifted a hand as Rebecca, horrified, interjected demanding details.

'They are unimportant at the moment. The main thing is that I owe both of them a great debt and I also gave my word to Jonathan's father, Aziz, that I would do all I could to help his career. I would be willing to take him back to Rome if necessary.'

Rebecca hesitated as she absorbed this last statement.

'Are you going back to Rome?' she asked.

'I have completed a report for Pilate which will satisfy him, though I confess does not satisfy me. So I have asked for another couple of weeks to continue investigating the case and he has granted me my wish. I have not given thought to my return to Rome, but I suppose there is an element of inevitability about it.'

Rebecca looked down at her hands again which were folded in her lap.

'I shall miss you,' she said simply.

'Rebecca …….' began Marc.

He was interrupted by a jolly voice announcing that the refreshments were ready. Whatever Marc might have thought of saying at that moment was to remain unsaid; he was not even sure what he did intend to say.

'So what is your next adventure going to be?' Daniel asked Marc.

His behaviour and demeanour was certainly not that of a slave. Perhaps Rebecca had given him his freedom.

'Tomorrow I shall go to Jericho to see if I can speak to Drusilla – a wife of Herod whom he married later. She may have some information about the value of the jewels. Then I shall head north to Capernaum. A man was imprisoned in the dungeons at Herodium a year or two after Herod's death. He was a guard, accused of attempting to break into the vault. He was released about seven years ago; I am going to find him.'

'In all probability he will be dead after such a long time,' said Rebecca.

'I know, but it's worth a try. I can't help feeling that Mariamne's lapis lazuli disappeared long ago. After that, I shall go to Damascus to see if I can find out more about who made the jewels and what their true value is.'

'Do you need Daleel's help?' asked Daniel.

'Not this time! I am still officially working for Pilate so I shall take Gaius as my witness. His leg is nearly healed.'

He did not add that he also wanted to know whether Pilate planned the solution to the theft himself.

'Please come back again and tell us what you find,' Rebecca pleaded.

Marc assured her he would. There were still things he needed to say.

Marc found Gaius practising his hobble in the grounds of the palace.

'You're looking good,' he shouted.

Gaius beamed.

'Yes! I'm mounting up this afternoon, to see if I can ride.'

'If you can, do you feel like coming north with me to Damascus?'

'I'd love to; it's my hometown, when?'

'I can wait a few days until you are ready.'

'I'll be ready tomorrow in that case.'

'I don't want your permanent disablement on my hands.'

'That won't happen! I'm too young and fit.'

'Two or three days will do!' Marc said firmly. 'I have some business in Jericho tomorrow.'

In the late evening Marc and Gaius rode out together through the eastern gate of Jerusalem and gently cantered and walked beyond the Garden of Gethsemane into the Valley of Kidron and up to the Mount of Olives. They passed the house of Deborah where Anthony had once resided with his wife and watched dark clouds gathering behind the tannery where Sabina mourned her son, no longer able to deny his death.

Rain fell gently, the outer fringe of a storm in the direction of the Dead Sea. A rainbow appeared, spanning the storm clouds, where remaining rays of the sun in the west refracted through the droplets. Neither man spoke a word except for the occasional grunt from Gaius as pain shot through his leg where the muscle had been torn away.

'Don't worry,' he said, as Marc looked at him with concern. 'The doctor says I will probably always have some discomfort, particularly at first, but I must build up what muscle is left.'

'If you are sure, but don't let's overdo it.'

They turned to look at the City of Jerusalem across the ravine. Slanting beams of sunlight struck its Temple through rifts in the louring clouds.

Riding towards the south gate they passed the house of Caiaphas, the chief of the Pharisees, where Marc had seen Jesus brought for questioning. He still could not understand the lack of due process of law that had taken place that night. The arrest was illegal and the trial was a mockery. Yet the prophet had seemed to believe he was fulfilling a purpose. Marc's inner eye saw his face once again and he found himself whispering, 'Forgive us!'

27

-Jericho-

That night the storm reached Jerusalem. Lightening shot across the sky hitting the earth indiscriminately, thunder roared directly overhead. The clouds were still black and heavy in the morning. Water ran down the streets so the cobbles were slimy and treacherous. Some parts were ankle deep in mud and the odour of sewers unable to cope with the quantity of water wafted through the air, more potently in some places than others.

As Marc led his horse through the palace gates, he was astonished to see Jonathan sitting on a wall nearby.

'Good morning, sir,' he shouted cheerily.

'What are you doing here?'

'I'm waiting for you.'

'How did you know I'd be here?'

'I wait just in case you need me. I come to look after you.'

'That is kind, but I really don't need looking after.'

'You are wrong. We all need looking after. Besides I want to help.'

'Have you got a mount?'

'Yes, look, I borrowed a mule from my uncle. I cannot go back – my brother instructed me to stay and watch out for you.'

Marc smiled, touched by the boy's sincerity.

'Do you know the way to Jericho?'

'Yes, I do.'

'Then you shall take me there.'

Jonathan, delighted, threw himself up onto his donkey. He rode bareback. The animal looked affronted at the onslaught and thrust his head into the air with a snort, but was willing to do as he was bid and they set off out of the eastern gate, where Marc and Gaius had ridden the night before.

When they reached the garden of Gethsemane the road divided. The lower road went to Bethany, the village where the young prophet had allegedly raised a man called Lazarus from the dead. The higher road led down to Jericho. The descent was continuous and steep, mountains and wild glens on either side. The sheets of rock were slippery and the rough mountain road uneven. They stopped at an old inn, scarcely more than a cube shaped block of stones with a doorway. The inn-keeper was hospitable and warned them to be vigilant, since the area was known for its plunderers ready to steal and leave their victims for dead.

Marc and Jonathan amused each other with stories from their own background and culture. The boy told of how they had to fight for suitable grazing. His father had a reputation when young for being a great warrior. He had fought many tribal battles for rights over prime land, but the victor was expected to be generous to the impoverished surviving women and children, who no longer had men to protect them. Aziz had acquired many foreign wives this way.

Jonathan had very definite ideas about this. He wanted one beautiful wife who shared his love of horses, sense of fun and love of adventure and, naturally, she had to be clever. Marc laughed heartily at the list of essential and desirable characteristics.

'You will be a lucky man if you find all of that in one woman.'

'Did you not find that in your wife?'

'Well, as a matter of fact, yes.'

'So why can it not be found again?'

Marc had no answer, but he thought of Aurelia, his wife, and unexpectedly a sudden desire for the presence of Rebecca overwhelmed him. He told Jonathan about his life; how he had become a bodyguard of the Emperor, and a judge in the courts of

Rome.

'That's wonderful! I hear the Emperor is a god and has to be worshipped. He doesn't seem to mind if you worship other gods as well, so long as you worship him.'

This comment entered Marc's consciousness like a knife. It had not occurred to him before that he had in a meaningless way worshipped the Emperor; he also knew that he would never be able to do it again.

The land became more desolate but Marc was no longer a stranger to the Wilderness of Judea. After several hours the steepest part of the descent was over, they emerged from the pass and the land opened up into the Valley of the Jordan, beautiful and fertile.

The river was full as it ran its course down to the Dead Sea – it was narrower than Marc had supposed. People sat on its banks. Some were bathing, washing clothes or watering their animals. All around there were signs of Roman influence, aqueducts and bridges. Flocks and herds were grazing to the north and east on vast plains. Across the valley the mountain range took on the appearance of a flat table from which rose cone shaped hills. Trees abounded.

Marc knew from his readings at Qumran that this place was closely linked to Jewish history – one of the first places of settlement causing many battles with neighbouring tribes. From their elevated position they saw the Jordan winding northwards, disappearing from sight in the deep cleavage of the mountains.

They walked across a bridge and stopped at a spring. The water was brackish and completely undrinkable. A voice called out to them.

'Use that one at the bottom of that mound over there.'
A man was indicating further down the road, at the edge of a copse at the base of a small hillock. He continued.

'The water there is lovely, sweet and pure. It's the one our old prophet Elisha healed.'

Marc took a drink, constantly surprised by the belief these people had in their old prophecies. As they followed the river round they saw Jericho outlined against the mountain of Nebo. Like Jerusalem, it was rebuilt by Herod and at its most splendid. The road leading to its main gate was lined with sycamores.

A disturbance caught their attention. It was outside the city, on a ledge with a drop of about twenty feet. Two men were holding the arms of a woman and she struggled as they dragged her towards the edge and, without hesitation, threw her over. There were several jeering onlookers. She remained still for a few moments lying on her back; then struggled to lift herself up on her elbows. One of the men took a small boulder, holding it above his head before casting it down onto the woman's chest. Her legs moved jerkily. The remainder of the gathering each took a few stones and threw them down onto her until she lay completely still.

Jonathan lost the colour in his face.

'And they call us barbarians,' he said, almost to himself. 'I wonder what she did to deserve being stoned to death.'

Marc made no reply but moved his horse onwards towards the imposing entrance. By the gates sat beggars, the blind and disabled, groaning for coins. They were mostly ignored, mocked or kicked for sport by young boys who overturned their cups and ran away laughing. One beggar stretched out his arms feeling for the lost coins. Marc stopped and picked them up for him and replaced the precious items in the container.

'Who are you?' said the beggar.

'Just a friend,' replied Marc.

'Are you the one they call Jesus, the son of David? Have you come back to heal me – as you did my friend Bartimaeus?'

'Heal you? No, I'm afraid not.'

'Have you not heard the story? He sat near here with me for many years. One day he shouted out to Jesus for mercy. "Rabbi, I want to see." His faith healed him and he left to follow the

218

prophet. I didn't believe then, but I do now. Oh, if only the preacher would come back; I ask God everyday for that to happen, so I won't have to spend the rest of my life in this miserable condition.'

'Do you think he is telling the truth?' asked Jonathan when they had walked out of earshot.

'Strangely enough, I do. I have heard so many remarkable things about the man who was crucified, nothing surprises me any more.'

'Why was he crucified when he was doing so many good things?'

'The answer to that lies in the realms of politics, religious power and jealousy.'

'I think I have a lot to learn about the world. I am not sure I really want to be involved, but I shall have to be if I want to make any impact on right or wrong.'

Marc looked at him. His young face was set determinedly.

The group who had just completed their gruesome stoning of the woman were walking behind them through the gates, laughing and shouting with the orgasmic rush of adrenalin instilled by their legally approved of killing. Marc was filled with disgust, though he had witnessed a reaction similar to theirs many times.

In the centre of the city the market bustled. Bazaars set inside surrounding colonnades sold anything from rugs to saddles. People from different nationalities were crowded into the space and different languages rose to uncontrollable crescendos as wrangling and negotiating took place. The sellers asked twice the value of their goods, whilst the buyers offered a half of their worth.

The verbal battles were so fierce that physical assaults, even murder, seemed imminent, yet each argumentative drama followed the same pattern, until eventually the players calmed down and a bargain was reached. Pickpockets prevailed, jostling their victims from side to side until their purses were dropped or lifted from among their clothing. The interactions were a fascinating display of human behaviour.

Marc turned to face the central part of the market place where skilled tradesmen and women were producing their wares. Two young men sat crossed legged on mats surrounded by leatherwork and tools. One held a round-edged knife in his hand, his long hair bound back so that it did not fall into his face as he bent over his work. He was cutting the leather and making holes for stitching. The other was sewing the seams together with great speed. He was lean with a seemingly large head. His hair was cut short and neatly framed a brown face with a prominent nose.

As though needing to stretch, he suddenly stood up. His tunic was tucked into his undergarment revealing muscly but ill-shaped legs that were bent too wide apart at the knee. He jumped up onto a concrete plinth to take a drink from the fountain behind him. Water spilt over his linen clothing so that it clung to his body. From where he stood, he looked down directly at his observer without acknowledgement. Then a commotion averted the man's gaze.

A young boy had emerged running from the back of a bazaar. The owner chased out swearing loudly with his arms in the air, declaring he had been robbed. Marc turned to see Jonathan take off through the crowd as fast as the tightly packed bodies would allow. He dived and weaved until he was out of sight, the mule standing patiently, the rein touching the ground.

Within minutes the manager of the market appeared, a portly figure with a ruddy face, accompanied by two soldiers bearing arms. The indignant shopkeeper was still complaining at the top of his voice. Marc watched in horror as two men came marching back down the street with Jonathan pinned between them.

'We have him!' they shouted triumphantly.

Marc approached.

'This boy is under my guardianship,' he said, surprised at the ease with which that statement slipped from his tongue, as naturally as though it were a fact. 'Let him go!'

'You should keep your ward under better control,' said the manager. 'He is a thief. We have our own ways of dealing with criminals around here.'

'I'm not the thief,' said Jonathan. 'I saw the boy who was and ran after him.'

'Liar!' called out several frenzied voices. 'Throw him in jail.'
The soldiers took charge and grabbed Jonathan roughly, fastening his hands behind his back.

'Stop it!'

A fresh penetrating and authoritative voice resounded across the crowd. Everyone turned to see where it had come from. The tent-maker, whom Marc had been watching, moved forward through the throng. He was short of stature but the bystanders stood to one side to let him pass.

'Let him go, he is innocent. I saw what happened. I was standing on the fountain and from that vantage point saw everything. I recognized the thief, I know him. This young man merely ran after him. He is not guilty.'

The manager huffed and puffed but he knew the tent-maker. He was a good customer who paid his taxes for the privilege of trading in the market.

'You,' he said, addressing one of the soldiers, 'go and fetch the captain. The rest of you come with me. I wish you to make statements and then I shall have the perpetrator arrested.'

He pushed his corpulent frame discourteously past the shopkeeper and disappeared into the back room, turning briefly to beckon all concerned to join him. He was anxious not to lose face by this incident and to stay fully in charge. The remaining soldier followed with Jonathan, Marc was closely behind together with the thin man, and the owner of the shop came last.

The witness, whose name was Saul, wrote down what he saw and named the thief; Jonathan drafted his version of events, Marc was also asked to sign. The captain arrived soon after. He clearly knew the tent maker and they exchanged a brief nod. The market manager seemed annoyed at this interchange, and hunched his shoulders twice in quick succession to indicate that he was in charge and would not tolerate delay.

'Captain,' he said, in a voice that carried as much weight as he could muster, 'an arrest is required and I should be grateful if you would carry it out at once. Our criminal will be busy congratulating himself on his success.'

The captain turned away and, with a slight jerk of his head, indicated to the two soldiers to follow him. They disappeared out into the street.

'Thank you for your assistance in this matter,' said the manager to Marc and Jonathan. 'I apologise for the mistake but I am sure you will appreciate that it was understandable in the circumstances.'

Jonathan nodded vigorously. The image of the stoning had been engaging his thoughts. Marc accepted the apology graciously seeing no reason to upset a senior member of Jericho's society since the outcome was satisfactory. The manager walked outside, equally relieved.

'It's a very good job you were watching, sir,' said Jonathan to the tent maker. 'I would have been in jail by now. Thank you very much, sir. I am most grateful.'

Saul looked at him quizzically. Then he addressed Marc.

'Where are you from?'

'Jerusalem. But before that, Rome.'

'Yes, I suspected as much,' he replied. 'I am a Roman citizen you know, inherited from my father, though my family are from Tarsus, which makes me Cilician. I come here to sell tents — business is brisk and I am sick of Jerusalem.'

'Why is that?' asked Marc.

'Have you not been there in the last few weeks?'

'Yes.'

'Then you'll have heard much said about a certain Jesus of Nazareth. I'm a Pharisee and he's challenged the Jewish faith. Says he is our Messiah – what presumptuousness! Anyone who dies as he did is cursed of God. He makes fools of our priests and twists the scriptures that have been our truth since the time of Abraham. His followers increase. They are insufferable.'

He spoke with such vehemence that for a moment Marc said nothing.

'But was he not also a Jew?'

'Oh yes. But he disowned his faith and made a mockery of it. He denies our traditions. But if you are from Rome, none of this will be relevant to you.'

'In fact, I think it is. I have spent some time reading your ancient Hebrew texts. They are full of significance. I wonder if some of them do not prophesy the coming of a Messiah.'
Saul visibly bristled.

'Those prophecies have yet to be fulfilled. But let's not talk of it any more – it makes me angry. Are you in need of a tent by any chance?'

'Yes, I am, as a matter of fact. I think we shall be staying tonight since the incident in the market has delayed my purpose.'

'And what was that?'

'I wish to speak to one of Herod's last wives whom I have been told is still living in Jericho.'

'And so she is,' remarked Saul. 'I have sold tents to many of her workers on the farm. What business can you possibly have with her? She is no longer young.'
Marc ignored the rude directness of the question.

'I'm investigating the theft of some jewellery from the vaults of Herodium.'

'Ah yes, I've heard of Herod's famous wealth.'

Just at that moment the captain reappeared.

Saul said, 'Well, did you catch him?'

'Yes, thanks to you, but he is a mere boy, suffering from starvation.'

'It makes no difference. The law says, "Thou shalt not steal!" He must learn his lesson.'

Saul moved his elbows outwards and flapped his upper arms rapidly twice, as though to emphasise the importance of his point. The captain replied.

'And no doubt he will, if he lives.'

He turned to Marc.

'I could not help overhearing your comment about Herodium. I used to be sent there from Caesarea to guard the vaults. It always seemed like a waste of time and money, but orders must be obeyed.'

'Can you remember anything unusual that might be worth investigating?'

'You mean any possible theft? Well, we were not encouraged to get to know one another. We were assigned in threes and drew lots to decide which two of us would stay. I was in the Italian regiment and assigned there maybe three or four times a year. We were forbidden to speak to one another. The Keeper of the Key was a man called Joel. I remember there was an incident around the time that Archelaus was exiled. I think one of the guards was imprisoned, but there were a lot of prisoners in those days.'

The captain paused and said thoughtfully, 'I heard a rumour that he was let out twenty years later, that would be seven years ago, but he will almost certainly be dead now. He was in a very sorry state by all accounts.'

Marc said, 'I wonder if you could help me further. I would like to speak to Herod's wife, Drusilla, if you could direct me.'

'That is easy,' said the captain. 'I will show you. I am riding out not far from there now.'

'Not before I show him my tents,' said Saul.

The working farm was set on a hillside of olives and vines - the building wide and white and beautifully maintained. In an enclosed field nearby were ten fine well-proportioned Arab horses. Marc and Jonathan leaned against a barred gate and watched them. A black gelding put his head over the top bar and shoved Jonathan's shoulder. The boy laughed and the horse repeated the action.

'He is wonderful.' said Jonathan.

'Would you like him?'

'Oh, sir, it would be too much to ask.'

'If you are coming out with me you need a proper horse to ride.'

Marc asked the foreman if the horses were for sale and whether they had been broken. The transaction was soon completed. Jonathan was overjoyed – a bridle was all he needed.

Marc asked if he might have an audience with the lady Drusilla. Eventually he was shown up some steps by the side of the building and onto the flat roof. Palm leaves swayed the other side of a low wall as the afternoon sun lengthened. A very elderly lady sat on a sofa, surrounded by large luxurious cushions. Her eyes held no warmth and her air was haughty. Curiosity alone permitted his presence. A servant announced Marc's arrival with excessive pomp. A nod of her head implied that she wished him to sit down.

'Forgive the interruption, ma'am. On the authority of Pontius Pilate, I am investigating the theft of your late husband's lapis lazuli jewels from the vaults at Herodium.'

The woman's face was sunken, her cheekbones prominent, her eyes almost too big for her head – they darted quickly to one side and back.

'I know nothing of a theft. My husband favoured me greatly and gave me a piece from his collection. I had no need to steal it.'

She raised her thin hand with its enlarged joints and tissue like skin, and moved a woollen shawl from one shoulder, revealing a huge and magnificent deep blue brooch with a central stone, surrounded by smaller ones. The stone seemed to have mystical properties, hypnotic in its effect, speaking to the onlooker of dark hedonistic mysteries. Marc thought the others he had seen were spectacular, but this was of a different quality all together.

'Forgive my impertinence, but some of the recovered jewels have proved to be fakes. Are you certain this is genuine?'

Marc felt the insult of his remark, but unexpectedly the woman laughed.

'This single stone could buy the whole of Jericho. Do you think Queen Cleopatra of Egypt would have entertained anything less? What nonsense is this?'

'How much of your husband's treasure did you inherit?'

'I didn't inherit any of it – I told you, he willingly gave me this brooch. It was his special gift to me.'

There was the sound of galloping hooves from the courtyard below and demanding voices. Footsteps ran up the steps and the captain appeared first. He bowed to Drusilla then spoke to Marc.

'You are Commander Marc Tiro, are you not?'

'Yes, as you say. You know I am.'

'Then I am arresting you for the murder of Silas, Keeper of the Key at Herodium.'

'But that is impossible. I was with him only yesterday.'

'Precisely, you are probably the last person to see him alive. He was found dead in the dungeon early this morning.'

28

Marc was now sharing a cell with the young thief and sat quietly considering his position. Someone must have had him followed to Herodium, known that he had been down to the dungeon with Silas. Perhaps it was the same person who had instructed Silas to imprison him. Silas had asked him to say nothing to the chief administrator or Pilate. Had Silas been manipulated - told to dispose of Marc in whatever way he could? But Silas had failed. On the other hand, he knew too much. Perhaps he was now dispensable, and accusing Marc of his murder must have been all too easy. He tried to think carefully whether anybody had seen him emerging from the palace – a witness. He had stopped briefly to speak to a gardener as he left, but had the man seen Silas? And furthermore would he be bribed to say nothing or even disposed of. Marc was a Roman citizen and would appeal to Caesar if necessary. He preferred to defend himself in Rome.

Food was brought and the captain called to express his regrets. Nothing could be done until he had instructions from Tribune Polybius. Marc felt dubious about the degree of support he would obtain from him.

Night fell and the open gap in the wall that allowed in air revealed bright shining stars against a black sky. The boy had refused to speak but now Marc could hear him quietly asking for protection, peace, wisdom, and for the truth to be told. That word, truth, pierced his memory. 'What is truth?' Pilate had asked Jesus, but there had been no reply. Perhaps because he knew Pilate would neither understand nor accept it.

There was no doubt that the boy was praying. Without comment, Marc joined in his supplication and they prayed together but separately until the early morning, when they were both blessed with sleep.

Marc awoke refreshed to find the boy watching him. The boy responded to a smile.

'Were you praying too?' he asked.

'I was.'

'And were you praying to God?'

'Yes.'

'Do you think he heard our prayers?'

'I'm sure he did.'

'Do you think he'll answer them?'

'In time, perhaps he will in his own way.'

'Do you want to know why I pray?'

'Yes, tell me.'

'Several months ago, a preacher came to Jericho. I saw him heal blind Bartimaeus – many of us did. It was incredible. I followed him and as he walked through the town a bad man called Zacchaeus climbed a sycamore tree to get a better view. He was a thief, like me, but much worse; he cheated people by charging them too much tax and was very wealthy. The preacher didn't seem to mind and asked to go to his house. Afterwards, Zacchaeus was so changed that I heard him say that if he had cheated anybody out of anything, he would pay back four times the amount. I thought if he can do it, then I must do the same.'

'So why were you stealing yesterday?'

'I wasn't. I was putting back the money that I stole, four times the amount. I thought I could slip in while everyone was busy but I was spotted.'

'Why didn't you say something and defend yourself?'

'Who would have believed me?'

There was validity in this question, so why did Marc believe him? Because he had heard him praying long and earnestly! He knew that in some way this boy's life had been transformed in the same way as his own. It was no use pretending that it had not happened to him as well because it had.

'I intended to pay back the money I had stolen and then, like Bartimaeus, I was going to follow the preacher. But they have murdered him. They had no right to do that. But if I get out of here I shall go to Jerusalem and find his followers. I have no family. My father was a Greek. He left when I was a baby, and my mother died of hunger last year.'

'What is your name?'

'Barnabas! People will come to hate me as they hated the man they crucified. I am older than I look. I shall avenge his murder by the Jews and the Romans.'

'Perhaps he would not want you to take revenge but to use your faith in him to change others.'

Barnabas looked at Marc.

'Perhaps, I shall have to pray and ask what I should do.'

'Shall we pray now?'

'Yes – it is the only thing to do. Otherwise there is no way out.'

The heat was sweltering. The summer sun, high and fierce, sent a burning beam of light and energy through the gap, heating the small cell and emptying it of air. Both man and boy had stripped to the waist, sweat poured from their brows and ran across their lips leaving the taste of salt on their tongues. The hours ticked away in prayer until late afternoon. The sound of bolts drawn across the wooden door broke their meditation. The captain entered and immediately removed his helmet, wiping his forehead.

'I have some good news for you. Both of you! Commander, you are to be released pending further inquiries by order of Pontius Pilate. You are to return to Jerusalem immediately. And you boy, for some reason the shopkeeper wishes to drop all charges. You are free to go but I warn you, you will not be treated so leniently next time.'

When they were alone, Barnabas commented on his freedom.

'I expect the shopkeeper realized that he had not been robbed. In fact, he probably made more profit than he expected. But he wouldn't say so, would he? He would make himself look foolish for making a fuss.'

'You can hardly blame him. Your reputation will take a long time to live down.'

'That is why I am not staying in this town. I need a fresh start.'

As they emerged into the encroaching evening sun, Marc rubbed his chin. The stubble felt uncomfortable, prickly and itchy. Jonathan was waiting for him with two horses and the mule.

'Sir,' said Barnabas, 'please take me with you as far as Jerusalem. I promise I shall not be a nuisance and I shall leave you as soon as we arrive. I know what I have to do.'

'Have we room for another?' said Marc to Jonathan.

'The more the merrier,' came the reply, although the smile was less easy than usual.

Some of the traders were packing away their unsold goods and avoided the small group like lepers as they walked through the market. Humiliating rotten tomatoes, thrown from behind, clung to their hair and oozed down the backs of their necks. They stopped to buy some food from a stallholder who either did not care or did not know. And then, as quickly as possible, the trio disappeared through the main gate, two on horses and one astride a donkey.

They headed quickly for the mountains to find a suitable place to camp before nightfall. Jonathan leapt about like a jackrabbit collecting firewood while Marc and Barnabas erected the tent bought from Saul. An hour later as they sat round the fire, the howl of a wolf sounded loud and clear not far away. Jonathan quickly turned his head to one side, jumped to his feet, put his hands to his mouth and responded. Within minutes out from behind some rocks stepped Daleel. There was much joyous greeting amongst them and introductions were made to Barnabas.

'So my friend, I was afraid I was going to have to break you out of that jail.'

'How did you know we had come to Jericho?'

'Come now! You need to ask me that? We know all things. Our eyes and ears are everywhere. We are your protection.'

'Did you also know that Silas has been murdered?'

'Yes. I heard.'

'Someone's stopping at nothing to get whatever it is they're after. I want to get to the bottom of this for Rebecca's sake as well as my own. She wants to clear Anthony's name.'

Barnabas interrupted.

'It's a man with the name of Anthony that I am looking for. That's another reason why I wish to go to Jerusalem, to return something that I stole from him – he didn't even realize I'd taken it from inside his cloak. I must now take it back. I know where he lives. I have his identification document too. It's most unusual to find someone carrying that around. I've never seen one before.'

'May I see it?' asked Marc.

Barnabas reached inside his tunic and drew out a small leather bag. Marc opened the identification and looked in astonishment.

'These belong to Anthony Avitus. When did you steal these?'

'It was the day before Jesus came to Jericho. The weather was mild – it's easier to pick pockets then because people wear fewer outer garments. The man was trying to attract the attention of a lady across the square. He was so agitated and preoccupied that he hardly noticed me brushing up against him.'

There was a long pause in the conversation as the implications of this chance encounter sunk in. They seemed improbable, yet this young man, whose life had been overturned so suddenly and completely, had unexpectedly thrown up the possibility of a whole new scenario.

'Do you mind if I keep this?' said Marc. 'I believe I may know the owner and I will certainly return them on your behalf.'

Barnabas looked pleased and relieved.

'I give them to you then. And I trust what you say. But there is more. This certainly needs returning.'

Barnabas put his hand inside his cloak once again. Something blue and sparkling flashed in between his fingers.

'He also had this on him! It has been worrying me so much – it looks very valuable.'

Marc felt he had never been so surprised. He simply could not believe that this young man had come across yet another piece of lapis lazuli – this time a small bracelet set in silver. He took hold of it as Barnabas opened his hand. Daleel and Jonathan moved near for a closer look.

'I will see that it is returned to its rightful owner,' said Marc. Barnabas visibly relaxed – grateful that a burden had been lifted from his soul.

Marc and Daleel sat late into the night keeping watch as the two young men slept in the tent.

'What do you make of all this?' began Daleel.

'I think that Sabina knew her son better than anyone. She never believed he was dead – only that he had gone off with some woman – and it looks as though she was right. But only one person could have put the belt buckle and ring on the finger of the corpse of whomever it was we found in the aqueduct, and that's Anthony himself. Perhaps he saw this as his chance of escape – he was guaranteed a valuable reward – sufficient to move away with a new love and not be found, yet still leave his wife with enough funds to survive. When Gaius and I went to see his wife, Deborah, a slave called Sarah told us they had been burgled recently. Perhaps Anthony did it after he was robbed of his prize. Maybe he had intended to leave his wife with some gold but had to go back and retrieve it for himself after Barnabas picked his pockets. He could have made it look like burglary.'

'You'd think he would have given up.'

'It would depend on the woman I suppose – perhaps he thinks he really is in love this time. Or maybe she's married and said she couldn't go back.'

'I wonder where he went.'

'That I don't know. But there's a chance he'll return home when the money runs out – unless of course his lady friend is an heiress.'

'I have met Anthony Avitus only once,' said Daleel. 'He didn't strike me as a thief or a murderer. Who do you suppose it is that he killed?'

'We don't know for sure that he did. It's possible it was some poor slave who had been employed to block up the tunnel. Maybe Anthony found the body and planted his own identification.'

'Why would he also place a map of Qumran on the body though, including some clues?'

'I really wish I knew the answer to that.'

Daleel thought through an answer.

'Unless, it was put there by the person who murdered the slave.'

'Maybe nobody murdered the slave. Perhaps it was an accident. The back of his head was split open. I suppose he could have fallen.'

'Are you going to tell Rebecca about her brother?'

'I think she has a right to know but I think I'll leave out the bit about the bracelet for the moment.'

'That may be for the best,' said Daleel. 'What are you going to say to Pilate about Silas?'

'Tell the truth, of course! There is no evidence that I killed him. It wouldn't hold up in a court. I would like to examine the corpse though. Just to see how he died. I'm still here officially to find the Herodian stones. I'm going north to seek the man who was imprisoned in Herodium, and then to Damascus. I want to find out more about this jewellery particularly why so much of it seems to be faked. I met up with one of Herod's last wives in Jericho. She has a brooch that Herod gave her personally before he died. She was totally convinced it was genuine and worth a fortune. Salampsio said that the necklace stolen from Marcellus was also original – seems strange that there are so many discrepancies in value.'

'Are you going alone?'

'No, Gaius will come with me this time. It was a condition of Pilate's allowing me to continue, I suspect. Besides, Gaius will be helpful – his father works in the jewellery trade.'

The flames of the fire gradually dwindled as dawn rose behind the mountains of Moab beyond the Dead Sea - the fresh cool air filled each of them with a new sense of anticipation.

Back in Jerusalem Marc's first task was to ensure Barnabas had some contacts. That was easy. Mary Magdalene welcomed him like a long lost brother when she knew he had encountered her beloved Jesus.

'You can stay at the house of Mary and Clopas,' she assured him. 'You will never need to steal again. The community of followers are growing daily and we take responsibility for each other, sharing food and other provisions as necessary.'

Barnabas was overjoyed. This was a new beginning, new friends, new family, new soul, all his wrongdoings forgiven and forgotten and definitely behind him. His life had been laundered. Marc, on the other hand, was unsure what would face him, but his own innocence gave him comfort and confidence. He made straight for the palace and an audience with the Procurator. But Pilate was so delighted with his investigator, who had so easily solved a problem of unmentionable proportions, that Marc need have no concerns.

'It's outrageous that you should have been so accused. I have had words with Tribune Polybius myself. He is to apologise for such inhospitable behaviour. He should never have taken the word of worthless slaves. They all denounced you, you know. They all said they had seen you with Silas going down to the dungeon. Of course you didn't murder Silas. I know that. What motive could you possibly have? It will prove to be one of his own slaves no doubt – using you to cover up his own deeds - a disgruntled lazy worker who has a strong dislike of discipline. I have ordered them all to be flogged until they tell us the truth. Someone will know what happened.'

Marc inwardly winced at this generalised method of punishment before guilt had been proven, but knew that this was the way of the world in which he was becoming to feel a stranger. He almost envied Barnabas, but there was much to be solved before he personally could begin to find peace.

'Pilate, I would like to see the body of Silas, if possible, to see how he died. I would also like your permission to interrogate the slaves from Herodium before you flog them. Just the threat may be enough to get them to tell the truth.'

'Very well, do as you suggest and good luck to you. In my experience slaves tend to say nothing until they have felt the force of the whip.'

'I will resort to that if I have to,' said Marc reassuringly.

'Good! Gaius tells me you two are to head north. Go and find out how Herod managed to deceive us all with his fake stones. It will make entertaining reading for the Emperor. He will need something to amuse him while he's languishing on Capri.'

Marc knew that Pilate was referring to the absence of Tiberius for nearly six years. He had withdrawn himself from Rome. Some said it had been because of the intrigues of Sejanus. Others said it was because of his bullying mother. Whatever the reason, he lived quietly in a villa, enjoying views of the Bay of Naples and Mount

Vesuvius.

Pilate continued.

'Don't bring me back any bad news! I shan't want to hear it. I have enough of that around here. I shall be returning to Caesarea after the Feast of Weeks, so if you take longer than two weeks, maybe you can both make your way back there – no need to return to Jerusalem.'

This parting comment filled Marc with a sense of depression. It hadn't occurred to him that he might not see Jerusalem and the people in it again. Soon after his return to Caesarea he would be expected to sail to Rome – his job complete.

Without deliberate consciousness he found himself outside the door of Victor's. He had no recollection of how he got there, his thoughts being preoccupied. Rebecca was working in her office. In the room beside the window was a large easel and she was busy drawing plans for tombs built inside a rock face. He stood on the threshold and watched her perched on a high wooden stool, using her pens skilfully in her slender fingers. The light shone down on her hair and highlighted half of her face accentuating her high cheekbones, aquiline nose and fine jaw. Her lashes were long and she sucked her lower lip thoughtfully as she fought to achieve a balance in her artistry, as perfect as her own.

Marc cleared his throat and she looked up, slightly startled, absorbed as she was. Her smile was instant and warm. She jumped down from the stool and walked lightly across the room to greet him.

'Marc, I have been so worried about you. I hear Silas is dead and his slaves have accused you. What has happened?'

'Don't concern yourself. It was all a mistake. I shall be asking them some questions to get to the truth of the matter. Can we talk somewhere privately?'

'Of course, come in and close the door.'

She indicated to him to sit on a couch on the right and sat beside him.

'I have come to tell you some good news – it seems that Anthony was seen not long ago in Jericho. The body we found was not his.'

'Are you sure?' she asked hesitantly.

'There is absolutely no doubt. I have his identification documents.'

'But that's wonderful news. So where is he?'

'That I don't know. It seems that Sabina was right, there was another woman involved and Anthony used the death of a slave to make it look like his own, so that no one would think to look for him.'

'By that I suppose you mean Deborah?'

Rebecca sighed.

'If only he had felt able to talk to me – perhaps we could have worked something out. Divorce is not forbidden – he could have divorced Deborah.'

'Many men are cowards when it comes to discussing their feelings, particularly if they think someone may be hurt by them. They can't face emotional outbursts and would rather pretend nothing was happening.'

'I don't know what he would live on with no income from his work here.'

'Well, it's possible the money will run out one day and then, who knows, he may be back.'

'Do you think I should tell his wife and mother?'

Marc hesitated.

'It may be best to say nothing to Deborah or Sabina for the moment until we find out more, but I will leave that to your discretion.'

'You're probably right. It would only lead to more speculation and expectation of his return, which may never happen. It's probably better for Deborah that she thinks he's dead. Is he still in

Jericho do you think?'

'It's unlikely. I think he would want to get further away than that.'

'He was always fond of Damascus. He used to say it was one of the oldest cities.'

'I shall be travelling north within a day or so. I will ask if anyone has heard of him but please don't hold out your hopes too high.'

'Will you be back?'

'I'm not sure, Rebecca. Pontius Pilate will be leaving soon for Caesarea so my work here will then be effectively over.'

'Promise you will come back and see us ………me.'

'Rebecca, I …. I want to tell you ….'

The door opened and Rachel burst into the room with a squeal closely followed by her friend.

'Come mummy, come and see what we have built. It is the best home ever. Marc, you must come and see too.'

The moment had passed yet again and somehow Marc doubted that there would be another, unless fate intervened.

29

The body of Silas lay on a stone slab. The mortician stood beside Marc shaking his head ruefully, examining the bruises.

'There are four knife wounds in the back and one, probably the one that killed him, in the left hand side of his throat. Each stab wound was made with a downward movement. One was in the middle of his back, deep and vengeful. The others were much lower down, shallower and more frenzied. They would have caused him to bleed but not necessarily to die.'

'Perhaps Silas bent forward after the first blow,' ventured Marc.

'Possible! It's almost as though the attacker became tired and was stabbing indiscriminately. This one here is no higher than his waist. The first wound is deep; maybe it was done with two hands. The three other wounds are shallow. Then this final blow in his neck was stronger again, almost desperate.'

The mortician added, 'The angle of entry of the knife indicates that his killer was much shorter than him. When Silas finally turned round to face his attacker, the knife penetrated his throat upwards from the left side of his neck.'

'How long do you think he has been dead?'

'The overall condition of the body suggested he had been dead about twelve hours when he was found, not much more.'

Marc considered this statement. He had left Silas in the middle of the morning – the body had been found very early the next morning - so he was probably killed late afternoon or early evening. He had visited Rebecca at midday on returning from Herodium – she could be a witness. In all probability the murder happened around the time that he and Gaius were riding in the Valley of Kidron, watching the dark clouds gathering prior to the storm. The thought of the body of Silas lying in the darkest recesses of the palace, reverberating with thunderbolts, lit by startling lightening, seemed to have the feel of judgement about it.

'Look at these lacerations on his leg,' pointed out the mortician. 'They look as though they were made after death. They hardly bled at all. And another curious feature of the corpse is these three long scratches on the right cheek. The middle one is deeper than that of the others and has torn the flesh.'

'Fingernails?' posed Marc.

'Yes, more than likely!'

The slaves who worked at Herodium had been arrested and brought to the jail. There were nine of them, three women, five men and a little girl, no older than six. Most of the men looked after the grounds but the women did the cooking and cleaning. Marc intended interrogating them all and took them out of the cell into a separate room one at a time.

The first was a short, elderly, thin, dark haired man. He fell flat on his face and shook.

'Get up! I need answers. You will be flogged if you don't cooperate.'

'Sir, I....I saw nothing. I work in the gardens on the south side of the palace. I rarely see who comes from the n...n...north. I don't see very well. My eyes are bad.'

'What gossip have you heard then?'

'Well, sir, I know that you came to visit the p.... palace and stayed one n...night.'

'And what of it?'

'Please, sir, I know nothing.'

'What kind of master was Silas?'

'Oh, he was g...g.... good, sir, very good.'

Marc stared hard at the man. He didn't believe him.

'I said tell the truth, didn't I?'

The man's eyes were wide open; his lips trembled.

'Well sir, he b....b....beat us sometimes, particularly the women. But they c....c....can tell you more.'

'Did you resent him?'

'We have no b...b...business resenting anybody, sir. We are nothing; we are worthless; we are worse than the d...d....dogs in the street.'

The second and third men had little more to add, but the fourth was the gardener to whom Marc had spoken as he left the grounds. He also had responsibility for the northern gate that stood in the miles of stonewalling that encircled the land surrounding the palace. He bowed his head as he walked through the door to avoid the architrave.

'Did you see Silas as I left, the afternoon he died?'

'No sir! I'm sorry. I saw only you.'

'Did anybody else come to the palace that afternoon?'

'I saw no one sir.'

'How did Silas treat you?'

'He was a good master, sir.'

'How did he treat the women?'

The slave looked up quickly and away again. Marc repeated the question.

'How did he treat the women?'

'They were looked after.'

'How well were they looked after?'

'He used them.'

'You mean for sex?'

'Yes.'

'And how did you feel about that?'

'It was his right.'

'And how often did he use them?'

'I don't know, sir.'

'Well, I think you do. Tell the truth or it will be the worse for everyone.'

'It wasn't their fault. He could do whatever he pleased.'

'I understand. Tell me, what pleased him most?'

'The girl, sir, she was his daughter by the slave Martha.'

'He abused his own daughter?'

'He didn't see her as his daughter, sir. To him she was just an animal to do with as he wished.'

Marc felt disgusted.

'How often?'

'Nearly every day, the girl had to go to him every afternoon, and then he would decide what to do with her, depending on how he felt and whether he was busy, or whether he had a visitor.'

'Did he rape her?'

'Worse sir, he said she was an animal; he tied her up by the neck and penetrated her like one.'

He suddenly realized he had said too much and started to weep.

'It's all right,' said Marc gently. 'I understand – you love her.'

'Yes, her mother is my wife.'

'Did you or your wife have a part in the killing of Silas?'

The man hesitated and decided not to answer.

'Did you or your wife kill Silas?'

'She had nothing to do with it – it was me.'

'And how did you do it?'

'I followed him to the dungeon in the morning and I stabbed him.'

'Where did you stab him?'

'In his back!'

'And how many times did you stab him'

'I don't remember.'

'Try harder.'

'Twice, yes, that's it. I stabbed him twice.'

'Twice in the back?'

'Yes sir!'

'I think you are lying.'

The man sobbed.

'Sir, I cannot remember I was so furious with him.'

'Were you standing up when you stabbed him?'

'Yes sir!'

Marc called in one of the soldiers whose height was about the same as Silas.

'Show me!'

The man raised his right arm and pretended to stab the soldier in the back – he was so tall that his fist came down at the top of the spine.

'You had trouble did you not coming through the doorway?'

'No sir!'

'You bent your head.'

'Yes sir!'

'Silas was stabbed in the back four times and once in the neck by a person much shorter than you.'

Before he had time to protest, Marc spoke again.

'Think carefully, please, did you see anybody else arrive or leave the palace that day after we spoke.'

'Oh sir, I'm very sorry but I didn't. You see, Martha, my wife, she's not well. There was some heavy furniture that needed moving and I went inside to help her. I wasn't supposed to ever leave my post, but very few people come, so I left the gate open just in case. Silas would have killed me if he had known. I feel I am to blame.'

'Why did you all tell Tribune Polybius that I must have been the killer?'

The man hung his head. It flopped onto his chest. When he lifted it his brow was furrowed, his eyes were rheumy.

'I'm sorry, sir,' was all he could say and he repeated it. 'I am to blame.'

When Marc turned his attention to the women, Martha confirmed what her husband had told him about the sexual demands of Silas on his slaves but she tried to make light of it, as if it was just one of those duties like sweeping the floor.

'I'd like to speak to your daughter alone.'

The woman looked alarmed and protested.

'Please sir, don't do it. You'll not get anything out of her, she can't talk.'

'Does she understand what you say to her?'

'Yes sir!'

'Then that will do.'

Before he interrogated the girl, he sent a soldier over to Rebecca's house asking if Rachel could spare some toys, especially one of her rag dolls. He stressed the importance. Within half an hour the soldier returned with just what was needed.

The slave girl sat on a stool in a corner, watching as Marc placed the toys on a mat in the centre of the room, together with a drink and sweet cake. He sat at a suitable distance and preoccupied himself with a puzzle. Eventually, with curiosity, the girl approached. She snatched the doll and cake and ran back, frightened that it would be taken away from her. When she realized that she was not to be punished, she relaxed, ate, and hugged the inanimate object.

Marc bent forward and placed his puzzle on the floor, resting his elbows on his knees, his hands hanging loosely between his legs. Lifting his head just a little, he looked up at her and smiled. There was no response, yet her eyes seemed to soften very slightly. She was not afraid. Perhaps, thought Marc, she has had so many traumas in her young life that her emotions have been numbed.

'Do you like the doll?'

She hugged it closer to her chest and swivelled her body from side to side moving from the waist.

'Would you like to keep it?'

She nodded.

'If you help me and answer some questions, I will give it to you.' He paused, allowing her to consider the suggestion. She stood looking at him.

'Do you know what has happened at the palace?'

She nodded.

'Did you go to see your master, Silas, on the day that he died?'

Another nod!

'Did you go to his room in the afternoons?'

No response.

'Did you go to his room that afternoon?'

She nodded.

'Was there anybody else in the room?'

She nodded.

'Was it another man?'

She shook her head.

'A woman?'

She nodded.

'Do you know the woman?'

She shook her head.

'Was it Martha?'

She shook her head vigorously.

'Did the woman speak to you?'

She shook her head again.

'Was she speaking to Silas?'

A nod!

'Was she arguing with him?'

Another nod!

'Did she do anything?'

She nodded again.

'Can you show me what she did?'

There was a long silence. The girl took the drink and bit into the cake. Marc sat still. Then she placed the doll on the seat propping it up, facing away from her. Marc looked directly at the soldier standing on the threshold and lifted his eyebrows. He responded, moving inwards to witness what was happening.

The girl lifted both her arms above her head and smashed them down onto the back of the doll, again and again. Then she turned the doll round, hit it in the neck, picked it up, wrapped her arms round it and sat down. The interview was over. She retreated back into her own world.

'My gods!' someone whispered. 'She saw who killed Silas.'

'But she was the only person who did,' said Marc. 'I need to speak to Martha and her husband again.'

They were both called and did not dare lift their heads as they were pushed into Marc's presence.

'Did you know that your daughter witnessed the murder of Silas?'

Martha sobbed and shook uncontrollably. Her husband tried to comfort her but was trembling himself.

'Please don't punish her, sir,' he pleaded. 'Let me suffer and die instead. She wouldn't have known what she was doing.'

'What are you talking about?' said Marc. 'I'm not accusing her. She saw it happen.'

'But, there was no one else around. She must have killed him herself. When we found her she had a dagger in her hand and was covered with blood.'

'What made you go looking for her?'

'It was mealtime. Silas never missed his food. He always released the girl first to give him time to bathe and cleanse himself before eating. We waited and waited and finally thought it best to remind him.'

Marc remembered the stab wounds in Silas' legs. This child was most probably left alone with the dead body and copied the behaviour she had seen. How long had she sat beside the corpse he wondered, two, three hours.

'I can assure you that the injuries inflicted on the body could never have been carried out by a girl so young – although a grown woman could have done it.'

'My wife didn't do it, sir. I was with her all afternoon.'

'And why should I believe you?'

'It's the truth, sir. We believed our daughter had killed the master.'

'How did the body get into the dungeon?'

'We moved it, sir. We all helped to get it down to the dungeon.'

'And then decided to put the blame on me?'

'Forgive the others, sir, please.'

The slave was overcome with sorrow and despair.

'Please take me and crucify me, let me die only. It was my idea. I must take the blame but please let the others go.'

Marc looked directly into the aqueous eyes of the slave who was prepared to die for his friends and family.

'I want you to come with me to the palace. I need to see where Silas died. The others will stay here in prison.'

Marc, together with the slave and two soldiers, rode immediately with great haste to Herodium. The daylight was long as midsummer was approaching.

They went straight to Silas' quarters to examine where he died. It was a plain room. The sun, low and refulgent, disclosed dark stains on the wooden floor, where the protectors of the young girl had vainly tried to mop away the blood.

Marc visualised the scene. Someone stabbed him from behind, injuring but not killing. The blow pushed him forward across a table and he was stabbed again at waist level and below. He had turned. The attacker moved backwards. He advanced on her, probably leaning towards her. She struck out with her left hand, scoring his right cheek with her nails. As he grabbed her arm, she brought the knife up with her right hand, stabbing him in the left side of his neck – the fatal wound. The body would have been covered in so much blood that it would have been impossible to determine where the wounds were.

'What did you do with the weapon?'

'We cleaned it and put it in the drawer. We believed it to be Silas' own dagger. None of us own such a thing.'

Marc found it, unconvinced that it belonged to Silas – it was too small and had a delicately painted handle. He scoured the room for anything that looked out of place. There was a small wooden box standing empty on a chest. The lid was inlaid with carved ivory and a metal lock was embedded in its edge. Whatever it had contained was gone. And then he spotted something else – a woman's scarf, made of light material, it had drifted under a cupboard, hidden from sight, spattered with blood.

'Do you recognize this?' Marc asked the slave.

'No sir, a scarf such as this could only belong to a lady.'

'Show me where you dragged the body.'

Blood stains again confirmed the slave's story. The body had been wrapped in a sheet and carried by the men down the steps to the dungeons. The slave admitted that the sheet was hidden, still waiting to be washed or burned by the women. So the entire household was involved in the deception, except that they had been deceived themselves. Not one of them had seen the intruder, the visitor who slipped through the gate to confront Silas, to put her demands, only to become so enraged that she was driven to murder.

There was no doubt in Marc's mind that this woman intended to kill. But what was her motive - jealousy or money? In his experience it was generally one or the other with women – men killed for power and prestige.

'How did you persuade the authorities that you just happened to find the body so early in the morning?'

The man could not meet Marc's eyes as he gave his answer.

'We said that the door to the dungeons had been left open and I went to investigate.'

'And they believed you?'

'Yes sir, they did.'

Marc felt very fortunate to have the patronage of Pontius Pilate. He felt sure it was due to the favourable report that he had produced. If he had proved to be a threat, Pilate would never have supported him in the way that he did.

Nevertheless, it was apparent that he had not been set up by anybody other than the slaves themselves, whose sole motive was to exonerate the child who, they believed, had murdered her father because of his abuse. But there was still the problem of finding the killer – the name of the owner of the knife and the scarf - who had mysteriously visited Silas, unseen, on the afternoon of his death.

It was nightfall by the time they reached Jerusalem again. Marc went straight to his room and wrote up his findings. Tribune Polybius would need a full report. He was unsure what fate would befall the slaves of Herodium – they had, after all, been guilty of conspiracy to obstruct the course of justice. He recommended clemency but it was not within his power to release them. He wrapped up the dagger and scarf, first to show them to Pilate and then to hand them over to Tribune Polybius. It was his investigation now.

The matter of the stones had been temporarily put to one side, but as soon as possible he would take the small bracelet for a valuation. Somehow he knew what the answer would be.

30

-The Scarf and the Dagger-

Marc went to find Pilate before he became too embroiled in the administrative matters of the day. He had accepted the report, did not recognize the dagger or scarf, but was nevertheless interested to know to whom they belonged.

'Polybius will be pleased, no doubt. He would not have been so thorough in his interrogations, but I suppose you did have a vested interest.'

The Procurator seemed to find this highly amusing and guffawed loudly, enjoying his own joke. Marc concurred.

'Don't forget,' added Pilate, 'next time you saddle up and move out, take Gaius with you.'

'I promise!'

The walk to the courthouse was invigorating. Early morning in Jerusalem brought a proliferation of interesting smells. The baker had started an hour earlier. Marc walked round that way. Large white delicious loaves replaced those made without yeast. Visitors were already sitting and enjoying their first meal of the day, absorbing the atmosphere of a large sophisticated city with a variety of cultures.

As he approached the Temple Mount he caught site of Mary. She was in deep conversation with a tall, well-built man with a mass of black curly hair. A fair-haired young man and an older woman joined them, and together they hurried off in the direction of the eastern gate.

The small shops were busy with customers buying vegetables, fruit, herbs, meat and other produce. This was a land of plenty.

The citizens were short of nothing. Marc felt no desire to return to Rome though he knew the inevitable would come.

He sat on a bench pondering the last few weeks. What had happened to his arrogance, self-certainty and pride? He knew it was those qualities that had brought him success in Rome, had helped him to reach heights of power that most could only dream of. He was a very wealthy man, but even that fact seemed of little significance.

It was time for the administrative centres to open and he walked slowly towards Antonia Fort where the jail and courthouse were housed. Tribune Polybius was in residence. He had heard of Marc's release on Pilate's orders and Marc sensed awkwardness in his manner. He looked up and smiled, but quickly looked down at his desk and shuffled some papers as if to indicate that he was busy and short of time.

'I understand you have interrogated the suspects from Herodium. Thank you for that. Crime does not stop and I have a mountain of cases to deal with. What did you find out?'

'The servants believed that a young girl had been responsible for Silas' murder and were trying to protect her. She was actually his daughter by a slave and he'd been abusing her regularly. However, as it turns out, she could not possibly have done it. She was neither tall nor strong enough, but she saw who did. It was a woman. This is the scarf and dagger of the murderer. Find who owns these and you have your killer.'

Marc placed both items on the table in front of Polybius. His face paled and his eyes glazed for a few seconds before he brought himself back to the reality of the moment.

'How can you be so sure? You only have the word of a young girl and a bunch of disreputable slaves whom you say have already tried to stop justice. I shall put the lot of them to death.'

Marc tried to sound unperturbed.

'This is my full report and that of the mortician, together with the confession. I have shown it to Pilate. Naturally I would not think of stopping the course of justice, but the slaves have been at Herodium for some years; they know how things are run, the intricacies and eccentricities of the building. It will be very inconvenient for Pilate if he has to train new people. What a relief it would be to him to know that the palace will continue to be looked after properly.'

Polybius sighed as though the weight of office was too heavy for his shoulders.

'I'll look into it and think about what you've said. I cannot guarantee that I shall have enough staff to go round all the houses in Jerusalem to find out who owns these items. No-one will admit to it anyway – complete waste of time.'

The sarcasm was evident.

'Perhaps, but executing the slaves won't bring us any closer either and the slave girl is practically mute.'

'Well, thanks anyway! No doubt you'll hear what my decision will be in due course. Er....I apologise, by the way, for any ill treatment you may have received in Jericho.'

Polybius spoke this sentence so quickly that it was barely coherent.

'I was well treated. In fact it was altogether quite an illuminating experience.'

Polybius shot a glance at him not understanding his meaning.

'I hope we shall meet again soon then.'

'Goodbye! And good luck with your investigation.'

Marc wondered if Polybius had some ideas about the ownership of the dagger or scarf; he mixed with the elite of Jerusalem's society and these were expensive items. But he was right in saying the chance of finding the owner was remote.

His next call was to see Theo, the jeweller.

'What, you again!' he said, as Marc entered his small premises.

'What have you got for me this time?'

Marc uncovered the small bracelet that he had carefully wrapped.

Theo's only comment was a grunt. He took longer than usual, but when he returned his conclusion was the same as for the others - a very good fake!

'There is something peculiar about this though. I would say the silver setting is hundreds of years old. I wondered if the original stones had been replaced, but in my opinion there's no sign of disturbance. I can't be absolutely certain, of course.'

Marc thanked him and paid him for his advice.

'Where are you getting all these pieces?' he asked.

Marc lifted his eyes without moving his head and pulled down the sides of his mouth.

'It's a long story!' he grimaced.

'Well, let me know the ending.'

The two chuckled as Marc left. He had no idea what the ending would be. His next morning visit was to Rebecca.

'I just wanted to thank you and Rachel for your help yesterday,' he said, as she ushered him into the garden. 'I have come to return Rachel's belongings – all except the rag doll.'

'Rachel was pleased to be of assistance, but why did you need them?'

'I thought it might help in the questioning of a young slave girl who was with Silas when he was killed. She was unwilling to speak, but the doll made her less afraid and we were able to find out what happened.'

'And what did happen?'

'It seems the murderer might have been a woman. We found some items at the scene of the crime, but the owner hasn't been identified yet.'

'What sort of items?'

'A scarf and a dagger! Polybius has them as evidence.'

'Does he have any idea who owns them?'

'He wouldn't say even if he did. There are a lot of wealthy women in Jerusalem. Why one of them would want to kill Silas is anybody's guess.'

'Jealousy?'

'You mean finding him with a young slave girl? Unlikely! Slaves are available for sex or any other service – boys, girls, men and women. Providing they are of a lower rank, no one thinks anything of it. Besides, Silas did not have any lady visitors according to the guard. I think he may have had something that the woman wanted – something more than his loving attention. We found an open, empty box on a chest in Silas' room. Something else is unusual as well. She must have been a good horsewoman and quite brave to ride all that way alone.'

'Or stupid!'

'I can't understand why nobody saw her. It was an amazing coincidence that there was no guard on the gate either when she arrived or left.'

'But she wouldn't have known that presumably in advance. She could easily have been seen. Perhaps she didn't care. Anger can make a person reckless.'

Marc glanced at her thoughtfully. Rachel bounced into the garden and gave him a chaste hug.

'Are you staying in Jerusalem now?' she asked.

'Alas! No!'

'Will you be back?'

'I'm not sure. I'm going in search of a man's family and then, possibly, to Damascus. After that I shall probably return to Caesarea.'

'Well, you can come back after that, can't you?' said the girl, for whom life was so simple.

'Well, when you put it like that, I suppose I could. Thank you for lending me some of your toys yesterday.'

'That's all right. Did you get what you wanted?'

'Yes, I did. And now it is up to the legal authorities to follow up the facts.'

'I'll see you soon then.'

And with that, Rachel skipped off.

'Will we see you soon?' asked Rebecca.

'I would like to, you must know that. First there are some questions to be answered. But I have a feeling I shall be back.'

Rebecca took his hand, lightly brushed her lips against his then quickly withdrew before he could say or do anything. He found his own way out.

Gaius was seated on a veranda at the palace. He had a pile of letters and reports in front of him and was dictating replies.

'Hello!' he shouted, as he saw Marc's tall figure approaching. 'By Jupiter, you do get up to some things when I'm not with you. I've heard about your interrogations. I think you've upset Polybius.'

'How do you know that? I only spoke to him an hour or two ago.'

'This place is the hub of all nosiness. One of his underlings brought me some documents. He said after you left the great tribune was pacing up and down uttering expletives that should not pass the lips and ears of those in polite society.'

'Good! I'm glad to hear it.'

'You have a real talent for upsetting the hierarchy. I wish you would show me how to do it.'

'It's not intentional. At least, I don't think it is.'

'What do we do now, then? I'm fighting fit and ready to go when you are. This paperwork is driving me daft already. I have been training a scribe to do the job so he can take over for a few days, if you still want me to come with you.'

'Do I have a choice?'

'To be honest, I don't think so. Pilate has instructed me to assist you as before. Do you trust me?'

The question was unexpected and Marc said nothing for a moment or two.

'Do I have reason not to?'

'No, actually, I believe that Pilate is genuinely glad to have you here. He sees you as some sort of ally – it's difficult to know whom to trust, as you know, but someone from outside has no personal axe to grind.'

'So are you my bodyguard or a spy?'

'Neither, I'd like to think I might be a friend. You have saved my life and for that I'm very grateful.'

'Just remember that I got you into the fix in the first place.'

'Well, yes, that's true. But be fair, I'm a young blood who has seen no action whatever. What have I done? My wars are on paper. Accompanying you is the most exciting thing that's happened to me.'

'In that case I feel sorry for you. You had better get up and be prepared for an adventure.'

31

-Sychar, Neapolis and Sebaste-

The air was fresh; dew clung to the grass in the palace courtyard. Marc had recovered the pieces of lapis lazuli from Stephen's care, separated them into two leather bags and fixed them to each of the saddled horses. If they made it to Damascus, he intended to try and find the truth behind the original collection designed for the first Cleopatra on the occasion of her wedding to the Prince of Egypt. Cornelius came out to say goodbye; Portius was with him.

'May the gods be with you! You'll need to keep your wits about you if you insist on travelling unaccompanied. Although by the looks of both of you, I wouldn't consider you worth robbing.'

Marc and Gaius had dressed in the garb of local peasantry. A mule carried their provisions. The beard that Marc had despised in the Jericho jail had now passed the stage of irritation and felt soft to the touch. Gaius looked younger than before – his face shone after his rest and was enlivened with eager anticipation of the journey to come.

'I'm glad to see you in such good health, Cornelius,' said Marc. 'I trust you will find things at home better than expected.'

'The house is nearly rebuilt, but I fear Julius is crippled beyond any hope and is badly deformed. It will be impossible for me to employ him as a charioteer but there is work he can do in the house. There are still no leads as to the culprit – I'd like to get my hands on him.'

Fleeting memories of that eventful night passed through Marc's imagination. The sight of Julius burning alive was vivid. The slave, who had so many hopes of gaining his freedom and riding his master's four Arabs to success in the hippodrome, stood momentarily at Cornelius' side with an air of arrogant subservience and then vanished in the morning reality.

Pilate appeared at the top of the nearby steps leading to a veranda.

'What a wonderful morning! I envy you all departing this place but I shan't be too far behind. I cannot wait to divest myself of this Jewish stench. I have your letters of authorisation. You may act on my behalf in Judea; Herod Antipas has given you his full support in Samaria and Galilee, Herod Philip in Iturea and Trachonitis. Herod Antipas has returned already to Tiberias. He wishes you two to stay with him when you reach the area. Take care! I trust you will find the jeweller whose predecessors faked the stones. The very best Etrurian wine will be waiting when we next meet.'

Marc and Gaius left the gates of the palace and followed the cobbled street to Temple Mount, then Antonia Fort, that forcing house of political contention, to the Damascus Gate, whereby they had first entered Jerusalem. The journey to Bethel was some ten or twelve miles to the north. After a while, from a small eminence beside the road, Marc stopped and looked back towards the Mount of Olives. Watery particles formed a pale purple mist, penetrated by glittering gold tints from the sun's early rays. The majestic towers of Jerusalem rose above the low cloud like a magical city.

The road followed the high central plateau that was the backbone of the country from north to south. A number of narrow treacherous passes crossed the spinal column from east to west. The land far to the west, on their left, skirted the Mediterranean Sea. In the East was the now familiar verdant green of the Valley of Jericho.

Numerous villages were strewn along the way; one, Marc recognized as Bethel, situated on a ridge with valleys on either side. The surrounding hills were dressed in fig trees. He looked more closely at this place that meant so much to Jewish worshippers in the early days, but for him had other memories. A large reservoir similar to that of Solomon's Pools came into view as they approached. Gaius was curious to see the spot where Marc had been assaulted, the place where Jacob had built the pillar to commemorate his dream of the angels. Then there it was in front of them – a circle of large stones with the monument in the centre. All was calm and peaceful. Yet Marc noted how close to the edge of a cliff they were. He dismounted and looked into the depth below, realizing how fortunate he had been that the narrow ledge had caught his fall.

They continued through barren slopes. The hills and mountains were formed in the shape of terraces with a drop to the left or right depending on which side the road ran. Sometimes, they would meet a shepherd with his flock coming the other way and be surrounded by sheep on all sides, unable to move for several minutes. They rested on the summit of a round hillock, sitting atop a knoll taking refreshments and lazily observing the surrounding rocky hillside. Close by was an old synagogue. A man emerged from a doorway, the lintel of which was decorated with a Roman amphora surrounded by wreaths of flowers.

'Those rocks are full of recessed tombs,' commented Gaius. 'Hundreds of them – some look very old – the fascia has crumbled.' Gaius spoke to the man as he passed them.

'Excuse me, sir. What's the history of this place?'

The man was a willing narrator and joined them, sitting on the ground.

'Many Jewish generations have worshipped here. It is believed this was once a sacred spot, the place where the Ark of the Covenant rested for a while.'

'What do you mean?' asked Gaius.

'When our patriarch Moses received the Ten Commandments for good living from God, they were written on tablets of stone.

They remained here for a long time inside a specially built wooden chest. It could strike a man dead who dared to touch it in an irreverent manner. It was even stolen once by our enemies, the Philistines, but they later returned it when they realized how powerful it was.'

'What happened to it?'

'Nobody is absolutely sure. There have been so many battles in these parts. Some say it was taken to Egypt. All I know is that God left this place when it went. Yet some of us older ones keep the faith.'

He stopped for a moment his voice choked with emotion.

'The Jewish priests of Jerusalem will have nothing to do with us Samaritans; they won't even speak to us. They say Samaria is full of wickedness. Shiloh was cursed – just look at it now.'

He spread his arm across the view of the poor homes of the village.

'Some of the great high priests of our ancestors are buried in those sepulchres. I pray that our guilt may be assuaged and that God will return one day.'

'I don't understand why the Jews in Jerusalem will have nothing to do with the Samaritans – you are all of the same faith,' commented Gaius.

'Hundreds of years ago, after the reign of Solomon, these lands were divided into two, Israel in the north and Judah in the south. The tribes of Judah and Benjamin lived in the south; the remaining ten tribes lived in the north. The dividing line was at Bethel where we worshipped. The Judeans worshipped in Jerusalem.

'Then Israel was conquered by Assyria. This stretch of land has always been vulnerable because it's a pathway to Egypt. But Judah was not attacked and they thought they were better than us because we had been overthrown and God had not protected us, but they were blessed. Their pride didn't last though. The Babylonians came from the east and overcame Judah. All the elite, wealthy, educated people were taken off to Babylon to work. After seventy years when the original population was dead, the descendants returned and rebuilt Jerusalem and worshipped their one true God in earnest. For some reason, that didn't happen in Samaria. Our people intermarried so that we are no longer pure – there are other gods worshipped here as well. That's why we are despised.'

'The Roman Empire is tolerant of all gods and all peoples,' said Gaius.

'Indeed, and there lies the problem. Our God says He is the one true God and we should worship Him only. Trying to appease all the gods of the Empire is not the correct way and will lead only to destruction.'

Gaius grimaced.

'I still think showing tolerance by accepting all cultures and religions is best.'

'Well, time will tell us who is right.'

The man smiled inquiringly.

'Where are you heading?'

'Damascus, if we ever get there. But first we're going to Neapolis and then hopefully Sebaste.'

'Ah, yes! Come over here with me and I'll show you something.'

They walked up a higher ridge and looked northwest across a broad plain into the distance.

'You see those two noble ridges – they are Mount Ebal and Mount Gerizim. Ebal is the mountain of cursing. It is rocky and barren. Gerizim is the mountain of blessing. It has good grazing right to its summit. There is a narrow valley between the two mountains and there you will find Neapolis. But that is the town's Roman name – we Jews call it the Vale of Shechem. It is where our great Father Abraham built his first altar when he arrived in the Promised Land. You will find a well near there at a village called Sychar, in the eastern end of the valley, built by our forefather Jacob. It is a special place, where our history began. May God go with you and give you peace.'

Having said this, he raised his arm in final greeting and left them.

Gaius said, 'What strange people these Jews are. They obviously don't know about our Roman Triad: Jupiter, Juno and Minerva. Nothing can be greater than their power, not to mention all the others. Where did they get all their ideas?   No wonder poor old Pilate hates having to govern them.'

An hour or two later they stopped at a rocky edge and from this elevated position was one of the most beautiful views Marc had witnessed since being in the country. In the distance to the northwest was the city of Neapolis. Delightful white storied buildings interspersed by occasional towers nestled between two magnificent mountain ranges. The pasture throughout the valley was good. Flowers had reached their maximum depth of colour, and the contrast with the barrenness of the land through which they had just ridden was startling.

Below them was the village of Sychar. They descended and headed towards it. Women were approaching. The first carried a jar on her head steadying it with one hand, holding a child's hand in the other. The second woman carried a very large container on her shoulder. She held it with both hands, one arm crooked over her head, which she leaned to one side to allow for the bulbous shape.

The well, which was the centrepiece of this activity, was barely marked except for a few built up stones around its periphery. Two men sat talking with a third, who was leaning on a staff. Smoke from a small fire rose idly into the air. Water pots stood beside them. As the women got closer the two men who were seated stood up. One of them kicked loose soil on the fire and they ambled away, still deep in conversation. The women compliantly waited until the men had gone. Then they went to work fetching water and filling their jars.

'Move away from the edge child,' said the mother. 'You know the well is very deep; it is dangerous.'

She had clearly given this instruction many times because the child did not even attempt to come close.

'Would you mind if we filled our containers?' asked Marc. 'We have come a long way and we're very thirsty and have nothing to draw water with.'

The woman at the well jumped and flung open her eyes. Then she bowed, pulling her headscarf tighter.

'Yes, of course, please let me help you, sir.'

'I'm sorry if we startled you.'

'Don't apologise to me, sir. You owe me no such courtesy. It's just that for the second time a stranger has asked me to draw water for him and the previous encounter changed my life.'

'I hope for the better?'

'Oh yes, sir. I met the Messiah. He told me so many things about myself. I went immediately back to town to tell the others and they came out to greet him. He stayed with us two days and because of what he said many of us became true believers. Have you met our saviour, sir?'

'Yes,' replied Marc, 'I believe I have. But you know he is dead?'

'I know he has been crucified but he's not dead. Several of our brothers and sisters from the south have told us they have seen him. Many people saw him ascend into heaven, it took place near Bethany not far from Jerusalem, quite recent it was.'

Marc was reminded of the conversation he had with Crassus. Two men had told Justin that they spoke to the risen Christ on the road to Emmaus. He had been so persuaded by their arguments that he planned to leave the troupe and move to Damascus.

'By Jupiter's teeth!' exclaimed Gaius, when the women had gone. 'Let's get to the city, back to some normality.'

So saying, he dug his heels into his horses flank and took off at a gallop down the valley. They passed olive groves where leafy branches overhung the road causing them to duck their heads, and gentle waterfalls where narrow brooks flowed over rocky slopes and orchards, rich with foliage.

As they reached the arched city gates the streets emitted the sounds of daily life gradually being replaced by the nocturnal. People pulling and pushing carts and animals were either leaving or returning for the evening meal. Several different languages could be heard. This was a key trading centre and looked very prosperous. Men and women laughed merrily in their separate groups having completed another successful day, the men mostly selling, the women mostly buying, but not exclusively.

An attractive woman of sophisticated and independent appearance stood in one corner of the square into which Marc and Gaius walked, now leading their mounts. She was packing away her fine purple cloth that had been displayed on a wooden stall with a canopy. A young man was helping her. Without any warning, a small group of men began yelling at one another. There was a scuffle, which before long turned into a brawl. One of the men was weaving about as though drunk. He pushed another hard on each shoulder causing him to reel backwards, falling fully across the stall, which collapsed under his weight. Rolls fell onto the ground and unravelled into dirt and animal dung.

The young man shouted at him and the woman tried in vain to rescue her cloth, but there were too many people around and it was trodden under foot. The canopy collapsed, landing on top of the man and snagging the materials, so they were ripped and torn at all angles.

Marc handed Gaius his reins.

'Hold this a minute. She needs some help.' Gaius grinned.

Marc reached down and hauled the man up, allowing him to straighten his clothing and smooth back his hair.

'Thanks!' he muttered ungraciously and made to move away. Marc put a hand on his shoulder.

'I think you owe the lady an apology and some compensation for the damage.'

'Well, I certainly shall not do either,' he said. 'I'm not paying. It wasn't my fault.'

He looked frantically around for the man who had pushed him, but he had already disappeared down a side alley.

'Regardless,' said Marc, 'you were partly to blame. It takes two to argue.'

The man lifted his arm, made a fist and swung at Marc's face.

'What business is it of yours?'

Marc stayed the blow, grabbed the man's wrist and twisted his arm round his back. He howled in pain, though in fact Marc knew it would be causing him little more than some discomfort.

'I'm making it my business. Now if I were you, I'd find some of those shiny coins you are carrying in that bag.'

The man reluctantly threw down some gold pieces onto the unfolded cloth.

'All right, all right – I apologise.'

Marc allowed him to shake himself free and then he was gone.

'I cannot thank you enough,' said the woman. The young man eyed him with a mixture of suspicion and awe.

'Think nothing of it. Let me give you a hand with this.'

It took some time before the mess was cleared up. Some of the wares were severely damaged and would not be saleable. The woman picked up the drapes and groaned, but with the help of Marc and the young man, they salvaged what they could.

'Thank you so much for your help! My name is Lydia. I came from Thyatira, near Pergamum in Asia, a few months ago to buy and sell materials. Neapolis and Sebaste are good places for trading. I don't think you're local either, are you?'

'No, I'm from Rome, Marc Tiro, at your service, ma'am.'

'Well, I thank you again Marc Tiro,' replied Lydia, with almost a light flirtatiousness in her voice. 'Who is your companion?'

'Allow me to introduce Gaius.'

He came forward smiling and bowed.

'Can we help you get your goods home?' asked Marc.

'I would be grateful for that, but I'm actually staying in Sebaste at the house of a friend. She is away, but this is her son, James.' The men acknowledged each other with a nod.

'That's fine. We are heading in that direction anyway. There's a garrison stationed just outside the city where we plan to stay.'

'Are you soldiers? You certainly don't look them.'

'Let's just say we are connected.'

Lydia had a wagon harnessed to two horses and with all four of them working together it was loaded in no time. She climbed up and took the reins with experience, and led the way through the centre of Neapolis and beyond, following the road towards Sebaste some six miles northwest.

They had been in the saddle for twelve hours, on and off, and although much of the pace had been slow and easy, Marc was concerned for Gaius. The younger man had insisted that he was well and had had plenty of time for rest and gentle exercise in the last few weeks. Nevertheless he was looking tired.

The road continued along the Valley of Shechem and then rose up the western side of the Mount of Ebal. It was rocky and barren, as the man from Shiloh had predicted, yet strangely beautiful. When they climbed a few hundred feet, the valley narrowed and the two mountains were drawn together. They reached a plateau and looked across at a similar plateau on the mount of Gerizim, as lush as their side was barren.

'Just look at that,' commented Gaius. 'It's as though people could shout to one another across the divide.'

James said, 'According to the Jews, their law was once read here by the priests standing on either side, so the people could hear in the valley below.'

'This place must have been used as a lookout as well,' said

Gaius. 'The town is very vulnerable to attack being so low in the valley.'

Lydia said, 'That is why Sebaste, or Samaria, as it was called before Herod renamed it in honour of Augustus, became the seat of government. It's on a flat-topped hill in the middle of a plain and can be more easily defended. It has withstood at least two sieges from Syria. There look, you can see the city from this ridge.'

Marc looked across to the undulating edifices built by Herod atop the hill of Samaria. Outlined against the sky, a double colonnade of Corinthian columns stretched the length of the city and followed the downward slope of the hill, sweeping round in a wide curve. The columns adorned temples, basilicas, a forum and hippodrome. Most extraordinary of all was the natural formation of a theatre where the topology of the hill dropped and curved into tiers. No doubt Crassus and his troupe were performing there.

Part way up the north-eastern slope was the Roman encampment. Marc gave notice of their arrival. Pilate had ensured they were expected. They left the mule, horses and all their belongings with instructions as to how each should be dealt with concerning health and safety; then they continued with James and Lydia. The sun was low in the sky as they entered the gates of Sebaste and rode to the western side of town to James' house, a multi-levelled building set in the hillside. Marc and Gaius were invited to sit on the rooftop and enjoy a jug of wine.

'Please stay and eat with us,' pleaded Lydia.

They heartily concurred and she went off to see what preparations were being made. James had lost his suspiciousness and was a perfect host. The floor was covered with highly patterned mats; exotic plants climbed into stony crevices concealing detritus and reached the overhanging ridge tiles, while highly coloured summer flowers hung from balustrades, exuding their heavy perfumes. A light breeze rested on their faces and the fading rays detailed the awe-inspiring vista from this elevated position. Gaius closed his eyes. From below was the sound of cicada in the long grasses, combined with desultory voices engaged in discussion about choice of food accompaniments. Very soon he was asleep.

An hour or two later, Marc walked alone back into the city. Gaius slept so soundly, it was impossible to wake him and James insisted he stayed the night. The same courtesy was extended to Marc but he felt he should return to the encampment, so he made his apologies. He reached a square filled with people watching a spectacle. A sorcerer was standing on a platform in the centre performing tricks. He ate fire, turned sticks into snakes and back again, and made two doves disappear. The crowd was entranced. Marc stood towards the back of the gathering.

'What's his name?' he asked the man standing next to him.

'Simon! He's a sorcerer and a very good one – he always attracts a large number of spectators.'

Simon lifted a burning torch into the air. The fire lit up the row of people at the back and glowed onto the faces. Marc started. He recognized the man from Sebaste who had fallen into Lydia's stall. He stood there passively absorbed by Simon's antics.

Marc moved further away into the shadows and was suddenly aware that he was not alone. Three men had approached him from behind, two moving to each of his sides. He felt a stinging blow to the back of his neck and immediately felt dizzy. He fell forward and was grabbed under each arm. The irregular cobbles swayed beneath his feet as he was dragged into a side alley.

32

-The Brothel-

Bright light was pouring in from the left. As Marc gradually focused, he could see a man above him lying in a bed. A soft smooth sheet covered him to the waist, but his arms and torso were exposed. There was a white band round his head and forehead, but he thought he could see wisps of dark hair poking out from around the edge.

A woman sat beside the bed with a bowl filled with water and a cloth. She dipped the cloth into the bowl, squeezed it out and wiped the man's face and chest. She was scantily dressed; her bosom rested on the edge of the bed, pushed upward, displaying a deep cleavage. Splashes of water dropped on her breasts as she lifted the cloth out of the bowl and ran down the cleft, forming a glistening pool.

Marc watched fascinated as the man moved his leg. The woman looked up and smiled.

'Ah! Did I see some sign of movement? Hey, Tone, he's coming round. Get in here.'

Her raucous voice brought Marc out of his reverie and he opened his eyes wide. He tried to push himself up on his elbows. The man above did the same. A sharp pain penetrated his brain and quickened down his spine. Marc slumped back and so did the man above. Enlightenment dawned.

'There, there, don't you go trying to move too much,' said the woman. 'You've had a nasty blow.'

Marc still could not remember what had happened, but he did have a memory of yesterday afternoon.

'Lydia?' he inquired.

'No, dear, I'm Prissi. Although we have got a Lydia, if you would like one.'

A man entered the door in the corner of the room and stood at the opposite side of the bed. Marc turned his head. He was shocked to see the man from Sebaste. His memory returned with a rush. Despite the pain, he lifted himself up hardly knowing what he was doing or saying.

'You can't keep me here against my will.'

'No! Of course not, my dear fellow! But please, don't worry yourself. You are not here against your will. I just happened to be present last night when some ruffians set upon you. I brought you here to recuperate. How are you feeling?'

'Why would you do that for me?'

'It was the least I could do after my atrocious behaviour yesterday. I was so angry with those other chaps that I'm afraid I took it out on you, quite unjustifiably. You can imagine my surprise though, when I saw it was you left in that alley.'

Not nearly as surprised as I am, thought Marc.

'Where is this place?'

'The best brothel in town,' said Prissi with pride in her voice. 'See those reflections above you, many pay a lot extra for that.'

Marc looked up again at himself and moved his leg feeling the coolness run across his skin. He began to feel more human and his faculties had fully returned. He turned his head and looked round the room. It was full of gadgets for sexual pleasure – mostly made of leather – but some of a spiky nature that were clearly intended for pain.

'I would like my clothes, please. Thank you for your administrations, but I really must be on my way.'

'Your clothes are just here,' said the man. 'But it is still early, and I would welcome your company at breakfast. Prissi, would you arrange something for us on the terrace?'

She moved reluctantly, having been looking forward to helping her patient into his clothes. However, she sighed and left, taking the bowl of water with her.

Marc slid his legs over the edge of the bed and placed his feet on the comfortable rug on the floor. He gingerly applied his full weight to them as he stood up. He could not resist one final glance upwards. He noticed with a degree of satisfaction how the layer of subcutaneous fat that he had brought with him from Rome had slipped away – as imperceptibly as it had come. The man handed him his clothes one at a time.

'I'm sorry if this has come as a bit of a shock, but I really couldn't just leave you there. I know what it feels like to lose your belongings. A thief stole all I had a few months ago – it distressed me greatly. I'm afraid those lads took everything you had.'

Marc smiled.

'No, they will have been disappointed. I was carrying nothing with me.'

'What good fortune! It could have been much worse.'

Marc thought what an amiable fellow this was. Not at all like the angry person who tried to land a blow to his chin the day before. He was almost childlike in his delight that Marc was feeling better and had lost nothing.

A short time later they sat on a charming terrace. Three girls, like Prissi, scantily clad, stood up as they arrived. The girls giggled and the man shooed them away like small children interrupting adult conversation.

'How long have you lived here?' Marc asked.

'Just for a few months, but they have been the happiest in my life.'

'Yes, I can imagine.'

'I was very unhappy in my previous life. My marriage had failed. Oh, it was my fault not that of my wife. I'm afraid to admit that I have....needs of a sexual nature that most women abhor or at least have no desire to satisfy. Since being here I realize I am not alone, and so am no longer ashamed as I once was. I lived in guilt and was deeply miserable as a result. My mother understood me though, strangely.'

'That at least must have been some comfort.'

'One day, when I was about thirteen, I found an odd looking whip. She openly told me what she used it for and confessed that when she was young she had been a prostitute. She was very successful apparently – made lots of money - ended up marrying the tanner who provided her with her leather gadgets and such like. They lived happily ever after. She understood my problems and supported me, but my wife did not have the same appreciation and I don't blame her for that. I am sure she is well rid of me.'

Marc had been listening to this confession with growing interest, trying to retain impassivity.

'There you are my darling Tone.'

Prissi arrived with plates of ham and eggs, bread and a jug filled with a sweet smelling beverage.

'How did you come to be living here?' It seemed a casual inquiry.

'I had intended to go off and live with a prostitute I knew before, but when I lost my money I lost her. I was going to Damascus but stopped off here one night. I had visited this place before as a customer so I was well known amongst the girls. Prissi said the manager had recently died. He had looked after them for several years. They need a man around. Yesterday is a case in point. Two of those rogues had left without paying and I followed them to Neapolis. That's what we were arguing about. Anyway, when she learned that I was planning to go to Damascus to seek my fortune, she invited me to stay here. It was the best decision I ever made.'

He gave a deep smile of contentment.

Marc took a large bite into the bread and munched with

evidential satisfaction not wishing to appear too eager to ask questions.

'What did you do before?'

At this the man called Tone became wary. Perhaps he realized he had said too much. Marc waited.

'Oh, I did a bit of this and that! I liked drawing best. But that's enough of me prattling on, what about you? Where are you from?'

'Rome.'

'And what is it you do?'

'A long time ago I did a bit of soldiering.'

'You certainly don't look like one now.'

'You're the second person to say that to me in two days,' said Marc affably. 'I'm more retired than working. I get the odd job to do.'

'Well I'd rather be here. You'd be very welcome to stay any time you know. Prissi has taken quite a shine to you, but we have a selection of younger wenches who will happily do anything you ask of them and more.'

'I might take you up on that offer. Thank you for your hospitality and for helping me to recover, but now I must take my leave, although I suspect I shall be back.'

Tone beamed. He had interpreted this statement according to his own values and had not guessed its true meaning. Marc knew that he must interrogate this man, but not alone. He needed a witness, at least, and help in case there was trouble. Anthony had possibly committed bigger crimes than adultery and Marc intended to find out exactly what.

He walked quickly back to the garrison. He was surprised how freely and openly the man had spoken to him about his lifestyle, yet he had given away no factual details such as his name, or where he had lived, or his previous occupation. Marc doubted the women at the brothel even knew that – they just called him Tone. The man could not possibly have suspected that such general conversational comments, which almost amounted to sales talk for a brothel, could have been linked together by a complete stranger to give vital clues as to his identity.

Marc went to the tent of the garrison commander and asked for support from one of his officers – since the outcome of his return to the brothel would almost certainly be an arrest. Three soldiers returned with him. Marc banged on the door. Prissi opened it. Delight lit up her face.

'Oh, how wonderful, you've come back and brought some handsome friends. Do come in.'

'We are here on official business, Prissi. Please stand aside, we must speak to Tone.'

The woman furrowed her brow.

'He's still on the terrace,' she said with concern in her voice, 'where you left him.'

Marc strode through to the back of the house where Tone was relaxing, enjoying the warmth of the sun on his face and legs. He sat bolt upright in astonishment as the men marched in.

'We are arresting you on suspicion of conspiracy to steal valuable jewellery,' said Marc addressing him. 'We have reason to believe that your name is Anthony Avitus, formerly of Jerusalem. Please come with us.'

The man looked terrified and started to protest. His anger rose and once again he tried to throw a punch at Marc, who stood deftly to one side whilst the soldier caught Tone's arms and tied them with rope. Prissi looked on with horror.

'I'm sorry,' said Marc to her, 'but I'm afraid we have authority to search your premises. Tell your girls to get dressed and come out on the terrace. We may need to speak to them.'

She was too frightened to argue. Two of the soldiers half pushing, half pulling Tone, took him back to the garrison.

'Show us the room where Tone sleeps,' ordered Marc.

Prissi took them through to a large room with shutters covering one wall, facing west. They were closed and Marc opened them to let in more light. He knew that Barnabas had stolen Anthony's papers, but there might be something else to connect him with his former life.

There was little in the cupboards, except a few clothes and the bag that Marc had seen him with yesterday, for collecting coins. Then he opened a small drawer. Inside was a piece of carefully folded linen. Marc opened it to reveal a dagger. It was identical to the one he had confiscated from Silas' room.

33

When Marc got back to the camp, Gaius was waiting for him.

'What's been going on? Trust me to miss all the excitement.'

'How are you feeling?'

'Much better, thanks! Obviously the long ride yesterday was a bit too much, but I'm fine now, after a good sleep. Lydia and James were very hospitable. Tell me what's been happening. I hear you've arrested someone whom you think might be Anthony Avitus. They've put him in a separate room waiting for your interrogation. It's caused quite a stir.'

'Come with me. I shall need a witness.'

Anthony, if indeed that was who he was, sat on a wooden chair in a cell that had been carved out of the hillside. There was anger and fear on his face.

'Are you Anthony Avitus? I should warn you, that if you are that person, you would be advised to confess it. Otherwise, we shall have to keep you here until someone who can identify you is brought from Jerusalem.'

'Yes, I am Anthony Avitus.'

'Were you previously a surveyor with the firm of Victor's in Jerusalem?'

'Yes, I was.'

'Tell us about the extent of your involvement with the planned burglary of jewellery from Herodium.'

'I wasn't involved.'

'Mr. Avitus, a body was found in a watercourse wearing your belt and identity seal. Both were identified by your relative, Rebecca

Victor.'

Avitus looked crestfallen. The style of living he had been enjoying – the best of his life – was crumbling in these few moments as a result of some careless talk. Yet he had given nothing of any great import away.

'How did you know?' he whispered.

'Just answer the question.'

Avitus sighed.

'Several months ago two men came to my house. I never saw their faces and they didn't give me their names. They just said that they were from the Essene community. They told me how, years ago, some valuable jewellery had been given to their forefathers to help with the struggle against Roman occupation; how they had been betrayed by one of their leaders, a man called John Hyrcanus, a Hasmonean, who kept the jewels for himself and had eventually passed them on to his granddaughter, Mariamne, who had married Herod. After both Herod and Mariamne died, the jewels remained in the vaults at Herodium.

'They said nobody wanted them, or even knew they were there, but the Essenes laid claim to them as the descendants of the Hasmoneans. The Essenes were planning one day to recapture Jerusalem, they said. I just saw that as a dream; it wouldn't be possible to oust the Romans. But their plan interested me because they offered to give me one of the baubles in exchange for doing very little, other than providing them with plans and showing them where to block the water flow, so that a cistern next to the vault would empty and allow them access to the wall. They intended to remove some of the stone blocks, get through to steal the jewels, replace the wall, then unblock the waterway and let the cistern refill.'

Avitus paused for reflection. Marc remained silent allowing him to collect his thoughts. He continued.

'My main contact was a man called Silas who was in charge of the Herodian household. He came with me to look at the underground channels to decide which ones should be blocked. He organised some slaves to do the work of blocking up the tunnel with concrete. After that, it was just a matter of waiting for the water in the cistern to be used up. That particular cistern fed the fountains in the northern gardens, so I knew it wouldn't take too long, although it was not possible to calculate exactly.'

Again he hesitated. Marc asked,

'Tell me about the body we found.'

Avitus answered quickly.

'I didn't kill him. I swear I didn't kill him. I told you how it was with my wife and me. I was desperate to get away. I had been having an affair with a prostitute, from Jericho, and I thought my reward for my contribution to the plan would be enough to set me up for the rest of my life. I could escape and still leave my wife with the house and gold so she could be cared for. I didn't wish her any malice – I just wanted to be out of the relationship.'

Marc noticed to his surprise that tears had formed in Anthony's eyes.

'Go on.'

'Well, one day I went to check how low the water had got. It was practically empty. There was a deep drop from the tunnel into the bottom of the cistern. On the edge of the tunnel was a body – I assumed it was one of the slaves. The back of his skull had caved in. I thought he might have fallen and someone had brought him back up. The edge did get very slippery.'

Marc noticed Gaius shudder. He still had vivid memories of how nearly he had met with the same fate.

'Rats were already showing interest in the corpse and his face was partly decomposed where it had been lying in the water. I saw this as my big chance. I put my belt on him with a distinctive buckle and put my ring on his finger. He was about the same size as me and I thought that my family would think I was dead. That would probably cause them less pain than knowing what had really happened.'

'Carry on.'

'Well, that's all I have to say really. I was paid. I was given a lapis lazuli bracelet and told that I would be able to sell it easily in Damascus. It would be enough for me to support myself for many years.'

'Who paid you?'

'Silas did. He had one or two pieces as his reward. He kept them in a carved ivory box with a lock on it. I saw it when he invited me to his room, the day he paid me off. He knew I was intending to leave Jerusalem, but he warned me never to speak of my involvement or the bracelet. But there was one person I had told of my intentions. That was my mother. She knew I was desperately unhappy. I didn't tell her everything, just that a man called Silas was paying me well to block the water at Herodium. I didn't tell her about planning my own death though. That bit of the tale came about by pure chance. I thought it best not to tell anyone. I wasn't even sure if they would find the slave's body. I just hoped someone would and mistake him for me. I always intended to write to her though when things had settled down.'

'The bracelet was stolen. Am I right?'

Avitus looked up in astonishment.

'Are you also some kind of sorcerer? How could you possibly know that? I told no one.'

'What did you do when you realized your fortune had gone?'

'I went back to the house and took my gold. I tried to make it look like a burglary. I had some regrets because I intended my wife should have it.'

This concurred with what Marc had been told by Sarah – that there had been a burglary not long after Avitus had left them.

'Did you place a pouch on the body containing a map of Qumran?'

'No I didn't. I've never seen a map of Qumran, although the two Essenes did tell me that was where they lived most of the time. But there was no pouch on the body; I would have noticed it.'

Marc unfolded the linen containing the small dagger.

'Tell me about this.'

Anthony looked at it and frowned.

'It was a present from my mother. She had two made — they were identical — she said it would always be a bond between us — she was rather sentimental like that.'

'How long have you had it?'

'About twelve years! I brought it with me for old time's sake. When a man is leaving his whole life behind, he must have a few things to jog his memory — to remember the happier times.'

'That will do for now. You will be kept here at the garrison until we can confirm your testimony.'

Anthony moaned. He had no choice but to accept his fate.

Marc did not tell him that he already knew or had guessed most of the confession. There was still the mystery of who had placed the pouch on the body. He felt convinced that it had been done deliberately to mislead him, but he needed more information and had no idea where he was likely to find it. A dispatch was sent immediately to Tribune Polybius in Jerusalem for the arrest of Sabina, the mourning mother. It was her dagger they found in Silas' chamber and therefore she must be questioned.

'How very tragic,' said Gaius. 'A mother thinks her son has been murdered, or at very least left for dead by the man whom he has seen as a means to his salvation. And in fact he is not dead at all.'

'Yes, I agree,' said Marc. 'Nevertheless, murder is murder, even though she might have done some people a favour by getting rid of Silas. Let's go and check on our horses and belongings. It's probably as well that we have been forced into staying at least another day, until we hear from Jerusalem. You could do with the rest and it's certainly not an unpleasant place.'

They checked their bags, which had been locked away safely. The last thing Marc needed now was for the jewels to be stolen before he had a chance to find out the mystery behind their true value.

Later that day, they strolled towards the theatre. Crassus was there, busy making preparations for the evening performance of 'Antigone' – a follow-up play by Sophocles about Oedipus' daughter by his mother Jocasta. He greeted his visitors with obvious pleasure.

'I didn't know you would be coming up this way so soon, sir.'

'Well, nothing was decided when I saw you last, although I had it in mind that should you still be here, I would come and see another of your splendid plays.'

'Please come tonight. Justin is playing the leading role for the final time and is very good. He has surpassed himself in talent – he becomes the character. You can be my guests of honour.'

'I promise we'll be here.'

As they left, Marc asked Gaius if he thought they should invite Lydia and James by way of thanks.

'That's an excellent idea! Let's walk over that way.'

'I know there are no markets today so they should be still at home.'

Lydia and James accepted the invitation gladly, and in the twilight that evening, all four sat in prime seats in the wonderful amphitheatre formed from the natural contours of the land.

Oedipus, having unwittingly married his mother, Jocasta, whose youth had been retained by wearing a special necklace, had several sons and daughters, who were also his sisters and brothers; one of them was Antigone. When Oedipus had learned of his sin, he put out both his eyes, went into exile and left two sons in charge. There was a battle for power between them and Jocasta's brother, Creon. When Creon became King, he ordered that the body of Antigone's dead brother should not be buried but left out for the dogs. She defied the order and was imprisoned by her uncle in a cave and left to starve.

Tiresias, a blind prophet, then enters to tell Creon he was wrong in sentencing Antigone to death and that if he does not listen to reason, he is doomed as Oedipus was. He runs to the cave in which he has imprisoned her, only to find that she has hung herself.

Creon's own son, who is in love with Antigone, commits suicide. Eurydice, Creon's wife, also takes her life when she hears of her son's death.

'Well acted, but a depressing story,' said James. Marc too felt uneasy, though could not quite identify why. He had read this story with his grandmother many times.

'Come and meet the cast,' said Crassus, eager to please.

'Well done, Justin,' said Marc. 'You played the part magnificently.'

'Thank you, sir,' he replied. 'I am glad we have met again. I want to offer you my sincerest apology.'

'I don't understand. You have no need to apologise to me.'

'Nevertheless, sir, I offer it.'

'That was a strange thing to say,' said Gaius, as they walked back. 'What do suppose he meant by apologising?'

'He must have been dissatisfied with his performance. I thought it was excellent. They must set themselves very high standards.'

'Yes, that must be it.'

Yet Marc had the feeling that was not what Justin meant. Maybe time would tell.

Sleep eluded him that night. The uneasiness would not leave him. He thought back over the conversation he had had with Rebecca when he returned from Jericho. He had advised that for the moment, it might be better not to tell Deborah and Sabina about their suspicions that Anthony may still be alive, although he had left it to her discretion. He realized that he had been a coward, not wishing to confront the women again, particularly when he was not absolutely certain about whether he would ever find Anthony, or if he would ever return voluntarily. He thought of Deborah's outburst of grief and Sabina's denial. Presumably Rebecca never told the women about the documents stolen by Barnabas from a man in Jericho.

The following day the despatch rider returned with a formal letter from Tribune Polybius. Sabina had been found dead, poisoned. A suicide note indicated that she could no longer suffer the grief of the loss of her son, or the shame of the murder of Silas, the man she blamed. When Anthony was told, his wails could be heard throughout the camp. He accused himself. He had intended to write and let his mother know he was alive. A few hours later, he was found hanging from his own belt in his cell.

34

The day they left Sebaste the weather reflected Marc's mood. The clouds hung misty, low and grey over the city. They were so close that it seemed they could be touched by an outstretched arm. Arrangements had been made to take Anthony's body back to Jerusalem. Rebecca had already been told. Marc dared not imagine how she must feel. He despatched a letter to her, expressing his sorrow of the circumstances of the deaths. He did not feel without guilt. Gaius could not understand his reasoning and perhaps a few short months ago Marc would not have understood it either.

They descended into the valley and picked up the road northward. Marc had inquired of the garrison tribune in charge of administration if records of soldiers from Capernaum three decades ago might still be kept. He acknowledged that even in outposts like Judea, there most probably would be lists of enrolled soldiers going back to that period, particularly at a large military station like Capernaum.

After riding steadily for between fifteen and twenty miles, they reached a town that seemed to be a main junction. It was luxuriant with fruits of different kinds and colours, irrigated by a huge waterfall coming from the hills beyond. In front of them stretched the Plain of Esdraelon. Now they had reached the northern boundary of Samaria and were entering Galilee. The whole area was flat and very fertile; riding was easy; they encouraged their horses into a comfortable canter and headed straight for the town of Nain. It was little more than a village but the two men stopped for water in the square. A young man stood in the middle of a group apparently the centre of attention.

'Well, you couldn't have been properly dead,' said one man sceptically.

'I tell you I was. You ask my mother. They were about to bury me. My mother was crying. Then he touched my coffin and told me to get up and I did, and started talking.'

'Yes, as usual,' said someone in the group, and they all laughed.

'Jacob, you saw it, didn't you?'

'I believe you,' said another gently. 'I was there. Let these old cynics have their day. We shall have ours, just you see. You can do nothing to convince those who insist on hardening their hearts.'

'Is that talk of another miracle, do you suppose?' asked Gaius, not expecting an answer. 'How much further is it to Tiberias?'

'Fifteen miles or so – shouldn't take too long if we keep up this steady pace.'

The Sea of Galilee, or Chinnereth, as it was known, was hidden from view until they reached the top of the hills on its western shore. The mountains on the east side were much higher, more like those that enclosed the Dead Sea.

Gaius said, 'Look how incredibly clear and blue it is. It looks quite calm; I thought this lake was known for its storms.'

'Apparently squalls come up suddenly. No one can be sure when they're going to happen, but I'm told they are quite violent.'

A steep descent led to the city of Tiberias stretched out below, now the capital of Galilee. From this height the gilded palace roof shone like a fallen sun. The forums, theatres and gladiatorial amphitheatres typical of the Greek and Roman mishmash were protected by defensive fortifications. When they reached the city gates, two soldiers barred their entry and asked to see their documents. One of them saluted.

'We are to escort you to the palace of Herod Antipas immediately. Please follow us, sir.'

They looked up at giant colonnades and spectacular temples

dedicated to every imaginable god. Herod and his wife Herodias exhibited delight, either genuine or feigned, as Gaius and Marc entered the great hall. Food and wine had been ordered. There was no question of them not staying the night and enjoying for a few hours the hedonistic lifestyle of the King and his consort.

'Herod Philip, my brother, wants to speak to you. He seems to think he may be able to help you with your investigation into the missing jewels. He lived at Herodium when he was growing up. As you probably know, the lands of our father were sectioned into three after his death. Archelaus had the best bits, Judea and Samaria.'

Herod pulled down the sides of his mouth exposing the inside of his lower lip. He raised his eyebrows and widened his eyes in disgust.

'The stupid idiot threw it all away – he couldn't rule a herd of goats. I was given Galilee and Perea but I'd have made a much better job of Judea. Still, my position was preferable to that of my brother Philip. He rules the northern territories and lives in Caesarea Philippi. We don't see him often – keeps himself to himself, particularly since I married my darling Herodias.'

He turned to his wife, rubbing his palm across her knee. She managed a smile, her boredom obvious and interest in Gaius evident. Herod seemed either not to notice or to ignore it. She was a dangerous woman. Marc remembered the story Nicodemus had told him of how she made her daughter ask for the head of John the Baptist, because he had poured scorn on the sinful nature of her matrimonial relationship. He did not like her but to behave as such would be suicide. Marc was well accustomed to being charming to those for whom he had no respect – the Roman senate had been his training ground. In those days it had been an essential part of the game. He bowed low as they retired after an evening of listening to Herod's tales of success.

They left early next morning before the household had time to stir and followed the shore road to Capernaum. As they rode northwards, the hills sloped less steeply towards the edge of the lake and eventually receded, leaving a populated area of great beauty and colour. Fishermen stood naked from the waist in their boats a hundred yards or so out into the lake, casting their nets from the sides and dragging them in, sorting fish, selecting the best and rejecting the worst.

Others rowed nearer to the shore, jumped out and, wading with determination, hauled in the boats, transferring their catches into large wooden baskets that were loaded onto the back of carts and taken off to the nearby villages. Nets were washed, mended and dried in a hive of economic activity. The Sea of Galilee was some thirteen miles long and seven miles wide – waves lapped onto the shore and the sails of boats that had ventured further out bobbed about at the mercy of the gusty winds. It was a picturesque and purposeful scene as they approached Capernaum.

The town lacked the grandeur of Tiberias yet had a spirit of its own. Jewish synagogues reflected Roman style building but there was little evidence of temples to other gods. Gentle green hills rose behind giving a feeling of peace but there was no doubt this was a thriving commercial centre, with a strong military presence. The Roman army was settled on the eastern side of the town. They were expected, greeted and treated to refreshments by the centurion in charge of headquarters' staff and training. He was no longer young and walked awkwardly as he led Marc to the payment office, leaving Gaius, who was engaged in an amusing conversation with one of the standard-bearers.

'I understand you are interested in a soldier by the name of Dimitri who may have served with the legion in the time of King Herod. I have looked at the records going back to that time. We had two legionaries who went by the name of Dimitri. They were both local recruits, granted Roman citizenship on enrolment. One has long since retired, living quite comfortably on his discharge payments, but the other was a volunteer. He went missing. It does happen, although I knew him and was surprised to learn that he had absconded. It was at the time Archelaus was persecuting the Jews – killed thousands he did. He saw them as a threat rather than people to be cajoled. I know Dimitri was deeply upset because he was called to put some of the pilgrims to death. He was a man who never minded the outcome of a fair fight, but murder was not his way.'

'Did you look for him at the time?' asked Marc.

'Oh, yes, of course! Never found him though. He probably got to the coast and took off in some small boat. Could be anywhere by now – may even be dead. It was strange though that he never returned to his family. He had close ties in Capernaum.'

'Do you know if he might ever have been sent to Herodium on guard duty?'

'It's possible, but there would be no record of that in particular. A soldier can be posted anywhere within the region for a short while. May I ask why you are so interested in him after all this time?'

'We have reason to believe he may have been wrongly imprisoned. There was certainly a man called Dimitri kept in one of the dungeons at Herodium for many years. If we could find him, he may be able to help us with an investigation into the theft of some valuable property from the vaults.'

'I knew Dimitri. He would never steal. He was very honest. But wrongly imprisoned …… that's a possibility I never thought of. Why would anyone do such a thing?'

'It's possible he saw the culprits and had to be got rid of. We know he was alive a few years ago, when he was released, but there is no way of knowing what condition he was in. Do you know where I might find his family?'

The centurion hesitated.

'What will you do if you find him?'

'Nothing, other than ask him if he can help us. Whatever he did or did not do, he has been punished enough. And if he is innocent, then may God help the perpetrators of such a crime.'

Marc suddenly realized what he had said. Not may the gods help, but may God help. He wondered if the centurion had picked up on his slip. Several moments passed.

'Are you a believer?' he asked.

Marc was greatly taken aback.

'What do you mean?'

'I mean are you a believer in the Lord Jesus Christ?'

'You mean the prophet Jesus?'

'Yes!'

'I saw him crucified, if that's what you mean, and I have heard tell of miracles.'

'He performed a miracle on my servant, a most valued member of my household, who was sick and about to die. I am a Jew you understand. I heard he was in Capernaum. He stayed here a lot of the time. Many of the local men became his disciples and travelled around with him listening to his preaching. All he had to do was say the word and my servant was healed instantly. Many people now believe he was the Messiah and the Son of God. I just wondered if you were also a believer.'

'I cannot be sure. I know that the man has influenced my thinking in some strange sort of way and I do believe that the miracles happened. I saw him being arrested, flogged and taunted. He said nothing in his defence – it was as though he knew what was going to happen and he allowed it.'

'Yes, he would certainly do that. He had a charisma like no other man. Yet he was full of humility.'

'I have also heard that he rose from the dead. I know people who are convinced of it. I met a woman at a well in Samaria. She told me how he changed her life and she had no doubt that he had risen.'

'And do you believe it?'

'To tell you the truth, I would like to, but I have a whole history of different cultural values to contend with.'

'You seem to be an honest and trustworthy man, Marc Tiro.'
The centurion hesitated, as though considering what to say next. He sighed deeply. Several more moments passed in silence. Then he spoke.

'I shall let you into my confidence. I'm afraid I have been less than honest with you. I do know what happened to Dimitri. Forgive me for lying to you but I have to be careful to protect his family. If you like, I will take you to meet Dimitri's wife. If she will not tell you what happened, then I will.'

Marc was confused and full of curiosity. So Dimitri had returned, but when and in what condition? Was he still alive? They walked through the cobbled streets and beyond the gates to the shore where stood a few wretched mud huts in a small hamlet. The centurion pointed to where an old woman sat by a ragged curtain that was the entrance to her home.

'That's Miriam – Dimitri's wife.'

Her clothes were mended and patched, her hair drawn severely back, her face was brown and deeply lined, yet there was a quiet dignity about her. She raised her eyes and lifted her arm with difficulty as she saw them approaching. The knuckles of her hands were swollen and disjointed; a wan smile crossed her lips.

'How are you Miriam?' asked the centurion kindly.

'Still full of pain, yet my spirit is good, thank you my friend. How are you?'

'I am well, Miriam. I have brought a visitor to meet you. He knows that Dimitri was falsely imprisoned. He would like to speak to him to find out what happened. He means us no harm.'

'You will not find Dimitri – he is safe.'

'Where is he?' asked Marc softly.

'He has gone to join followers of Our Lord.'

'Can you tell me what happened to him? Did he return to you after they let him go free?'

Miriam looked at the centurion who returned her gaze with a smile and an encouraging nod.

'When he was released he was covered in a disease. He was blind and his tongue had been split so he could no longer speak. They sent word to us to fetch him. My son and nephew went to find him in Jerusalem and brought him back to me, but he was not allowed to stay – the people here were afraid of his disfigured body and he was sent away to beg.

'Then one day he met Jesus who laid hands on him and he was completely healed. The scales fell from his eyes and his body and his tongue became whole. I wanted him to stay but he would not. He said that as long as he stayed, I would be in danger from those about whom he knew too much. They still live and have power to hurt us. He would tell me nothing about what happened to him. I know nothing of use to you. All I know is that Dimitri has joined the followers of Christ and has moved to Damascus where many of them have gone.'

Tears filled her eyes and she sobbed quietly for a moment or two. The centurion put his arm on her shoulder and waited. The sorrow passed and she recovered herself, dabbing beneath her eyes with her apron.

'Promise me you won't hurt him if you find him,' she said, looking directly at Marc.

'I promise.'

35

Marc returned to the garrison reluctant to reveal to anyone else what he had just heard. Gaius was still enjoying the company of his new friends.

'Did you find him?' he asked jovially.

'No! We need to head for Damascus, but we'll stop at Caesarea Philippi first.'

Gaius reluctantly roused himself. He still felt unfit and stretched as he stood up.

'It's beautiful up there,' commented the standard-bearer. 'It's where the source of the Jordan lies and the city itself is new and luxurious. You'll make it by evening if you keep going.'

Gaius tweaked his mouth sideways, nearly closing his eye and made a disapproving noise with his lips.

'That's what I was afraid of,' he said. 'Thanks for your hospitality. Maybe we'll see you on the way back.'

The land was hilly as they moved northwards away from the Sea of Galilee. Green and pleasant valleys abounded. The whole region enjoyed prosperity and was well populated with villages every two miles or so. They reached an old stone bridge where the main road continued on eastwards to Damascus, but another continued north towards Lake Huleh – much smaller than the Sea of Galilee, less than a third of its length and half its breadth at its widest point. Tall grasses and reeds grew profusely in its waters.

From its northern shore the land opened up into a swampy plateau from which Mount Hermon, some seven or eight thousand feet in height, could be seen in the distance. Brilliant white tops were clearly defined against a deep blue sky, contrasting the coldness of the summit with the unbearable heat they were now enduring in the afternoon sun. Gaius stopped, wiped his brow and took a swig of water.

They rode towards the southern side of the mountain until they reached a gorge, at the end of which was a massive sheer face of rock. At the base, the mouth of a large wide cave gushed out water in torrents; here was the source of the River Jordan, a thousand energetic chattering springs found their way through deep dark recesses from the top to the bottom of Mount Hermon and converged together, making a deafening roar. Marc admired its grandeur. To the left of the cave, sited on a plateau above it, stood an impressive white temple, dedicated to the Greek god Pan. Worshippers could be seen moving up and down the steps that stretched the full width of the portico, supported by four large Corinthian pillars.

Gaius, who was at the point of feeling faint, climbed down to a place where a natural circle of rocks formed a protective pool, and he slipped into the cooling clear water with relief. Marc looked down into the darkness of the water that reflected in detail the rocks and shrubbery on the other side of the gorge, creating an upside down world where the sky emerged from the depths.

Refreshed and anxious to complete the journey they emerged into a place of great trees and undulating grassy banks where small streams and waterfalls separated the land. There before them lay the fortified city of Caesarea Philippi. In all its splendour, it could not compete with the magnificence of the rock formations that nature itself had created.

Once again they rode through triumphal arches into the city where Greek and Roman influence was much in evidence. The palace was even more grandiose than that in Tiberias, with no expense spared to dignify the deity of the Emperor.

They were shown into a room with marble floors and a balcony overlooking the city. Lights emanated from the square white homes of the populace, set against black, purple and orange brush strokes caused by the sun falling below the horizon. Gaius leaned on the balustrade with relief.

'I'm really tired,' he admitted. 'I hope our audience with King Philip can wait until tomorrow.'

'I think that is most probably what will happen. If he had been keen to welcome us tonight, I think we would have heard by now.'

There was a knock at the door and two slaves dressed in white tunics appeared. They bowed simultaneously.

'Your baths are waiting, sirs. We are here to serve you.'

The bath was an oval pool with steps leading downwards from the edge. Constant underfloor heating maintained a relaxing temperature. Delightful oils were available and warm towels. A scrub was followed by a massage for both of them, lying face down side by side on two couches. Fresh clothing was provided and when they returned to their room, a table was covered in comestibles of every kind, together with the finest wine. Of the king, however, there was no sign.

'Life won't seem the same back in my small house in Caesarea,' commented Gaius. 'I'm getting too used to this.'

'I think there'll be something we're expected to do. Rarely is anything for free.'

'Oh!' replied Gaius, 'I hadn't thought of that. Still at least we get to sleep first.'

Early next morning the slaves arrived to help them dress and provide morning refreshments. They were informed that the king wished to see Commander Tiro alone in his quarters as soon as they were ready. Gaius was to be shown round the libraries within the palace.

Shortly afterwards Marc entered the king's presence. Philip was taller than his half brother, Herod Antipas. His face lacked the flabbiness and his bearing was altogether more upright and steadfast. On first impressions Marc liked him. He had no female consort, only his two black bodyguards stood at the door, giants of men with biceps so large their arms could barely meet across their chests.

'Welcome,' he said. 'Forgive the informality of our meeting. I find the great hall not conducive to speaking frankly.'

'Whatever you wish, sir,' said Marc.

'I have heard about your exploits Commander. I know that you are here to investigate the missing jewels that once belonged to my father Herod and stepmother Mariamne. I understand that you have come to the conclusion that they were stolen recently by Essenes, seeking revenge on a dynasty that had no right to their ownership.'

'That is correct, sir.'

Philip smiled.

'And we both know that is a lie, do we not?'

Marc felt a small surge of alarm pass through his chest as the adrenalin rose in his body. However, he remained outwardly calm.

'I see you are invested with a perception not attributed to many, sir.'

Philip looked at him directly. He took a few moments to decide whether or not the comment was made by a sycophant or whether it was a genuine concurrence. He decided this man was not of the former kind and therefore it was meant as the latter.

'Pontius Pilate is well pleased with your conclusion, but I sense it did not please your intellectual prowess and suspect it was made as a matter of political expediency, otherwise you would not be making this journey.'

'The facts pointed to the conclusion, yet you are right, there are certain incompatible elements.'

'Tell me about them.'

Marc took a deep breath and released it slowly while he took stock of how much he should reveal, but there was something about this king that made him seem trustworthy.

'We found a pouch in relatively good condition on the badly decomposed corpse in the aqueduct. I have reason to believe it was added to the body some time after death. It contained a map with clues to the whereabouts of some of the pieces of jewellery.'

'Do you have them with you?'

'Yes, I do, sir.'

'Let me see them.'

Philip looked at each one in turn, allowing the light to reflect on the stones.

'I understand these are not of value. Do you believe they are from the original collection?'

'I cannot say, sir. But Salampsio, Queen Mariamne's daughter, suggests that the necklace at least might have been.'

'How is Salampsio?' interrupted Philip, smiling and changing the subject.

'She is fine, sir.'

'Good, good, I remember her well. I always liked her. She had an amusing sense of humour. I seem to remember this necklace. It was a favourite of my father. Mariamne wasn't his only wife to wear it. Tell me where you found these.'

'The necklace belongs to a man from Jerusalem called Marcellus, who claims he bought it for his wife whilst travelling in Judea – he couldn't remember exactly where. The bracelet was given to the architect Anthony Avitus for his part in the plot. The crown was given to us by a man from Mamre who found it in a tree.'

'In a tree!' exclaimed Philip.

'Yes sir, it was one of the clues. However, he found it fifteen years ago on his son's birthday.'

Philip leaned back in his chair, stretching his elbows behind the seat and exercising his shoulders to release any tension. There was a long silence as he absorbed what he had just been told.

'Well, well, that rather supports what I have always thought.'
Marc lifted his brow.

'May I be so impertinent, sir, as to ask whether you have a theory on the matter?'

'I do have some ideas, which is the reason why I wished to see you. You may know that my half brother, Archelaus, took over Judea and Samaria when my father died. He had to leave because of too many altercations with the Jews. But he was a greedy man, and I don't believe that he would have gone into exile in Gaul twenty-seven years ago empty-handed. He had access to all our father's valuables although in theory there was a Keeper of the Key working with the Roman guard to stop any of us gaining access.

'We were told that none of it belonged to us but to the Emperor, collateral for all the loans he had given my father to rebuild Jerusalem. Archelaus, however, would have known better than any of us what was in the vault, particularly after the inventory was taken. It would not have been beyond him to bribe the Keeper of the Key, although I understand that the man doing the job at the time had impeccable credentials and reputation.'

'That would be Joel, sir.'

'Yes, I remember now. I visited Archelaus once in exile. He was living in Vienne and we met in the nearby coastal town of Narbonne. He was always selfish and would have enjoyed life wherever he went.'

'The jewels were not among his possessions when he died, eleven years after his exile.'

'I am aware of that. Nevertheless, I believe he took them. I have absolutely no proof. It is mere conjecture on my part. What I don't understand is why someone would go to elaborate lengths to pretend that they had been stolen only recently.'

'Perhaps it was to stop us finding out exactly when they were taken, to muddy the waters.'

'That's entirely possible. But it also means that the person or persons who stole them are still alive, so someone must have helped Archelaus. I wish you to carry out an assignment for me. I want you to go to Baalbek. It's a city north of Damascus. I have reason to believe that there is a man living there, called Rashidi – an Egyptian. He is very old – I'm hoping he's still alive. It is said he was descended from the last of the Ugarit kings, Ammurapi. His family have been jewellers for hundreds of years. He will know the origin of the Herodian stones if anyone does. Go and find him and ask him.'

Philip paused, looking once again at the jewels.

'Get another reliable valuation on these pieces you have shown me. Since you have unleashed this snake pit, I want to know the truth. Were my father and the Queen of Egypt herself deceived as to the worth of the jewels? I would also like to know what has happened to the rest of them. If you find them, I would appreciate you bringing them to me first. I would prefer they were not taken to Pontius Pilate or to my half brother. I shall see they are returned to their rightful owners. But no one is to know that, including your young friend. Do you agree?'

Marc looked across at the two bodyguards who were feigning disinterest.

'I am not hopeful of finding the rest of the collection but I shall do what I must should they come into my hands.'

King Philip seemed to assume that what he knew he must do is give them to him and nodded assent, pleased that Marc was in agreement. In fact, Marc intended to make a considered judgement should the eventuality occur, although he instinctively trusted Philip. He wondered who the king meant by the rightful owner - presumably Emperor Tiberius – perhaps he wanted to gain some favourable points of his own.

Philip turned to one of the bodyguards.

'Baraka, take our friend to the main part of the palace and allow him to browse around.' Then to Marc he said, 'I know you are a learned man, well read with an interest in history, you may find things to entertain you in the palace.'

Marc bowed and left. Baraka towered over him by at least a foot. Gaius was still in the library and Marc wandered down to the great hall. Along each side were three rows of pillars the bases of which were shoulder high. Philip had commissioned marble busts of every warlord and successful politician throughout the Republic and Empire to be placed in niches along the walls. Two giant bronze statues of Augustus and Tiberius stood half way down facing each other.

He came to each sculpture in turn. Some he had known personally but others were long dead. Gaius Julius Caesar was unmistakeable, the epigraph beneath read, 'I came, I saw, I conquered.' Marcus Cato, born a peasant but who became a military and literary success, was graced with the words he frequently declared in Senate debates, 'Carthage must be destroyed.' Marcus Tullius Cicero, who had given Marc's great, great grandfather his freedom, was among them.

Then, there was a face that had a strangely familiar proud bearing; it was Lucius Cornelius Sulla, otherwise known as 'Felix' – the fortunate, the general who had seized the dictatorship of Rome over a century ago, and who had had such a strong influence on the young mind of Julius Caesar. Beneath the plinth was the epitaph he had given himself:

'No greater friend, No worse enemy.'

36

Gaius and Marc had enjoyed King Philip's hospitality for the rest of the day and night; he was anxious to show off his creation to visitors he knew would appreciate the culture and artistic flair of his newborn city. Marc had mused over the epitaph that was the third clue on the Qumran map. Did it mean that more jewels were to be found beneath a bust of Sulla, if so, where? And the reference was not from ancient scriptures like the others, it was distinctly Roman rather than Jewish. He did not divulge his find to Gaius, preferring to contemplate the question himself.

'What did the king have to say to you?' Gaius inquired when they had met up later the previous morning.

'He was interested in the value of the jewels. He couldn't understand why they appear to be of no particular worth.'

'No, well, it must come as a bit of a shock to the family knowing that their heirloom isn't an heirloom at all. What does he want us to do?'

'Find someone who can tell us a bit more about their history.'

'Did he give you any clues as to where he thinks they might be?'

'No, he's as much in the dark as we are.'

'So I didn't miss anything then?' said Gaius jokingly.

They set off for Damascus before sunrise, deciding to journey across the lower reaches of the west side of Mount Hermon, rounding its northern edge and heading east through the gorge of the River Abana. Like the Jordan it was fed by the spring melting of the winter snows from the summit. The alternative would have been to return south to the point where the road had parted and they both had an instinctive preference for moving forward.

They rode down into the hollow valley of Coele-Syria alongside a narrow stream for several miles, keeping the mountain on their right. The heat became unbearable towards midday and Gaius stopped frequently to soak his kerchief and squeeze the cool water over his neck and face.

As they grew nearer to the northern end the land rose quite steeply, forcing the road to change direction sharply from left to right. A stream, that earlier in the year had climbed this far, was now little more than wadi with a stony bed. The journey was wearisome and lacked variety except for the occasional plateau, sparsely vegetated with bushes.

Then the path turned the edge of an escarpment and entered the gorge of the River Abana, uplifting and cooling as it plunged enthusiastically and noisily between the rocks until, tired of its labours, it transformed into a tranquil valley filled with trees and birds. The two men stopped beside the flowing water, and extended their bodies across the refreshing grass under the shade of a tree with copiously filled branches. The horses sensing the restfulness walked into the waters edge, picking their way amongst the stones, and slaking their thirst.

Images of the last few weeks came into Marc's thoughts as he lay in the shade. Rebecca – how was she he wondered. How did she now feel about the suicide of her stepmother and half brother? He felt her brief seductive kiss and smiled. Daleel and Jonathan – he missed their company, and Aziz. He remembered Salampsio sitting on her balcony, reminiscing about her childhood at Herodium, and Anna, Joel's wife – distraught over her husband's alleged suicide. And Claudia, Pilate's wife, how gently she had treated Anna! What a contrast to Deborah, Anthony's wife, with her long suffering servant, Sarah, and Sabina, his mother. He tried to analyse his feelings about the events of his life since he stood beside the captain on the deck of the ship docking into Caesarea harbour.

'Come on!' he said to Gaius, jumping up suddenly. 'If we stay here too long we'll both be asleep.'

Gaius stood up slowly and fetched the horses, noticing the swiftness of the current and how the water formed small whirlpools round the exposed rocks. They followed the bank as far as they could, but often the trees were too thick to pass and they were forced to move inland. The width of the river varied, sometimes as much as fifty or sixty feet, and at others so narrow that branches from opposite sides met and entwined into an impenetrable mesh. But eventually, as the sunlight elongated into evening shadows, the old city of Damascus loomed before them, picturesque and alluring. Gaius breathed a sigh of relief.

'It's good to be home. It's good to be home.'

They entered by the western portal, Gaius leading the way to another archway that marked the beginning of Straight Street. It is not particularly straight, thought Marc, as they rounded another bend. Then Gaius turned right into a courtyard filled with vines, pomegranate and fig trees. Outside torches bathed the stones and foliage in a warm glow. As he slid off the side of his horse, an elderly rotund woman ran from the back of a large imposing house.

'Oh, master, can it be you? It has been such a long time. It is so good to see you.'

Within minutes, loving, welcoming people surrounded them. A tall grey haired man emerged from a garden at the back and put both arms round his son. When introduced to Marc he treated him with easy good nature.

'Father, this is Commander Marc Tiro from Rome. He has been helping Pontius Pilate solve the disappearance of some jewels and I've been assisting. Marc this is my father.'

'Please call me Abel.' The voice was deep and lilting. 'I'm glad to see my son is in such good company. Come in. Leah, bring refreshments.'

They entered a delightful terraced room, furnished with carved willow chairs covered with soft comfortable cushions. Several glass oil lamps on bronze stands danced into life, one by one, as Leah circulated with a taper. Within minutes she conjured up fruit, bread, cheese and wine.

'Master Gaius, I have seen you looking better.'

Leah peered into his face carefully as the glow from a nearby lamp caught his cheeks.

'Your mother would never forgive me if I did not take care of you. Please eat something. You look very tired.'

'You always did fuss too much, Leah. If mother were alive, she would tell you to let me be.'

Gaius smiled but when Marc looked into his eyes, he had to agree that he did not look at all well. Perhaps the journey had been too much for him.

'I tell you what I'll do, I'll take to my bed early and tomorrow I shall be as handsome as ever, you'll see.'

'Mind you do then, sir,' said Leah, determined to have the last word.

'So, tell me about your exploits.' Abel decided to change the subject.

'So much has happened, father, since I saw you last. Marc has brought some excitement to our lives. That is for certain.'

'What sort of excitement?'

Gaius spoke of the parts he knew about and Marc realized how much the younger man had missed. Because of his accident in the tunnel, he had not been to Qumran or Mamre, or on a later visit to Herodium, or to Jericho or Bethel. Much of what he said he had heard second hand and it was not entirely accurate. Nevertheless, Marc allowed him to continue since his father was deeply impressed by the tale he had to tell. Leah, who was listening in the other room, came in as fast as her legs would allow when he told of his accident.

'There now,' she said, almost triumphantly, 'I knew there was something wrong.'

'Leah, I'm fine. If anything, I became too unfit lazing around the palace so long. I am young and strong and need plenty of exercise. I missed out on the wars unlike those a few years older than me. Very few battles are won by the pen.'

'I wouldn't be too sure about that, son; it's the way the world is going. Battles are expensive and drain economic resources. The populace doesn't like that, not the wealthy ones at any rate and they're the ones who end up paying through taxes. They're also the ones who choose the leaders in the end. No, sometimes the spoken and written word has more power than weapons of war.'

Marc said, 'It's true. More battles were won in the Senate by verbal argument than ever were won on the field. And it's far less bloody.'

The evening was spent idly talking about politics, until Gaius excused himself and went to bathe and then to bed. Marc and Abel were left to while away their time in conversation.

'So how are you finding Judea after living in Rome, quite a change I would imagine?'

'I think there's a tension between Rome and the Jews that might erupt before long. Neither party understands the other. Religion is clearly its basis. Your average Roman does not appreciate the Jewish obsession with one God, or with the influence that God has in the life of an individual. Romans hedge their bets by worshipping many gods. As they conquer more nations, the more they add to their collection and the more they have to appease.'

Abel nodded agreement.

'It stands to reason that if the invader is successful, then his god must be more powerful. But the Jewish God always said that he would stay faithful to his people and would always reclaim for them what they had lost. Centuries ago Jerusalem was taken by the Babylonians and the Jews sent into slavery. It was prophesied that

they would return and return they did. And now look at the city —
it is more magnificent than ever, thanks to King Herod and Roman
expenditure.'

Marc interrupted.

'Yet the Essenes, a radical Jewish sect, are convinced that there
will be another revolution.'

'I wouldn't want to be on the Jewish end of that. The Romans
can just as easily demolish Jerusalem as build it.'

'And they would do it too. It would be razed to the ground.'

'Come let us not worry about that tonight. Have some more
wine and please do tell me about these jewels. You know my family
have made jewellery for several decades.'

'Yes, Gaius told me. Have you heard of the stones that were
inherited by Mariamne, Herod's wife?'

'The history of jewellery is not my speciality, only what is
currently fashionable and what I can make and sell. My jewels are
mostly glass paste impressed in moulds, not precious stones. But
they make me a remarkably good income. It is merely a way of
increasing the coffers. I'm not ashamed to say it. Very few of us
today have only a small interest in acquiring the goods that the
Empire can provide for a price.'

'That's true. I'm no different. I have an independent income
from lucrative olive groves on the outskirts of Rome. None of it is
thanks to me, but to the hard work of diligent grandparents. It
gives me a way of life that few can afford.'

'So what do you propose to do with your revelation of that
fact?'

Marc hesitated at the incisiveness of the question. He liked Abel
very much.

'What do you suppose I should do with it?'

'That is up to a man's conscience. It is not for one to advise
another, since the first would then be obliged to accept his own
advice, or else he would be a hypocrite.'

'Hypocrisy is not a defect that seems to worry many, particularly those in high office.'

'Sadly that is true. But it does not prevent lesser mortals from having scruples.'

Marc laughed out loud.

'Are scruples affordable?'

'The older one gets the more easily one can afford them, particularly if one has already amassed sufficient for one's needs.'

'How true you speak.'

There was a pause in the conversation as both men refilled their wine glasses and enjoyed the advancing hours of the night.

'Can I ask you something more specific?' said Marc.

'I will answer if I can.'

'Do you know of a man called Rashidi? He lives in Baalbek, but would be very old. He was originally from Ugarit. His family was very wealthy, having been specialists in jewellery.'

Abel looked thoughtful for a moment, then stood up and walked to a cupboard in the corner of the room. He opened one of the doors revealing drawers for keeping papyrus rolls. He searched for several minutes before finding what he was looking for.

'Yes, here it is. I thought I knew the name. We wrote to him several years ago, or rather his great grandson, about a valuation of some jewellery owned by a client. I have found his reply – it has an address; I rarely throw anything away, one of my faults, although it can come in useful sometimes. But as for Rashidi himself, he is most probably dead by now. We haven't had reason to contact him since.'

Marc copied down the street name where Rashidi's shop was situated.

'Why do you wish to see him? I assume it has something to do with the missing stones?'

'We have found some pieces of the collection, but the stones themselves are not genuine lapis lazuli. I wondered if he could tell me why not.'

'Have the stones been stolen and replaced?'

'The jeweller in Jerusalem thinks the settings are original and have not been tampered with, although he could not be sure.'

'May I see them?'

Marc gave them to him. Abel took them to the light for a closer inspection.

'I am no expert in this matter, as I said, making up to date fashionable jewellery is my trade, but these have settings unlike any I have seen. They must be hundreds of years old. The stones are very fine and certainly look like lapis lazuli to the naked eye.'

'Do you think they have been tampered with?'

'I would say not. But this quality is a little out of my reach.'

'I must go to Baalbek as soon as possible and find this man. It is a royal instruction.'

'Is it really? How intriguing. One can no longer call it a search because there have been too many misfortunes along the way. It has become more of a quest, the quest for the Herodian stones.'

The wine was affecting both of them, but that did not prevent Abel calling Leah to bring another flagon. She fussed around him.

'It is good to see you so relaxed, master. But I must say I feel worried about young Gaius.'

'Madam, you worry too much. Now get you off to bed and leave the world to us men to do with as we will.'

37

-Baalbek-

Despite the quality of the wine, Marc woke with a hangover befitting a wild party. The light that filtered through the shutters was too much for his eyeballs and he turned over, feeling instantly sick. However, he managed to recover sufficiently to bathe and dress and look respectable.

'Plenty of fat, that's what you need when you've drunk too much,' said Leah, as he appeared in her cooking area on the way to the rear of the house.

'That's most kind, but not just at the moment! I think fresh air may be more of what I need. I'm taking a walk – won't be long.'

Straight Street ran from east to west, bisecting the city. Stately pillars and trees edged its walkways, on either side a mixture of residential homes and small bazaars. A myriad of offshoots led to narrow alleyways and lanes. Heavily embroidered materials hung from lines strung across the front of shops. Perfumes, of so many varieties, mingled together and filled the air, reminding Marc of his first visit to Cornelius' distillery.

In the darker recesses of the stone entrances, figures worked industriously with needles, threads, hammers, chisels and nails to produce pillows, slippers and leather sandals, jewellery of silver and bronze and carved wooden boxes. Marc watched a man decorating a plate by hollowing out an area of bronze, filling the hole with glass powder and heating it so that it fused, forming an overlay of enamel. Another skilled worker was carving animal bone, making bracelets and knife handles. A lathe was turning, producing a wooden bowl. Blades, knives and swords were on display. There was something to watch and enjoy at every corner.

The fortified walls by the eastern gate were so thick that houses were built within them. Raising his hand to his forehead to protect his eyes from the ascending sun, Marc saw two small children leaning from an embrasure, pointing and laughing at the morning pedestrians, their elbows fighting one another for space within the opening. He smiled at their enthusiasm.

When he looked away, the pupils of his eyes had contracted and the scene was shaded in grey. A figure appeared from one of the doors in the lower part of the wall and hurried up Straight Street. The gait, the uprightness and the bounce of the head were familiar. Surely, it was Justin from the acting troupe. Crassus had said that Justin intended to move to Damascus.

'Justin, Justin,' he shouted.

Was it imagination that the figure halted slightly on hearing his voice? Whoever it was did not look round, but increased in pace and turned into a by-way out of sight. Vision gradually returned as Marc followed into the dingy road, where the closeness of the buildings would not allow the sun's rays to penetrate, but there was no sign of the figure. By taking a road to the left and then left again, he emerged back onto Straight Street to the west of Abel's home.

Leah was frying thin strips of pork and he realized not just how much better he was feeling, but how hungry he was.

'Is Gaius about yet?'

'No sir, I'm quite worried about him. It's not like him to stay in his bed until this time. The master has already left. I wonder if you would mind looking in on him just to make sure he's all right?'
Gaius was lying on his back, his breathing irregular.

'Are you not feeling well?'
At first there was no reply. Then Gaius opened his eyes but with little interest.

'Good morning, my friend! No, but I shall improve later.'

'Are you in pain?'

'Some, yes, in my chest and arms. I don't feel able to move too well. I must be stiff from all that journeying.'

Marc suspected that this was not the case but said nothing. As he approached the bed, he could see that Gaius was sweating profusely and was clearly in more pain than he was admitting to.

'I think you need the doctor, old man. You're really not looking too good.'

'No! I don't trust them.'

'In that case, I'll fetch Leah.'

Despite his protestations Leah duly arrived.

'Master Gaius, I am going to get your father.'

Gaius was beyond arguing by this time and Leah set off for the shop where Abel had already ensconced himself for the day's trading. He was deeply concerned for his son and brought a doctor to examine him.

'His heart is not beating properly.'

'So what does that mean?'

'It may mean nothing. He is perhaps overstressed. For now, he must be kept quiet and given a sedative and painkillers to ensure rest. I will return tonight.'

Marc sat by Gaius' bed and read to him until he fell into a sound sleep. He recalled the hours he had done the same for his father.

'Please don't let this hold up your journey,' said Abel, later that evening. 'Gaius is young and will recover. He will be well looked after. You need to pursue the truth that you are looking for. You have been instructed to go to Baalbek to find Rashidi, please go. I will send a man with you.'

'Thank you for your concern, but I'll be safe. I'm quite used to this country now.'

'I think you are unwise. As your host, I cannot possibly allow you to travel alone.'

Marc did not argue any more. He looked in on Gaius who was sleeping soundly, and went to bed.

When he emerged the next morning into the delightful room he had first entered the evening before last, he was astonished to see Abel and Gaius both tucking into Leah's morning meal, enjoying the usual banter.

'Good morning! You see, I am much better. I told you I would be.'

'I'm very pleased to see you up and about. You had us all very worried yesterday.'

'The pain has passed, just a small matter of overindulgence. I am raring to go.'

'That's not sensible, son. I strongly disapprove of what you're doing. The doctor was very specific about you having rest.'

'T...sh, I have had enough of rest. It was nothing I tell you. What do doctors know anyway? Are we off to Baalbek today, Marc, or Heliopolis as the Greeks would have us call it – the City of the Sun? Not that there's much left of Baal – that god has been replaced by Jupiter since the Romans conquered the east.'

Marc felt decidedly uneasy about taking Gaius with him.

'Supposing you have a relapse, I am not qualified to know how to help you.'

'It's no use arguing. My mind is made up. I haven't come all this way to not finish what we came to do. If I have a relapse, I give you full permission to ride on and leave me.'

'Don't talk so stupid,' said Leah. 'You know you shouldn't be going.'

'Hold your tongue, woman. Why my father hasn't got rid of you years ago, I really cannot understand.'

Leah pursed her lips. She knew that Gaius was only joking. Yet there were times when even teasing could be hurtful.

'Oh, I'm sorry, Leah. You know I didn't mean it. What would any of us have done without you?'

Leah smiled. She felt better, yet a frown set into her forehead and refused to move.

'Now then woman, ask that lazy grandson of yours to get our horses ready.'

Abel shook his head and had one more remonstration with his son, to no avail. So in the end, he could do more than wish them both well.

'Pack the tent. You'll need it tonight. The final descent into Baalbek will take you four or five hours and is probably best left until tomorrow morning.'

'Yes, I remember it father. This is one journey in which I can take the lead. I shall keep our Commander safe, you see.'

The contours of the journey were similar to what they had already experienced. They followed a river then crossed a stifling hot plain and through a gorge. On the other side, the river ascended steadily through orchards and vineyards that were terraced against erosion. A mountain gave rise to magnificent waterfalls that tumbled over rocky crags and joined the water in the river, so that it deepened and increased its flow.

The climb suddenly opened out into a vast plain, the centrepiece of which was a dark lake that reflected the sky, the occasional white cloud and the surrounding peaks. The lake fed the countryside, which was rich and fertile as a result. An hour later, they reached a small village from which they could look down on the city of Baalbek and its enormous temple to the god Baal.

On several occasions, Marc had the feeling someone was following and watching them. But each time he looked, he could see no one. He was not prone to having an imagination but so much had changed since he had been here. After eating, the two men sat looking at the bright stars. Gaius was rubbing his chest.

'Have you got the pain again?'

'I must have eaten too much bread.'

'Have you had this trouble before?'

'No! Not in quite the same way! Please don't worry about me.

I told you, I'm just unfit. What do you expect to learn from this fellow Rashidi?' Gaius was anxious to change the subject.

'I'm hoping he may be able to tell us the history of the Herodian stones and why there is a mystery about their value.'

'Did you ask my father?'

'He said he is not an expert in that field. Herod Philip seems to think that Rashidi can provide us with an answer – assuming he's still alive.'

'What will you do when all this is over?'

'Return to Rome, I suppose.'

'And what then, work in your olive groves?'

Marc hesitated.

'To be honest, I don't know what I shall do. Retirement seemed like a good idea at the time.'

'Perhaps fate has a path for you to follow that you don't know about yet.'

Marc laughed.

'And what will you do, Gaius? Isn't it time you found yourself a nice young woman to marry and have children? It's what most people do you know.'

'Yes, yes, my father and Leah are always badgering me about it. To tell the truth, I haven't quite found the right person yet, although there have been one or two. I was in love once with a freedwoman. It would not have been allowed for a free person such as me to marry a freedwoman until Augustus made it possible. I was named after him you know. Gaius Octavius he was known as originally.'

'So what happened to the freedwoman?'

'Oh, I messed about so long that she went off and married someone else. She has three children now. Don't worry, I will marry someday, and I shall come to stay in Damascus permanently. My father is getting older and I am his one remaining son. I shall have a duty to take care of him.'

Marc unexpectedly stood up.

'Did you hear that noise?'

'What noise?'

'There was a rustling in those bushes. I think we're being followed.'

Marc felt uneasy. He took out his dagger and scouted around, but there was no sign of anyone.

'There is something I should tell you,' said Gaius, when he returned. 'I was going to ignore it, but it has been troubling my conscience and has made me feel quite sick at times.'

'Whatever is it?'

'Marcellus! His servant came to see me and offered me a great deal of money to kill you.'

Somehow Marc was not surprised.

'Did he say why he wants me dead?'

'His servant said that he and his wife hated you. Everything and everybody you connect with seems to end up worse off was the way he put it. He is afraid you will ruin him and his reputation.'

'Why should he think that?'

'Obviously, it must be something to do with the necklace. He didn't reveal how he got it, but he certainly doesn't want you to find out. I can't think why he would assume I could be bought. He obviously doesn't know me very well. I'm sorry. I should have told you before. I hope I haven't put you in danger. Let's keep watch tonight. I'll take the first shift.'

Marc agreed, but had no intention of relaxing, which was just as well, because Gaius had fallen asleep within half an hour. However, the night passed without event.

It was only on approaching the temple the next day, after making the descent in the morning, that they realized the full extent of its elaborate architectural design, its colossal pillars and exquisite stonemasonry. It dominated everything around it. A woman sat on a step beside one of the columns, a mere speck in comparison. She wore a headdress consisting of a colourful scarf covering her hair, with a chain of coins hanging across her forehead, down either cheek and under her chin. Numerous golden chains of varying sizes adorned her neck. Beside her, was a large basket filled with flowers that she was selling to visitors and worshippers. Marc stopped beside her. She stood up, bowed slightly and smiled.

'Can I help you, sir?'

'Yes. Can you tell me where I can find this shop?'

Marc leaned across his horse's wither and showed her the name of the road Abel had given him.

'Yes sir! Go to the end of this road and turn right. You will come to a square with a fountain. Go straight across. Take the first turning on the left and the shop is about half way down. I doubt you will find Rashidi the Elder there though.'

'Where is he?'

'His great grandson will give you directions. But I believe Rashidi has retired to a retreat in the cedar forests.'

'Thank you for your help. Here's a coin for your trouble.'

'Thank you, sir.'

Rashidi's great grandson's workshop was filled with bronze figures of a bull-like creature – the god Baal. On a long table to the left, clay identity seals for use on documents were drying and, beside them, a sculptured design of grapevines in gold relief. The young man was busy fixing gold coins to chains, similar to the one worn by the flower woman.

'That's an unusual design,' said Marc.

'It's a copy of those worn in Egypt. It seems very popular, sells well and has become quite the fashion in the city.'

'My name is Marc Tiro. Forgive me for asking, but I am seeking your great grandfather, Rashidi. Do you know where I might find him?'

'He doesn't want to be found these days – he is living out what is left of his already generous life in peace and quiet.'

'Nevertheless, it is important that I speak to him. I won't keep him long, but I need some information about some lapis lazuli jewellery that was made hundreds of years ago. King Herod Philip is certain he can help us since he comes from Ugarit, where the stones originated.'

'It sounds like the sort of thing that would interest him. If you care to wait a few minutes, I'll take you there. I don't think he'll see you if you go alone, but he might do so if I am with you. But you must promise not to tire him. He is very elderly.'

'No, indeed not, I'm grateful to you.'

Half an hour later they left the city to travel further northwards. The valleys were beautiful and the higher they climbed the more plentiful became the cedar trees, until they were in the middle of a forest. The trees were huge, even bigger than Abraham's Oak at Mamre. They reached a summit and looked back across a deep green sea of branches, beyond which lay the ocean.

After a couple of hours they came to a pass protected on both sides by mountains. To the left a stairway had been hewn out of rocks and around the base several people, men, women and children sat chatting or in prayer. Many of them had brought food and drink that had been spread out on the ground.

'These are people from the local village,' explained Rashidi's great grandson. 'They come with their problems to ask the inmates here to pray for them. Sometimes, they wait to see if the prayers are answered immediately. There are always a goodly number of them.'

At the top of the stone steps, a door led into a round tower from which foliage draped and hung down providing shade. Behind the tower was a second tier to the building and then a third as each layer was built higher into the rock face.

A figure wearing a long grey robe stood at the entrance. He instantly recognized their young guide, and allowed them to enter the cool, round, stone room that lay beyond. They were invited to sit on wooden benches while Rashidi was informed. The man returned to say that Rashidi was at prayer, but would join them shortly. Meanwhile, they were offered juice in wooden goblets. Marc noticed that Gauis looked ashen and was grateful he was resting. He wished he could have been persuaded not to come on this journey and feared for his health.

Rashidi was bent over at the waist. His face was deeply lined. It was impossible to tell his age but he could have easily been over a hundred. Nevertheless, he had all his faculties and hugged his young relative with enthusiasm. He was not quite so enthusiastic about the visitors, but was civil and invited them into the room beyond the porch.

'I am sorry to disturb you,' began Marc, 'but I have been investigating the theft of some lapis lazuli jewellery that belonged to King Herod. The jewels were originally made for Queen Cleopatra the first. The stones themselves may be as old as a thousand years. I have brought some to show you.'

He reached inside his cloak and pulled out the samples that he had and showed them to Rashidi. The old man's eyes lit up and he smiled imperceptibly. There was no doubt he recognized them and was enthused by their appearance.

'Well, well, well!' he kept repeating.

'You know of them?' asked Marc.

'Oh, yes! They were the finest examples that had ever been found. Magnificent!'

'But strangely, it seems the stones are not genuine.'

Rashidi laughed.

'That's hard luck then,' he said. 'It seems you've got the bad batch.'

'Could you explain what you mean?'

'As you say, the stones were mined out east over a thousand years ago. One particular mine was discovered where the stones were of an exceptional quality, the very best. Deep blue and gold with a mysterious allure – that's how they should be – magical. They were all brought to Ugarit to be sold. It was the main trading route on the Syrian coast to Egypt and elsewhere. But then, the mine dried up.'

Rashidi paused and allowed his mind to focus.

'The king of Ugarit, as there was in those days, was unwilling to admit it. Instead he found inferior stones that looked like lapis lazuli – particularly if they were mixed up. And that's what happened. Most of the stones would have been genuine but some were not. He kept them all together. Trade was based on trust and no one questioned the king's word.

'It wasn't until years later that the deception was discovered, by which time the stones had been sold on. Nobody wanted news like that to spread abroad. Imagine what would happen to the prices. It was in no one's interest to reveal the truth and have large fortunes devalued. Only one or two of the very oldest wealthy trading families got to know about it, mine was one of them, and everyone kept quiet.

'It's a story that was passed down in hushed tones from generation to generation, although I must confess, I never mentioned it to anyone. I think I rather forgot about it. It was only word of mouth anyway.

'Now my guess is that the people who made the jewels for the young princess would have wanted the very best, and asked for the stones that had been excavated hundreds of years before from that excellent mine. Some of the king's false ones will have been included. Whoever designed and made up these pieces must have known about it, but was either bribed heavily to keep quiet, or it may have been in their own interest to do so. They would be long since dead. Their descendants may not even know about it. Well, well, well, this has really improved my day.'

The old man started to chuckle. It was so infectious that the rest of them laughed with him – even Marc. It was somehow a relief that the answer to the problem that had been puzzling him for so many weeks turned out to be so simple. The last question though was not so easy to answer. If the stones in the pieces he had in his possession were not genuine, what had happened to the rest of them that were?

38

-The Drowning-

Having camped one more night in Baalbek, they rode out of the city the way they had come in. Gaius was musing.

'It's strange that we seem to have collected the jewellery that is made of the fake stones. It's as though someone took all the good ones and kept them, and put all the bad ones together.'

'Someone certainly knew what he or she was doing. Trouble is we don't know when it was done. Maybe even Herod himself had it arranged that way.'

'Now there's a thought! It still doesn't explain who stole them though or whether the thieves knew about the separation of the genuine from the false. I see the flower lady is still sitting on the steps. There's something not right about this place, but I can't quite understand it.'

Oddly enough Marc had been thinking the same. Maybe it was the colossal temple that was so dominating – he could not be sure. He still had the feeling that they were being watched.

'How are you, any better?'

'I'm fine, just don't worry about me.'

Several hours passed before they had climbed out of the city and back to the flat plain where they could make up some time. They had decided to try and make it back to Damascus before dark and had to ride hard wherever the going was easy. They reached the area of waterfalls and crags and traversed the terraced orchard and vineyards.

It happened just before they reached the gorge. It was as unexpected as a thunderbolt. Rocks from above loosened and cascaded down on the two riders. The blows hit them directly on their heads and both of them were knocked unconscious.

When Marc regained his senses he was aware of deep discomfort in his wrists and arms. He tried to move his legs. They felt heavy and when he attempted to draw them up, it was as though he was dragging a large weight. He laid his head down thinking this must be an effect of the blow to his head. He relaxed until he could focus more clearly and opened his eyes.

He was lying on a broad ledge close to the rock face. The sound of the river was immediately below. He could not move his arms and legs because they were bound with rope. He lent back and edged himself into a sitting position. A rock was attached to his ankles. It had been criss-crossed with rope to keep it in place. Further down the ledge, Gaius was laying similarly bound, but he was motionless. Two men appeared round the corner of the escarpment. Marc looked up at them but it was difficult to see their faces with the sun behind them.

'Ah, so you have recovered from your little accident. Good. You will enjoy your experience all the more. I'm not sure about your friend though.'

A glimpse of blue shone from the man's fingers. It was easy to see what he had found.

'This is more than we expected. How grateful we are to you for giving us such lovely jewels for so little effort.'

'Is that all you want?'

'You have more?'

'Yes, in exchange for our lives.'

'Well, you see, now if it was up to me I might be prepared to bargain, but my friend here, he feels better when he has seen death. He gets a real boost from it.'

Marc realized how dire the situation was. He was helpless to release himself in this position and was very worried for Gaius, who still had not moved. In fact, he could see no sign of breathing either.

'Do you know what it feels like to drown? After the panic is over it is very peaceful. Your mind floats away. You will like it, I promise. So much better than dying by the sword – that is so messy. This way there will be no bloodshed.'

Marc's fingers searched for a small sharp broken piece of stone at the base of the rock where he was sitting. If he could hold his breath for long enough then maybe he could cut through the rope. He started to inhale deeply and slowly, trying to expand his lungs and relax at the same time. He knew that if he panicked he would use up more air, and his reflexes would force him to gulp in water. He must delay the urgent need to breathe under water. Even so he knew his chances were slim.

He found a small piece of rock with a sharp edge and held it in his fist. He sat horrified as the two men rolled Gaius to the edge. The man who had done all the talking put his boot on the lifeless form.

'You can watch your friend go first.'

He shoved him with his foot and Gaius went over. His body made a loud splash as it entered the water.

'Now it's your turn my friend.'

Marc took one last long slow gasp of air as they each held him under his arms and dragged him forwards. The water made a loud noise in his head as he was dragged quickly downwards. He could not see at first, but as he sank to the bottom and the mud settled around him he opened his eyes.

He knelt on the riverbed and looped his hands under his bottom until they were near his feet; he was grateful for his loss of weight in the last few weeks. He grasped the rope attached to the rock, as best he could, in the fingers of one hand and started cutting with the improvised implement he held in the other. He forced himself to think positively. The rope was made of loose fibres that began to disintegrate. It felt like an eternity but could not have been more than a minute or two.

Then something banged into his side so that he unbalanced and dropped the stone. The white face of Gaius was looking straight at him – the eyes were wide and staring, the mouth hung open. Marc gasped and inhaled water. He started to cough, inhaled again and then felt his throat constrict. Unconsciousness wafted over him as he began to struggle, followed by a euphoric feeling that he was being lifted towards the glittering light above.

He coughed. His throat opened and water began to spurt into his mouth and trickled out, running down the side of his face. His chest hurt as something pushed down on it. He coughed again and more water emerged, until he regained consciousness. He was lying on the riverbank. He caught sight of the legs of a horse, its hooves covered by running water. His brain started into action and he remembered what had happened. Gaius! Where was Gaius? He shouted out his name.

'Take it easy.' The voice was deep and resonant. A large black face was peering down at him. Two large black hands lay across his chest.

'Baraka! What are you doing here?'

'I have King Philip's instructions. I was told to look after you, sir. I was nearly too late.'

'Where is Gaius?'

'I'm sorry, sir, I couldn't save him. I think he was dead before he went into the river. There was no water in his lungs.'

Marc sat up. Gaius lay a few feet away. He crawled over and put his hand on his neck. There was no pulse. He leaned across and closed the eyelids then slumped back heavily, looked at the body in deep sorrow and wept. He thought of Abel and Leah. This would devastate their lives. How would they cope, knowing that Gaius was no longer in the world?

'I think he may have been killed by one of the rocks, sir.'

'Where are the two men who attacked us?'

'One of them ran away. The other is dead.'

'You killed him?'

'Yes. He has a knife in his back. I threw it from the riverbank when I saw him push you in. He never knew what hit him. The other man didn't stay to find out.'

'Thank you, Baraka! You did well.'

'I didn't save Master Gaius.'

'I think Gaius has been unwell for a long time. The doctor said his heart was weak. A shock like this would have been enough to kill him, I'm sure. It may have happened at any time.'

They carefully wrapped the body in a blanket. Marc climbed up to look at the dead man. He didn't know him although there seemed something vaguely familiar about the face; it was just one of those marauders that they were forever being warned about. He disentangled the jewels from where they were still entwined in the white fingers, and used his foot to push the body into the river, where it would eventually end up in the gorge and cut to pieces on the rocks. The fate intended for him.

'Have you been following us since we left Caesarea Philippi?'

'Yes, I have sir! I felt sure you had seen me at least twice. I think you must have heard me. It wasn't easy staying out of sight when you were crossing the plain. I had to wait until you reached the other side before setting off – that's why I was so far behind you, else I might have been able to stop this happening.'

'Baraka, you have saved my life. I am forever in your debt. Gaius was a young man, but he was ill. He should never have come on this journey – but he was so keen it was impossible to stop him. He died in action. He always wished for a more active life. You did all you could. It's important now that we get him back to his family so that he can have a proper burial.'

'Yes, I agree, sir! But I think it would be well to make camp and rest now – head back tomorrow.'

This was good advice. There was nothing more they could do now. It was a difficult night, despite hearing Baraka's exciting stories of how his forefathers had been sold into slavery, achieved fame as gladiators and ultimately their freedom. Marc could not avoid looking towards the body of Gaius and reflecting on their relationship over the last few weeks and months. He had learned something from the young man. He had an enthusiasm for living that had not been tainted by the love of power.

He recalled the evening they had visited Gaius' house in Caesarea. How he had refused the grandeur of living in the palace, preferring a simple existence, gaining pleasure from a few beers and a cocktail of fish pieces in garum sauce whilst sitting and looking out at the sea. There had been evident delight that lit up his face when he arrived at the home of his father. He would never forget his willingness to engage in adventures and his hope of one day meeting the right woman.

It was a shame that their friendship once had been marred by the suspicion engendered by the political circumstances of their employment. The overriding question of trust had been ever present. Yet, Gaius had warned him about Marcellus. He could have accepted the commission that was offered to him. There had been plenty of opportunities along the way. Marc genuinely hoped there was a spiritual life after death and that Gaius was now enjoying it.

Baraka went with Marc to the house on Straight Street. Marc asked him to stay and recount the circumstances of Gaius' death to Abel, and insisted he should take credit for trying to save his son. Leah came running out into the courtyard as she had done before. She stopped when she saw the body lying across the saddle of the horse. She looked at Marc then at Baraka, confusion written on her face.

'Where is Gaius?' Tears were forming in her eyes. When Marc dismounted and said her name she burst into sobs, bringing her apron to her face to hide the ugly distortions of sorrow.

'Why did you take him with you? Why? Why? You knew he wasn't well.'

She moved to the body and touched the locks of hair that protruded from the blanket.

'Oh, my darling boy, what will your father say?'

Abel was fetched. The stoicism with which he endured his distress was remarkable. Perhaps he felt fortunate to have had his son for so long. During the course of the Roman advance on the western and eastern world, there had been thousands of young men who had never reached the zenith of maturity.

'What happened?'

'Let's go inside. This is Baraka, a personal bodyguard of King Herod Philip. He tried to save your son. I would like him to tell you himself.'

Abel nodded and led the way. Gaius' body was brought onto the terrace and laid on a long wooden table.

'I was instructed by my master to follow Commander Tiro and your son, to make sure they were safe and to report back if anything happened concerning their investigation.'

Marc looked at him. So it was not just for their protection. Philip was not certain he could trust him, wanted to make sure that if he found the rest of the jewels they were returned to him.

'I followed them here and then to Baalbek. On the way back, I got behind, because they crossed a plain and I was anxious not to be seen; that was a specific instruction. When I arrived at the river the two attackers had already bound them and fastened rocks to their legs. Gaius was the first to be pushed in. I threw a knife into the back of the one who appeared to be the leader and dived in. It was difficult to see, the water was murky. The current had already dragged them several yards down river towards the gorge. Then I saw them both.

'I pulled them out together and treated your son first but I couldn't revive him. There was no water in his lungs and I truly believe he was dead when he hit the water.'

Abel walked across and briefly held Baraka's upper arm.

'You did your best and I am grateful. Allow me to reward you.'

'No sir! That would not be right. King Philip treats me well.'

'Then you must stay and eat with us and rest. You can return tomorrow. I need to make funeral arrangements. Gaius would like to have been treated like a Roman officer, and so he shall be. Marc, would you be so kind as to send a dispatch to Pontius Pilate – he needs to know. I wonder if he would like to come. Perhaps he could help us with the eulogy.'

Marc recalled how Pilate had first suggested to him that Gaius be his guide and adviser. He could hear his voice echoing in his ears, 'I would like you to meet a young administrator who, I believe, shows great promise as an investigator. His name is Gaius.'

Guilt crept over him like a paralysis. Abel interrupted Marc's thoughts as though he could read them.

'You did what you could. Gaius died as he would have wished.'

Perhaps it was because Abel had a few spectres of guilt himself that he understood. Marc knew they would pass. They always hung around death like a black cloud, as they had when his wife died and then his father, but once the last rites were spoken they dissolved and only good memories remained.

39

-The Funeral-

Baraka returned to Caesarea Philippi taking with him a letter from Marc to Herod Philip, reporting on what Rashidi had said. Abel also sent a letter telling the king about the bravery of his servant, how he had saved Marc's life and that the death of Gaius was unavoidable since it was suspected that his heart had a defect.

The funeral was organised by a professional undertaker. Gaius was to be taken to the family mausoleum in the cemetery that had served his ancestors for many generations. Pontius Pilate, Flavius, his chief of staff, Cornelius Sulla, Marcellus and Polybius were all to be present at the ceremony. Abel was most gratified by their patronage. Gaius would have been pleased and that was all that mattered.

Marc was to stay as a guest of Abel until after the funeral. He spent his time walking round the city in the vain hope of finding Dimitri. The only clue he had was that the man had become a follower of the teachings of the prophet Jesus. Small sects of believers were starting to evolve, but they met in secret even though they were far from being a threat to anyone.

One evening he returned to the house from which he had seen the person who looked like Justin emerge, hoping that he might catch sight of him again. The door of the house that was embedded in the Damascus fortified walls opened; a figure stood on the threshold. It was a young woman carrying a small basket covered in a cloth. He watched her walk into Straight Street and followed. The likeness to Justin was remarkable and then it dawned on him that this may be Justin's sister, perhaps his twin. It would explain why the young man was willing to move to Damascus and leave the group of actors that had seemed to become his family. The girl stopped on a corner and turned right, up a side street, and then left down an alley that brought her along the backs of some spacious houses. She entered through a small wooden door in a wall.

Marc waited for a few moments and then did the same. Beyond was a large unkempt garden that had turned into an attractive wilderness. Exotic trees and shrubs had overcome the landscape and orange blossom filled the air. Stepping-stones led to the back of the house. There was no one in sight. Feeling like an intruder and having no pre-prepared explanation as to why he was trespassing, he made his way stealthily across the grass.

He could hear voices from within. At first it was difficult to identify where they were coming from. Just in front of him was a grate that aerated a cellar below the house. He stooped to listen. Now there was singing, or rather, praising in song. The top of a head unexpectedly appeared. The hair was not long but dark and curly. It was the young woman. She was moving down a circular stairway below the grating, steadying herself on an iron banister as she descended.

Pleasurable murmurs greeted her. She was expected, and he could see some movement as another woman put her arms round her and touched her cheek with the side of her own. He sat in the twilight listening. He heard someone say, 'This is my body' and then, 'This is my blood.'

What kind of sacrifice was taking place, he wondered. Marc had heard how hundreds of burial urns had been found at Carthage after it finally surrendered to Roman might. Bones of babies and young children dedicated to the goddess Tanit and her consul Baal had been unearthed during rebuilding projects. Gaius had said his father was a Phoenician nobleman. Marc knew from history that these people had originally colonized Carthage. It came to him why he had felt so uncomfortable in Baal. It was a sense of evil – Gaius had felt it too. Is this what is going on in that lower room, he thought. Should he not be stopping it? But before he could make up his mind, it was all over. People were hugging each other again with a kiss on the cheek. It was time to go.

Later that evening over a good wine, he asked Abel about child sacrifice.

'I haven't heard of it being practised here recently, although I know it did go on. The Romans don't approve of it, as you know. There was some of it happening in Northern Africa but not after they were conquered. If it's taking place in this city, it should be reported, especially if it is happening in a main street. Which house was it?'

Marc described the position as well as he could.

'Well, I know nearly everyone here and that sounds to me like it belongs to a man called Judas. I always thought he was harmless enough; he's lived here quite a while, not the type to go in for child sacrifice. But you never know. Perhaps you'd better investigate a bit further.'

'Do you know of any other services to a god that offers blood and body?'

'No! Can't say I do. But I don't take it too seriously myself. There are some strange cults about. There seem to be new ones every week. It's become quite the fashion.'

Marc did not like the idea of Justin, or his sister come to that, being involved in something offensive although he knew it was really none of his business. Nevertheless, he decided he probably owed it to Crassus to keep an eye on the young man if he was here.

It was two nights later that he saw the young woman again. She looked down as she walked and did not see Marc approaching her. This time he challenged her.

'Please don't be alarmed; I mean you no harm. My name is Marcus Tiro. I am looking for a young man called Justin. You look so much like him. Do you happen to know him?'

She would not look him in the face but she did not need to. She was identical to the actor he had congratulated on his emotionally engaging performances.

'Please let me go, sir. You're blocking my path.'

'Tell me if you are related, please.'

'I am not related to him.'

'Do you know who I mean, then?'

'Please let me pass.'

Marc had no choice. He was not in the business of intimidation, although he might have been at one time. He decided instead to go to the house he had seen her come from. An elderly woman opened the door. She smiled as Marc introduced himself and then frowned at the question as though racking her brain for an answer.

'I don't know of any Justin.' She seemed relieved but was anxious not to disappoint.

'I do have a young lady staying with me whose name is Candace. But she's out at the moment.'

Marc thanked her. He went to the house he had visited two nights previously, but this time he went straight to the back and knocked. There was no reply. Presumably no one could hear. He tried the latch, pushed open the door and stepped inside, aware that he was now an unwelcome visitor. He crossed the room to the stone steps leading to the cellar.

When he was about half way down, he knelt to get a better view. No one saw him because they all had their eyes tightly closed. A man at the front was reciting, 'Forgive us our sins as we forgive those who sin against us, and lead us not into temptation.'

Marc was struck by the feeling of great peace and goodwill that had settled on the assembled company. He quietly walked down the rest of the steps and through an archway into a small vaulted room, joining some people at the back. They were not afraid of him and smiled in welcome. The leader took a small round loaf of bread, broke it and blessed it.

'This is my body; eat this in remembrance of me,' he said.

He passed a tiny piece to each person present. While they were still slowly eating, he took an earthenware cup and filled it with red wine. 'This is my blood, spilled for you; drink this in remembrance of me.' They passed round the cup and each took a sip, including Marc.

Later, the members went upstairs where refreshments had been laid out, juice, fruit and nuts. The young woman, whom he now knew as Candace, looked at him uncertainly. She spoke to the leader who patted her gently on the arm and said something to reassure her. Then he approached.

'You are welcome, brother. My name is Judas. How should we address you?'

'Marc Tiro.'

'Come! Help yourself to something to eat. Have a drink. Please do sit down and tell me something of yourself.'

Marc submissively did as he was bid. He felt obliged to justify his presence.

'I am looking for two people. A young man named Justin who recently came here after leaving a troupe of actors, and the other, a man called Dimitri.'

'Why do you wish to see them?'

'Justin I have met on occasions after his performances and wish to let him know I am here. I thought he might be pleased to see someone he knew. The young lady with you looks so much like him that I thought she may be his sister. As for Dimitri, that's another matter. I understand he has had a terrible injustice meted out to him, but that he was healed by a miracle of the prophet Jesus, and may now be able to tell me what happened.'

Judas turned to the young woman.

'Candace. Don't be afraid of the truth. This man will not harm you. Come here.' She approached.

'Marc, I am delighted to introduce you to Candace, otherwise known in a previous life as Justin, one of our much loved sisters in Christ.'

He was totally dumbfounded and stared at the girl in amazement. She explained.

'You know, sir, it is impossible for women to be actors. It is socially unacceptable. There is nothing I would rather do than portray the tragedies of the characters you saw me perform. I have never had a womanly figure and it was very easy to pretend to be a young man.'

'Does Crassus know?'

Marc immediately felt stupid. That was the sort of fatuous question that normally he would have despised.

'It's all right! I know the answer. He must have known since you worked with him for so long.'

'Yes. He is a good man and protected me well.'

'So why have you left him?'

'It was a very hard decision. But when I saw the prophet being crucified and the skies went dark and the lightening struck at the moment of his death, somehow I knew.'

'Knew what?'

'That he was the Son of God – the only God and the one I shall follow until the end of my days. And then when I heard he had risen, I was even more convinced, particularly since so many people saw and spoke to him. I heard about this place in Damascus. There are a number of people who feel as I do. We call ourselves Christians. Jerusalem has become a bit too dangerous. If we all stay we'll be too noticeable, and the Pharisees were very much against Jesus. They are hardly likely to look favourably on the development of our sect.'

'That's true.'

Marc thought of the deep suspicion and hatred on the faces of the priests on the first day he and Gaius had arrived in Jerusalem. That was the day that Gaius jumped on Barabbas and Marc had confiscated his knife. He smiled at the memory of Gaius' face afterwards. 'Well, I got my man.'

'I'm sorry for deceiving you,' she said.

Marc remembered her saying she was sorry once before, so this must have been what she meant. Yet he was convinced he caught sight of a glance that passed from Judas to Candace, a frown and twitch of the mouth, but she shook her head, barely noticeably, in a stubborn refusal, despite a disapproving look from her mentor. Marc could not even begin to guess what that was all about and decided he was definitely better off not to enquire.

Should he pursue the question of Dimitri? He had the impression that if Judas wished to tell him, then he would. Perhaps he knew the man but needed to speak to him first. His disclosure was of greater political importance than that of Candace's revelation and could have more serious consequences. He left, promising to return.

Abel supplied his guest with information about the most highly praised and long-standing family jewellers in Damascus. Marc visited each in turn. They were all particularly interested in the necklace and confirmed that a few, though not all, of the stones had been replaced at some time. It was understandable that the jeweller in Jerusalem had been confused. The setting was original and had a value because of its age and design, but the stones were of little value. Each firm was intensely interested in the history of the collection, but no one was willing to admit that their ancestors might have been involved in such a deception so long ago. Even if they had something to hide, there would be no point in confessing to it now.

The day of the funeral came and the dignitaries arrived amongst much pomp and ceremony. Abel was gracious and welcomed them to his house although they were staying at a garrison nearby.

'My deepest sympathies,' said Pilate, well rehearsed. 'Your loss is our loss. Gaius had a great future. I miss him very much.'

'I am deeply honoured that you should all see fit to attend the funeral. My son would have been most gratified.'

'How goes your investigation, Marc?' asked Cornelius with much more bonhomie than would normally be expected. 'Have you found what you are looking for?'

'Part of the mystery is solved. I now understand why some of the jewels have no value.' He explained what he had learned from Rashidi. The look on the face of Marcellus was a mixture of disbelief and anger.

'That is the most outrageous deceit I have ever heard.'

Marc said to him, 'Now that you are here in Damascus, perhaps you could find the jeweller from whom you bought the necklace and ask for a return of your money.'

'I really cannot remember. There are so many bazaars – it was a long time ago. Besides, my wife likes it.'

Marc knew that this man had offered Gaius a considerable sum of money to kill him. It was not improbable that he had tried before, but this was no time to challenge him with that information. It would have to wait.

Mourners from Gaius' extended family, wearing masks of his ancestors, led the procession from the central forum, followed by the body carried on a bier. A eulogy was read praising his life and achievements. The dignitaries rode in chariots.

On arrival at the site of cremation, outside the city gates, various rites were observed. Coins were placed over the body's eyes to pay the boatman, Charon, to carry him across the river Styx in the underworld, and food and drink was offered for the journey. It was doubtful if anybody in attendance actually believed the concepts behind the rituals, but they were performed nevertheless. Gifts and some of Gaius' personal belongings were cremated with him. The ashes were to be placed in an urn and entombed with those of other family members. The full period of mourning would last nine days after which there would be a feast celebrating Gaius' life.

Marc noticed a man watching the cortege. Fear seemed to strike him and he dodged quickly into the crowd.

The illustrious visitors returned to camp to bathe, ritually purifying themselves against the pollution of death. Duties called them back early next day. Their apologies were made and thanks exchanged.

Later that evening, Marc sat with Abel and Leah, reminiscing about Gaius. It was cathartic for them to talk about him and they wanted to hear as much as possible about that part of his life of which they knew very little. Leah both sobbed and laughed intermittently.

As they relaxed there was a desperate knocking on the door. Leah rose and returned with a soldier from the garrison.

'Sorry to disturb you, sir! I have been sent to ask you to come immediately. It seems Marcellus has been poisoned.'

40

According to the doctor, Marcellus had imbibed a large quantity of henbane. There was nothing to be done. Earlier in the evening he had bought some wine from a merchant who came to trade with the encampment. No one could remember seeing him. It must have been someone with a grudge against the Romans. Marcellus had invited Cornelius to come and share a drink with him and by the time he arrived, his friend was already very drunk. Cornelius had taken only a few sips when Marcellus collapsed. Cornelius said,

'He was sweating profusely; his breathing was fast and shallow. He couldn't move and then he passed out completely.'

'You had a lucky escape yourself. There was poison in your glass too,' said the doctor.

'When I realized what was happening I drank plenty of water to dilute anything that had entered my stomach.'

'Someone is trying to kill us all,' declared Pontius Pilate, in a high state of agitation. 'There have been attempts on nearly all of us. It is really too much. Doubtless I shall be next.'

'I do hope not, sir,' said Flavius in a pandering tone.

Pilate shouted. 'Then find out who is doing it. Marc, what do you know of this?'

'I regret I know nothing. I am as shocked as you.'

'I want you to find the wine merchant. He must be to blame. We must return tomorrow. Marcellus' wife will want to arrange the funeral. I am leaving you to investigate further.'

The party left the following morning. They had arrived in confident pomp and splendour but left disconcerted and sapped of energy. Marc was to join them in a few days. There was something he wanted to do first. Later that evening he went to the house of Judas. No prayers were taking place but a number of friends were seated in a circle in the back room, enjoying companionship. Marc was delighted to see Barnabas, the young thief with whom he had shared a cell in Jericho. The boy jumped up in surprise.

'What are you doing here, sir?'

'I might very well ask you the same thing.'

'I've come to listen and learn more about the teachings of my Lord. Jerusalem is not exactly dangerous but uncomfortable. The Pharisees are everywhere, discrediting his name and life. On the other hand, for us he has become our life. But tell me, how come you are here at the house of Judas?'

'It's a long story. Right now I need to find a man called Dimitri. I know he came to Damascus; it's most urgent that I speak to him.' Judas stood up and welcomed Marc.

'You are right, Dimitri was here, but he has left.'

'Did he say where he was going?'

'No. He trusts no one at the moment. Not even me. He just seemed afraid.'

'Do you know what it was that made him fearful?'

'Not exactly – but I think he saw someone he recognized. More important, he thought the person might have seen him – that's all I can tell you. Now please join us for a while, there is nothing you can do this evening, so rest.'

The invitation was welcome although it was disappointing not to find Dimitri. Some of the answers lay with him. He hoped for his sake that he had not been involved in the poisoning of Marcellus.

Marc asked Barnabas, 'Where is Mary – the woman I took you to in Jerusalem? Is she joining you in Damascus?'

'Mary Magdalene has gone back to her village,' said Barnabas. 'It lies on the western shore of the Sea of Galilee, about half way between Tiberias and Capernaum. Many of the early disciples lived in Capernaum. They go back to visit their families from time to time. Some of them, like Simon Peter, had good fishing businesses and members of their families have kept them going. They are the most amazing men. Can you imagine spending three years travelling with Jesus and listening to his wisdom every day?'

'I'm glad you have found a faith, Barnabas. I'm not sure I could ever have your level of commitment. But perhaps I have too much history of another kind that I'm carrying around with me and need to offload it first.'

'You couldn't be carrying around more guilt than I. Remember I made a living from stealing from others and had no conscience about it whatsoever. Some of the women I have met were once prostitutes – it's not easy for a woman without a husband to make a living – but they have given all that up in the name of their Lord. They feel no guilt because they have been forgiven.'

'It's a wonderful concept.'

'Give it time, sir. Give it time.'

'Is Candace around? Has anyone seen her?'

'Not in the last couple of days,' replied Judas. 'There are different people here at different times. Our numbers are growing quickly.'

It was probable that Candace had already revealed everything she knew, but another conversation with her before leaving would have pleased him. Marc knew he had to go back to Capernaum. It was possible Dimitri might have returned to his family, as the other disciples did from time to time. Surely he would want to make sure they were safe.

'I shall be leaving tomorrow morning,' said Marc, 'but I expect we shall meet again.'

'Before you go,' said Judas, 'will you allow us to pray with you and for you, so that you are kept safe?'

Marc hesitated but could see no harm in their doing so. The

assembled company stood round him, some of them placing their hands on his shoulders and Judas led prayers. They asked for his forgiveness, for his safety and that his eyes may be opened. They thanked God for his life and for his presence amongst them.

Marc felt a strange sensation of warmth throughout his body and found he too was asking for forgiveness for the arrogance and pride with which he had led his life. His jaw began to shake uncontrollably as if he was nervous, yet he felt calmer than he had ever felt before. The prayers ceased and hung thickly in the air as though reluctant to go. But eventually the group moved away from him and laughter began to fill the room and everyone relaxed. When Marc later looked back on his life, he decided that was the moment it truly began, but for now there was a mission to be accomplished.

Abel and Leah were sorry to see him leave so soon. He was not sure whether fate would bring them into contact again but hoped it would. Abel told him he should not travel alone yet Marc had no fear. He was certain that he would be protected until he had learned the truth.

He followed the road southwest out of Damascus, keeping Mount Hermon on his right. There was no need to take the road directly west, the one he and Gaius had travelled together, because he had no intention of returning to Caesarea Philippi. He remembered crossing a stone bridge with Gaius north of the Sea of Galilee but south of Lake Huleh, where the road forked, and went almost directly northeast to Damascus. They had not followed it at the time but now he intended to use it.

South of the city was a plain through which flowed another river that had its origins in the summit of Hermon. How much that mountain contributed to the well being of this whole area! He rode all day through the region ruled by King Philip, camping overnight at the fountainhead of a stream where a rocky overhang protected him.

He thought of the look of death on the face of Gaius and remembered the dying face of his own father. It occurred to him how not long after a body breathed its last breath, the essence of the individual disappeared, as though some spirit of life inhabited a being for a short number of years and then left. Surely there is more to it than that. Why struggle, fight and obtain wealth if that is all there is to life?

'What a complete waste of time,' he said out loud. Waste of time, waste of time, waste of time; the echo reverberated. What was the point of justice? What was the point of war, of power? What was the point of procreation if all it achieved was the generation of more misery? Show me what else there is. Why are we here? What should we be doing while we are here? These were big questions and ones he could not answer before falling into a deep sleep.

The next day he reached the stone bridge and headed south towards the northern shore of the Sea of Galilee. He watched the fishermen with interest and wondered if any of them had been followers of Jesus. Reaching Capernaum, he took the road round the outside of the city walls to find the small wretched hamlet where Dimitri's wife, Miriam, lived. There was no sign of life at the mud hut. She was not sitting outside as she had been before. The ragged curtain was down.

Marc dismounted and walked towards the doorway. He called out but there was no reply, so he moved the curtain to one side and entered. There was nothing there other than some straw covered by a blanket in one corner and a few cooking utensils, hanging over a now cold open fire. A hole in the mud roof allowed the smoke to escape. He went back outside – it was surprisingly quiet – no hens feeding on corn in rapid thrusts of their beaks.

'Is Miriam all right?' he asked a man leaning on a gatepost opposite.

'Who wants to know?'

'My name is Marc. I came to visit her a while ago. A friend of hers who is a centurion introduced us.'

'Ah! I know of him. Don't remember you though. Anyhow, she's all right. So now you don't have to worry do you?'

'Has her husband been to visit her?'

The man pushed himself away from the post and turned and walked into his hut. He was giving nothing away. Then Marc did something that he realized he had done once before. He called on the Lord. Where is she? Show me the way. Please, show me the way.

As he turned to look at the sea, a vision of the face of Mary Magdalene came into his mind. What was it Barnabas had said? She had returned home for a visit – a village along the coast between Tiberias and Capernaum. Could it be that Dimitri had taken his wife to live there? If he thought he had been recognized, then he would want to do something to keep his wife safe. She was too crippled to go far, but just round the coast – that was a possibility. The more he thought about it the more logical a solution it seemed.

There were numerous villages along the coast, as he well knew. He entered a hamlet called Taricheae, and then he saw her. She was standing at a vegetable stall filling her basket. He walked up beside her.

'May I carry those for you?'

She looked round in alarm and then relaxed in joy as she saw him.

'Commander, this is a surprise! How well you look.'

'And you Mary. You look quite radiant.'

'How on earth do you come to be here?'

'Actually I was looking for you. Barnabas told me I might find you somewhere along this coast. I confess I left the rest to good fortune. I need to speak to a man called Dimitri. Do you know him?'

'Yes, he and his wife are staying with me. He is very afraid. He may react badly to seeing a stranger.'

'I am not here to harm him.'

'No, I believe you won't do that. But he is under a considerable strain.'

'Can you speak on my behalf?'

'Yes, I'll try. But what's more intriguing is how you came to meet up with Barnabas again.'

'I saw him at the home of Judas in Damascus.'

'Have you been attending meetings at his house?'

'No! Not really, although I have been there when he passed round the bread and wine.'

'That is indeed amazing. Our God works in mysterious ways. I'll tell Dimitri. I think it may appease him. Follow me. I'll show you where I live, but don't come in until I tell you.'

Marc stood outside the threshold of a house made of crushed baked clay. He could see the walls were plastered and covered in whitewash; the floor was made of stone blocks and wood. He waited as the sun reached its height and began lowering, reflecting on the water. Mary called to him and he walked into the room – his eyes needed to adjust to the gloom within compared to the brightness he had just left.

A tall thin elderly man stood in front of a fireplace. Miriam sat on a stool in the corner to the left. Another man, probably in his forties, had positioned himself much nearer the door, on the right, and still had his dagger in his hand. Mary stood in the centre of the room facing the door. She smiled and walked towards her guest taking his arm and leading him in.

'Please sit down,' she said indicating a chair. 'You are just in time for a bowl of stew.'

Seeing that Marc was unarmed the man beside the door relaxed and put the dagger back in its bronze scabbard.

'Allow me to introduce you. Marc, this is Dimitri and his wife you already know. This is Dimitri's son. Nobody is to talk about anything serious until we have finished eating.'

Marc looked into Dimitri's face. It was careworn and scarred, yet his eyes had a light that he had noticed in Mary, Judas and Candace and several of their friends. They exchanged pleasantries. Marc told them how he came to be in Judea and some of the hazards he had experienced whilst trying to solve the mystery of the stones, including the sad death of Gaius. Dimitri told him of how he had met the Lord Jesus who had healed him. It was not until they were relaxing after the meal that Marc dared approach the subject on his mind.

Dimitri said, 'I know why you are here. I know what you want to ask me. I have scarcely dared to talk of it. But I trust you. Don't let me down.'

'I won't. If I can, I will see that justice is done.'

'I was a young man when I was asked to join the Roman army. I was not unhappy about doing so. We had experienced many years of uprising and killing under Herod and then Archelaus, who ruled over Judea and Samaria. They had murdered so many Jews, their own kind that Roman occupation didn't seem too oppressive to me at the time, and I thought I could help. I was stationed at Capernaum but was sent on several assignments in the area. One of these was to guard the vaults at Herodium palace. It was the job I liked least. I worked with strangers and I always hated being underground.'

Marc made sounds of acquiescent sympathy.

'It was a week or two before Archelaus was due to go into exile. I had arrived early and walked to the lower level. One of the others was already there. We always took lots to see which two of the three would stay. He told me to go, that the other chap was on his way and they would be happy to do it. I hesitated. I very nearly agreed to it and how I wish now that I had, but then I remembered that someone told me to be wary about this kind of offer – it was

344

being used by those in senior positions to trap the likes of me.'

Dimitri stopped and took a deep breath. His wife leaned over and took his hand.

'It's all right Dimitri, you know you are safe now. Nothing will ever harm us again. Trust the Lord.'

His voice wavered as he began again.

'I heard the third guard descending and turned towards the man to ask if he had the sticks so we could take lots, but before I had the chance, he hit me hard in both eyes. I thought it was with his fists at first. I didn't realize that he had rings on his middle fingers with sharp protruding stones in each. My eyes were bleeding, I could see nothing and later I lost my sight completely. But I never forgot the last face that I ever saw, before I was healed that is.

'The third man obviously knew the other. In fact, I had the feeling that two men had arrived but I couldn't be certain. They forced open my mouth and sliced my tongue. There was a shout from above and they bundled me into one of the cells and locked the door. That was the moment that my life, as I knew it then, ended. I never understood why they didn't kill me. Perhaps they were going to but were interrupted and didn't feel like coming back later to finish the job. Or perhaps they knew they had done enough damage to me that I would never be able to tell anyone anyway.

'But strangely enough, I was looked after for many years and quite well. A woman came and bandaged my wounds to stop the bleeding. She washed my eyes and mouth each day so they didn't become infected and I'm sure that's why I lived. Food was provided through a shutter in the bottom of the door. My fear gradually turned to resignation and then to determination to stay alive until they let me out. I found a sharp stone and felt my way along the wall marking out each day. I was there nearly twenty years. But my son can tell you the rest.'

Dimitri's son looked disconcerted but continued.

'One day a man came to the house. He wasn't a soldier, more like a slave. He simply said that my father would be released from prison the following week. I was to come and fetch him and never to speak of it to anyone or my whole family would be killed. I believed him. My cousin and I went to Herodium. I did not recognize my father. His eye sockets were closed. He was unable to speak although he still had a voice and made noises. Worst of all he was covered in a skin disease that looked like leprosy. I suspect that was why they wanted to get rid of him. Someone had bothered to go in and see what was happening.'

Marc thought he knew who that someone had been. The new man who took over about seven years ago and wanted rid of prisoners.

'What did you do?'

'We brought him back here but the neighbours were angry and threw stones at us, so we built him a hut, well away from the city and took him fresh food each day. Then something amazing happened. A young prophet who came from Nazareth started performing miracles of healing. My cousin and I heard him preach. It was spellbinding and what he had to say made so much sense. Then the prophet came to live here. Some of his early disciples were from the town. There was a fisherman called Simon, his brother Andrew, and our friends James and John. These were people we had grown up with and knew quite well.

'Each day we saw him drive out evil spirits and then one day he healed Simon's mother-in-law of a fever. We were convinced that if only we could bring father in front of him, he would be healed. Our opportunity came. Jesus took such pity on father when he saw him. He said to him, 'Be clean!' and the disease just disappeared. Then he touched his eyes and mouth. Father could not believe it and neither could my brother and I. It was absolutely miraculous.'

The man looked towards his father and tears rolled down his cheeks. Mary put her arms round the son.

'You have done well,' she said gently.

Miriam decided to continue the story.

'The trouble was we soon became afraid that someone would discover Dimitri had been healed, and think he might talk about what had happened to him. No one ever came though. Perhaps they were confident that he would not be believed. It happened so long ago. And then Dimitri began to follow Jesus and soon after I began to follow the Lord too.'

'So tell me, Dimitri, what happened in Damascus?' said Marc.

'I saw the man who put out my eyes. He was riding in the procession with the rest of you. I don't know his name, but he is of stocky build and has put on a lot of weight since I saw him last. He was to the left of Pontius Pilate. I doubt he knows who I am, but I cannot take the risk.'

Marc noted that Dimitri talked about Marcellus as though he was still alive.

'How do you feel about him now?'

'Strangely, I feel very little now. I admit I felt afraid when I saw him and my first thoughts were to get back to my family and make sure they were safe. But as for the man himself – well, God has been so good to me that he has completely healed my body and redeemed my soul. It has helped being here with Mary for a couple of days. She strengthens my faith and takes away my ghosts. I have forgiven him – I will leave him to God to deal with in whatever way he feels fit.'

'The man you are talking of is called Marcellus. He is from Jerusalem. Just now his body is on the way back.'

'His body – what do you mean?'

'He died the night of the funeral. He was poisoned, by someone who brought wine to the tent.'

'And you think I may have done it?'

'Did you?'

'No. I did not. In the name of my Lord Jesus Christ, I did not kill the man.'

'I believe you,' said Marc. 'There will be no more recriminations. What happened to you was wrong and to be deeply regretted. I thank God that you have found healing and peace. As for Marcellus, the Lord has already pronounced his judgement.'

Mary smiled. 'Do you know that you sound like one of us?'

Marc was startled.

'Do I? Perhaps that is no bad thing.'

But his mind was still troubled. If Dimitri did not kill Marcellus then who did?

41

-Confession-

The sky was clear and fine mist heralded another good day. Shouts and laughter emanated from the shore where the fishermen were returning from the night's trawling. There was no way of knowing how far ahead Pilate and his contingent would be. They would most certainly have stayed with Herod Antipas at Tiberias. Marc had no particular desire to catch up with them – quite the reverse – so he stayed with Mary and her friends another day. Mary was delighted. This was, after all, the man who with his companion had saved her from rape, and possibly worse, that fateful night in Jerusalem. She felt that she owed him a great deal and was quite certain that the hand of her Lord had been in the entire incident. Marc felt that might be the case too, particularly since it had led to the arrest of two of the thieves who had broken into Marcellus' house, both of whom had been crucified with Jesus.

The Galilean hills were rich and green; the view was restful but active and entertaining. He sat looking out across the sea, reassessing what he knew and what he did not know.

Was the attack on Dimitri made at the same time as the theft? It would make sense to believe that was the case. Who was the woman who knew he was there? Dimitri had been released seven years ago and had been imprisoned twenty years. So maybe Herod Philip was right in his assumption that Archelaus was responsible for the theft. But what had he done with the stones? They were not amongst his personal possessions when he died, so he must have sold them, but an exchange of that kind would have been spoken of. Perhaps the jewels that remained in Jerusalem were used to reward those who helped him. That may account for why Marcellus and Joel had some of them.

Marc allowed all the information to accumulate in his mind, then lay back on the grass and rested, allowing his brain to sort out the information. By the time he walked back to Mary's house he felt an urgency to return to Jerusalem. There was someone he needed to see.

The sights and sounds of Jerusalem were familiar and comfortable as Marc rode through the Damascus Gate. He went straight to Herod's Palace to register his arrival. Pilate was in a very disagreeable mood, never having expected to still be in the city.

'How is Aemilia?' asked Marc.

'She's hysterical as usual. That woman is extremely tiresome. It makes me so grateful that I had the good sense to marry Claudia.'

Interesting the way Pilate expressed that notion, thought Marc, attributing his fortune to himself rather than fate looking kindly on him. He suspected Claudia may have had some regrets but that was none of his business.

Pilate continued, 'She actually seems more upset about her necklace than she does the death of her husband. She hates you with a vengeance. Take my advice, keep out of her way.'

Does she hate me enough to conspire to murder me? Marc thought. All because of a piece of worthless jewellery!

'It would be better if you didn't go to the funeral,' continued Pilate. 'I'm sorry to have to tell you that, because I know you have come all this way especially. But I really think the woman is mad. One look at you and it may tip her over the edge. It would be disgraceful if she made a scene. She'll be bad enough as it is.'

That was enough to satisfy Marc.

'Don't worry! I'll not go anywhere near the place.'

As he walked back into the garden, he caught sight of Claudia. It had been a while since he spoke to her and she was just the person he wanted to see.

'Claudia, how are you?' He walked up to her and squeezed her hand.

'Marc! How lovely to see you. What a dreadful business this is with Gaius and now Marcellus dying like that.'

'I shall miss Gaius. He always had such a positive attitude towards life.'

'Indeed he did. And how strange it is that Marcellus was poisoned. Who do you suppose did it?'

'I suspect Marcellus had more enemies than we know of.'

'Do you think he was a bad man?'

Marc had an image of a young Marcellus gouging out the eyes of Dimitri.

'I think he was capable of cruelty, like the rest of us. Claudia, I have a great favour to ask you. Will you come with me to see Anna again?'

'Anna? Yes, of course, I would love to see her, but why?'

'She might not have told us all she knew and will be more willing to discuss the past if she has a good friend with her. She trusts you.'

'Are you asking me to be disloyal to her?'

'No! But I feel close to finding the truth of the Herodian stones and I'm sure she can tell me what I need to know.'

'If I hear it too, will I be able to cope with it?'

'You're a strong woman, Claudia. You know that it's within all of us to do good and evil. But I believe you also understand the power of forgiveness.'

'Are they the only clues you're giving me?'

'Do you remember Salampsio telling us she suspected there had been an arrest of a guard while she was still living at Herodium? Well, I found him. His name is Dimitri. He was imprisoned in the dungeon for twenty years. Silas released him when he took over the job of Keeper of the Key. It was probably on somebody else's orders – the chief of staff, maybe. Dimitri was blind and mute.'

Claudia gasped. 'It makes you wonder how we can inflict so much pain on one another. It will be fear that caused it.'

'Do you also remember the prophet Jesus, the one you dreamed about the night before he was crucified?'

'Yes, I do. How could I forget? I sent a warning to Pilate to have nothing to do with him, but he didn't take any notice.'

'Perhaps that's because fate had already decreed that Jesus should die. Nevertheless, I have been hearing a great deal about him. He healed Dimitri of all his afflictions so that he's now fit and healthy although getting on in years.'

'That's an amazing story. And you spoke to Dimitri?'

'Yes!'

Claudia paused, realizing the implication of this.

'So you know who did that terrible thing to him.'

'It was Marcellus.'

Claudia fell silent not knowing what to say.

Marc said, 'He wasn't alone. And there was a woman involved as well. Someone helped Dimitri while he was in prison.'

'What are you suggesting?'

'That Joel was involved at the time and that Anna helped Dimitri.'

'Surely you can't imagine that Joel would be so cruel. You forget, I knew him! He may have been extreme in his views but he was a god-fearing man. He would never have done such a thing to another human being.'

'I'm sure you're right, and I don't think he did, but I believe he was part of the plot to steal the jewels. Dimitri said that Marcellus tried to bribe him to leave, but he was suspicious that it was a trap to get him into trouble and so he refused. If he had gone when asked, he would never have been attacked.'

'So you think Joel didn't know what was going to happen.'

'I don't think anyone really intended it. That's probably why they put Dimitri in prison rather than killing him. They hadn't planned on murder.'

'Do you think Anna may know who else was involved?'

'I do. Herod Philip thinks it was his brother Archelaus.'

'Taking valuables from the vault before he was exiled?'

'Yes.'

'When do you want to go and see Anna?'

'Can you come now?'

'Give me half an hour. I'll meet you by the gate.'

Anna heard the knock and shuffled slowly across the room. Her legs and feet were particularly painful today. Her wizened face broke into a large smile when she saw Claudia on her doorstep.

'What a surprise! Please come in. And Commander Tiro is with you. How are you Commander?'

They perched on some hard chairs; Anna apologised for the lack of hospitality, but she had very few coins left and was too crippled to go out.

'Is someone looking after you?' asked Claudia.

'I have a neighbour who looks in occasionally and will buy me some food once a week. But I am not worried. I feel now that my time is very close. I am glad you have come, if you had left it longer I may never have seen you again.'

'Please don't say that, Anna. You have plenty more years left.'

'No, my dear, I do not. Neither do I crave them. A person somehow knows when the end is getting close. Please don't worry about me or be fearful. I am ready to go. In fact, I want to go. Since Joel left me, there is very little to live for.'

'Anna, we have come for a purpose.'

'Yes, I know. I was expecting that you would be back. I knew your Commander would not be satisfied and he would guess.'

'Guess what?'

'That I have information he would like to know. I should have told you before but I was too concerned with protecting my husband's reputation. Now I have come to realize that it doesn't matter. He will be forgiven – he was not a bad man, just a bit misguided perhaps. But I believe that he would have wanted me to tell you and, when you know, I can die in peace and he can rest.'

'I am sorry, Anna, this must be very painful for you.'

'Not as painful as living with the knowledge! You probably have learned most of the story by now anyway and I know that I can't tell you everything, but what I have to say will help you.'

'Please tell us in you own time,' said Claudia. 'Stop if you find it too difficult.'

'Joel was a young man on fire for his God. He was honest and became disillusioned by the secular and hypocritical ways of the Pharisees and the Jewish leaders of the Sanhedrin. He joined the Essenes and became totally committed to their cause.

'When he heard that the lapis lazuli jewellery had once belonged to Cleopatra and been given to the Hasmoneans to fight the Romans, he was incensed that it now languished in the vaults that he had been engaged to protect and that it belonged to Augustus.

'He often spoke of how he had access since he was Keeper of the Key, but did not have opportunity because Roman soldiers were always present outside the vault. One day, his boss approached him. He had just been appointed chief administrator when the first governor came to Jerusalem, one of his tasks was to oversee Herodium. I don't think the arrangement has changed.'

'No, it hasn't,' confirmed Marc.

'He asked him if he would be prepared to join in a plot to steal Mariamne's jewels. After all, he argued, they were doing no good where they were. Nobody seemed to want them. Herod had been dead two years and nobody had bothered to come and get them. It was all true, and made perfectly good sense to my Joel. He did not even see it as stealing. To him, it was putting right a wrong. He was to receive some of the jewels for his trouble, and all he could see was that he would be benefitting the Essene cause. They were busy accumulating wealth for the time they would need it to stand against the occupying enemy.'

Anna paused and took a few deep breaths as though to calm herself. Claudia took her hand and smiled. The old lady seemed reassured and continued.

'Joel's boss told him that there was a conspiracy from the highest level. Joel assumed that it was from Archelaus himself. He had been almost a prisoner in his own palace after the Emperor decided to replace him. He knew he was to be exiled any day. Joel never saw the Romans as his superiors – not in his heart – and would probably have preferred to work for Archelaus, despite his evil ways.

'The day arrived for the theft to take place. Then it all went horribly wrong. Marcellus arrived and Joel gave him the key, but the innocent soldier with him, called Dimitri, refused a bribe to leave, and insisted lots were drawn. Marcellus had not anticipated this and hit him with both fists in the face, damaging both his eyes.

'The second man to arrive sliced his tongue so he would never be able to tell anyone, and they shoved Dimitri in the dungeon. When Joel learned what had happened, he was dreadfully upset. He couldn't believe the state of the man. I offered to help. For nearly twenty years I looked after him and made sure he had food. Nobody ever mentioned him as though he had never existed. I think it was assumed he had died. Joel never let anybody know what I was doing and no-one ever asked, until Silas was appointed. He came the year Pontius Pilate arrived in Jerusalem. He had the dungeon scrubbed from top to bottom and told Tribune Polybius, of course.'

'Polybius?' queried Marc.

'Yes. He was Joel's old boss at the time of the theft, although he had moved on to other things. I thought you knew that.'

'So Tribune Polybius was the second man?' said Claudia.

'I don't know for sure. Remember that Joel was not directly involved, other than releasing the key, which was bad enough. Anyway he got no reward for doing it. The man at the top argued that the job had not been carried out smoothly and that there was now a risk of being discovered.'

'How did Joel come to have a crown and anklet?'

'It was strange how that happened. He received his reward eleven years later. He had always assumed he had been duped. He was totally ashamed – that's why he stayed, so that we could look after Dimitri as best we could. He would definitely have died otherwise. The jewels appeared on the doorstep in a bag. I thought he was given them to keep him quiet because he had started to talk about the incident more and more with me. Someone wanted to make sure he kept his mouth shut and giving him the jewels would ensure that, wouldn't it?'

Anna looked to Claudia who nodded in agreement.

'He took them to Qumran and marked them on the copper scroll, then hid them, each with a scriptural clue for future Essenes to find. People who do not know the scriptures would be unable to decipher them. He felt somehow more at peace then – knowing he had contributed to the cause. He talked about it less. Nine years later, when Dimitri was released, he seemed even more at peace. He prayed everyday for forgiveness and I think he was beginning to forgive himself, which is much more difficult.'

'So what happened to destroy his peace?' asked Claudia quietly.

'Last summer, two men came to the door. They said they were Essenes and we invited them in. They knew about the jewels, although would not say how. They wanted Joel to tell them what clues he had left and what they meant. He didn't want to tell them. He said that when the time was right, they would be found. Meanwhile they should rest where they were. Then one night the men came and fetched him. He had no choice but to go with them. I never saw him alive again. They had tortured him. His fingers were broken on one hand and his nails were ripped out. I knew he would never hang himself.'

Anna started to weep. A few minutes passed.

'I don't really have anything else to tell you. I don't know what the two men did with the information, or even if my Joel told them. But I suspect he did. He was not a brave soul - just an ordinary man who was led astray, but suffered for it. Do you know what has happened to Dimitri? Did he die?'

'No, he didn't. He was healed completely, thanks to a man called Jesus,' said Marc.

'You mean the man who was crucified with those two thieves?'

'Yes.'

'Well, well! I have heard that people are now following him saying he is the risen Lord. I'm afraid I'm too steeped in the old scriptures to believe it, although they did prophesy that a redeemer would come to save the Jews.'

Marc remembered well what he had learned at Qumran.

'It's true that it was predicted,' he said.

Anna continued. 'I can't think that Jesus is our Messiah. But history may prove me wrong.'

Claudia said, 'Anna, we are just going to get you some provisions and I'll cook you something before we go.'

Anna smiled. 'Please don't trouble yourself my dear.'

'It's no trouble. We'll not be long.'

Marc and Claudia walked in silence to the bakery and then bought fresh vegetables and fruit. When they returned, they knocked once again on Anna's door. But this time there was no reply.

42

-A Promise Fulfilled-

They spent some time informing neighbours of Anna's death; Claudia was to take care of the funeral arrangements. The two returned to the palace in doleful mood. Cornelius met them coming up the steps.

'Watch out Marc!' he warned. 'Aemilia is waiting for you on the rear terrace. She refused to leave when she learned that you had arrived from Damascus. She's in a foul temper.'

'Well, I suppose I shall have to face her sometime.'

'I'll come with you,' said Claudia. 'You never know, the presence of another woman may calm her down.'
Cornelius chuckled.

'I doubt it, my dear! I doubt it very much. Good luck to both of you!'

Aemilia was pacing up and down. As soon as they arrived she addressed Marc.

'I hold you totally responsible for the death of my husband. Totally! We were happy before you arrived with your impertinent questions and arrogant ways. You had no right to interfere with our lives.'

'I deeply regret your loss and your distress.'

'Distress, distress, you understand nothing. You should have died at Bethel. It's a pity Gaius didn't kill you and leave you to the wolves. I positively prayed to every god under the sun that it should happen.'

'And I thought it was your husband who desired my demise.'

'My husband, my dear sweet loving generous husband, he

wouldn't hurt a fly.'

'No, he just destroyed an innocent man's eyes with his fists,' said Claudia, her voice wavering.

'What are you talking about? How dare you! How dare you make insinuations about my poor tender husband! He's not even been buried yet.'

'Marcellus was neither poor nor tender. There may be much you do not know about him.' Claudia was upset.

Aemilia screeched. 'I have only ever had two things of value to me, my husband and my necklace. Both have been taken from me. One I shall never see again and the other I never want to see again. You are both hateful.'

Pontius Pilate strutted onto the terrace having been disturbed by all the noise.

'Now madam, I have heard enough. I will excuse the insult to my wife by your present grief. But please do not call here again. Your acceptance in our society was due to your husband's status only – not by any right of your own. You are no longer welcome after this behaviour.'

Aemilia departed, sobbing as loudly as she could. Marc actually felt sorry for her.

Pilate addressed his wife. 'Claudia, I don't know what you have involved yourself in here and I don't want to know, not just at the moment in any event, but I would appreciate it if you would now desist.'

'Some things are just too important to ignore,' she said. Then with a small bow, she took her leave.

'Marc, you know how grateful I am to you for what you have done. But our society is fragile. Tempers fray easily.'

'Yes, particularly when murder and deceit are involved.'
Pilate looked at him for several seconds.

'Very well, have it your way. But be careful. I will not tolerate Claudia's involvement.'

'I won't involve her any more. Please accept my apologies!'

Pilate's reasonableness could only be explained by the concern he felt for his own position, particularly since Marcellus had died under suspicious circumstances. An unfamiliar dark mist of depression crept over Marc. He fetched his horse. There were some friends he wanted to see.

He went out of the western gate, near the almost permanent encampment where Crassus and his group had stayed, and followed the road to Emmaus. Jonathan saw him coming long before Marc reached the farm, and galloped out to greet him. It was like coming home. Daleel was not far behind. The men could not have been more heartened by the sight of each other. Daleel and Jonathan wanted to know every detail of the journey that had taken Marc to Damascus and he left nothing out.

'Now I must tell you my news,' said Jonathan. 'Come out back.' There, in a makeshift paddock, were the four beautiful black horses that had belonged to his father, Aziz.

'What are they doing here?'

Daleel said, 'Jonathan has ridden them in the hippodrome south of the city. He didn't win but he came second. Admittedly it's not Rome, but there were a lot of competitors. There was a man watching who looks out for young new talent. He was so impressed by Jonathan's performance that he invited him to race at Caesarea next week. It's a very great honour being so young.'

'Well done! I'm proud of you,' said Marc.

'My father has given his approval. It is a big race; the prize money is good. If I can win, it will pay for my education. Or perhaps it will take me to Rome to visit you.'

'Who says I'm going?'

'You have a son.'

'Perhaps I can persuade my son to come here.'

'No! That would not be right. His home is in Rome. You should allow him to stay until he is old enough to make up his own mind.'

Marc laughed but did not scold Jonathan for his bold statement. The boy was probably right.

Later that night, when Jonathan was asleep, Marc discussed with Daleel what he had learned about Anthony Avitus, Joel, Dimitri, Polybius and Marcellus.

'Well, Marcellus has been punished. Do you know who poisoned him?'

'Dimitri denies it was him.'

'And you believe him?'

'Yes, I do.'

'Do you truly believe that he was miraculously cured?'

'Yes.'

'Well, I suppose these things do happen. We have some very good curative herb mixtures that heal all sorts of diseases.'

Marc realized that this was one area that was not worth pursuing with Daleel. He would not understand.

'Are you going to challenge Polybius?'

'Yes, if I get the chance. Anna thought he might have been the second man present. He may know who murdered Joel.'

'If I were you, I wouldn't bother. The theft was a long time ago. You'll just put his back up and end up getting yourself killed. Too many people have gone that way already.'

'Well, I'll sleep on it.'

Next morning, when he arrived back at the palace, Cornelius was waiting.

'I've been looking for you. Claudia told Pilate that she visited Anna yesterday and that her husband Joel was involved with a theft at Herodium, just before Archelaus left.'

'Yes, that's correct.'

'Do we assume that Archelaus was behind it after all?'

'Certainly looks that way.'

'She also said that Tribune Polybius might have been there.'

'That is also what Anna claims.'

'And are you prepared to believe the words of a deranged old woman who was at death's door?'

'It's not for me to believe or disbelieve. I am merely seeking the truth.'

Cornelius snorted.

'Well I think you had better look in more reliable places.'

'Thank you for the suggestion.'

'Glad you see sense then.'

Marc looked down, rocked back on his feet and glanced at Cornelius by raising his eyebrow.

'Are you acquainted with the phrase, "No greater friend; no worse enemy?"'

The cleft of Cornelius' brow deepened further.

'It sounds familiar! Is this another of your riddles?'

'It was the epitaph of your ancestor and namesake.'

'What of it?'

'It was a third clue written on the map of Qumran found on the slave's body in the aqueduct near Herodium.'

'How did you discover it was an epitaph?'

'It was written beneath a bust of Sulla in the hall of Herod Philip's palace.'

'And what do you think it was trying to tell you?'

'I don't know. The other two clues were from old Jewish scriptures, the third clue was something of an anomaly.'

'I can't help you. If it's a guide to another piece of jewellery, I shouldn't bother. Firstly, there are probably several busts of my ancestor – he was a famous general after all. And secondly, if the other clues are anything to go by, you'll only find more of the useless, worthless stuff.'

'Do you have any idea who could have killed Marcellus?' asked Marc.

'No, I don't. Undoubtedly it will be some disgruntled citizen who hates Romans. Marcellus was just unlucky. Nobody considers the fact that I might be dead as well. I drank some of the wine, you know. It was just fortunate that I had only just arrived and therefore had no more than a few sips.'

'That was fortunate indeed.'

Although Marc had made his comment without a trace or hint of sarcasm, Cornelius eyed him with suspicion.

'You're not suspecting me now, I hope. Really Commander Tiro, I always thought you were a good investigator but this is going too far.'

'It hadn't even crossed my mind.'

Cornelius looked disconcerted.

'That's good then. Make sure you don't go accusing me of anything, or Pilate, come to that. Remember, it was us who invited you here in the first place. We'd hardly be doing that if we were in any way to blame, and paying for the privilege of being found out.'

'No indeed.'

Placated, Cornelius relaxed.

'I'm returning to Caesarea as soon as this wretched funeral is over. I really can't abide them. I'm entering the chariot race at the hippodrome next week.'

Marc could hardly contain his surprise and said so.

'Why what's the matter – think I'm too old, do you? I have a magnificent set of Arabs. You know that, you've seen them. Julius, poor fellow, is no longer able to ride. I intend to have one last go as a competitor. It's an important race. I have spent a lot of time getting fit again. I'll show them that I'm still the best.'

'I wish you luck then.'

'I am inviting you to attend. In fact, I insist upon it. Have my seat in the central section for honoured guests. I shall have no need of it.'

'I look forward to it.'

'You must come and stay in my newly reconstructed house.

You can tell me if you think it's an improvement on the last one. Julius is expecting you. He still works for me, though I warn you be prepared for a shock when you see him.'

Marc thought carefully about whether or not to approach Tribune Polybius. Cornelius was right. He had only the word of Anna, and although he had no doubt about her honest belief, she had not been present. Nevertheless, Polybius was Joel's chief at the time and had encouraged the theft. Marc was no further towards knowing who the two men were who claimed to be Essenes. There were still vital pieces missing in the puzzle. However, a walk to Antonia Fort confirmed that Tribune Polybius was not in the area, and not expected for another three weeks. There was doubt about whether he would be in Jerusalem for the funeral of Marcellus.

Later that afternoon Marc made a visit he had subconsciously been avoiding – to see Rebecca, not knowing whether she would blame him for the suicide of her stepmother and half brother. He had thought of her often, and as soon as he set eyes on her he knew why. The fair curls sat high on her head; just the occasional few tumbled over her cheeks and down the nape of her neck. She was wearing the dress that she wore the day he first met her. Her voice was soft and inviting as she asked him to sit in the garden with her. Daniel and Rachel were nowhere to be seen.

'I have come to say how sorry I am about Anthony and Sabina. I only wish I could have stopped it happening.'

'I blamed myself. I should have told Sabina that Anthony was alive.'

'I am equally to blame. I suggested that you not do so.'

'I know. But the final decision was mine. I thought it best not to say anything because of Anthony's unpredictability. Sometimes it's easier to bury the dead than accept that the living no longer love you. I would have told her, once you had found him. Meanwhile, we could not be sure what had happened to him. Or at least that was how I rationalized it to myself. Anthony certainly loved his mother, even though he was ambivalent about his wife. He was like a child – not quite mature. He always wanted what he wanted immediately. It would not occur to him that a relationship needed working on to be a success. With his mother it didn't matter, because she would always love him no matter how badly he behaved. With wives it is different. They expect more.'

'And probably get less.'

Rebecca shrugged. 'Perhaps they do.'

'I have thought of you constantly while I was away.'

Rebecca looked down at her hands folded in her lap.

'Marc, please do not say any more at this moment because I don't know how to reply to you. I think I could love you, but I loved my husband and he was taken away from me. I have become a new person since then and I have not yet decided on the direction of my life.'

'Well, should you ever decide that it might be worth moving a little in my direction, will you promise to let me know?'

'Yes, I will, I promise. But you are likely to leave soon and I might never see you again.'

'I can assure you that if I thought I might be able to spend some more time with you, wild horses would not prevent me from coming to Jerusalem. The empire is not that large.'

Rebecca smiled, leaned across and kissed him on the mouth. He momentarily felt weightless and euphoric. He reached round the back of her neck and pulled her face closer, returning her kiss with a passion that surprised even him. He felt like an immature boy and could not decide whether he despised himself for it or was grateful that he was still capable of such feeling.

A banging door, somewhere from another life, made her draw away quickly. Rachel bounded into the garden anxious to tell her mother about the pony ride that she had just enjoyed with Daniel. It occurred to Marc, once again, that this man was more than a simple slave but might live his whole life in a state of unfulfilled love. Maybe that was enough for him. With a woman like Rebecca perhaps a few crumbs are better than nothing at all.

Salampsio had just finished her late afternoon meal when her slave went to answer the outer door. A voice rose to the terrace where she was enjoying the ambience of the evening. Recognizing it immediately, she ran a palm across her hair and adjusted her dress.

'Marc, it's lovely to see you! Come! Sit with me and enjoy some wine.'

'It's good to see you looking so well Salampsio.'

'It takes me longer each day to look like this. Once it took two minutes, now I need two hours.'

'The effect is the same – enchanting as ever.'

'Commander, you wouldn't be trying to satisfy an old woman's ego, would you? I know flattery when I see it. But I love it just the same.' She gave one of her girlish giggles.

'I have come to fulfil a promise that I wasn't sure if I could keep. But I now need a good home for a splendid necklace, a bracelet and anklet if you would like them.'

'Commander, I would love to have them. I don't care if they have no value – they have priceless memories and that's more important. Did you find Drusilla in Jericho?'

'Yes. She showed me a brooch that Herod had given her before he died. I confess it had a rare quality – almost hypnotic. But I learned from an old jewel expert called Rashidi that some of the stones in your mother's collection were fake, but by no means all. It also looks as though the main theft took place just before Archelaus was exiled. He might have even taken the stones with him. Herod Philip seemed to think he stole them out of spite, or possibly because he needed the money.'

'And how did he pass the guards?'

'He had help. Marcellus was involved and possibly Tribune

Polybius, although I have not had a chance to confirm that. Joel, I'm afraid, was part of the plot as well. His motives may have been purer than the others, but he was nevertheless a thief.'

'This is a closed society. More people know about things that have gone on in the past than they will confess to. They watch one another's back because they all know something about each other.'

'Or end up killing each other to retain silence.'

'That's true too. Do you think that's what happened to Joel?'

'Yes, I do. But who did it is still a mystery.'

'I'm sorry you didn't get all your answers. What will you do now?'

'Travel to Caesarea. I'm going to a chariot race. Cornelius is entering, and also a young man I met a few weeks ago. And then I shall return to Rome. I shall just have to get used to the idea that I have failed to solve this crime in its entirety – it'll do me good – teach me some humility.'

'You never know, the answer may yet be out there somewhere.'

'That's being very optimistic but I'll try to keep reminding myself.'

They laughed and enjoyed one another's company for an hour or so until Marc took his leave. Salampsio stood up slowly and put her arms round him.

'If you were my son, I would be very proud. And if you were my husband – well, there now, my thoughts are unmentionable.'

'Take care of yourself – and enjoy wearing your jewels.'

'I will. Farewell and thank you.'

43

The day of the funeral came and went. Tribune Polybius sent his apologies. Pilate was in a very good mood. He was going back to Caesarea until his next compulsory visit. He was ready. Marc did not go back with the main party but chose instead to ride with Jonathan, Daleel and their brother Nadeem. Each of them led one of the four magnificent black horses that Jonathan was due to harness in the chariot race. He was immensely excited.

'I never imagined that I would have the opportunity to do this. I am so lucky,' he repeated regularly. Marc had some serious doubts. He thought of Julius – another young man who had been full of hope – he had recognized the dangers though. So many charioteers had been killed. Still, if his father and brothers were supporting him, there was nothing to be done but give him all the help he could. They travelled more quickly than Pilate's party because they did not have the hindrance of the carriage required for Claudia. She had so often protested to her husband that she would prefer to ride herself, but he would not hear of it. His wife should be afforded a status befitting his own.

Approaching Caesarea, the long narrow structure of the hippodrome with its semi-circular end came into view. A camp had been established nearby for the competitors who had travelled a long way, similar to those provided for pilgrims entering Jerusalem.

Jonathan rode up to the monstrous base colonnades and strained his neck backwards to see the top of the building. Stewards directed them through the archways that led down to stables below. The whole place was thronged. Veterinaries were examining

368

hooves and hocks. Stable boys replaced straw and hay. Bets were being taken – vast amounts of gold coins were exchanged. Blacksmiths were glowing over red hot braziers; sizzling steam emerged from nearby buckets of cold water as the heated iron cooled. Saddlers with nails in their mouths hammered and stitched and mended bits of broken bridles and harnesses. Smells of horse, leather, smoke and sweat combined to fill the air with something essentially masculine. This one sport supported several industries and provided work and income for hundreds of people.

Once the horses were safely housed, the four of them walked through a central arch at one end of the stadium and into the long U-shaped arena. Men sweeping the surface were diminutive beside the colossal central barrier, lavishly sculptured with obelisks, which divided the track. Turning posts were situated at each end. They were standing near the starting gates - Jonathan counted ten – from which the four horse chariots drove to the right counter-clockwise for seven laps.

Markers in the shape of huge ornate golden eagles were tested, one by one, each dropped down as a lap was completed. On either side were tiers of seats for the spectators. Half way down the right hand side was a pillared roofed and balconied veranda, set apart for important people. This no doubt was where Cornelius had his seat, alongside Pontius Pilate. Musicians were practising trumpets, horns and drums to be played before the race started, to rouse the spectators' competitive spirit.

'I've been told I can practise here tomorrow morning,' said Jonathan, the excitement in his voice barely containable. 'Please come and watch me, master Marc.'

'Certainly I'll be here, and the day after tomorrow to see you win.' The feelings of trepidation were well hidden.

Marc had told Cornelius that he would stay at his new home, now completed due to the free labour of a multitude of slaves, and took the road he had travelled with Julius on first arriving in this land. The then burgeoning blossoms had fulfilled their promises of extrovert colourful displays, and were now showing signs of tiredness. But apart from this much was still the same, with roadside haggling trade and the constant need for refreshing life-giving water from the local wells.

Marc caught sight of the back of a figure in the grounds as he approached the new house. It was identical to the last in every detail. The same wall surrounded the grounds – only the gardens still showed signs of damage. The figure stood up and looked behind him. Seeing a visitor, he donned a headpiece made of thin white material that veiled his head and face. A full-length tunic covered the rest of the body. No hand hung from below the left sleeve. The figure opened the gate and allowed Marc to ride up to the portal before dismounting.

'Cornelius told me to expect you, sir. Everything is prepared for you.'

Marc could see very little except one eye that was partially closed.

'Thank you, Julius.'

They walked into the replica atrium, turned into a corridor on the right and into a room similar to the one in which the attack with the dagger had taken place. The furnishings were different, however, much simpler and less flowery. As usual, the bath was soon ready and waiting. Marc told Julius he needed no further assistance and the disabled slave gratefully retreated. However, a meal was waiting for him with a jug of wine.

He went to bed early and slept fitfully. A bright light flickered and in a trice he was on his feet. There was a shadow at the door holding a torch in its right arm. The similarity to a previous occasion was stark – his dagger was ready for any onslaught.

'Don't be alarmed!' It was Julius' voice. 'I want you to see what you saved and I want you to understand why I despise you for it.'

He allowed the light to fall on his naked grotesque body. The skin of the torso was shrivelled like an old tree trunk. One arm was skeletal; a limp lump of fingerless flesh hung where a hand had once been. No hair crowned his head, just a blackened scalp. The left side of his face was horribly distorted and the ear was missing. Marc could find no words and none were required. Julius simply wanted him to look. His legs were relatively untouched, though he had no testicles. He looked like a ghoul from the grave, yet he was still a young man. After a few moments he turned and walked away. Marc stood, wondering, tears of pity wet his cheeks.

Neither man made any reference to the incident. It was as though Julius needed to do what he did to get over a point, after that, there was no more to say.

Marc kept his promise to Jonathan and spent most of the next day advising, watching and admiring. The boy's ability was astonishing. He handled the horses with the skill of a professional and they responded readily to his every command. They were swift and worked together as a team, intelligently supporting one another to best effect. The race was programmed for late afternoon the next day. Jonathan's colours were white, as instructed by the man who had supported his entry. Of him, however, there was no sign. After circulating the course several times, they walked the horses back to the stables to rest. Cornelius' dapple-grey Arabs were being harnessed for a practice run.

Cornelius approached them. 'Good day to you! We've just arrived. Don't tell me you're taking up the challenge Marc?'

'No, I'm here to support my young friend, Jonathan.'

'Well, well, and I thought you would be supporting me.'

'May the best man, win.'

'Or boy, it would seem. Yes, I'm all in favour of that. Come and watch, see what you think.'

Daleel and Marc sat in the side seats as Cornelius and his 'Arabian beauties' flew round the circuit; their leader, Zeus, dominated the team with power and style. Cornelius pulled up beside them, barely out of breath.

'You see I have lost none of my magic touch, have I? Tomorrow it will be a battle of youth over age. And what a battle it will be.'

Excitement and anticipation filled the hippodrome. It was impossible to be insensitive to the aroused emotions and tensions that magnetized the atmosphere. Appearance was as important as skill and both horses and riders preened and plumed to look their best.

Marc felt he needed a break from the hubbub, which somehow heightened his awareness of ominous portent. As he walked out from under the main base colonnade, he saw a man coming towards him whom he felt sure he knew. The man obviously recognized him and waved. Marc waited until he was closer – to his utter astonishment it was Judas.

'You look surprised to see me. I was told I might find you here. Can we talk somewhere in private?'

'Yes, by all means! I know a little place where we can get a drink down by the harbour. But what on earth are you doing here?'

'I'd rather not talk now – let's move away from this place, you never know who might be listening.'

Marc could hardly contain his curiosity but did as Judas had asked. They walked by the end of the road where Gaius had once lived and down the hill to the harbour, to the bar where the two of them had enjoyed a beer what now seemed like such a long time ago. They ordered some drinks and took them outside, away from prying eyes and ears.

'I came to find you because you were not told the whole truth when you were in Damascus. It was not my business to tell you but the person involved has now asked me to come and plead her case and ask for forgiveness.'

'Plead her case? I assume you are talking about Candace.'

'Yes.'

'I don't understand. I know that she pretended to be a man in order to retain her acting career, but I can hardly blame her for that, in fact I applaud her courage for doing so. Many young women would have not even attempted what she did.'

'There is rather more to it than that. Candace carries with her a very great sin, for which she requires your absolution.'

'Mine!' said Marc incredulously.

'Yes. She tried to kill you.'

Marc was stunned into silence as he tried to absorb this piece of information.

'You had better continue because I am at a total loss to begin to understand why or how or when. I hardly know her. Surely I have not upset her so much that she would want to kill me – there must be some mistake.'

'There is no mistake about what she did. She burned down the house where you were staying and tried to impale you with a dagger, although I believe its blade was not intended for you. A few nights before, you had been at a performance of "Oedipus Rex" with Pontius Pilate, his wife Claudia and a man called Cornelius Sulla. Am I correct?'

'Yes.'

'And you were all introduced to the cast were you not?'

'Yes.'

'Candace was brought up in Greece but had very little memory of her early childhood. That night, as she was introduced to Cornelius Sulla, parts of her life came flooding back. She recognized him as the man who murdered her mother. He came to their house one day, where the two of them lived alone. He slit her mother's throat. Candace was then ten years old and witnessed it happening. Realizing she had seen him, he picked her up in his arms, looked her full in the face, apologised saying he was sorry, just as he did during their conversation at the theatre, then threw her against the wall with his full force and left her for dead.'

'Is she absolutely certain it was Cornelius? That's quite an accusation to be making against the man.'

'She says she is completely sure.'

'The events have come back to her in waves. She remembers him pulling her mother's necklace from her throat as he murdered her and assumed he was stealing it. I heard your assignment here was to search for stolen jewels from Herodium. Could there be a connection?'

'It's possible. Where was she living at the time?'

'I asked her that but she didn't know. Her earliest recollection is sailing for Greece with the woman whom she thought, until now, was her mother, who always treated her with loving care and attention as though she was her own daughter. The woman's husband, she assumed, was her father, but now she's not sure. The trauma of what she witnessed must have been so terrible that her young mind blocked it out in some way. She has written to her presumed mother in Greece and is awaiting an answer. It will be sent to Crassus here in Caesarea if it comes. She did not know at the time that she would be moving to Damascus.'

'Can she remember her mother's name?'

'No, I'm afraid not. She may never have known it; she was very young. I suppose it's possible the woman wasn't her real mother. She is totally confused as to her identity and background. She is hoping the woman in Greece can shed some light on it for her.'

'How did a young woman manage to do the amount of damage that she did?'

'She had learned how to walk again after her injuries and deliberately engaged in all kinds of sport to strengthen her body. She became a superb runner, even entered the girl's foot races at Olympia. She learned to throw the javelin, ride and climb. She had the figure of a young boy and never quite developed the normal womanly traits. Perhaps that too was due to her injuries, or the trauma, who knows? She was strong and fast.

'She found the house where Cornelius lived and observed the movements of its occupants. Knowing the dogs would give her away they had to be dealt with. The slaves bought the dogs' meat from the local stall and fed them at night. She dressed as an old woman pretending to help out the farmer, poisoned the meat she set on one side specially, and that same night scaled the wall and set fire to the house, using hay from the stables. She assumed that it was Cornelius lying in the bed when she threw a dagger at you.

'Please understand her heart was full of hatred. She was out of her mind with desire for revenge and simply did not heed the consequences. Only God can heal that kind of obsession and he did so, the moment she saw Jesus die on the cross.'

'I'm glad she has found some kind of peace. But does she know what damage she caused to the slave Julius?'

'She talked only of the fact that she had tried to kill you and failed, for which she is very thankful. What happened to the slave?'

'His body is barely recognisable as human, yet for some reason he has been spared.'

'She'll be deeply distressed to know the extent of his injuries. She believes that God was watching her that night and saved her from killing or seriously injuring anybody.'

'I wish I could bring her comfort, but the truth may preclude that if she wants to know it. God may have been watching over her, but not Julius.'

Judas looked worried.

'It's no good! We mere men cannot take sin of this kind upon our shoulders. What do you think? Should I tell her?'

Marc was reminded of another occasion when he had advised someone to keep quiet and it had led to two suicides. He thought of how presumptuous he had been then. Marc shrugged and shook his head slowly.

'I am not qualified to give an opinion on such matters.'

'I will pray about it. Can I give Candace a message from you?'

'Yes! You can tell her that her actions are understandable in the light of her suffering and desire for revenge – nevertheless, against the law. Though I hardly think Cornelius will bring charges against her in view of the provocation, so she need have no worries about that. It was only his property that was damaged, if we want to take a purely legalistic approach and include his slave. His house has been restored. As for my part, I absolve her completely. In fact, thank you for enlightening me – it clears up one more part of the mystery. Did Candace also try to poison Cornelius using a viper?'

'Actually, she did mention that. Something happened on the way to Jerusalem did it not? She said that when she realized he had not died in her arson attack, it seemed like providence when he was bitten by the snake. She was hoping he would die. I'm sure she would have told me if she had been responsible for another murder attempt. I rather think on that occasion, it was pure misfortune, unless someone else put the snake in his bag.'

'Thank you for coming to tell me this. Where are you staying?'

'Oddly enough, with a friend, also called Cornelius, and his family. I think I may yet persuade them to turn to the Lord. I will pray that you have peace and that you will now know what to do.'

'Yes, I know what I must do.'

After Judas left, Marc sat looking out to sea as the sun dropped behind the horizon. The sky was magnificent but its beauty was lost on him. He struggled to understand why Cornelius had called him to Judea to uncover a plot that it seemed he had been involved in himself. A possible answer struck him, a solution to most of the apparently contradictory bits of information that he had collected along his journey. Only confrontation would provide the answers.

He needed time to think, to plan what he was going to do and say. With a heavy heart he walked back through the city to find some rest in the camp with Daleel and Jonathan.

44

-The Conspiracy-

Next morning, early, Marc rode up to Cornelius' house. The man was walking in the grounds and waved cheerily opening up the gates. There was no sign of Julius.

'So, you stopped out all night – hope it was worth it,' he jested. Marc dismounted.

'I need to talk to you, I want your advice.'

'What's happened? Come through.'

Marc could hardly countenance the man's affability. Did he have no scruples? Of course not, why should he? Was he any different to the Senators of Rome?

'I believe we have finally got to the bottom of the missing Herodian stones.'

'How interesting, do continue.'

'I'm reaffirming what I said to you a few days ago. It was Archelaus who masterminded the theft. Herod Philip alerted me to the fact that it might be him. He supports the view.'

'But Archelaus was exiled twenty seven years ago.'

'The theft took place shortly before he left.'

'I worked for Archelaus. He entrusted me with everything. I would have known about it. I really think you have been listening to too many stories.'

'I didn't realize you were so close to him. Nevertheless, I have two witnesses who concur.'

'I know about that stupid old woman who was married to Joel. Who's the other one?'

'A soldier called Dimitri.'

'Impossible!'

'Why do you say that?'

'Because I'm sure none of it can be true.'

'Can you persuade me otherwise?'

'Yes. I was Archelaus' right hand man. He did nothing without consulting me. He trusted me. I would most certainly have known if he had planned such a thing.'

'It seems then that, on this occasion, he did not take you into his confidence. Perhaps he thought you would not go along with it. It appears he gave the task to Marcellus and Tribune Polybius.'

Cornelius narrowed his eyes. He looked like a man finding it difficult to contain his anger.

'Archelaus would never entrust anything to those two – they were totally incompetent.'

'Did you work with them?'

'Yes! They did as they were told.'

'Well I rather think, Cornelius, that they may have outwitted you. You see, together they enlisted the help of Joel to provide the key. The two of them, plus Dimitri, were put on guard duty. Marcellus tried to bribe Dimitri to leave them but he was suspicious that it might have been a plot to discredit him, so he refused. Marcellus gouged out the man's eyes and Polybius sliced his tongue. He was left to rot in a nearby dungeon but Anna looked after him for nearly twenty years. When Silas arrived, he was released. His skin had become ulcerated. I met him and have his testimony.'

'You expect me to believe that you have a statement from a man with no tongue?'

'He recovered.'

'Preposterous!'

'His story confirms what Anna had to say. She was in charge of all her faculties before she died, and Claudia is a witness.'

'So, if all this is true, what happened to the stones?'

'Archelaus duped his co-conspirators and took all the jewels with him. Marcellus and Polybius were to be rewarded with a share, but they received nothing.'

'That must have been extremely vexing for them.'

'Yes, it must. But after Archelaus died, eleven years later, one of them went looking for the jewels. They were not among Archelaus' estate because he had given them away.'

'You're guessing. You cannot know that for sure.'

'It's a good guess though, wouldn't you say?'

'So, to whom did he give them?'

'A woman, a woman with a child, perhaps his own child!'

'How do you know all this?'

'Do you think I'm right then?'

'No! It's pure conjecture.'

'Well, here's a bit more. Let's assume Polybius went to find the woman. Supposing he murdered her and murdered her daughter and stole whatever jewels she had in her possession. And then he had them valued and discovered the truth, that they were worthless. He didn't know at the time that over a thousand years ago the mine supplying these particular stones had dried up, and the king of Ugarit had substituted some rather inferior ones of his own. When the collection was commissioned by the family of Cleopatra I, on the occasion of her marriage to one of the Ptolemies of Egypt, a highly reputable jeweller from Damascus who was asked to complete the design was bribed to keep quiet about the secret. I rather think that Archelaus discovered this and had the jewels rearranged. Those that were worthless he gave to the woman, whoever she was.'

'Go on.'

'Polybius brought what he found back to Jerusalem and gave some to Marcellus and Joel in return for their silence. After all they were in it together, weren't they? But he omitted to tell them they were worthless. Joel took his two pieces and hid them, left some old scriptural clues as to their whereabouts for future Essenes to find.'

Cornelius' face had a look of hatred. He would kill me right now if he dare, thought Marc.

He continued. 'Marcellus' wife thought her necklace was highly valuable. That's why she behaved as she did – she could barely face the truth. She even offered to pay Gaius to kill me, holding me somehow responsible for the revelation.'

Cornelius interrupted him.

'She's always been a very silly woman. If what you are saying is true, why did you write a report to Pontius Pilate saying that the theft must have been recent, that it was accomplished by entering through an underground aqueduct and draining a cistern next to the vault, and that it was carried out by two Essenes.'

'Because that is what I was meant to believe. In fact, one of the pieces was found fifteen years ago, so they couldn't have been hidden recently could they?'

'How do you know that?'

'I have spoken to the man who found a crown, the one that was given to Joel to keep him quiet. Polybius is a very clever man. He must have known that Pilate intended to open up the vaults, so he sent two men, pretending to be Essenes, to ask Anthony Avitus for his help. Avitus was bribed with some of the false jewellery, a rather attractive bracelet. Silas was in on the plot as well. He was Avitus' contact and rewarded him when his job was done. It was easy. All they had to do was to make sure a surplus slave was killed, and leave a pouch with a map of Qumran and some clues on the body. Oddly enough though, the pouch had freshness about it, as if it had been added later. Probably Polybius put it there just before I arrived. He would have wanted to make sure that it was in a readable condition. Of course, no one realized that Avitus had an agenda of his own. He left his own belt and ring behind so that his family would think he was dead. He believed the jewels he had been given were priceless. They were his retirement to a different life.'

'I really have heard enough of this rubbish.'

'I questioned Anthony Avitus in Sebaste. It is undeniably true. He had told his mother a certain amount of the story. She knew that Silas was his contact and assumed he had killed her son. She murdered him and then committed suicide out of grief and shame. Unfortunately when Avitus learned of what his mother had done, he too killed himself.'

'Good riddance to both of them! Scum like that deserve to die.'

'What about the scum who murdered an innocent woman and her daughter?'

Cornelius turned away and became seemingly preoccupied with the garden.

'So what advice do you want from me?'

'There's no doubt that Archelaus, Marcellus and Polybius were very devious. The plot was cleverly conceived and executed. Marcellus was becoming too jittery about the truth – his wife could not have helped with her incessant nagging. Polybius most probably put poison in Marcellus' wine – the easiest way of shutting him up. I have had the Tribune arrested and I would like your help and experience in his interrogation. He will be reluctant to answer my questions, bearing in mind he was only too willing to have me arrested for the murder of Silas.'

'It sounds as though you know it all already. What else is there left to ask him?'

'We know there were two other men involved – the two Essenes. I am assuming it was they who wanted Joel to tell them where he had hidden the crown and anklet. If the clues were to be believable and genuinely Essene, it would be easy to use the ones he had already devised. The trouble was Joel did not want to tell them. They were required to torture him for the information, went too far and Joel died of asphyxiation so they tried to make it look as though he had hung himself.'

'The man committed suicide.'

'I don't believe he did; it was entirely against his beliefs. Anyway, I was then meant to come along, find the clues, find someone from the Qumran community who could interpret them for me and find the jewels. Once I discovered they were worthless, nobody would be interested in what had happened to the rest or to the Essenes. Pontius Pilate was delighted. Nobody could blame him for being incompetent, not when the Emperor had spent nearly thirty years guarding something that was worthless, the joke would be entirely on him.

'The question remains, did Pilate know of the plan, not the old conspiracy but the recent one? If he didn't, someone went to a lot of trouble on his behalf. I suspect Polybius protected Pilate in order to retain his own position. Pilate is clearly indecisive and unstable in many respects so I think Polybius secretly wields all the power around here, wouldn't you say? It would have been very inconvenient for him to have Pilate shamed and replaced. One never knows who the next replacement might be. It's often better to have power behind the scenes than up front. That way someone else takes the blame if mistakes are made. It's better to be number two than number one. Anyhow, you haven't answered my question, will you help me interview Polybius? I'm sure he will tell you the truth.'

Cornelius said nothing.

'There is one more witness.'

'Who is it? You cannot possibly have any more.'

'The young woman who Polybius left for dead, she is alive and well. She was in Damascus when we all went to Gaius' funeral. She spotted the man who murdered her mother and recognized him after all these years. She is absolutely certain it is the same man and will be coming to identify him. So you see it is important that you are there to witness all these events.'

Cornelius sat down heavily and observed his opponent. There was a long pause as though he were considering his next move. A snarl of hatred overcame his face.

'Do you really think that Polybius or Marcellus would have the brains to dream up a plot like that? Do you really think that the mealy-mouthed Polybius and simpering Marcellus would risk their stupid little necks for Pontius Pilate? Do you really think that Polybius has any power to wield around here? I am the controller.'

'Are you saying they are not capable of such deceit?'

'They're capable of deceit all right but they have no real guts. They are like whimpering children when the going gets rough. They want constant reassurance that their spineless backs are well covered.'

Marc did not respond. He looked at the floor and then raised his head to watch Cornelius out of the corner of his eye, and waited.

'You must think you are extremely clever, Commander, working all this out. But you are wrong. You missed the third vital clue that you seem to have ignored, Lucius Cornelius Sulla. I did it all for him. He fought and won authority in Rome, died peacefully having achieved power. Archelaus vowed half the jewels would be mine, enough to raise an army and dethrone Augustus. How dare he appoint himself as a god?

'People like my ancestors and I were the true sons of Rome, not cowards like Gaius Octavius, who always seemed to be missing when the real action started. He even had the audacity to call himself Gaius Julius Caesar Octavianus, even though he was only Caesar's great nephew. Then, when Caesar was deified and subsequently adopted him, he became "divi filius" – son of a god – and finally "Augustus" meaning reverend. Yes, I was the one who masterminded the theft although Archelaus asked me to do it on his behalf. He had his own reasons wanting to get his own back on Augustus for deposing him for merely doing a good job. Rome was too great to be allowed to succumb to Emperors. I was younger, fitter and angry. You were right in your assumption that Archelaus left with the jewels – he did not keep his agreement, not to be trusted as a man of his word. My reward did not come.'

Cornelius hesitated. He seemed calmer as though talking about it was having a soothing effect on him.

'When he died I went to Gaul, a town called Narbonne, to find out what had happened to the jewels that had been pledged to me. I discovered he had given them to one of his fancy women, so I waited, and yes, I killed her. So what? Many people got killed during the wars; another useless whore was neither here nor there. I must admit I felt bad about the girl. I had a daughter of my own once you know.'

Marc noticed his instinctive glance at the wall over the fireplace where a picture had once hung.

'But she died as well. We all die sooner or later. When I took the jewels to be valued, I was told they were worth nothing. I killed the jeweller too – I thought he was trying to cheat me, offer me a pittance for them. I brought them back with me and used them to keep Marcellus and Joel quiet. I didn't tell them they were worthless and they never asked. That ridiculous wife of Marcellus thought her necklace was worth a fortune. She became quite obsessed with it. That's why she reacted so badly when you took it from her. I doubt she'll ever recover from the shock of finding it was of no value. Marcellus was angry with me when you found out and informed him. He wouldn't shut up about it. He thought I had replaced the stones and kept the originals for myself. He's made my life a misery since you came here.'

'Is that why you killed him?'

'Yes, I poisoned him to shut him up.'

'And what happened to Joel?'

'Joel was delighted to have two pieces of the jewellery. He hid them and left two clues for his useless cause. His only problem was himself and his own conscience. But I did get the idea to dupe you from what he did with his jewels sixteen years ago. When Pilate said he was going to open up the vaults I knew that he would find the stones missing. I had enough time to block up the tunnel, drain the cistern and make it look as though the theft was recent. I thought by using Joel's authentic clues the two pieces he had hidden would be found, valued as worthless and Pilate would be off the hook. Brilliant, don't you think? And that's exactly what happened. Everything went just according to plan.'

'And Polybius?'

Cornelius sneered. 'He knew there was a plan to steal the jewels, that's all. He wasn't involved beyond that. He wouldn't risk his skin with the messy stuff. I told him things had gone wrong and Archelaus had taken the stones. He wanted to distance himself from the rest of us – too worried about his precious career.'

'So you were the third man.'

'Yes. I made sure Dimitri, as you call him, would never speak again.'

'Who were the two Essenes?'

'My trusted servants, Portius and Julius, who else? I knew you would want to find a plan, so the two of them visited Avitus at his home, making sure that nosey slave of his wife's overheard them. I didn't underestimate your intelligence. Although I confess I did not expect you to actually go to Qumran and study the ancient texts, I thought Anna would help you out there, or some other religious addict.'

'How did Joel die?'

'Julius is over enthusiastic where torture is concerned. Joel wouldn't tell them the clues or where he had hidden his pieces. They put the pressure on a bit too much. He did eventually give in, but they managed to kill him in the process. It was probably just as well at the time. The man was becoming a nuisance and would have confessed all very soon.'

'And the slave in the tunnel?'

'That was the work of Portius. We needed a body to leave the clues on – a blow on the head ensured that he was too injured to walk. Portius left him at the top of the tunnel, knowing the rats would do the rest – it couldn't have been too pleasant being eaten alive.'

Marc inwardly shuddered at the callousness.

'What was the point of the third clue?'

'I confess that was probably a mistake. It was pure vanity on my part. You asked me the riddle that Oedipus had to solve. After that, I couldn't resist putting in one of my own. Don't ask me why. Perhaps I secretly wanted you to find out that it was me who was responsible. Who knows the workings of our minds? That's why I was missing when my house burned down. I just paid a quick visit to Herodium. The pouch that Portius and Julius had left on the slave's body was deteriorating so I replaced it – I didn't want the map and the clues to be destroyed. That seems to have been a mistake too.'

'Did you not notice that Avitus had placed his own seal and belt on the body?'

'No! How could I be expected to know that the man had a plan of his own? Besides, I had never met him personally. Silas was the go-between. I gave him the last remaining pieces that I had. He kept one and gave the other to Avitus as a reward for his contribution and silence. I had no idea that the surveyor intended to use it as an escape route. Now, I have a question for you – a puzzle that still has not been answered. Who burned down my house? Tell me that if you can.'

'It was done by the girl whose mother you killed.'

'Rubbish, a mere girl could never do such a thing.'

'She wasn't just a mere girl though. It seems she had to learn to walk again. Her sport and exercise made her fast, strong and agile. She was more than capable of scaling the walls and setting fire to the house. She mistook me for you.'

'Well, well! Another of your lives that was saved! Do you have any left? I still don't quite understand. It must have been me she recognized at the funeral in Damascus. So what made her burn down my house when she did?'

'You actually met her a long time before then. Do you remember the introduction we had to the cast after we had been to the theatre? There was a young man in the line up who asked you what you learned from the play. He asked you if you agreed that the gods punish the proud but punishment brings wisdom.'

'I remember. But, as you say, that was a young man.'

'It was a young woman in disguise. She had courage and purpose. It seems you may have indirectly given her that.'

'So then, there you are, I did some good after all.'

Marc said, 'One more question, why did you choose me?'

'Ah, I knew you would be a worthy opponent. I was setting my wits against yours. Besides, if you uncovered my plot Tiberius would trust you. It would have been too easy to dupe others and there would have been no challenge. But there was more to it than that. I hated the way you exposed Sejanus. He was our one last chance to do away with the Emperor Tiberius. Senators were ready to step into the breach. It would have been the end of the Empire and a return to a Republic or maybe something better.'

'What you are saying is treason and cannot be ignored, nor can your actions.'

'Yes, yes, I realize that,' said Cornelius cursorily. 'But I would appreciate it if you would wait until after the race. You know that I'm going nowhere else. You have the offer of my seat, so you will be there at the end. Come now, as sons of the Empire you can at least grant me a last wish.'

45

-The Chariot Race-

The full brightness of the sun was declining in its intensity by the time the race was due to begin, but the land still reflected retained heat. The uneasiness of Marc's mind was affecting his ability to see the occasion as mere entertainment. The crowds were pouring into the seats, intoxicated by the atmosphere and expectation of thrills.

'Master Marc,' shouted Jonathan seeing him walking through the hippodrome.

'I have seen the man who selected me and invited me to come here to ride, but he wouldn't talk to me. He pretended to ignore me as though he had never seen me.'

'That sounds very strange! What did he look like?'

'I don't really know. He didn't look like anyone in particular. But he was leading the dapple grey Arabs.'

'Was he young or old?'

'He seemed quite young.'

Portius! What was he doing selecting charioteers? Could it be Cornelius who had recommended Jonathan's entry in the race? Marc was confused. Perhaps Cornelius wanted to ensure that he had good opposition. Was everything in life a game to him?

Aziz had arrived from Mamre.

'I'm delighted to meet you again Commander. You see how brave and strong my son has become. I knew that coming here would be good for him. What do you think of my stallions?'

'Magnificent. They respond to Jonathan as though he were one of them.'

'Yes, they do. Together they will win today.'

'I hope so!'

'It will be so!' laughed Aziz with the confidence of certainty.

The whole place was humming with excitement and busier than previous days when preparations had been taking place. Jonathan was ready. He was wearing a plain white linen sleeveless tunic with leather protection strapped over his shoulders, and a helmet. Leather covered his wrists to his elbows to strengthen and support his arms; there was a similar belt round his waist.

He was filled with pride.

'This is the best day of my life.'

Marc hoped it would end that way.

Trumpets started playing a stirring march and the riders mounted their flimsy chariots. Horses vied for space neighing, whinnying, rearing and pulling against the harnesses that held them tightly together. The teams also felt the emotion of the event. They were trained to compete and loved to win.

Jonathan saluted and took his place in the line up of ten four-horse teams. Marc spotted Cornelius in the familiar red, trimmed with gold, matching the harness. He noticed that, as Julius had described, he wrapped the reins round his waist. He was glad to see that Jonathan had not done so. He could not dispel a feeling of foreboding but Aziz, Daleel and Nadeem did not appear to have the same concerns. The four of them sat together not far from Pontius Pilate. Pilate smiled and waved at Marc and was about to beckon him over until he spotted his companions; then he merely nodded, unwilling to invite the others to sit with him.

The teams walked out in procession led by three soldiers dressed in lavish cloaks and carrying resplendent flags. There hardly seemed sufficient width for all the charioteers, but they managed to keep in harmony as they paraded once round the circuit to the sound of trumpets and cheering from the hundreds of supporters that packed the arena. Some fans were sitting precariously on the central barrier with legs dangling over the edge. The trumpeters stood behind them; above their heads were the golden eagles designed to measure each round.

When they returned to the starting line, there was a hush of electrically charged anticipation. Some teams started before the flag was down and the riders had to back them up to the line. There were looks of disapproval, frustration and boredom. Pontius Pilate stood up and addressed the crowd.

'Today our entries are from across the Empire.'
He read out the names of the places represented and the supporters cheered loudly as he came to each one.

'We welcome you all and trust that the best man will win.'
He waited until the crowd was quiet then with a flourish gave the signal to begin and the starting flags were dropped.

There was immediate confusion. Two charioteers collided and took several minutes to disengage, amidst much swearing and swipes with long whips whilst the others took off. Soon the noise of hooves was so thunderous that even the cries of the crowd could not drown them out.

The third eagle had dropped when one of the chariots took a turn too sharply. A wheel caught the base of the turning post and the chariot was flipped into the air, expelling its occupant. He flew over the top and landed in front of the next set of charging horses and was briefly trampled. Men with a stretcher came to fetch him from the track, as quickly as they could.

Meanwhile the horse kept running without a rider. The chariot became disengaged from the harness and was thrown with the full force of the speed with which it was travelling into another team, injuring the lead horse which stumbled, taking the rest with him. The harnesses became twisted as the horses fell in disarray, legs in the air struggling to get free but becoming more entangled with every movement. Their rider, bleeding from his legs and temple, tried in vain to help them. Part of the harness snapped; one of them was released.

Scared and pumped full of adrenalin, he bolted across the track straight into the next set of galloping animals. They did not hesitate for a moment, and the horse lay unable to move except for raising his head, death inevitable. The wheels of the chariot had bounced over his body throwing yet another rider.

Jonathan's team of blacks was close behind. They leapt over the fallen horse in harmony and Jonathan was thrown into the air slipping over the front. His leg caught on the cross bar and he managed to pull himself back into the chariot.

Aziz, Marc, Daleel and Nadeem were on their feet. The crowd made noises of sympathy. They were living vicariously and loving every moment, waiting for disaster to titillate them without any pain or inconvenience to themselves.

With three teams down, there were seven left. On the fifth lap two charioteers came too close together on the turn and their wheels became hitched, unable to separate. As the teams moved in different directions a wheel from each chariot was pulled off and the vehicles both dropped on one side wrenching bolts. Twisted metal now obstructed the track whilst the two teams of horses continued unaware. Another charioteer, not seeing the obstacles before rounding the turn, charged directly into them.

The scene was chaotic as the injured were carried clear, whilst others tried to remove broken chariots before they caused further disasters. Single riders charged after the runaway horses in an attempt to guide them out of the way. The remaining teams, with more space to manoeuvre, were racing faster.

Cornelius was half a circuit in the lead with Jonathan in second place at the end of the sixth lap. The crowd was standing, cheering and waving. Then as Cornelius turned the corner for the final lap something extraordinary happened. Marc thought about it many times afterwards and could only come to the conclusion that Cornelius' move was quite deliberate. He threw both arms up in the air, stood tall making triumphant fists and allowed himself to be dragged over the front of the chariot. The reins that were tied round his waist became tangled in the harness and for the full length of one circuit, his own beautiful horses trampled him, turning the body over and over until they were stopped and Cornelius laid on the track a bloodied mess.

Portius ran to his master without a thought for himself. Jonathan was unable to rein in since the blacks were sensing victory and moving like Pegasus. They hit Portius full on. He was caught up under their hooves and dragged by the chariot. The young man rode passed the winning post, but with no pleasure in his heart, although the crowds were jumping up and down in excitement. Those who placed bets on the outsider had just won a fortune.

Jonathan came to a stop. People ran onto the track to congratulate him but Daleel and Nadeem reached him first. The boy was weeping amidst his joy.

'He ran out in front of me. I could not stop in time.'

'It was not your fault. This is a dangerous sport,' said Daleel.

'But he was the man who selected me. I would not be here if it were not for him.'

He had no time to think too long because the crowd was already insisting he should claim his prize. He was picked up and carried on the shoulders of two unknown men to the bottom of the steps where Pontius Pilate was waiting to crown him.

'You are the youngest man to ever win this prize,' he said. 'Congratulations! You have set a record today and will be forever famed. Your name will spread throughout the land and many will want to challenge you. Accept this wreath of laurels and enjoy your moment of victory.'

The crowd went wild particularly all those young men who aspired to be like their heroes in the ring and here was one the same age as themselves.

Some hours later Jonathan, his father, brothers and Marc sat assessing the events of the day. Cornelius was dead. The doctors said he had received severe blows to the head, which had crushed his skull. It was generally thought that Cornelius, seeing the finishing line in his sight, raised his arms to indicate his success. Marc was certain that this was not the case but kept quiet. It simply would have required too much explanation. Portius was still alive but had lost one of his legs. He would spend the rest of his life on crutches.

Aziz and Nadeem took a hard line on the matter. Everyone knew the risk – it was bad luck. Jonathan and Daleel took a different view; the victor struggled with the idea that he had crippled a man for the rest of his life. Marc decided that one day he would tell Jonathan and Daleel the whole story. They might not feel quite so sympathetic if they knew that Portius was responsible for crippling a man himself, and then leaving him to be eaten by rats. One thing was certain, both Julius and Portius would spend the rest of their lives as beggars without the protection of their owner.

Despite the accident, life for Jonathan had now changed. Not only was he a national hero, he had a considerable sum of money in his own right.

'Master Marc, I would like to come to Rome with you. I want to be educated; I can afford to pay. My brother Daleel has done his best with me, perhaps enough for me to know that I wish to learn more. Will you please let me come? I will be a companion for your son and I will do everything you wish. I will work for you as well as attend to my studies. I beg you, take me with you.'

Marc looked at Aziz. He was surprised to see that tears filled the old man's eyes, whether it was from pride or sorrow at an impending loss was difficult to say.

He said, 'Well Commander, I remember you made me a promise in exchange for my crown.'

It was undeniably true. Would it do any harm to take the boy with him? He certainly had talent and it was a shame not to develop it. Felix knew that he would always be his true son and heir, so jealousy was unlikely. But there was another reason for taking Jonathan with him, one that was buried more deeply in his psyche, a link would be maintained with this land.

'All right, I'll do it.'

Jonathan leapt to his feet and hugged him. Aziz put an arm on his shoulder; Nadeem and Daleel beamed with pleasure.

'When can we come to visit then?' said Daleel.

'My friend, you will always be welcome. I have not forgotten that I owe you my life.'

'And me!' said Jonathan, pretending to pout.

'Yes, and you, and I have Nadeem to thank also. And you Aziz, for helping me to solve my problem.'

'When can we set sail?'

'That will depend on the boats. But I promise we will be on the next one to Rome.'

46

-The Herodian Stones-

There was not another boat to Rome for several days. Pontius Pilate insisted that Marc stay at the palace. He was reluctant to do so, but at least he had access to writing materials and he wanted to complete the record of what he knew. How Pilate chose to deal with that knowledge was up to him. All the perpetrators except for the Tribune had met with an unfortunate end. Marc suspected that Polybius would choose to retire; otherwise he would always be at the mercy of Pilate, with the threat of revelation of his involvement in the theft of jewels that technically belonged to the Emperor. Men had been crucified for less.

There remained only one overriding question. Where were the real stones? Just at this time Marc felt so weary and drained that he no longer cared. They had caused too much misery and death. Furthermore, Pilate did not seem too worried about them. He had received a message from Tiberius to find the money himself for his new building work, but there were no recriminations concerning the loss of the jewels. Pilate was already making plans to strip Temple Mount of its gold.

'You would not believe the amount of gold that is built into that place,' he told Marc. 'Not all the Jews are poor you know; many bring gold to the Temple. It is used for adornment.'

'With respect Pilate, do you not think that may cause further trouble?'

At one time he would have gone on to express concern for the governor's safety and protection. Once, he could flatter with impunity. It had been a normal part of his life, a means of survival.

Now hypocrisy brought him only distaste.

'I have had enough of being told what to do by people I govern. If they want to become martyrs because of my decision then this time I shall let them.'

Marc thought the decision very unwise. Nothing propels people into riots faster than martyrs to a cause. He suspected that the pot would soon boil over and that Pilate's days were probably numbered.

The day before the boat was due to arrive he went to see Claudia. They met in the garden.

She said, 'I hear you are to take the hero of Caesarea with you to Rome. Is that sensible?'

'I think so. The boy has remarkable talent in ways other than controlling horses. He insists he wants to use his winnings to pay for an education. He is so keen it would be a travesty to deny him.'

'You are a very kind man Marc Tiro.'

'If indeed that is true, I confess it has not always been so.'

'I wish you luck with your new project. Make him a man in your own mould and he will do well.'

'It is you who are kind, ma'am.'

'Maybe I am and maybe I'm not! But regardless my hands are tied to do anything outside this life I have chosen for myself. I hoped it would not be so, but my role is set. Your life is still open to do with what you will. Make sure you deal with it wisely.'

'I will ma'am! And I hope most sincerely that we shall meet again.'

Aziz, Daleel and Nadeem were standing on the quay where Marc had once watched the disembarking passengers wondering what the next few weeks would bring. Now he knew, but he was not yet at peace. The crewman was still shouting, but this time the ropes were released and the anchor was raised. He stood watching the three figures until they blurred into the background and then disappeared altogether. Jonathan went below to investigate the boat. Marc remained looking out to sea, enjoying the wind on his face. He heard a soft voice behind him.

'Hello, Commander.'

He turned and was looking down at a small hooded figure. The hood was thrown back to reveal a shock of curly black hair – it was Candace.

'Candace! I thought you were still in Damascus.'

'I am going home. My …… mother is dying. I must go to her. I hope I am not too late.'

'You know, don't you, that Judas explained your circumstances to me.'

'Yes, and I am grateful for your forgiveness.'

'Have you heard that Cornelius is dead?'

'Yes, I understand he died in the ring. Did he ever confess to you what he had done?'

'He did. He was misguided in many ways. But I think he ended his own life rather than face disgrace.'

'I am sorry to hear that. Do you think there was any redemption in the man?'

'Well, it was an extraordinary circumstance, but it seems he sent his slave Portius to pick out potential charioteers. He selected young Jonathan, who is aboard somewhere; he is coming back to Rome with me.'

'Yes, I heard. Was he not the winner?'

'He was. Yet Cornelius allowed it to happen.'

'Why do you suppose he would do that?'

'Perhaps he realized his life was over and he wanted to give someone else a chance.'

'If that is true, then maybe there is some saving grace for him. Did Judas tell you that I had written to the woman I always knew as my mother to ask her for an explanation?'

'Yes! Did you ever get a reply?'

'I did. It came to Crassus when he returned to Caesarea. I would like you to read it. You will find it enlightening.'

She slid her hand inside her cloak and drew out a letter. Marc read every word.

My darling Candace

You know I love you more than life itself, yet my conscience is troubled by my deception. I have brought you up as my daughter – I know you can remember nothing else, but I must confess to you that you are not of my flesh and blood, although I love you as much as it would be possible to love my own. It gives me great sadness that I am not your natural mother. The man you came to know as your father was my husband. There I have said it, I owe you the truth.

When you were young we taught you as much as we could. Do you recall those gentle exercises that helped you learn how to walk? The strolls on the beach that increased each day until you ran so fast that the very air was confounded. You were like the wind itself and outran us all. How proud we were to see you grow so strong and healthy and how we thanked our gods for their great mercy.

You developed those fruits that we all admired so much: kindness and gentleness, love and patience. You learned the plays of the Greek scholars, performing for us in the garden with your friends. We so enjoyed those pleasant summer evenings. What a pleasure it was to hear the elevated words of the playwrights enlivened by enthusiasm and feeling.

Just before your fourteenth birthday you were chosen to run in the girls' foot races at Olympia to the goddess Hera. You lifted your tunic to your knees and ran like no other, your hair hung long and loose down your back flowing behind you. There was no competitor who came anywhere near you. As the victor you were well honoured. I am looking now at the bronze statuette inscribed with your name.

Do you remember your pony? You rode him fearlessly. You climbed trees and rocks with ease and swam like a little fish. No parents had a more loving, able or intelligent child – either son or daughter.

After your father, sorry, my husband, died, there were just the two of us. I am grateful for the lessons I learned from you during that time. How not to be anxious, how not to take insults personally but to see them as the other person's problem, how not to be so insecure as to believe I had nothing of value to say. Your care and support of me seemed to be the reverse of how life is intended, the child taught the adult. How wise you were! You recognized my needs and I loved you for your faithfulness. I was so pleased when you had the opportunity to travel and act even though you could not be yourself because of our social rules. Yet you made as eloquent a young man as woman. I trust you have found happiness.

I am afraid my days are now limited – in fact by the time you read this letter I may be dead. There is nothing to be done. My time has come and I am grateful for what I have had. There is only this one thing left for me to do and I hope with all my heart you will forgive me for it.

I came to know you when you were a baby. At the time you were living in Gaul near Narbonne. I was your nurse and then your teacher and came to see you every day. Your natural mother was very beautiful. Her name was Simone. She was a lady of noble Jewish birth from Judea. She mixed with those in society who are honoured for their wealth and status rather than their inner qualities.

She had an affair with a Roman soldier thinking that he would marry her, but, when she became pregnant, he refused. Soldiers were forbidden to contract legal marriages during their terms of service. Her family was disgraced and sent her away to live in Gaul where she had some distant relatives. Then you were born. She wrote to your father to tell him he had a daughter in the hope that he might change his mind. She had one letter from him wishing her well. She always kept it.

Meanwhile, a man of even higher nobility had also noticed her beauty and desired her. His name was Archelaus, the King of Judea. He ruled badly and was sent away in disgrace to live out his life in a foreign land. He chose exile to Gaul and lived at Vienne, not far from Narbonne. Your mother always suspected he had deliberately followed her. Although he was known for his cruelty, your mother brought out the best of his character and I have no doubt he loved her, in his own way. She became his mistress out of necessity because he provided support for her and her baby. She insisted that the two of you came together. He could not have one without the other.

Archelaus employed me to look after both of you. I feared for you at first because I thought he might try to have you killed, but as you grew to look more like your mother he actually came to love you too, even though you were not his natural child. You were affectionate with him and made him laugh. In fact, you treated him as though he was your father. There was no reason why you should think otherwise. I don't believe he had any children of his own. He spent many happy hours in your company. Maybe he was not a bad man in every respect. I suppose none of us is.

However, he insisted that your mother write to your real father to tell him that you had died and that she was now the lover of Archelaus. The only explanation for this was that he feared he might come looking for you. She knew that your father would hate her for it, but dared not go against Archelaus' wishes.

He was generous to both of you. He provided clothes and gave her many gifts of jewellery. Sometimes before she became ill, her hair would be full of sparkling stones that brought out the shining light of her deep blue eyes. She had long dark curly hair, just like yours and a fine curvaceous body. Not like mine, I'm afraid, with my thick waist and short torso. Still my husband never did mind that, so I was very fortunate. He loved me the way I was.

She walked with an upright gait, as you do, my darling. Nobody could fail to notice the gloss of her hair as it swayed from side to side. Sometimes though, beauty can be a curse and can lead us into situations that we would prefer not to be in. But when you were born your mother loved you dearly. She would have died for you. However, after a few years, she became unwell and required a lot of rest, even though she was still young.

I shall tell you how she died although I know that it will pain you, but you have a right to know. I arrived at your mother's house one afternoon to give you your lessons as usual. The rooms were quiet and I called out but there was no reply. The scene that met my eyes in the bedroom I shall never forget. The *whole room was torn apart as though a beast had been searching for its prey. Your poor mother had been killed with a knife. But she had obviously been sleeping just before it happened and I doubt she suffered at all. The lovely necklace that she always wore had gone from her throat, so had everything else that her lover had given her.*

You, my poor darling, were also close to death. In fact, when I looked at your young body I thought you were dead. Someone had thrown you against the wall and smashed your bones, yet the gods preserved you for some greater fate in life.

Blessedly you could remember nothing about that fateful event and never did recover your memory. It was as though those earlier years had never existed. Neither did you ever query them. Life began for you a year later when you were able to focus your mind once again. The previous years had gone; the mind had blotted them out for the sake of self-preservation.

Three months before your mother was murdered, Archelaus wrote me a letter, which I was instructed to open in the event of his death. I believe he must have known because he died a few days later. He told me that should anything happen to him, I was to take you both back to Greece where I was born and to live out my years with you and my husband, as unassuming as possible. If your mother died he wanted me to change your name to mine. I think he really feared for your lives and wanted to protect you. My husband and I planned to go but your mother became so weak herself that we did not think she would survive the journey. If we had known what was going to happen, we would have taken her, regardless.

Archelaus also told me a secret that I was not to reveal to you until I myself was near death. He said I would know when the time was right to do so. I believe it was for your protection that he asked me to take these precautions. There are many greedy and dangerous people in this world who take what is not theirs and kill without a second thought. Not that I have met any personally but I have witnessed the results of their terror, and know enough to be afraid of them.

Archelaus' father was a powerful King called Herod. The King owned artefacts that made him fabulously wealthy and used materials and labour from the Roman Empire on the strength of this. After he died, the Emperor Augustus claimed the goods that Herod owned in the place of what he owed the empire. Yet the Emperor had no need of them and left them in the vaults at the palace of Herodium near Jerusalem, believing them to be safe, particularly since they were guarded. Knowing that he was about to be exiled, Archelaus stole jewellery from the vault that had once belonged to his stepmother, Mariamne. At the time he saw no wrong in what he was doing. They were his after all by inheritance.

When he reached Gaul he had them valued. Strangely, some of them were so rare and precious they were beyond price, whilst others, although being of great beauty were of very little worth. He separated them. Those that were not of great value he gave to your mother to wear everyday because she admired them so much. The others, for the sake of safety, he removed from the settings and gave them to you.

I know you will be astonished at this because you did not know that you had them. They were in a most unlikely place yet you touched them every day of your young life and have them still. They are the stones that you played with. I watched you many times as you threw one of them in the air, picking up as many of the others on the floor as you could before the airborne stone fell to the ground. You loved that game and played it until you left home taking the stones with you. It was maybe as well you did not know that you owned such a great fortune. Archelaus wanted you to have it. I must leave it to your own conscience as to whether or not you feel that you are entitled to keep it.

Although I shall not meet you again, I hope you will think fondly of me and forgive me for my great sin and for keeping from you vital information on your life. Perhaps, as Archelaus judged, the time would be right some time and now is the time. Great wealth, like great beauty, is a blessing as well as a curse. The stones caused the death of your mother. Someone knew they were in her possession and killed her, nearly killing you too. They little suspected that what they sought lay in front of them on the floor. But you have been given a second chance to do what is right. Officially the stones belong to the Emperor. Unofficially they are yours, a present from the man who wished he was your father. Ask the gods for advice and assistance and may they bless you mightily.

I am tired now and my eyes are failing. My love endures forever no matter what becomes of me. I will watch over you if the gods permit it. One last thing, I have enclosed the one letter that your father wrote to your mother.

Look after yourself my darling daughter, if I may be so bold as to call you that, from the woman who will always think of herself as your mother.

Sylvia.

Marc finished reading the letter and handed it back to Candace.

'This must be a shock to you after all this time.'

'Yes, but not as great as this one.'

Candace handed him the letter from her natural father. It was old and frayed at the edges as if it had been folded and unfolded many times. Marc was careful not to damage it. The words were few and to the point.

Dear Simone

I thank you for letting me know that we have a daughter. Please forgive me for treating you so badly, but my career means everything to me and I would make a very bad husband and father.

I wish you both well.

Cornelius Sulla

Marc nearly dropped the letter in surprise.

'My dearest Candace, your story gets worse.'

'I know! What will God think of a person who has tried to kill her own father? The situation is not so far removed from that of Oedipus is it?'

'What will God think of a man who murders the woman he once loved and his own daughter? That's more like Antigone.'

'It's no wonder I loved the Greek tragedies. My life so far has been like them. Cornelius must have hated my mother after she told him she was the lover of Archelaus. Perhaps the two men knew each other.'

'They did. Cornelius told me he was his right-hand man. I suppose he must have felt betrayed. I know it is wrong but it is a phenomenon that some men, even though they may not want a lover themselves, don't want anybody else to have them either, particularly not someone whom they know.'

Candace said sadly, 'I feel almost sorry for him, learning that his child had died and that his ex-lover was now the mistress of someone else, someone he knew, must have been hard. No wonder he had no compunction in murdering my mother. And he probably thought that I belonged to Archelaus. Do you know he said he was sorry as he was trying to kill me?'

'He told me that he had a daughter who had died. Before the house was burned there was a drawing over his fireplace of a young woman. I assumed that it was her. Come to think of it, the girl in the picture had long dark curls. Perhaps he drew it himself as he imagined you to be. One of his sleeping rooms was feminine in décor. Maybe subconsciously it was yours. Even the most dedicated career men eventually want to reproduce themselves and have a desire for children. It is an inevitable force of nature.'

'It would be nice to believe that he loved the thought of me, even though he never knew me, but somehow I doubt it.'

'Nevertheless, it might be easier to hold onto that belief.'

'Well, all I can say is that I do truly forgive him. It is incredible to think that I have held some of the most precious stones in the world in my hands. I'll show you.'

Candace felt inside her cloak and brought out a very large bag tied at the top. She opened it.

'Hold out your hands.'

Marc cupped his palms upwards and Candace poured out some of the contents. Marc was mesmerised; his eyes riveted.

'They are truly beautiful. They seem alive.'

'I think they are alive,' said Candace. 'But I also believe they are filled with evil. I didn't used to think so, of course, but their effect is hypnotic, not healthy for a mind given to greed, envy or pride. Look how much damage and death they have caused.'

'They have certainly done that.'

He thought of the catalogue of deaths: Simone, Cornelius, Marcellus, Joel, Silas, Anthony Avitus and his mother Sabina. Gaius too had died indirectly because of the stones and so had Anna; Portius and Julius were damaged for life, Dimitri and Candace had suffered for many years and there was an unknown slave, whose bones now lay at the bottom of a cistern.

'What have you decided to do with them? Are you going to keep them, or do you think we should return them to the Emperor?'

Candace looked him fully in the face and smiled. It was a smile of peace and knowing. She picked up one of the stones from Marc's hand and dropped it into the sea.

'Is this what you really want?'

'Yes. It is what Jesus would want me to do. They are stones of darkness.'

'Yet, has not the light overcome the darkness?'

'I believe you may be right; out of evil arises goodness.'

Marc leaned over the edge of the boat and let the stones slip through his fingers. They were the same colour as the deep blue water and seemed to merge into their new home without complaint. Candace took the bag and tipped out the rest.

'This will be our secret,' she said.

'If you had asked me to do this a few weeks ago, I would have had you arrested. But now I agree. It is the right thing to do.'

He put his arm round her and squeezed her shoulders. She put her head briefly on his chest. They stood looking at the waves that had just swallowed a fortune. A woman's voice interrupted their individual thoughts.

'Commander Marc Tiro!'

Marc turned round to see someone he recognized. It was the lady whom he had rescued in Neapolis, after Avitus had fallen onto her stall and spread her cloth everywhere.

'Lydia! This is a surprise.'

She smiled at him in delight.

'Can anyone join this party?' she asked.

'Of course, let me introduce you. Lydia, this is Candace – she is going home to Greece – Candace this is Lydia from Thyatira. That's right isn't it?'

'Certainly is,' said Lydia. 'I have been trading here for several months, but I am really ready to go home now.'

She joined them and Marc had a lady on each arm.

'Well, well, you are lucky, Commander Tiro. You arrived alone and now you are returning with two beautiful ladies.'

It was the captain – the one who had brought him to this Promised Land of the Jews. They laughed. The captain stood beside Lydia. Jonathan came back on deck and he too joined them, standing next to Candace. The five of them looked to the west. Yes, thought Marc, we are going home. But in his heart he knew nothing would ever be the same.

Postscript

Pilate pursued his project of constructing more aqueducts from the pools of Solomon to Jerusalem. He used Jewish sacred funds to do so, provoking riots. He sent his soldiers into the crowds, armed with weapons but disguised as civilians, killing a great number of people.

Rome deposed him three years after the crucifixion of Christ and he was sent into exile. Very little is known about him after that, although some legends say that he committed suicide.

The high priest, Caiaphas, was also deposed by the Roman authorities in A.D.36.

---

i   Zechariah 9:9
ii   Jeremiah 7:11
iii   Isaiah 53:3-9
iv   Psalm 22:14-18
v   Zechariah 12:10
vi   Psalm 34:20
vii   Psalm 25:2
viii   1 Corinthians 10:13